Tara Bond grew up in Surrey, England. She read History at Cambridge University, before working in various ~~ible~~ office jobs. She lives in London with her hu~~sband~~, and loves reading and writing, as well as watchi~~ng mo~~vies and TV ~~box~~ sets. Her guilty pleasures are coo~~king~~ and chocolate desserts.

Also by Tara Bond

Beautiful Liar

TARA BOND

Sweet
DECEPTION

**SIMON &
SCHUSTER**

London · New York · Sydney · Toronto · New Delhi

A CBS COMPANY

First published in Great Britain by Simon & Schuster UK Ltd, 2015
A CBS company

1 3 5 7 9 10 8 6 4 2

Simon & Schuster UK Ltd
1st Floor
222 Gray's Inn Road
London WC1X 8HB

www.simonandschuster.co.uk

Simon & Schuster Australia, Sydney
Simon & Schuster India, New Delhi

A CIP catalogue record for this book is available from the British Library

Paperback ISBN: 978-1-4711-1163-1
eBook ISBN: 978-1-4711-1164-8

Typeset in the UK by Hewer Text UK Ltd, Edinburgh
Printed and bound in Great Britain by CPI Group (UK) Ltd, Croydon, CR0 4YY

Simon & Schuster UK Ltd are committed to sourcing paper that is made
from wood grown in sustainable forests and supports the Forest Stewardship
Council, the leading international forest certification organisation. Our
books displaying the FSC logo are printed on FSC certified paper.

To My Readers

Prologue

Eight years ago

'Ah, Charlotte, there you are!' My mother's voice boomed out as I walked into the drawing room, the last one to arrive. I froze, automatically straightening my shoulders, as her eyes swept over me, assessing my appearance. She looked elegant in a cream linen suit, and I knew she expected me to try to live up to her high standards.

After a moment, she gave a brief nod of approval, and my body relaxed as I exhaled.

'I like that dress on you. It suits your figure.'

I bit back a smile. It was hardly a surprise that my mum was a fan of the navy coatdress – after all, she'd bought it for me that day, commenting in her usual none-too-subtle way that it would probably be nice if I wore it when we went out that evening. To be honest, I'd rather be in jeans and a

1

t-shirt, but I trusted my mother's choice implicitly. A successful human rights lawyer, she always looked neat and stylish, and I aspired to be just like her. Unfortunately that was pretty much a pipe dream. While her petite frame and poker-straight, glossy dark hair made her seem effortlessly chic, my heavier build and untameable mousey curls meant I was unlikely to ever attain her polish and sophistication.

'William?' She turned to my father, who was sitting on the couch, reading the newspaper. 'Tell your youngest how good she looks.'

'I don't need to.' My dad glanced up from his paper, and winked at me. He was a neurologist, equally as successful as my mother in his field, but while she was sharp and businesslike, he was softer, cosier, like an academic. 'Charlotte always looks beautiful.'

I could always rely on my father for support. He was much more approachable than my mother – less intimidatingly perfect. While he was undoubtedly an attractive man, tall and trim with salt-and-pepper hair, there was just enough hint of a middle-aged paunch to make him seem human.

'Let's have a look at you,' my sister Kate chimed in. She was curled up on one of the armchairs, her long, slender legs tucked beneath her as she texted on her mobile phone. I looked enviously at the simple white dress she was wearing, feeling suddenly over-dressed and chunky in my own dark ensemble. Kate was the lucky one, who took after our mother. Sometimes it was hard not to feel bitter about that.

My sister finally sent her message and then looked up to smile at me. 'Good job, Mouse. You scrubbed up well.'

I cringed at her use of my hated nickname. It didn't take a genius to work out why I'd been branded with it – in my overachieving family I was the quiet one, the shy girl who lurked in corners. I often felt like the ugly duckling in a family of swans.

'Well, now we're all here, shall we open the bubbles?' As usual my mother took control. 'What do you say, darling?'

Sighing, my father folded up his newspaper, and headed over to the sideboard, where a bottle of champagne rested in an ice bucket. Tonight was a celebration. Kate had just finished her second year at medical school, and she'd found out this morning that she'd come top of her class in the end of year exams. We were going out to a nearby restaurant to celebrate – it was in a country hotel, where we always went to celebrate family occasions. For me, those tended to only be birthdays, never the academic successes that came so easily to my siblings.

The only person missing from the family gathering was my brother, Christopher – or Kit, as we all called him. Like our mother, he'd studied Law at Oxford, and now, having just finished his one-year Legal Practice course, he was taking a well-earned break before he started his training contract at one of the big corporate law firms. Not that I'd personally have called climbing Mont Blanc much of a 'break', but my brother loved sport and any kind of physical challenge.

My father eased out the champagne cork with a loud pop. Bubbles fizzed over and he quickly picked up a flute to catch the liquid. He poured three glasses – for him, my mother and Kate – and then turned to me.

'And how about you, Charlotte?' At seventeen, I was still a year too young to drink. 'Perhaps a small glass just for a toast.'

'Thank you,' I murmured, as he poured out a measure that was a third the size of the others.

'To Kate,' my mother said, and my dad and I echoed the words, as the four of us clinked glasses.

I took a sip of the champagne. It wasn't my first time drinking it, but for whatever reason it hit my throat the wrong way, and I hiccupped. My hand clamped over my mouth as my family turned to look at me.

'Oh, Mouse!' My sister laughed indulgently. 'Very elegant—'

The phone rang, cutting off her words. No one moved to answer it. Kate's friends and admirers all used her mobile, and I didn't really have anyone who'd be calling me.

My father sighed. 'Don't trouble yourselves. I'll get it.'

He put his glass down, and headed across the room. As he lifted the receiver, he automatically checked the caller identification. 'International. It must be Kit.

'Hello. Kit, my boy—' His cheery greeting froze on his lips as the caller began to talk. The smile dropped from my father's face, and his expression grew serious. 'Sorry – what are you saying?'

A knot began to form in my stomach. Whoever was on the end of the line spoke again, and my father's eyes darted over to where the rest of us stood, waiting, watching. He swallowed, hard, as though trying to clear a lump in his throat. 'Just hold on a second.'

He turned from us and disappeared from the room, closing the door behind him. He began to talk again, but we could only hear the muffled sound of him speaking and couldn't make out the words.

Mum, Kate and I all exchanged worried looks. None of us spoke. It was as though we sensed this wasn't the time to speculate on what was going on.

We waited in silence as the minutes ticked by. Finally everything went quiet in the hallway. We watched as the door handle bent and my father walked back into the room. His head was bowed, and he was still clutching the phone in his hand.

'William?' My mother was on her feet, her arms wrapped protectively around her body, already anticipating bad news. 'What is it? What's going on?'

There was a long silence, when all I could hear was the sound of my own heartbeat filling my ears, and then he finally raised his eyes to her.

'It's Kit.' He spoke slowly, clearly, as though trying to make an effort to enunciate every word. 'It seems there was an accident. An avalanche. Kit was buried in the fall. The rescuers managed to dig him out, and they airlifted him to hospital. The doctors did everything they could . . . But Kit . . .' His voice broke a little, and then he tried again. 'Well, I'm afraid Kit's dead.'

Chapter 1

Present day

I burrowed further under my duvet, trying to block out the incessant ringing. I wasn't sure where the shrill sound was coming from, but it was the last thing I needed after the tequila shots I'd downed the previous night. All I could think about right now was the incessant throbbing pain hitting me right between my eyes, beating away like a pulse. I just wanted the noise to stop, so I could fall back to sleep, and hopefully wake up hangover-free in a few hours.

It was only when I heard my flatmate, Lindsay, throw open her bedroom door, and stomp across the hallway, that I finally figured out the source of the noise – it was our intercom. That was when the pieces fell into place.

It was *him*, of course; the bane of my existence – here to ruin my day.

As Lindsay answered the intercom, I closed my eyes, and willed her to pretend that I wasn't in. She knew how much I hated these occasions, and had been known to lie on my behalf more than once. But it was too much to hope for today, I realised, as I heard her tell him to come up. Lindsay was a good friend, but she didn't like to get up before midday, and I knew she'd hold me responsible for today's early morning call. This was her revenge.

She didn't bother waiting for him to climb the five flights of stairs up to our top-floor flat. Instead, I heard her leave the door on the latch, and then on the way back to her room, she threw something against my door, to make sure I was awake – from the thud it sounded like a shoe.

'Charlie? Mr No Fun's here,' she called out. I flinched at the volume. 'You might want to make yourself decent. If that's even possible . . .'

I heard her bedroom door slam shut, as she headed back to sleep. Lucky her.

As though I didn't have enough problems already, the mattress next to me shifted, and I froze as a warm, hairy leg brushed against my bare skin. I came out from behind the pillow, peeled my crusted eyes open and saw a man lying next to me, naked apart from a sheet pulled over his middle, mercifully preserving his modesty. My alcohol-addled brain couldn't exactly place him right now, but he was an attractive guy, if you liked that rough, rock-band look. His hair was way too long; his nose and lip were pierced, and both arms were covered in tattoos. He was entirely my type.

I couldn't remember much about last night, but it didn't take a genius to figure out what had happened. I worked behind the bar at a pub in Camden, and he was typical of our clientele. No doubt I'd served him, we'd got talking, and then after my shift we'd headed on somewhere to continue drinking, before one thing led to another. It wasn't the first time something like this had happened – in fact, it was kind of a weekly event for me. I was just surprised I'd let him stay over. Most of the time, I kicked them out straight after the deed was done. It was the best way to avoid that awkward morning-after moment, where the guy felt obliged to pretend he was going to call, and I felt obliged to pretend I wanted him to.

But I didn't have time to worry about getting rid of my unwanted guest right now. I had far more pressing problems with my other male visitor, who I'd just heard coming into the flat.

I'd just about managed to sit up and pull on my black kimono dressing gown when the door to my bedroom door was thrown open by my self-appointed protector – and gigantic pain in my butt – Richard Davenport.

Even at this time in the morning, Richard was the epitome of a young, successful businessman. Tall and tanned, no doubt from Saturday mornings on the tennis court, he was, as always, impeccably turned out in chinos and a blue button-down shirt. He never seemed to step out of the house looking anything less than perfect, and today was no exception – his dark hair was short and neat, his strong jaw clean-shaven, and I could smell the fresh scent of his shower gel from where I sat hunched over on the side of the bed, reeking of my own signature aroma of fags and booze.

I'd known Richard for most of my life. He'd gone to the same boarding school as my older brother, Kit, and they'd been best friends since they were eleven. I'd never had much to do with Richard growing up. After all, I was five years younger than him and Kit, and a girl – he'd barely seemed to notice me. But when I'd moved to London seven years ago, that had all changed. I guess out of some sense of duty to my brother, he'd taken it upon himself to keep an eye on me, which entailed phoning every few weeks to check up on me, and making sure that I attended the obligatory family get-togethers. Which would explain his presence in my flat today.

Of course his interference irritated me no end. At twenty-five years old, it wasn't like I needed a babysitter. I wasn't sure why he couldn't just mind his own business.

It was hard to believe he was only thirty, a mere five years older than me. The contrast between us couldn't have been greater. I didn't need a mirror to tell me how I looked – I'd had enough mornings like these to know that I had mascara and eyeliner smeared round my eyes, and my bleached hair was sticking up all over the place. I no doubt resembled something even the cat wouldn't bother to drag in.

With a strength I was surprised I could muster, I forced myself off the bed and stood to face him, my arms folded across my chest. 'You could've knocked.'

Irritation at being woken, and the pounding in my head, put me on the defensive. But if I was hoping he might apologise, I clearly had no chance. He looked just as furious as I felt.

'And you could have answered the door. I've been ringing that wretched intercom for twenty minutes.'

'Yeah?' I affected a bored look. 'Well maybe you should've taken the hint and left.'

'Oh, no, Charlotte.' I winced at his use of my full name – only he and my family ever called me that these days. To everyone else, I was Charlie. 'Not today. It's your parents' thirty-fifth wedding anniversary party. You're going, even if I have to drag you there, kicking and screaming.'

I didn't doubt that he would, so I wisely kept my mouth shut. I felt too fragile to be getting into one of our arguments this early in the day.

Richard cast a quick glance around my room. I could sense his disapproval, and I felt a twinge of guilt at the state of the place. Lindsay and I were lucky enough to live in a top-floor warehouse conversion in the heart of Shoreditch.

Even though the area's relentless gentrification meant it was no longer considered cutting-edge, it was still a decent enough area for going out, with lots of good bars and clubs. Our flat was pretty impressive, too – it had double-height ceilings, exposed brickwork and original iron beams. Obviously under normal circumstances the apartment was well out of our price range, but luckily for us a school friend of Lindsay's owned the place, and when his lucrative banking job took him to Hong Kong, he'd let us stay here for a fraction of the market price – I suspected because he had a crush on my friend. We'd repaid his generosity by completely trashing the place.

My room was by far the worst. Dirty plates and mugs were scattered across every surface; it was impossible to see the polished concrete floor with all the clothes strewn over it; and there were two used condoms on the bedside table. Oh, well – at least Richard should give me points for practising safe sex. It still amazed me, my instinctive sense of self-preservation – no matter how drunk I was, I always managed to insist on taking proper precautions.

Richard's eyes finally settled on the naked man in my bed – taking in his long, greasy hair, the piercings and tattoos.

'And who might this be?' Richard made no effort to disguise his distaste. It didn't bother me in the slightest. I'd never made any attempt to hide how I lived my life, and while this might be the first time he'd been so directly confronted with it, I didn't give a damn if he had a problem with it. If anything, I hoped this might make him stop coming round. It wasn't that I didn't like Richard, I just resented his interference in my life, and went out of my way to remind him of that every chance I got. It had become a game – whenever we saw each other, I'd try to push his buttons, being deliberately rude and ungrateful, and he'd do his best to ignore me. One day I was sure I'd find his Achilles' heel and get him out of my life for good. Until then, I'd just have fun goading him as best I could.

I followed his gaze to my unwanted bedfellow and shrugged. 'Your guess is as good as mine.'

Richard's nose wrinkled at that, which was exactly the reaction I'd been trying to elicit. In fact, I knew exactly who the tattooed guy in my bed was. It had come back to me now – his name was Gavin, and he was the lead singer in a band who'd played at the bar a few times. But it amused me to try to shock calm, unflappable Richard.

My bed-mate was by now wide awake and struggling to sit up. His eyes were wide with apology and fixed firmly on Richard. 'Aw, shit. I didn't realise she had a boyfriend, mate.'

'He's not my boyfriend,' I said automatically.

'And if I was, you wouldn't still be in that bed. Trust me. Mate.'

Richard's silky-smooth voice belied the threat behind his words. I could see Mr Rock Band swallow, hard, and I bit back a smile. Richard might act and dress all corporate, but at six foot three and 180 pounds of pure muscle, it was clear he wasn't someone to pick a fight with. Even if you didn't know he had a black belt in Taekwondo.

He turned his attention back to me, his gaze sweeping over my kimono and dishevelled appearance. 'I take it you're not intending to attend lunch looking like that?'

'Of course not. Give me fifteen minutes to have a shower and get ready.'

'You have five. We're already late.'

He didn't need to bother adding that it was my fault we were in that predicament. Earlier that week, when he'd phoned to arrange to pick me up, we'd agreed that I'd be outside, ready and waiting when he arrived. Personally I thought he should have known better than to expect me to be so willing.

'Fine.' I wasn't about to argue with him, but I had no problem teaching him a lesson for being so inflexible. 'If that's how you want it . . .'

Before he could figure out what I was about to do, I loosened the tie on my kimono and slipped it from my shoulders, letting it drop to the floor so I was standing there stark naked.

Perhaps it wouldn't have been such a statement if I had the kind of boyish figure that fashion models possess. But instead I had Jessica Rabbit curves, which I'd given up trying to hide a long time ago. Even Richard, the master of self-control, couldn't help letting his eyes linger on my 34C breasts a second longer than he should have. I watched his jaw tighten, which was pretty much the biggest reaction I ever got from Richard, and then he averted his eyes.

I crossed the room, walking deliberately by him, and started hunting in my drawer for underwear.

'Jesus, Charlotte,' he muttered.

I turned back to him, affecting an innocent look. 'What? I'm just getting ready, like you asked.'

His scowl deepened. 'I'm not in the mood for your games today. I'll wait downstairs in the car for you. Be there in five minutes, or I'll come back up and drag you out. If you choose to act like a child, then I'll be forced to treat you like one.'

He swept from the room before I had a chance to reply.

Once he was gone, Gavin let out a long sigh of relief. I started at the sound – I'd almost forgotten he was there.

'Wow.' He shook his head. 'That's one tightly wound asshole.'

'Tell me about it.' I turned back to my underwear drawer, selecting the only clean bra and panties left in there. I put them on with my back to Gavin, but he didn't seem to get the hint that I just wanted him to shut up and quietly disappear from my life.

'Well . . .' he drawled. Why was it that men felt obliged to make conversation with their one-night stands? I blamed all those movies that suggested women got upset if a guy didn't automatically start proposing when they slept together. I forced myself to face him. Gavin had on what I presumed was the most polite expression he could manage. He scratched his head a little, looking beyond awkward. 'I guess I should get your number or something. Maybe we could hang out sometime.'

'Yeah.' I spoke with exaggerated seriousness. 'We should totally do that. Maybe go for dinner and a movie. We could hold hands and everything.'

'Huh?'

It took all my willpower not to laugh at his obvious confusion. It was clearly his looks rather than his quick wit that had attracted me last night.

'Look,' I said, as I wriggled into a denim miniskirt and pulled on the cleanest white tank top I could find. 'Let's not pretend last night was anything other than what it was. We got drunk, I invited you back to my place, and we shagged. To be perfectly honest, I can't remember much about the whole evening, but I'm guessing that we both got what we wanted out of it. So, as far as I see it, that's pretty much the end of our involvement.'

I couldn't help enjoying the look of astonishment on his face. He obviously wasn't used to the women he bedded behaving this way.

'So you're saying you're happy with what went on last night. You don't want anything else?'

Ten out of ten for catching on quick. I'd obviously picked up the equivalent of a dumb blonde.

'That's exactly what I'm saying,' I said with exaggerated patience.

He looked at me with the kind of undisguised admiration that should be saved for whoever cures cancer. 'You know something? You're a really cool girl.'

'Yeah? My parents will be so proud.'

I reached for my biker boots, my footwear of choice, but then noted the sun streaming through the Velux windows that lined the ceiling. It was late September, but it looked more like mid-summer, and so I slipped on a slightly grubby pair of cream pumps instead. I dug through the pockets of the jeans I'd had on last night, found my purse and keys, and chucked them into the busted-up faux leather bag I took everywhere.

'Help yourself to tea, coffee, and whatever we have in the fridge,' I said, as I made my way out the door. It was meant to be a good exit line, but it seemed to throw Gavin even further.

'What? You mean, you don't mind me staying here once you've gone? That's a bit trusting of you.'

'Not really. If you even think about disturbing my flat-mate, she'll stab you in the eye, and—' I gave a pointed glance round the room – 'if you can find something worth stealing in here, then you're more than welcome to it.'

The intercom sounded then, Richard's way of letting me know that my five minutes was up. I popped briefly into the bathroom, deciding he'd rather I took the time to brush my teeth and gargle some mouthwash than have me breathe stale alcohol fumes all over him for the two-hour drive.

Once I'd finished, I made the mistake of looking in the mirror above the sink. Panda eyes stared back at me. Why couldn't I ever remember to take my make-up off? I ran a hand through my bleached hair. I was still getting used to it. I changed the colour every few weeks – I'd been everything from bright pink to ebony black. Platinum blonde wouldn't have been my choice, but I'd told Lindsay to surprise me, and she had. If my skin had been more tanned, maybe it would have looked tartier – but the white blonde against my Casper-the-friendly-ghost colouring gave me an Emo, edgy look, and made my eyes look an even more unnatural corn-flower blue than usual.

A wave of exhaustion washed over me, which had nothing to do with how little I'd slept last night. I so wasn't prepared for this day – lunch with my parents and two hundred of their closest colleagues and friends. I could just imagine my mother's face when she saw me – her trouble-making youngest daughter, the university dropout who worked in a bar – turning up hung-over and in a ridicu-lously tiny miniskirt, amongst a sea of overachievers in floral dresses and suits. Ah, being the black sheep of the family was always a fun role to play.

I took a deep breath, mentally shaking myself out of my moment of self-pity. Then I grabbed some face wipes and stuffed them in my bag, sprayed on a liberal amount of deodorant that I feared still wouldn't mask the smell of fags and booze, and headed downstairs to see what the dreaded day would bring.

Chapter 2

I emerged from our flat and ran down the five flights of stairs to the ground floor. My hand trailed against the roughness of the exposed brickwork walls as I went. I could have done without all the jolting around, as my head was still pounding, but it was the quickest way to the bottom. There was a lift – one of those old service elevators, lovingly restored – but at this time on a Sunday morning, it would be experiencing peak-time use, as the other occupants headed out for a leisurely brunch.

Downstairs, in the small lobby of the building, I found Richard sitting on the antique leather chesterfield couch, waiting for me. A well-groomed brunette sat next to him. It didn't take a genius to figure out that this was his latest girl-friend. He was a serial monogamist, and he definitely had a type – they were all conventionally beautiful, intelligent . . . and somewhat bland. Posh Pashminas, as Lindsay and I liked to call them. The kind of Home Counties' girls who spent their whole life doing the right thing, without ever questioning if it was what they really wanted – they went on skiing holidays; knew how to scuba dive; enjoyed the theatre; had probably taken a year out to travel to India. All before completing a degree at one of the 'good' universities and finding a prestigious graduate job in London – law, banking or management consultancy – to tide them over until they could get married.

To me, they were perfectly boring, their lives devoid of any real passion. To Richard, they made the perfect girlfriends.

I cast a look over his latest. She was model-tall and slender, with chocolate-brown hair that fell in Kate Middleton waves around her shoulders, presumably the result of a professional blow-dry this morning. She rose with Richard, and I took in her tailored cream dress, that fell demurely below the knee. She was perfectly attired for a late-summer luncheon party. This was the kind of daughter my mother longed for. She was probably only a couple of years older than me, but next to her, I felt like a teenager again.

She greeted me with a friendly smile, and held out her hand. 'You must be Charlotte.'

'Charlie,' I corrected automatically, ignoring the hand. That threw her. She glanced over at Richard and frowned, obviously upset about having got a detail wrong. That was the other thing about his girlfriends – they were all perfectionists and overachievers.

'Oh, right, of course. Charlie. It's lovely to meet you at last.'

Richard's girlfriends were never entirely sure how to treat me. I suspected he described me as something like a younger sister, so they invariably started off trying to be pleasant to me, wanting to win me over. But it quickly became apparent to them that they were never going to get on with me, so after a while they settled into just being as polite as possible whenever I was around – or ignoring me, which worked, too.

I turned to Richard. 'So this is your latest.'

'Petra Hawthorne,' she filled in.

I looked back at her, seeing a chance to cause trouble for Richard. 'I've stopped learning the names of Richard's girlfriends. Every time he drags me down to one of these family occasions, he has a new one. He never seems to keep them for longer than six months.'

'Which is five months and twenty-nine days longer than you keep your boyfriends,' he fired back. Then he seemed to notice Petra, who was looking between us frowning, clearly perturbed by our sparring. I'd guess that if there was one quality she lacked, it would be a sense of humour.

Richard rested his hand on her small waist. 'Don't worry, darling.' His voice was smooth and reassuring, but I could hear an edge to it, which I knew was directed at me.

'Charlotte's just kidding around. Pay no attention to her, I certainly don't.'

'Oh right,' Petra forced a smile. 'I see.'

He ushered her outside, shooting a frown at me over his shoulder, a clear signal to behave. They did make an attractive couple, I admitted reluctantly as I followed after them. Very grown up and sophisticated. Trailing behind them, I felt a bit like their wayward teenage daughter, and for the first time, I began to wish I'd made a bit more effort this morning – at the least that I'd had time for a shower.

I'd heard Richard had a new car, and when I saw it my heart sank. Outwardly, it was impressive – a sleek Mercedes-Benz, CL-class coupé, in a dark silvery-grey. But basically it was one of those two-door sports cars, really only meant for a couple, with a cramped seat in the back for those occasions when you had an extra passenger. I didn't deal well with confined spaces, and just the thought of being cooped up in there for more than five minutes made my heart start to beat faster.

Confirming my fears, Richard opened the door, and pulled the driver's seat forward for me to climb in the back. I just looked at him.

'What's the problem?' The amusement in his voice belied his innocent face.

'You seriously expect me to spend the next two hours squashed up in the back?' It would take at least that to get to my parents' country house in Hampshire.

'How else are you planning to get to Claylands?'

I stared at him for a long moment, contemplating whether I dared head back inside. But finally I gave in and clambered into the back seat, muttering a few choice oaths under my breath as I did so.

I shifted around, trying to get comfortable, as the other two got in. Richard put the key in the ignition, but before he started the car his gaze caught mine in the rear-view mirror.

'The seatbelt's there for a reason.'

I sighed with exasperation, but did as he said and fastened the seatbelt. At this point, I just wanted to get the whole day over with as fast as possible.

As we started on our journey, Petra kept up a steady stream of bright, polite chatter – everything from how lucky we were to have such good weather today, to where they'd been for dinner the night before, as well as expounding about her job as a PR executive at a FTSE 100 company, which apparently she *absolutely loved*. We'd only been driving for about fifteen minutes, and had just reached Chelsea, when Richard began to slow the car.

'It's just over there.' Petra pointed to an upmarket florist's shop.

'Why're we stopping?'

Petra turned to me with a big smile, clearly still trying to win me over. 'I ordered some flowers for your parents, and I just need to nip in and collect them. I know how important your mum and dad are to Richard, so I wanted to get them something really lovely.'

It took me a second to figure out that it was a present for their anniversary. That was probably something I should have done, too. Oh, well. Too late now. Maybe she'd let me put my name on the card . . .

But just as that selfish little thought was going through my head, I saw the look of gratitude that Richard shot Petra, and I felt ashamed. My mum and dad had been good to him over the years, and he'd never forgotten their kindness. As my brother's best friend, he'd always been welcome at our house. But then, when he was nineteen, his parents had died in a plane crash. He hadn't had any siblings or close living relatives, so my mum and dad had made it clear that he was to treat their home as his own, and there'd always been a place for him at Christmas and Easter. After my brother died, they'd made a point of keeping in touch with him. In return, he seemed to have made it his mission to keep an eye on their wayward youngest daughter.

Naturally Richard offered to go and collect the flowers – because he prided himself on being a gentleman – but Petra insisted on doing it, so she could check they'd got the order correct. I watched as she got out of the car, and ran delicately across the road in her heels.

'So what happened to Prince Charming?' Richard said after a moment.

It took me a second to figure out he was referring to Gavin, my overnight guest. 'He'll see himself out.'

He frowned at me in the rear-view mirror. 'Aren't you getting a little old for these one-night stands? You do know that you don't have to sleep with every loser who crosses your path.'

His words didn't bother me. I'd heard it all before. As far as I was concerned, it was up to me how I lived – and no one had the right to judge me. 'Have you ever considered that it's about me, not them? That maybe I just like sex, but I don't want a boyfriend? And that someone like Gavin allows me to have that – a great time in the bedroom, but with no strings attached.'

'Is that so?' Richard raised a sceptical eyebrow. 'Because given the state you were both in this morning, I find it hard to believe you derived any pleasure from whatever took place in your bed last night.' I wished I could contradict him, but frankly I couldn't since I had no memory of what had happened. 'And anyway surely sex isn't just about physical gratification – it's much more about expressing emotional intimacy.'

'Oh, yeah?' My lips twitched into a smile. 'Is that what your girlfriends tell you? Maybe you're just not doing it right.'

'Ha, ha. Very funny.' He rolled his eyes, as if to suggest I was being childish, but I ignored him. This was far too good an opportunity to tease him.

'Or have you ever thought it might just be the women you're dating?' I went on, inclining my head towards the florist's shop. 'I imagine Little Miss Uptight likes it missionary with the lights off.'

Richard didn't bother to respond. He was too smart to rise to such obvious bait. So instead I leaned forward, folding my arms along the headrest of the passenger seat, and resting my chin on my hands, so my head was turned directly to him. If I was going to goad him, I needed to try a little harder.

'Or maybe I'm wrong. Perhaps Petra likes to get a little dirty in the bedroom. For the moment anyway . . . It's probably all part of her ploy to hook you into marriage, isn't it?'

Richard's dark eyes flicked over to mine. 'Trust me, marriage is the last thing on Petra's mind. She's focused on her career right now.'

'Oh, please,' I scoffed. 'Come on. Even you can't be so naïve to fall for that line.'

As much as he might irritate me, Richard was what most women would deem a 'catch'. He was good-looking, charming – if a little uptight – and, most importantly of all in these situations, he was seriously minted.

His father had run a successful advertising business before he died, and as his only child, Richard had inherited all the shares. He'd continued with his plan to finish his degree at Oxford University, allowing the management team to run the company. But then when he graduated, he entered the business and began to learn the ropes. I'd never shown much interest, but from what my parents said, he'd assumed control two years ago, on his twenty-eighth birthday, and the company had expanded greatly under his stewardship.

Unsurprisingly, given all of that, he had been featured in *Tatler* as one of their 'Most Eligible Bachelors' for the past few years. It caused me much amusement, but there were women out there who took it deadly seriously. Every girl that Richard dated was desperate for him to put a ring on her finger. For all her practised nonchalance, Petra was undoubtedly salivating at the thought.

'Trust me,' I said. 'She's after a big, fat diamond on her left hand.'

He shrugged, refusing to be drawn. 'Even if she is, that doesn't mean it's going to happen.'

'Oh, really?' I lifted an eyebrow. 'How can you be so sure about that?'

'Because I'd need to propose, and right now I have no intention of doing so. I'm too busy with the company to even think about settling down.'

'Perhaps.' I pretended to muse on this for a moment. 'But what if she gets pregnant?'

He flicked a look over to me. 'She won't,' he said flatly.

'How can you be sure? Because she's told you she's on the pill? Or is she letting you "take care of business"? Either way, no contraception is one hundred per cent infallible.' I affected a shocked look, placing a hand to my mouth in a gesture of surprise. '*Oh, Richard darling, I have no idea how this happened.*' I mimicked Petra's high-pitched voice. '*I didn't want to get pregnant, you know that, but now that I am, whatever shall we do?*' I paused. '*Marriage, you say? Well, I'd never given it much thought. But now that you mention it, I've had my eye on this little diamond ring in Boodles—*'

'Okay, okay.' Richard cut me off. He was trying to sound like he didn't care, but I could hear the irritation in his voice. 'That's enough. I get the idea.'

I would have gone on further, despite what he said, but Petra came out of the florist's then, carrying a huge bouquet of white and pink roses and lilies. Usually Richard would have been straight out of the car, opening the door for her, but now I saw him hesitate for just the briefest of moments. Whatever I'd said had done the job. He wouldn't be able to look at Petra in quite the same light from now on. I felt a pang of remorse, but quickly quashed it. This was payback for him dragging me along to my parents' lunch, and no less than he deserved.

There was a tap on the window, as Petra tried to get his attention. 'Would you mind helping me, darling?' I could see from the quizzical look on her face that she was wondering why his assistance wasn't as forthcoming as usual.

'Sure. Of course.' He got out of the car, and helped her arrange the bouquet in the back, on the seat next to me.

'Lovely flowers, aren't they?' Petra said, once they were settled back in.

'Hmm.' Richard was non-committal as he started the engine up.

Petra frowned. This obviously wasn't the response she'd been expecting. She put a hand on his wrist.

'Is anything wrong, darling?'

'Why would it be?' His voice was polite but cool. 'I'm just concentrating on driving.'

'Oh.' She forced a bright smile. 'Of course.'

She removed her hand, and turned to look out the window. They lapsed into silence.

I snuggled down in the back seat, trying to get as comfortable as possible in the cramped space, and closed my eyes, allowing a little satisfied smile to play across my lips. Now that I'd ruined Richard's afternoon, I could happily go to sleep.

The jerk of the car as it went over a speed bump woke me. My eyes flew open, and I saw that we were on the country road that led to Claylands, my parents' house. I'd slept through the whole journey.

'Gosh, it's even more beautiful than you told me,' Petra cooed at Richard from the passenger seat, as we pulled up to my childhood home.

Even I couldn't disagree with that. My mother liked to refer to Claylands as 'the cottage', but in reality it was a grand Georgian house, with ten acres of land attached, as well as stables and a barn conversion for guests. The long driveway was already lined with cars – my lie-in had obviously made us one of the last to arrive – so Richard dropped Petra and me at the house, and then went to park.

I could see Petra was impressed as we entered the wood-panelled hallway.

A young man, dressed in a white suit that designated him as one of the catering staff, stepped forward to take our names. 'Ah, yes.' He frowned a little when he heard who I was. 'If you'll just wait here for a moment, I'll get your mother. She asked to be alerted to your arrival.'

'Of course she did,' I muttered as he hurried off.

My parents weren't exactly filthy rich, but they were certainly well-off by most people's standards. They were both leaders in their respective fields of law and medicine, and that inevitably had brought financial rewards. That didn't mean I had money, though. My mum and dad were great believers in the idea that everyone should make their own way in life. Ever since I could remember, they'd told us children that we would never inherit a penny from them – they intended to donate everything to charity. They would happily pay for our education, but after that we were on our own.

Friends often thought I'd be bitter about them withholding their money, but frankly I thought their reasoning made sense. From the moment I'd been kicked out of university at nineteen, I'd been supporting myself, and I was quite happy to do so. I suppose it would be easy to argue that I would always have a safety net if anything went horribly wrong – but anyone who thought I'd go running back to Mummy and Daddy if I messed up didn't know me very well. I'd rather gnaw my right arm off than lose my independence.

'What a lovely picture.' Petra's voice broke into my thoughts. I followed her eyes up to the family portrait on the wall. It had been painted nine years ago, around the time of my sixteenth birthday. It showed my mum and dad, along with Kit, who was twenty-one at the time, Kate, who was nineteen, and a 16-year-old me. I had on a tartan skirt and red blouse, buttoned up to the neck; my mousey brown curls had been blow-dried straight into a sensible centre parting, and I was smiling into the camera, looking fresh-faced, sweet and happy – almost unrecognisable compared with the unashamedly slutty and cynical 25-year-old standing here today.

'You must have had an idyllic childhood here.'

I didn't say anything. It just went to show how deceptive appearances could be.

Speaking of which . . .

'Charlotte, darling!' My mother appeared then, looking as elegant and stylish as ever. She was fifty-nine now, but could easily pass for a decade younger. Her smooth English rose complexion appeared almost unlined, and her dark brown hair showed no grey hairs, simply falling into a perfect bob. Still as trim as ever, she was sporting a well-cut duck-egg-blue suit, which made her look somewhere between a businesswoman and a very youthful mother-of-the-bride.

She came over and kissed me on both cheeks. My mother was nothing if not scrupulously polite. 'I'm so glad you could make it.' Once she'd finished the perfunctory embrace, she stepped back to survey me. She took in my low-cut tank top and tiny skirt, and frowned, wrinkling her perfect button nose a little. 'Though I thought I told you it was something of a formal occasion . . .'

And there it was. The inevitable criticism.

My mother switched her attention to Petra. 'And you must be Richard's new girlfriend.' I could see straight away that my mum approved. She beamed as Petra handed her the huge bouquet of roses and lilies. 'Oh, how lovely! That's so thoughtful of you. And there was no need, after that wonderful case of wine you and Richard sent. Amazing that you found something dating back to the year of our wedding!'

'It was Richard who arranged that,' Petra said.

'Of course it was,' I muttered. 'Thoughtful as always.' It was hard to admire these gestures when they showed me up so completely.

As if on cue, the man himself appeared. My mother beamed as she spotted him.

'Oh, Richard, it's so good to see you,' she said, as they embraced. 'And thank you for bringing Charlotte.' I grimaced at the way she talked about me as though I was a child.

'Where's Dad?' I asked. I needed him to control my mother's inevitable jibes, and his absence was leaving me vulnerable to attack.

'He's out in the garden, along with the rest of our guests. In fact, I hate to hurry you all, but I think we really ought to go through. We're just about to serve lunch, which I know probably seems like something of a rush, but unfortunately you are the last to arrive so you've missed most of the drinks reception.'

My mother shot a pointed glance at me, leaving everyone in no doubt that she knew exactly who was responsible for our tardiness. Without further ado, she linked arms with Richard and Petra, and led them out into the garden.

I didn't make any move to follow them. Instead my gaze shifted to the front door, as I wondered if I had the guts to cut my losses and leave right now. But then I heard my mother calling my name, and with a heavy sigh, I abandoned my thoughts of escape and headed out to the party.

Chapter 3

I could hear the sounds of chatter and laughter growing closer as we walked through the house. There were several ways to reach the garden, but by far the most impressive was through the beautiful drawing room, and so that's where my mother guided us. It set the scene for the day well. The French windows that lined the exterior wall had been thrown open for the occasion, and the delicate cream voile curtains fluttered in the soft breeze.

As we stepped outside onto the patio, I blinked against the harsh white light of the sun. It took me a moment to focus, and then I was finally able to take in the scene before me. It felt like a garden party from the Edwardian era, with guests scattered across the manicured lawn, a sea of floral dresses and suits, while waiting staff circulated with trays of Pimm's and Buck's Fizz. At the end of the garden, there was a huge white marquee, where lunch would be served.

When my parents were initially planning the party, my mother had stated in no uncertain terms that she wanted to eat outside – after all, the garden was her pride and joy, and she took every opportunity to show it off. But the late September date had meant the weather was a risk, so she'd been forced to agree to a marquee. Although looking around at the clear blue skies today, it seemed we could have done without the tent – even the English weather hadn't dared to disappoint my mother.

'Sweetheart!' I turned to see my father, walking towards us. My face lit up with a smile – the first genuine one of the day – and I forgot how much I didn't want to be here, as I ran and threw myself into his arms.

As we embraced, I couldn't help thinking how frail he felt. He'd had a heart attack three months earlier, and the subsequent bypass surgery had taken a lot out of him.

I drew away a little, my eyes scanning him. 'How're you feeling?'

He smiled down at me, his soft brown eyes crinkling at the corners. He'd aged noticeably these past few months, and now looked every one of his sixty years. He still looked good for his age, but there was a weariness about him that worried me. It probably didn't help that he was dressed more like a professor than a successful neurologist, in navy trousers and a tweed jacket, which made him seem more vulnerable, like a bumbling intellectual.

'Oh, I'm fine,' he said. 'Apart from this blasted diet your mother's got me on.'

'Still?'

'Yep. No red meat, cheese or alcohol. And far too much fish, vegetables and salad.' He pulled a face. 'Sometimes I wonder whether it's worth it to stay alive!'

'Yeah, I can see that.' But as much as I sympathised, at least it explained some of the weight loss. He'd always been a big man, who liked the good life a little too much. Less of the port he loved would be a good thing if it kept him healthy.

'Of course you'd know all this if you came to visit more often,' my mother joined in, pulling herself away from her conversation with Richard and Petra.

'Oh, Eleanor, leave her alone.' As usual, my father came to my defence. 'She's young. She should be out enjoying herself.'

'Well, she certainly knows how to do that,' my mother retorted.

Even though her criticism annoyed me, I did feel a little ashamed. I'd always got on well with my father, and I hated how sporadically I saw him now. Before his heart attack, he'd spent two days a week working in London, and we'd regularly met for lunch or dinner. But for the past three months he'd been confined to Claylands while he recuperated. That meant the only way I got to see him was if I came here, which meant I'd be stuck with my mother, too. Needless to say, my visits had been minimal.

Before I could respond, my sister came over to greet us. Kate looked as stunning as ever, her bright eyes and radiant skin a testament to her healthy lifestyle. A registrar in oncology, her career was going well too, and she was already talking about becoming a consultant. At twenty-eight, she seemed to have it all.

'Charlotte! What have you done to your hair?' Kate looked slightly appalled as she eyed my bleached locks. Her gaze ran over my tight top and tiny skirt, and she frowned her disapproval.

It wasn't exactly a surprise that she felt that way. Kate's sense of style had always been more conservative than mine, and that was putting it mildly. In a strapless pale-pink sundress, with a cream pashmina covering her shoulders, she looked fresh and youthful, if a little conventional for my taste.

'So you finally made it, Charlotte.' Kate's boyfriend, Toby, appeared at her side. 'We were about to send out a search party.'

To soften the jibe, he flashed his movie star smile, and I tried hard not to think about punching out his set of perfect white teeth. Like my sister, Toby was a doctor – a promising plastic surgeon. He was the original blond, blue-eyed boy – tall, athletic and handsome – the perfect match for my perfect sister, as everyone was constantly telling me. Seeing them together was yet another reminder of what a fuck-up I was.

Toby cast a pointed look around. 'Still no boyfriend then, Charlotte?' His tone had that irritating tinge of surprise mixed with pity that was clearly meant to make me feel deficient.

'I planned to bring a date, but he was too exhausted to get up this morning. Guess I wore him out last night.'

My comment was met with an embarrassed silence. Toby gave a brief shake of his head, as if to say, 'typical', while Kate sighed wearily.

I watched as Toby snaked a comforting arm around her waist, and she tilted her head to gaze up at him. My eyes narrowed at the sickening display of affection between them. It was hard to believe I'd once had a schoolgirl crush on my sister's boyfriend. It was something I'd definitely rather forget.

I tore my eyes away, and looked round at my family. It was funny, seeing us all together. It made my brother's absence even more pronounced. Although it was eight years since Kit died, the loss still weighed on us all. On occasions like this, it was hard not to feel like someone was missing. I saw my mother looking over at Richard, and wondered if she was thinking the same.

My parents had always adored Richard, but I think their bond had intensified since Kit's death. My brother and

Richard had been alike in so many ways – both of them smart, good-looking and sporty – and at the boarding school they'd attended, they'd been natural competitors. It had never caused friction between them, instead spurring them on to try harder. It had also led them to make the fatal decision to climb Mont Blanc together. Richard had somehow survived the avalanche that killed Kit, and I think it had connected him to our family forever. Just as he was without parents, my mum and dad were without a son. I think they all tried to fill the void in each other's lives.

'Right.' My mother cleared her throat, and forced a bright smile. 'Let's go in for lunch.'

With a deft signal to the catering staff, she began to make the rounds, ushering everyone towards the marquee.

'Shall we?' My father offered me his arm, and we began to make our way down to the huge tent.

As we stepped inside the marquee, I allowed myself a small smile. My mother had outdone herself once again. The interior looked exquisite. There were about twenty round tables, covered in crisp, white tablecloths, with low centrepieces of cream avalanche roses. The walls were draped in ivory gauze, and white peonies festooned the arching ceiling. Every little detail had been attended to. It could easily have been the scene of a beautiful – and expensive – wedding.

I was seated with my family and a few close friends at the head table. All the other tables were set for ten guests, but on ours there were only nine of us: four couples – my parents, my sister and her boyfriend, Richard and Petra, my father's colleague, Winston Hammond, and his wife, Grace – and then me on my own, the odd one out as usual.

I took my place between my father and Grace Hammond. I'd met Grace on occasions like this before. She was a sweet, motherly woman, who lived in the shadow of her somewhat overbearing husband.

As the waiters began to pour water, and bring round baskets of bread, Grace turned to me. 'And how are you, Charlotte? It's been such a long time, I hardly recognised you.' Her eyes ran over me, and then she stopped, frowning at my back. 'Oh.' She blinked. 'What's that you've got there?'

Damn. She'd spotted my tattoo. If I'd thought more, I would have covered it up today – it was easier than answering questions about it. But she was looking at me expectantly, so I had no choice but to turn a little to show it to her. It was just below my right shoulder, a drawing of a single rose . . . but it was more than that – the flower seemed to resemble a person wracked with sorrow, standing up on its thorny stem, its bloom drooped over like a bowed head, shedding its petals as if it was dripping blood or crying tears.

The whole table had stopped chatting and turned to witness our conversation unravel. I could sense poor Grace was searching for something to say.

'I've never seen anything quite like it. Have you, Winston?' Her husband grunted. I could tell she was at a loss as to how to continue, but then her expression cleared a little. 'Although of course, you're an artist, aren't you? I suppose this sort of thing is normal for you creative types. I must seem like an old fuddy-duddy.' She laughed self-deprecatingly, but no one joined in.

'Actually, I wouldn't really call myself an artist.' I tore off a piece of ciabatta and dipped it in some olive oil. 'I didn't even finish art school. I got kicked out at the end of my first year.' I popped the bread in my mouth and started to chew it slowly. I sensed this was going to take her a while to digest.

'Oh.' Shock registered on her face. Cranfords didn't fail at anything. 'So what are you doing now?'

'Working in a bar.'

There was silence. My mother took a long sip of water. Poor Grace looked around the table, obviously hoping someone would help her out. But mostly there was just an embarrassed silence.

'So what are your plans?' she tried again. It was obvious she couldn't quite believe that was all I was doing. 'Are you going to reapply to university?'

'Not if I can help it.'

There was a marked silence from everyone else at the table. They were all suddenly preoccupied with buttering their rolls or pouring more water, clearly embarrassed by the line of questioning.

'Oh, yes. Of course.' Grace turned to the table and shrugged. 'That's what all the young people do these days, isn't it? Take some time out to "find themselves".' She laughed a little. 'I'm so old-fashioned and out of touch.'

She launched into a long story about one of her children's friends, who had spent several years in India, before coming back to London and settling down to work in investment banking. I think the message was that they shouldn't give up hope on me, but I doubt it made my family feel any better.

The waiter came round, and offered wine. I'd been about to refuse – the tequila hangover wasn't sitting well with me – but when I spotted the disapproving frown on my mother's face, I couldn't resist letting him pour a glass. I lifted it, and offered a toast to my mother.

'Hair of the dog,' I said, before forcing myself to take a large sip just to irritate her. Her lips pursed, and I forced a smile. But as soon as she turned her attention to Toby, I pushed the glass away.

Lunch dragged on for what seemed like forever. It was a light summer menu of a smoked salmon starter, followed by lemon zest chicken, accompanied by baby new potatoes and crisp green beans. By the time the plates had been cleared, almost two hours had passed. I wondered about trying to make an escape for a quick fag break. But before I could do so, the waiters started serving plates of Eton Mess dessert and filling up the champagne flutes on the table – a sure sign that the speech part of the festivities was upon us.

When everyone had their glass filled, my father got to his feet, and the room slowly fell silent. I was pleased he was getting to talk for once – my mother's feminist zeal meant she was forever taking charge, just to prove that she could. It was nice to see my dad taking centre stage for a change.

He started by thanking everyone for coming, and then began to talk about himself and my mother as a couple – how they'd met and fallen in love, married and begun to build a life together, supporting each other's hopes and dreams along the way. It was lovely to hear him reminisce like that, and I could see the guests around the room smiling at his anecdotes.

'And best of all,' he said finally, looking tenderly towards Kate and then me, 'she gave me three beautiful children, Christopher, Catherine and Charlotte. They have given us both so much pleasure over the years, and it has been a joy to watch them grow up.' He paused, and I could feel the room tense a little, as everyone knew what was inevitably coming next. 'Of course, sadly our wonderful son Kit was taken from us far too soon.' People's eyes dropped to their tables, suddenly unable to watch my father. It was funny how uncomfortable grief made everyone. I kept my head up, and watched my brave father plough on. 'However, as much as we miss him, we still cherish the memories that we have of the time we did get to spend with him, and feel proud of the tremendous young man he had become.'

There was the faintest catch in his voice. He bowed his head a little, and waited for a beat to collect himself before turning to my mother. 'So, my darling wife Eleanor, I'd like to thank you for a wonderful thirty-five years of marriage, and I can only hope for many more.'

He raised his glass of champagne, and all the guests did the same. As I reached for my flute, I was surprised to find tears gathering in my eyes. I quickly brushed them away with the back of my hand. I hated the idea of anyone seeing me cry. But as I turned my attention back to my father, I felt someone's gaze on me. I looked over, and saw Richard watching me from across the table. He'd clearly seen my display of emotion, and I felt my cheeks flush. But instead of teasing me, he raised his glass in my direction, and mouthed 'To Kit'. The gesture brought a small smile to my face, and I raised my glass back.

The moment was broken as my parents kissed, and the room burst into a round of applause. With the speech finished, my mum and dad sat back down. But before lunch could resume, my sister's boyfriend, Toby, got to his feet.

'If you wouldn't mind,' he began, 'I'd like to say a few words, too.'

I sighed loudly enough for people at the next table to turn and cast disapproving looks at me. I ignored them. I couldn't stand Toby, and I didn't care who knew it. Apart from my mother, he was the main reason I avoided family get-togethers. It was typical of him to try to steal the limelight today. It was my parents' anniversary, and he had no business standing up to make a speech.

'Thank you, William, for that wonderful speech,' he said, before anyone could object. 'And thank you both for inviting us all to your home today to celebrate this glorious occasion with you.' I couldn't help rolling my eyes. His words sounded hollow to me, devoid of any real sentiment. 'I was lucky enough to meet your eldest daughter, Kate, almost eight years ago now. As when you two met, I was instantly smitten, and like you, I've wanted to make our union permanent.'

He paused dramatically, and dropped down onto one knee. There was a collective gasp around the room as everyone worked out what he was about to do. My hand tightened on the stem of my champagne glass, gripping it so hard that I feared it might snap right off.

'And so, Kate,' he went on. 'In front of all your friends and family here today, I'd like to ask whether you'd do me the honour of agreeing to marry me.'

Kate's eyes were wide and her mouth open, in an almost cartoon-like picture of surprise. It was quite obvious to anyone looking at her that she really hadn't known anything about Toby's proposal today. I felt a twinge of sympathy for my sister. It was a difficult position to put her in – she really didn't have much choice but to accept, unless she wanted to humiliate him. For a split second, I hoped she might just do that. But then she seemed to finally pull herself together, and the stunned look on her face dissolved into a tender smile.

'Yes.' Kate spoke so softly that only those of us sitting close enough to her could catch what she was saying. But the happy expressions on the faces of the newly betrothed couple and my parents left no one in any doubt as to what was going on. 'Yes, of course I'll marry you!'

As she stood and threw her arms around Toby, the room broke into another round of applause. And then it seemed everyone was on their feet, rushing to shake Toby's hand and kiss my sister's cheek.

I was left sitting alone, watching guest after guest congratulate Toby and my sister. As I stared fixedly ahead, I raised the champagne flute to my lips and downed the contents in one go.

'Charlotte?' I'd been so absorbed in the scene that I hadn't noticed my mother appear beside me. She ducked her head towards me, so no one could overhear her words. 'You need to go over and congratulate your sister and Toby.'

'Do I have to?'

'Yes, you do.' She sighed, and shook her head in exasperation. 'I don't know what your problem is with Toby. The two of you used to get on so well.'

'Yeah? Well, that was a long time ago.' My mother just gave me a look – the one that said she wasn't getting into an argument over this. I sighed in defeat. 'Okay, okay. I'll do it.'

'Good.'

My mother waited, clearly intending to make sure I went through with it. I sighed again and slowly got to my feet. There was a crowd around my sister, and I would have hung back, but when other guests spotted me, they cleared out of my way, mistakenly believing that I was eager to reach the happy couple. When Kate spotted me, she rushed over and flung herself into my arms. She was shaking with excitement.

'I really wasn't expecting this!' She pulled away, and I could see her eyes were bright and her cheeks flushed with happiness. I felt a pang of guilt that I couldn't feel happier for her. 'I can't believe I'm engaged!'

My sister didn't seem to notice my lack of response. She was too caught up in her big moment. She gave me one last hug, and then a second later she was swallowed up in a crowd of well-wishers.

With my duty done, I turned away, eager to get back to the safety of my table. But before I could move, Toby appeared in front of me.

'Charlotte, could I just have a moment?' he said, with what I presumed was his best impression of sincerity.

I crossed my arms over my chest, the classic defensive posture.

'What is it?' My voice was as cold and unfriendly as I could make it, and he winced at the tone.

'Look, I know we haven't always got on. But I hope now, with me marrying your sister, we can put our differences in the past.' He paused, his blue eyes growing solemn. 'For Kate's sake, if nothing else.'

With that, he reached out and squeezed my arm. My whole body tensed as he touched me. He couldn't have sounded more sincere during his little speech, but I didn't believe a word of it. It was embarrassing to think that I used to have a crush on the smarmy bastard. I felt ashamed of my 18-year-old self for having such poor judgement.

I didn't trust myself to speak, so I just fixed him with a glare. He immediately released my arm, and without a word, I brushed past him and hurried back to my table.

I felt a moment of relief as I slipped back into my seat. And then a knot of anxiety began to form in my stomach. I felt so detached from the festivities. My sister's engagement had made me feel even more isolated from my family than usual. There must have been over two hundred people surrounding me, and yet I'd never felt so alone.

By chance, a waiter happened to be passing nearby with a tray of freshly filled champagne glasses.

'Hey, wait.' He stopped, allowing me to reach up and grab a flute. I downed it in one, and put the empty glass back before grabbing another, plus a half-filled bottle that he'd brought with him for top-ups. He looked shocked by my behaviour, but clearly didn't know what to do about it. I flashed him a smile. 'That'll be all for now. I'll get back to you if I need anything else.'

I glanced around to check no one had noticed what I'd done. They hadn't – they were far too busy discussing the big announcement to pay any attention to me. So I poured another glass of champagne and started to drink. It was the only way I was going to get through the rest of the afternoon.

Half an hour later, everyone had finally returned to their seats. Clinks of cutlery against porcelain could be heard as the guests began to eat their dessert. I picked up my fork, and half-heartedly scooped up some of the Eton Mess, but the gooey meringue seemed too sweet after all the champagne. Pulling a face, I pushed my plate away, and instead surveyed my surroundings, looking for something to occupy me.

Conversation buzzed around me, none of which I felt like joining in with. My mother was busy talking to my sister and Toby, no doubt already making wedding plans, while my dad was occupied with Richard and Petra. Grace had excused herself to visit the ladies' room, which left just Winston and me unoccupied. He'd also finished with his pudding, and was sitting staring into his coffee. I would have turned away, imagining we had nothing to say to each other, but then I noticed his fingers tapping away in time to the song that the jazz quartet were playing.

I slid over into Grace's seat, and elbowed him to get his attention.

'Hey.' He looked up, startled to find me addressing him. I nodded towards the band, who were seated on the other side of the room. 'You like the song?'

'Uh . . . yes.' He looked a little taken aback by the question, but then he appeared to relax, as though he'd assessed my interest as genuine. 'It was actually the first dance at Grace's and my wedding.'

'Really?' My surprise wasn't faked. It was hard to imagine Winston having any kind of sentimental moment.

His mouth softened into a small smile. 'Yes. I was dreading it, you know. All those people looking at me. So I took dance classes, to surprise Grace on the day. Became pretty good at it, too.'

'Wow! I'm impressed.' Then a thought occurred to me. 'How about you show me some moves?'

Winston laughed a little, 'Oh, no. I don't think so—'

He obviously didn't think I was serious. 'Come on. I insist. Let's show them how it's done.'

As I got to my feet, I stumbled a little, feeling dazed. I'd worked my way through the rest of the champagne, without anyone having noticed. The bubbles had gone straight to my head, no doubt partly because last night's alcohol wasn't fully out of my system, so I felt more drunk than I should.

I tried to focus on Winston, who hadn't made any move to get up. 'Come on,' I repeated. 'What're you waiting for?'

'Honestly, Charlotte.' His eyes darted nervously around, as it dawned on him that I was serious. 'I really don't think this is a good idea—'

I grabbed his arm, ignoring the horrified look on his face. 'Don't be shy. It'll be fun.'

I tried to haul him up. Horrified, he pulled back. For a moment, a tug of war went on between us, and then I heard the sound of cloth tearing. A second later, the arm of his suit jacket ripped from its seam, sending me stumbling backwards.

I felt the ground slip from beneath me, and I grabbed at a tablecloth, trying to steady myself. But it was too late. I crashed onto the floor, landing hard on my bum, and dragging the contents of the table down too.

As the cutlery and plates clattered to the ground, there was a collective gasp of shock from around the room, as everyone turned to see what the commotion was about. With me flat on my back, and Winston clutching at his damaged suit, I could only imagine what the other guests made of the situation. I saw the looks of horror on everyone's faces, and for some reason it struck me as funny, and I started to laugh, big, hysterical guffaws that seemed out of place in the shocked silence of the tent.

Grace had reappeared and now rushed to her husband's side. All around me, anonymous hands were helping me up, asking in concerned tones if I was okay.

'Don't worry, everyone,' I said, as I straightened up, brushing off my skirt. My tone was overly loud, and I was feeling no pain, no doubt due to all the alcohol. 'I'm fine. Nothing damaged apart from my ego.'

Before I could even think of my next move, Richard appeared by my side, catching hold of my upper arm. Everyone no doubt assumed he was checking I was all right, so no one noticed as he whipped me round to face him, his disapproving dark eyes searching mine.

'How much have you had to drink?' His question was rhetorical, more of a rebuke than anything else. He shook his head. 'Couldn't you let your parents have this one day without ruining it?' I wanted to explain what had gone on – that I hadn't intended for any of this to happen. But he'd clearly already made his judgement, so instead I dropped my eyes, unable to stomach his reproachful gaze. I heard him sigh. 'I think it's time I took you home.'

I wasn't about to argue with that.

He looked around the room. At first I wasn't sure what he was doing, but then I saw Petra. He inclined his head, and she came over to join us.

'We're leaving.' His tone was brusque.

'So soon?' She sounded disappointed, but then her eyes darted between us, and she seemed to sense there was something going on and shut up.

My parents were on their way over to check on Winston. Richard guided me across the room, skilfully heading them off. His grip on me was firm, but he needn't have worried – I wasn't about to object. The sooner I got out of here the better.

He made our excuses to my parents, saying he had to get back to London to do some work that night.

'And pass on our apologies to Kate,' he said smoothly, casting a glance towards my sister, who was apologising profusely to Winston and Grace. 'She seems to have her hands full at the moment, but I'll call her during the week to catch up.'

'Of course. We're just sorry you couldn't stay longer.' My mother's eyes moved to me, making it clear that she knew I was the reason for our abrupt departure.

My father looked at me with concern. 'Are you okay, poppet?'

I felt a twinge of guilt for making him worry. It was the last thing he needed in his condition. 'I'm fine.' I managed a smile. 'You don't need to worry about me.'

With that, Richard caught me by the arm and led me out. It was probably just as well – I'd already caused enough damage for one day.

Chapter 4

Brakes screeched, and the car came to a sudden halt, throwing me forward so I woke with a start. For a moment I couldn't work out where I was, mostly because it was now dark. I sat up and looked round and saw that we were stuck in traffic on the Euston Road, just coming up to Kings Cross. That meant I'd slept the entire way back to London – no doubt courtesy of all the champagne I'd drunk at lunch.

Richard glanced back at me. 'You all right?'

I nodded, too groggy to form a sentence.

The Mercedes inched forward. All around us, horns blared, as drivers became increasingly frustrated with being overtaken by pedestrians. We'd hit the Sunday night rush hour, as everyone flooded back into London after the weekend. The mood in the car was quiet and tense. Even Petra didn't attempt any conversation – I think she could sense that Richard wasn't keen to engage in idle chatter.

'Can you drop me at The Nick?' I asked, breaking the silence. It was the bar where I worked, and spent most of my free time, too. I'd planned to go home and change before heading there, but at this rate it was going to take another forty minutes to get back to the flat.

Richard raised a sceptical eyebrow. 'Have you got a shift tonight?'

'Seeing a band.'

He sighed. 'Fine. Just tell me where I'm going.'

I directed him towards Camden, where The Nick was located just off the main high street. It was quite a journey for Lindsay and me to get there, but it was one of the best venues for up-and-coming rock bands, so we considered it worth the trek.

Ten minutes later, Richard turned right onto a dark, cobbled alley. The Nick was buried at the end of the street.

He pulled up outside the bar. Two guys with shaved heads and tattoos covering their arms walked past us. I could see Petra's hands automatically tighten on her handbag, her eyes widening with fear. The skinheads gave us a look of undisguised curiosity – I was certain they'd never seen a hundred-thousand-pound sports car parked outside The Nick before – and disappeared inside the bar.

'Well?' I made no effort to keep the impatience out of my voice. 'Are you going to let me out some time tonight?'

Petra went to say something to Richard – presumably to tell him that she didn't feel safe here – but he put a reassuring hand on her wrist, to say that he had it all under control.

He made no move to get out of the car, but instead turned in his seat so that he was facing me. 'So what's your plan, Charlotte?' His voice was more reasonable than usual. 'Are you meeting Lindsay here?'

I shrugged. 'She said she'd try to drop by later.'

'I see.' His face remained impassive, but I could tell that my answer hadn't made him happy. He ran a hand over his face, clearly trying to choose his words carefully. 'Look, Charlotte, I'll be honest with you. I don't like leaving you alone at a place like this.'

I pulled a face. 'Why? What's the big deal? I work here most nights.'

'I know that.' He spoke with slow deliberation, obviously trying to be reasonable and avoid a fight between us. 'But tonight you're not working. You were drinking earlier and you seem – how shall I put this? – upset. I don't like leaving you in this state.'

'In what state?' I could see he was genuinely concerned, but that just annoyed me even more. Why did everyone insist on treating me like I was a child? 'I had a few drinks earlier, but where's the crime in that? I'm over eighteen. I can make my own decisions—'

'I understand that—'

'Yeah? Then when are you and everyone else going to start realising that I can take care of myself?'

I glared at him, challenging him to disagree with me. He looked at me for a long moment, but seemed to think better of arguing back.

'Now,' I said. 'Will you let me out of this car so I can get on with my evening?'

Finally he did as I asked, and opened the door and stepped onto the pavement, bringing his seat forward to allow me out.

I grabbed my bag, and clambered from the car, my tiny denim skirt riding up my thighs as I did so. I could see Richard's jaw tighten at the sight of my exposed skin, and I hurriedly straightened my clothes, before heading for the bar.

'Charlotte?' His voice stopped me just as I was about to go in. I turned back to face him. He was still standing by the open car door. His eyes were serious and filled with genuine concern. 'You know that if you ever need anything, you can call me. I won't judge.'

The sincerity in his voice threw me. I swallowed hard. I could cope with the bickering between us, but any sympathy or real feeling just didn't feel right.

'Yeah?' I jutted my chin up, wanting to get us back on our normal footing. 'Well, don't wait by the phone.'

With that, I turned away and headed towards The Nick. Right now, all I wanted to do was forget today ever happened.

I pushed open the double doors and stepped into the bar. Immediately the smell of stale beer and cigarettes hit me. There may have been a smoking ban in place for years now, but it had been far longer since The Nick had last been refurbished, and the tobacco odour still lingered on the shabby furniture and peeling paint. A long time ago, the building used to be a police station – hence the name – and in honour of that, there was police paraphernalia around the walls: old truncheons, handcuffs and helmets.

Strangers tended to be quite disparaging of The Nick. Tourists often stumbled in here by mistake, looking for a quintessential English pub, and invariably headed straight back out again. It was, in all honesty, a bit of a dive, and had that unmistakably early nineties grunge feel to it. But the great music made it a cool place to hang out.

I looked around the room, searching for a familiar face. The place was heaving, which was always the case on nights with live bands, and it took me a moment to spot Lindsay. She was sitting up at the wooden bar, talking to one of the other staff, Steve, who was on duty tonight. Even though she had her back to me, I knew immediately that it was her – she was kind of hard to miss, with her shocking-pink hair. It was a bold colour, but somehow she managed to pull it off

– I think it was because she kept her hair short, in a pixie cut that framed her pretty face, so it wasn't too much. It also suited her wild demeanour. She was a pocket rocket: just a fraction over five feet and bird-like thin, she made up for her small stature with her big personality.

I walked over to where she sat, and hopped up on the stool next to her, making the mistake of resting my arm on the bar, right on something sticky. I quickly peeled my skin away, and rubbed at it with a napkin. Sadly the place never felt particularly clean.

As Steve hurried off to serve a group at the end of the bar, Lindsay swivelled round to face me. 'So look who finally decided to make an appearance.' She folded her arms, and pretended to pout. 'Although I don't know if I want you sitting with me. I still haven't forgiven you for this morning. You know the rule – if you're going to have guests round that early, then make sure they don't bother me.'

'Yeah?' I fired back. 'Well, I still haven't forgiven you for letting Richard in. I thought we had a deal – he comes over, and you tell him I'm out. You're meant to have my back.'

We mock-glared at each other for a moment.

'Hmmm.' She pretended to muse on the subject. 'So I suppose we should just call it quits then?'

'That seems like a good idea.'

We grinned at each other. Lindsay and I had been friends for the past eighteen months, ever since I started working at

The Nick. Back then we'd both lived near the pub, in separate flat-shares. My first week working there, we'd gone out clubbing after our shift ended on Saturday night, and hadn't got home until the Monday afternoon. Those thirty-six hours of mayhem had bonded us for life. She was the only person who could keep up with my partying.

With Steve busy serving someone, I leaned over the bar and helped myself to a bottle of tequila and a shot glass. As I downed the clear liquid, Lindsay raised an eyebrow. 'Bad day?'

'The worst.' Another shot.

'Want to talk about it?'

'No.'

'It might do you good . . .'

I thought about it for a moment. I wasn't usually much of a sharer, but Lindsay looked genuinely interested.

'It was pretty much the usual boring waste of a day – except this time my sister got engaged to that tool of a boyfriend of hers.'

The bitterness in my voice took even me by surprise. Lindsay must have picked up on it, because she arched an eyebrow. 'So? Why do you care? I know the guy's a dick, but it's not like *you* have to marry him. Anyone would think you were secretly in love with him, or something.'

I froze as she said that last part. It was meant as a joke, but the thought that this might have crossed anyone's mind sent a shiver through me.

'You're right.' I turned away from her, and poured another shot. 'I'm making a big deal about nothing. Let's forget it. I'd rather just drink.'

'Yeah?' Lindsay frowned. 'I'd have thought after last night you'd have had enough.'

I was surprised to see that she seemed serious. 'What are you – my mother?' I elbowed her in the ribs. 'You're meant to be my drinking buddy, my partner in crime. I've had enough judgement from Richard today – I don't need another babysitter.'

She didn't smile at that like I'd thought she would. In fact, she looked like she was about to say something, but before she could, the owner of the bar, Malachi Gold, appeared.

Despite the Jewish name, Malachi was pure East End. A former boxer, he'd retired ten years ago, with enough takings to buy this place. He was a character in his own right. He wasn't especially tall – maybe five foot eight – but he was built like a brick wall. No one messed with him.

He came over to where Lindsay and I were sitting, and planted his meaty forearms on the bar. He nodded at me. 'Thought you had the night off.'

'Plans changed. I can help out if you want.' The bar looked busy – well, of course it would be, with Oblivion headlining. And I could do with something to take my mind off today.

His eyes narrowed. 'You been drinking?'

I squeezed my thumb and forefinger together. 'Just a little-itty bit.'

'Then stay that side of the bar.' He picked up the tequila bottle. 'And do me a favour, stay away from this.'

Once he'd left, I rolled my eyes at Lindsay. 'What is it with everyone today? It's like you all took party pooper pills. If I didn't know better, I'd say you'd been taking tips from Richard.'

She said nothing. I waited for a moment, and then slid from the stool.

'Anyway, the gig's about to start. You coming?'

Without waiting for her to answer, I headed towards the backroom, where the shows were always held.

The backroom was even more rammed than the bar. Health and Safety would have had a fit if they'd seen the groupies packed shoulder to shoulder, sweat on foreheads, jackets piled on the chairs at the back. I stripped off my jumper and threw it in the mix. Then I grabbed Lindsay's hand, and shouldered my way through the crowd so we were nearer the stage.

Just as we got there, the lights dimmed and a huge roar went up from the crowd. The band ran out on stage, five guys in black leather. One of them stepped up to the mic – coal-black hair to his shoulders; tattoos covering his arms and stretching up his neck. He looked like trouble. Just my type.

'My name's Brett.' He had to shout into the mic to be heard. 'And we're Oblivion!'

As they started to play, the room erupted, and the crowd surged forward, cheering and punching the air. But my eyes remained firmly riveted on Brett. I'd just found my evening's entertainment.

Once the band was finished, Lindsay and I streamed outside with the rest of the crowd, and fought our way to the bar. As Lindsay ordered for us, my eyes scanned the room for Oblivion's lead singer.

It didn't take long to find him. He was standing across from me, looking flushed with the thrill of performing, surrounded by a gaggle of girls in push-up bras, who were fluttering their false eyelashes up at him.

I nudged Lindsay. 'Hey. I'm going to make a new friend.'

She followed my eye-line and groaned.

'Ah, Charlie, no. Not again . . .'

But I was off before she could finish.

I pushed my way through the groupies, ignoring the irritated looks that they flashed me. I was a woman on a mission, and I didn't care what anyone thought. I tapped Brett on the shoulder. He turned, giving me the once-over.

'What can I sign for you?' His eyes settled on my ample bosom, and he flashed a wolfish grin. 'Maybe your bra?'

The other girls giggled as though this was the most outrageous thing they'd ever heard, but I didn't even crack a smile. It took a lot to shock me these days.

'Actually, I was wondering if you wanted to join me for a drink?'

I could see he was taken aback by my directness. The groupies scowled, clearly aware that they were fast losing his interest.

Brett studied me for a moment. I stared right back. I might not be as attractive as the other girls, but I had one key advantage that they lacked – I wasn't impressed or intimidated by this guy. My indifference made me interesting and desirable.

'Sure,' the singer finally drawled. 'Why the hell not?'

I got us a bottle of tequila, while he found a table in the corner. We'd been there for about an hour when the guitarist came over, and said something to Brett, before heading back to join the rest of the band.

Brett downed the rest of his drink, wiping the back of his hand across his mouth. 'Look, we're heading off now. Some dude's got a party going near here. You want to come?'

It was on the tip of my tongue to accept, but then I caught sight of Lindsay. We got up to some crazy stuff, and so, early on in our friendship, she'd insisted that we always stick together if we went to parties or clubs. That meant I was going to have to run this by her, and try to convince her to come along. 'Just give me two minutes.'

I got up – stumbling a little as the alcohol hit me – and headed over to where my friend was sitting at the bar, chatting to some regulars we knew.

'You ready to go?' she said, as I approached.

'Not exactly . . .'

I quickly told her what I was up to. She was already groaning and shaking her head before I finished.

'Come off it, Charlie. Not again. Last night finished me off. I just want to go home and sleep.'

'You said that yesterday, but after a few drinks, you were fine.'

'Yeah, and I was also so hung-over today that I couldn't meet up with Adrian. He's meant to be coming round later to stay over, and I'm not letting him down again.'

Adrian was the guy she'd been seeing for the past few weeks. He was nice enough, a softly spoken English teacher, who seemed a little shy. But I was surprised she was still seeing him, to be honest. Lindsay was like me. Men were for the night, no longer. And Adrian in particular seemed far too tame for her. He'd been invited along this evening, but had stayed in to mark essays. Hardly a surprise – I couldn't exactly see this being his scene. As soon as Lindsay got rid of him the better, if you asked me. But if she wanted to keep him around for a while, then that was her business. I just wasn't about to let it affect my plans.

'Fine,' I said. 'Go home to Adrian, if you want. No one's stopping you.'

I turned to leave, but before I'd made it even a step, she caught my arm. 'You seriously think I'm going to let you head off to an unknown address with some guys we've never met before?' She nodded across the room to where the band was standing by the door, all tattoos and black leather, waiting for me.

'I'll be fine. You worry too much.'

She swore under her breath. 'What is with you? It's like you have a death wish or something.'

'Just trying to have fun.'

She gave me a sidelong look. 'Is that what you call it?'

I didn't bother to reply, just turned to head over to Brett.

'Hey,' I heard her call after me. 'Wait up. I'm not letting you go alone. I couldn't live with myself if something happened to you.'

'Fair enough,' I threw back over my shoulder. 'But if you're coming, you better get a move on. We're leaving right now.'

The walk to the party was pretty much a blur. I was vaguely aware of Brett's arm around my waist, supporting me, as we headed away from busy Camden Town, and into a quieter, more residential area. Lindsay, who'd called to cancel on Adrian, walked in front of us, talking to the rest of the band.

It was after midnight on a Sunday, so the streets were pretty much deserted. We walked on until we finally reached a small row of Georgian townhouses, which would have been quite impressive if they weren't so dilapidated. Only a few of the buildings had lights on. In fact, several of the properties were boarded up, as though they'd been repossessed and were now standing empty, and the walls were covered with colourful graffiti.

Brett led us to the grubbiest house, which looked like some kind of squat. Music and voices drifted out to us, telling me that we were in the right place.

The bell had been ripped out, so we just had to hammer on the door until someone came down to let us in. It was a guy, who looked like he could have been the sixth member of the band.

'You made it!' He high-fived Brett as we traipsed in.

We followed the noise up a flight of stairs. The interior was just as dilapidated as the exterior, with peeling paint and broken floorboards. The first room we came to was a small, dirty kitchen, where Lindsay and the band settled in. I helped myself to a warm beer – the fridge wasn't working – but then Brett appeared by my side.

'I've got something better than that.' He held up a bottle of vodka. 'Wanna find somewhere more private to drink this?'

He didn't need to ask twice.

The party seemed to be spread across the house. It took a while, but finally Brett found a large, empty room at the back. It was lit by dozens of candles stuffed into wine bottles, the wax dripping down the glass necks, making the place seem more atmospheric. Huge velvet curtains hung from the windows. That looked like a great combination with the naked flames. If a fire broke out, we wouldn't stand a chance.

There were some battered sofas and beanbags around the side of the room. Brett plonked himself down on the most hideous orange cord sofa I'd ever seen – something that looked like it had been dragged off the street.

I went over and flopped down next to him, nodding at the vodka in his hands.

'Care to share? Or are you already breaking promises?'

'I'll just get some tonic—' He made to stand up, but before he could, I swiped the bottle from him and swigged from it.

The clear liquid burned my throat. I stopped to cough, and then drank more down. Brett watched me with widening eyes.

'Je-sus,' he said, as I handed him back the bottle. 'For such a little thing, you've got the constitution of an ox.'

I gave him a lazy smile. 'That's not my only talent.'

He blinked, clearly not used to girls being so forthright with him. 'Well, that's good to know.'

He took a swig of vodka himself, as I produced a packet of cigarettes, and lit one for us to share.

It took us five minutes to finish the cigarette, and almost half an hour to down the rest of the vodka – most of which I think I consumed. With the last drop finished, I laid my head back and closed my eyes. The vodka mixed with tequila and champagne was beginning to make my head spin.

Brett took it as an invitation, and began to kiss me. It wasn't entirely unpleasant, and I was too out of it to really put up much of an objection. Soon I was on my back on the sofa, with him on top, his hand pushing under my t-shirt as he ground against me.

'You like that?' His voice floated through to me, making me aware that he was pawing at my breasts. 'Feels good, doesn't it?'

I moaned obligingly, because that's what I knew I was meant to do. But the truth was, I was too drunk to feel much of anything – which was just the way I liked it.

I felt the whole thing moving on – clothes coming off, breathing becoming more laboured. I'd done this so many times before. But gradually I became aware that something wasn't right. I shifted beneath Brett, trying to get into a better position. His body pressing down on me was making me feel sick. I tried to think back to when I last ate – it was lunchtime. Perhaps all that booze on an empty stomach hadn't been the best idea.

I broke my mouth from his, and managed to say, 'Hey.'

'What?' He raised his head, frowning. 'Something wrong?'

I tried to nod, and put my hands on his chest. 'Yeah . . . I need you to get off—'

'Huh?' I wasn't surprised he didn't understand what I was saying. My voice was muffled, and I knew I was having trouble forming words.

With all the willpower I could muster, I forced myself to form each word. 'Get. Off. Me.'

This time, he did as I asked, and rolled away. I struggled to sit up, hoping to feel better. But instead the room started to spin.

I tried to focus, but everything looked pretty blurry. I could just about make out Brett, who was frowning at me in concern. 'You don't look so good. Do you want some water?'

It took me a moment to process the question. 'No water. I want—' I didn't managed to finish the sentence. Instead, my stomach heaved, and without any warning, I threw up all over the floor.

Brett jumped back squealing, as I splattered his shoes and leather trousers with chunks from lunch.

The rest of the house must have heard the commotion, because a second later, the door was thrown open.

'Oh, gross,' some guy said from across the room, as I threw up again.

'Ugh. The smell.'

'You better clean that up,' someone else called over to me.

But I was oblivious to the abuse.

'Bathroom?' I managed.

People shouted directions, moving out of my way as I stumbled from the room. I couldn't seem to focus as I staggered along the hallway, and I kept knocking into the wall. Behind me, I could hear laughter, undoubtedly aimed at me, but I didn't care. At the end of the corridor, I pushed open a door, and fell into a tiny WC. Even in my state, I could see it was filthy – the sink was hanging off the wall, and the porcelain toilet was cracked and the bowl stained. A lone light-bulb hung from the ceiling, adding to the dinginess.

I collapsed in front of the toilet, and began to throw up again.

I was still vomiting a couple of minutes later, when someone knocked at the door.

'Charlie?' I heard the hinges creak open. 'Are you okay in there?' It was Lindsay. Brett at least had had the good sense to get her.

I was retching too hard to respond.

'Oh, shit.' She came up behind me, holding my hair back as I continued to throw up. She was an old hand at this.

The vomiting seemed to go on forever. Just as I thought it might be stopping, I felt my stomach begin to contract again.

After what seemed like an hour, I finally collapsed back on my haunches, sweating from the exertion of the constant vomiting. It seemed like even the dry-heaving had stopped.

'You want to get out of here?' Lindsay said.

I didn't have the energy to reply. Instead I grabbed the sink with both hands, and used it to haul myself to my feet, dislodging it even more with my weight. I stumbled a little, and Lindsay caught me. I decided to lean against the cool wall for support. 'Am fine.' My words sounded slurred, even to my own ears. 'Just give . . . a minute.'

Lindsay was peering at me with a worried expression. 'You really don't seem fine.'

'Been like this 'fore.'

'This is different.' She peered at me. 'You look really sick, Charlie. I seriously think we need to get out of here.'

I tried to open my eyes to glare at her, but it was too much effort. 'When did you stop being fun?' I said instead.

'There's being fun and then there's being an idiot.' I tried to walk past her, but Lindsay moved in front of me. 'Where do you think you're going?'

'Brett.' I'd wanted to say a whole sentence, but I could only manage that one word.

'Oh, no, you're not.' She crossed her arms. 'I'm not letting you out of here with him.'

'And what you gonna do 'bout it?' I said. Or at least that's what I tried to say. Unfortunately my brain didn't seem to quite manage to co-ordinate with my mouth, so it came out as a jumble of sounds that weren't quite words.

'What the hell?' Lindsay squinted at me. 'Jesus, Charlie. How much did you drink?'

I grinned at her. She was making such a big deal about nothing. 'I'm fine,' I started to say. But somewhere along the way the room had started swimming. I had no idea what was going on, but something didn't feel quite right.

I swayed a little on my feet. For some reason, I couldn't quite manage to focus. I stumbled backwards a little, and banged against the wall. I just about had time to make out the distressed look on Lindsay's face, and then I sank to the floor.

Chapter 5

The first thing I was aware of when I woke up was what felt like the mother of all sore throats, stretching all the way down my oesophagus to the throbbing pain in my stomach.

My eyes cracked open, and I saw immediately that I was in a hospital bed, in what looked like a private ward. An IV was feeding fluids into my arm. Vague images flitted through my mind from the night before – the wailing siren as I was rushed to hospital; the agony of a tube being forced down my throat; the constant pain and indignity of vomiting . . .

My eyes swept the room. At first I thought I was hallucinating, but there was Richard, sprawled out in the easy chair in the corner. I groaned to myself. The last thing I needed was him and my family getting involved. They'd never let me hear the end of last night.

I tried to sit up in bed, attempting to be as quiet as possible, so as not to disturb him. But the movement must have somehow dislodged my IV, because an alarm sounded. Richard's eyes flew open.

'You're awake.' He didn't appear at all disoriented. Instead, he was up and out of his chair straight away, long limbs stretching, as he came over to stand by my bed. The expression on his face was one of concern rather than disapproval. 'How're you feeling? Is there anything you need?'

I wasn't entirely sure what time it was, but I sensed he'd been here all night. His jeans and jumper looked crumpled, and his usually clean-shaven face was darkened by a five o'clock shadow. It was almost enough to make me forget about my predicament – it was the first time in years that I'd seen him looking anything less than perfect.

'Am okay,' I managed. My voice was little more than a croak. My throat felt sore and scratchy, and it hurt to talk.

'You might want to give your voice a rest for a bit.' He gave a wry smile. 'I hear having your stomach pumped is a bitch.'

I frowned, taking in what he'd just said. 'Thought they'd stopped that.'

'What?' He arched an eyebrow. 'Shoving a tube down patients' throats? Yes, nowadays they have less barbaric ways of dealing with alcohol poisoning – putting an IV in and rehydrating patients usually works. But in your case they made an exception. Because you'd consumed so much alcohol they were worried you might die.'

His voice was deceptively light. I dropped my eyes to where my hands were resting on the white sheets of the bed. It was bad enough that I'd managed to drink so much that I'd landed myself in hospital, but now I had to face the fact that I was worse than the normal idiots they got in here. To say I felt ashamed was an understatement.

I would have asked him some basic questions – like *where am I* and *what am I doing here*? but I'd kind of figured the answers out for myself: I'd collapsed; an ambulance had been called; my stomach had been pumped; and at some point Richard had arrived and had me spirited to a private room in whatever hospital I was in. That was all fairly self-evident. However there was one thing I couldn't figure out.

'What're you doing here?'

'Lindsay called. She panicked after you collapsed. She didn't want to worry your parents, so I guess I was the next in line.' He must have seen the question in my eyes because he shook his head. 'And no, I haven't told your mum and dad what's been going on. The doctors were pretty certain you'd be fine, so I decided not to worry them. Enough of us were already having a sleepless night over you.'

I didn't know why he'd bothered coming if he was just going to try to make me feel bad. I was already feeling sore and embarrassed. Unfortunately, my voice wasn't up to any arguments right now.

'Home?' I said, instead, hoping he'd pick up on my pidgin English.

'Tomorrow. And I'll be taking you back to my place for the night.'

The horror I felt must have been obvious from my face, because he held up his hand. 'No arguments. The doctors think it would be best for you to have someone watch over you for the first twenty-four hours after you're discharged, and there's no one else who can do it apart from me.'

'Lindsay?' There was a tinge of desperation in my voice. The thought of Richard and me being confined in one place for any length of time wasn't a good one. I wasn't sure I could take his judgemental attitude for that long.

'Lindsay doesn't have time to play nursemaid. She has an interview tomorrow.'

This was news to me. I wondered why she hadn't mentioned it, but Richard was already speaking before I could process the thought. 'I, meanwhile, have arranged to work from home. So, I'm afraid you're stuck with me.' He folded his arms, in a gesture that said: *deal with it*.

I felt suitably contrite. He'd obviously rearranged his schedule – his very busy schedule – to accommodate me. I hadn't meant for my stupid behaviour to cause everyone else such problems. I managed a sheepish smile. 'Thank you.'

He gave a brisk nod of acknowledgment. 'Good. That's more like it.'

Right then, a pretty young nurse bustled in. 'Ah, you're awake at last,' she said brightly, in a pretty Irish lilt. She walked over to deal with my beeping IV. 'That's good. Now, let me get this sorted out for you . . .'

As she began to examine the IV pump, Richard turned to me. 'Look, I'm going to push off now, if that's all right with you? I just wanted to be here when you woke up. But now *I* need to get some rest.' He inclined his head back to the easy chair. 'That contraption wasn't meant for sleeping.'

He hesitated for just a moment, and then dropped a quick kiss on my forehead.

'I'll be back tomorrow,' he told me. Then, after thanking the nurse, he left.

'There. All done,' the nurse said, as she finished fixing my IV. She turned to me and beamed. 'You're a lucky girl, aren't you? Your boyfriend's a sweetheart.'

'Not boyfriend.' I probably should have been resting my voice, but that was the last thing I wanted people thinking.

'Oh, really?' The nurse's eyes brightened with interest. 'In that case, is he single? He's one of the good ones, I warrant. He was here all night, making sure you were all right. I could do with a man like that in my life.'

I wasn't in the mood to hear about Richard's virtues. So I clutched at my throat, and pulled a sad face, as though I was in too much pain to reply. Then I closed my eyes and feigned sleep.

'So you're alive then?' Lindsay's loud voice jolted me out of my doze. I opened my eyes to find her standing in the door of my hospital room, looking distinctly unimpressed – with me, I imagined. Frankly, the feeling was mutual.

'Yeah. I hung on long enough to scream at you for calling Richard,' I threw back at her, although my croaky voice unfortunately made my retort sound less sharp. 'Seriously, Lindsay . . .'

My friend rolled her eyes, and walked over to perch on the end of my hospital bed. 'I think the words you're looking for are: "thank you, Lindsay, for making sure I didn't choke on my own vomit and die a horrible, premature death."'

I grunted. 'After spending tomorrow with Richard, I'll probably wish I'd carked it.'

Lindsay usually found my dark humour amusing, but this time she reached out and slapped my shin, hard.

'Ouch!' I wrinkled my nose. 'What the hell was that for?'

'Don't even joke about dying.' Lindsay spoke through gritted teeth. 'You have no idea how scared I was last night.'

The anger in her voice drew me up short. I didn't know what to say. Lindsay wasn't the type to sound so serious.

'Oh, come on, Linny.' I used a pet-name she hated to try to lighten the moment. 'Don't be so melodramatic. I'm fine. No permanent damage – I promise.'

'Yeah? Well, maybe not to you. But I lost years off my life last night worrying about your silly, drunken arse. So don't you ever pull a stunt like that again. Because next time I might not be around to look after you.'

'Next time I'll make sure I'm with someone who lets me sleep it off instead of calling an ambulance.' I knew I should have kept my mouth shut, but I couldn't resist the dig. So I'd had a few too many drinks? Where was the harm? I felt like everyone was making a big deal about nothing.

Lindsay's lips pursed, and she looked like she wanted to contradict me, but then seemed to think better of it. 'Fair enough, you ungrateful cow. I came here to cheer you up, not give you a hard time. So let's talk about something else.'

I eyed the duffle bag she'd brought with her, which was now on the floor by her feet. 'What's in there?'

'Change of clothes, pyjamas, magazines, toothbrush . . . Why? What were you hoping for? A bottle of vodka?'

I managed a grin. 'That's right. Hair of the dog.'

Lindsay started to laugh then, and I joined in, but unfortunately the motion hurt my throat and stomach more than I'd anticipated.

'Ow!' I stopped abruptly, my hand coming up to clasp the

base of my neck, as though that might help ease the pain. 'Remind me not to do that again. It hurts like hell.'

'Good.' My friend smiled sweetly at me. 'It serves you right.'

Lindsay stayed for another hour. After she left, I spent the rest of the day napping. Richard was as good as his word, and turned up at ten the following morning to collect me, looking far more refreshed than the previous day. It took until midday for me to finally be discharged, which meant I got to listen to him conduct business for his advertising firm in my room for two hours, while I flicked through the gossip magazines that Lindsay had brought in to me.

Once I'd finally been discharged, Richard helped me out to his car. At least this time I got to sit in the passenger seat as he drove us back to his place. Fortunately, with my throat the way it was, there was no opportunity to chat. Instead, he continued talking business on his hands-free phone, as I stared out the window.

Ten minutes later, we reached Canary Wharf, the business district where he lived. He owned a penthouse in one of the luxury blocks located on the river. We pulled into the underground car park of his apartment complex. At this time of the day, it was pretty full. Most of the people who owned flats here worked in the area, and were only in London from Monday to Friday, driving back to the country at weekends. The vehicles reflected the wealthy status of their owners, and I reckoned there wasn't one under a hundred grand.

We caught the lift up to his apartment. I'd been there a couple of times before, and it was just as I remembered – more like a show flat than a place to live. Like most of the flats in these modern developments, the centrepiece was an open-plan living space. It reflected his personality perfectly, looking modern and neat to the point of compulsiveness. The decor had a distinctly masculine feel, with clean lines, a neutral colour scheme and dark wood furniture. There were no pictures around, and no personal effects.

'Cosy.' I held my hand to my throat as I spoke, trying to stop it hurting. 'Needs a woman's touch.'

He raised an eyebrow. 'Having seen the state of your room the other day, it certainly doesn't need yours.'

I wasn't feeling up to a retort, so I pulled a face.

After that, Richard took me on a quick refresher tour. He showed me how to operate his flat-screen TV and gave me a rundown of the gadgets in his state-of-the-art kitchen, telling me to help myself to anything I wanted. The fridge was packed with fruit and vegetables – not a ready-meal in sight.

'You shop?' I couldn't keep the surprise out of my voice.

'Order online.'

'Thought you ate out all the time?'

'I like to cook, too.' Before I could ask more, he said, 'I'll show you where you're sleeping.'

I followed him upstairs to the spare room. It had its own en-suite bathroom, complete with Molton Brown toiletries and a spare bathrobe. While he went to put my bag in the walk-in wardrobe, I sat on the bed, sinking into the plump mattress. I stroked my hand over the soft duvet. The linen was virgin white, and either hadn't been used before or had been professionally cleaned. It might be austere, like a hotel room, but it was also extremely comfortable.

'So have you got everything you need?' As Richard came back into the room, I sprang to my feet. I'd got so caught up in my surroundings that I'd almost forgotten he was there.

'Yeah . . . I think I'm all set.'

There was a silence. I stuffed my hands in my pockets, and studied the floor. I hated to admit it, but it was quite nice to be somewhere with a well-stocked fridge and some-one to look after me, rather than in the mess that was our flat. While it might be a bit impersonal here, it certainly had everything you could want. I knew I ought to thank Richard, but it was hard to bring myself to do it. It was gall-ing to have to admit that I'd needed him.

Luckily I was saved from thanking him by the sound of the intercom. Richard frowned. It was clear that he hadn't been expecting anyone.

'I better see who that is.'

While he went to answer the door, I decided to get ready for bed. Lindsay had packed my overnight bag, and she'd put in my favourite pyjamas – a pair of red shorts with white hearts on them, and a white tank top with matching red trim. They were old but comfy. Just as I pulled them on, I heard my stomach rumbling. I hadn't been able to eat much over the past day, sticking mainly to soft foods, but I remembered seeing some Häagen Dazs in Richard's freezer. That would do me fine.

I eased my way back down the stairs. The door to the living area was pulled to, but I didn't give much thought to it as I walked in – until I saw Petra and Richard standing in the middle of the room, glaring at each other, clearly in the middle of a fight. Hearing me, they turned, startled. I was equally shocked. I stood still, gawping at them for a moment, before recovering.

'Sorry. I just came down to get something to eat.' I pointed at the fridge, just in case they hadn't got the point.

Richard ran a hand through his hair. 'Sure. Of course.' But his eyes were on Petra, who was in turn staring at me – and she didn't look happy.

Her gaze ran over me, and I was suddenly aware of how short my shorts were, and the way the tank top emphasised my boobs. It probably would have been a good idea to wear that towelling robe down.

She looked at me with undisguised hostility. 'Well, you certainly appear to have recovered quickly.' It was clear she didn't think this was a good thing. I wondered what her problem was – while I was certain my dress code violated her sense of decorum, I wasn't sure it warranted this much venom. 'Richard made it sound like you were at death's door.'

'Sorry to disappoint.' It was meant to be a joke, but her lips tightened.

She glanced over at Richard. 'I think that's my cue to leave.'

'Petra—' he started, but she was already walking towards the door.

'Don't go on my account,' I couldn't resist calling after her. She turned to glare at me, and then she was gone.

Richard disappeared after her. I shook my head, confused about what the hell had just happened.

'Not my problem,' I muttered under my breath, and headed to the freezer, like I'd originally intended.

A moment later Richard reappeared. Clearly whatever had gone on, he hadn't been able to smooth Petra's ruffled feathers.

I leaned against the kitchen counter, and opened up the tub of Pralines and Cream. 'So what was all that about?' I said, helping myself to a large spoonful.

He frowned, as though I was being dense. 'What do you think? Petra wasn't exactly pleased when she heard that I had a woman other than her coming to stay with me. I told her she had nothing to worry about, and then she turns up to find you parading around my flat half naked. It didn't exactly reassure her.'

'Are you serious?' I laughed. 'She thinks something's going on between us? That's ridiculous!'

He raised an eyebrow. 'Is it?'

'Of course it is! I mean, you're not exactly my type.'

'Oh?' He cocked his head to one side. 'And what makes you think that you're mine?'

It took me a second to work out what he meant. Then I flushed as I realised exactly what I'd said – that the only reason we weren't sleeping together was because I didn't want to. Like I was some kind of femme fatale who could have any guy she wanted. 'I didn't mean it like that . . . I just, well—'

'I know what you meant, Charlotte.' Thankfully Richard abruptly cut my jabbering off. 'I was just teasing you. Now—' his voice was crisp, his attention clearly moving elsewhere – 'I should really get on with some work. So if you don't need anything else—'

'I'll be fine.'

He left the room without another word. Once he'd gone, I looked down at the tub of ice cream in my hands. My appetite seemed to have deserted me. I put the Häagen Dazs back in the freezer, and headed upstairs.

★   ★   ★

I managed to keep myself occupied for the rest of the day. I was still quite tired, so I dozed a lot, and the times I was awake, I mostly read – Lindsay had remembered to pack the thriller that I was halfway through. I pretty much managed to avoid seeing Richard. I was able to make it up and down the stairs by myself, so I just went to the kitchen to fix myself drinks, or get soup or ice cream when I fancied it – I was still sticking to soft foods because of my throat. Richard was holed up in his study, but he popped his head out whenever he heard me moving around, just to make sure I was all right. Other than that we kept pretty much to ourselves.

I went to bed early that night, and managed to sleep all the way through, so when I finally woke the next morning, I was surprised to see that it was after ten. I stretched in the comfy bed. The soreness and grogginess seemed to have almost gone now, and I felt like my old self.

I decided to skip breakfast and head straight to the shower. Given that my presence had already caused an argument between Richard and Petra, I thought the sooner I got out of here the better. I'd already messed up enough of his life.

Lindsay had packed my least outrageous outfit: jeans and a V-neck grey jumper. I'd just finished getting dressed, when I heard a knock at the door.

'Come in,' I said.

It was Richard, dressed more casually than usual in jeans, too, and a t-shirt, with a mug of what smelt like coffee in his hands.

'I heard you up, and I thought you could do with this,' he said, handing the hot drink to me.

I took a sip. It was milky and sweet, just the way I liked it. I was quite surprised he'd remembered.

'Thanks. That's perfect.' I sat down on the edge of the bed. The first burst of energy I'd felt that morning had faded slightly, and I was feeling a little unsteady on my feet. Maybe skipping breakfast wasn't the best idea.

Richard continued to stand, his hands resting lightly on his hips, as he regarded me with concern. 'So, how are you feeling this morning?'

'Pretty much back to normal, thanks.' I felt almost touched by his concern. Perhaps he wasn't as bad as I'd been making out, after all.

'Good. I'm glad to hear it,' he said. Then the sympathetic expression dropped from his face, and his eyes hardened. 'Because after that little stunt you pulled the other night, we need to have a serious talk.'

Chapter 6

From where I sat on the bed, I eyed Richard warily. 'What do you mean? A serious talk about what?'

'About what the hell's going on with you.'

'Oh, God, you're not serious, are you?' Before he could answer, I scrambled off the bed, and began to stuff my belongings into my bag. 'Look, I'm grateful for you coming to the hospital and looking after me, but I really don't need a lecture.'

'Fair enough.' He leaned back against the wall, folding his arms. 'That's entirely up to you. By all means, leave. But—' his voice took on a darker tone – 'as long as you understand that the moment you step out of that door, I will be straight on the phone to your parents.'

I was in the middle of lacing up my trainers, but hearing that, I stopped what I was doing, and looked up at him, and laughed. 'Seriously? That's your big threat? You're going to tell my parents on me? What do you think I am – eight years old?' I finished with my shoes and grabbed my bag. 'By all means, call my parents. Be my guest. Because I really couldn't care less.'

With that, I made for the door.

'Fair enough.' Richard's voice floated after me. 'I'll call your parents. I'll speak to your father – your very sick father, who is still recovering from a heart attack. And tell him that his youngest daughter drank so much that she needed her stomach pumped. That she nearly died.'

At that, I stopped in my tracks, and turned back to face him. 'You wouldn't dare.'

He arched an eyebrow. 'And why's that?'

'Because you care about my parents. You wouldn't put my dad through that. You wouldn't risk worrying him and causing him to have another heart attack.'

'And what should I do instead? Wait for his youngest daughter to drink herself to death? How do you think he'd feel then?'

'Oh, please,' I scoffed. 'Don't be so melodramatic. I can take care of myself.'

'Really? Because it didn't seem like it the other night.'

He really wasn't about to let this go. 'Okay. What do you want me to say?' I shifted my bag from one shoulder to the other. 'I made a mistake. I went too far. But it's not going to happen again—'

'How do you know?'

'I just do.' Even to my ears that sounded childish, so I searched for something to add. 'I've learnt my lesson. I'll be more careful next time. It was just a—'

'Just a what?' Richard prompted, after I stopped. He was studying me closely, and I could see he was genuinely interested.

'It was just a very bad day.'

'What – attending your parents' wedding anniversary?'

I looked away, unable to fully explain, not even to myself. 'There was other stuff, too.'

Richard regarded me for a long moment, and I could tell he was weighing up whether he was prepared to let it go. 'I'm sorry, Charlotte,' he said eventually. 'But I'm worried about you, and about what you're doing to yourself. So I can't let you walk away from me today without trying to get a few things sorted out.'

I could see his resolve. I felt a knot of anxiety beginning to form in my stomach. This was the last thing I needed – Richard Davenport trying to take charge of my life.

'Seriously? What business is it of yours what I get up to?'

'I'm making it my business,' he said quietly. 'Because of your brother.'

That drew me up short.

'Kit?' I managed, once I'd recovered from my surprise. 'What's this got to do with him?'

Richard pushed off from the wall then, and started to pace the room. 'When we were up there on the mountain, and he'd been injured, he knew that his chances of survival weren't great. He asked me then to look after you all – his family. And I promised that I would. That I'd take care of you all.'

This was the first I'd heard of it. I opened my mouth to speak, but nothing came out.

Richard stopped pacing then, and turned to me. 'I'm not about to let your brother down. And I'm not about to let your parents down either. They've always been good to me, and I can't stand by and watch them lose another child. It was hard enough for them the first time.' He took a step toward me, so I could see the pain in his eyes. 'To lose their eldest child, their only son. It took everything they had in them to get through that; to find some way to live again. How do you think they'd cope if they lost you as well? It would destroy them.'

I dropped my eyes to the floor then, unable to hold his gaze any longer. I knew what he was saying was true. We'd all struggled with our grief after Kit died. My mother had tried to hide her pain by throwing herself into work, but the anguish of losing her only son was always there, casting a shadow over everything. And then there was my father. He was by nature a happy, contented man, but he'd never been quite the same since that awful day eight years ago. The doctor had said his heart attack may have been brought on by the stress of my brother's death.

I loved my parents. I might have my differences with them, but that didn't mean I wanted to hurt them – not the way they'd hurt over Kit. I couldn't bear for them to worry about me. If something I did caused my father to have another heart attack and die, I could never forgive myself.

I hesitated for a moment. Then I let my bag slip from my shoulder and I walked over to sit on the bed.

'So – what is it you want me to do? In return for you not informing on me to my parents.'

There was an occasional chair opposite the bed. Richard sat down too and leaned forward, resting his muscular arms on his legs. 'I want you to come and work for me for the next three months.'

'You what?' I spluttered.

'I want you to give up working at The Nick, and try having a normal job for a while. A job that requires you to get up early, go into an office, and work from nine to five. A job that requires you to be responsible. And a job that takes you away from the culture of drinking, drugs and sleeping around, which unfortunately seems to have become a huge part of your life.'

I glared at him. I hated being told what to do. Plus, I liked my life. It worked for me. 'So basically you don't want me to have any fun for three whole months?'

I saw the corner of his mouth twitch a little when I said that, and then he appeared serious again. 'I wouldn't put it like that exactly. I just want you to have some time away from your self-destructive lifestyle. I think it would do you some good.'

I stared at him for a long moment. Frankly, I couldn't think of anything worse than having to work at his uptight company, among a whole load of Richard clones and brown-nosers. But I knew him well enough to sense when he was serious about something, and I could tell he meant it about this.

And the alternative was that he'd call my parents, and I couldn't have that.

'All right,' I said finally. It was only three months, after all — and then I could go back to doing whatever I liked. 'I'll do it.'

'Good.' His voice was brusque, as though he'd known that I was going to cave in all along. 'And I want you to see a therapist, too.'

'A what?' My voice was a shriek.

'You heard me.' His eyes were deadly serious.

'Oh, no.' I shook my head to make my point. 'There is no way I'm going to see a shrink. The job I'll do. But no therapy of any kind.'

'Then we don't have a deal.' He took out his iPhone, and held it up for me. 'If that's your final word, I'll call your parents now.'

I just stared at him. He had me over a barrel and he knew it. 'Are you serious?'

'Deadly.' He held my gaze, unflinching, for a second. But then he must have seen how distressed I truly was at the prospect of going into therapy, because his face softened. 'Come on, Charlotte. You must know yourself that something isn't right. The way you act — it's like you're on a path to self-destruct. You never used to be like this. You used to be sweet and responsible—'

'Yes, because I was a child! Has it ever occurred to you that I just grew up?' I spread my arms. 'That this is just me.'

'I don't believe that. I think there's something going on with you to make you behave this way — some underlying problem. I thought it might be because of Kit's death—'

'It's not,' I said flatly.

I could tell he didn't believe me. 'Well, whatever's going on, it needs to stop. And I think seeing a therapist will help. At least I hope it will.' He stopped, clearly waiting for me to object. When I didn't, he went on, 'Just one hour a week. That's all I ask of you. For the duration of the time you work for me.'

He paused then, letting his demands sink in. He must have known that this was pretty much my worst nightmare — a boring office job and weekly therapy for the next three months. I didn't know how I was going to get through it. I wanted to say no, to leave right now, but unfortunately the alternative was so much worse – I didn't want my dad to know about what was going on. I just couldn't put that on him right now.

'So – what's it to be?' Richard said eventually, obviously knowing my inner debate was nearly at an end.

Put like that, it wasn't even a choice. 'Fine!' I spat the word out. 'You win. I'll do whatever you want for the next three months. As long as you keep what happened the other night to yourself.'

'Good.' He gave a brief nod. 'You made the right decision, Charlotte. I promise.'

'Well, you didn't exactly leave me much choice, did you?'

'That was the idea.'

He held out a hand for us to shake on the deal. I ignored it. After all, seeing the self-satisfied smile on his face, it was taking all my willpower not to punch him.

'Can you believe that asshole?' I said to Lindsay.

It was an hour later, and I was finally back at my flat. My friend had made sure to be in when I got home, just in case I was still suffering any after-effects from my misadventure the other night. Now we were sprawled across the battered sofas in the sitting room, clutching mugs of tea, as I recounted the agreement Richard had forced me into.

There seemed to be no end to his control-freak nature

since I'd landed in hospital. He'd insisted on driving me home, even though I was well enough to get the Tube. I'd wanted to object, but his threat of telling my parents hung over me, so I had to go along with him. It was irritating, the way he was treating me as though I was some fragile little girl who needed looking after.

It had been a silent journey back, with me still fuming about how he'd manipulated me into agreeing to his demands. I was relieved when we finally pulled up outside my apartment block. I needed some time away from him. His parting shot had been to remind me to be at the office at nine on the dot on Monday morning.

Now, I gave Lindsay a pleading look. 'Seriously – you have to help me think of a way to get out of this.'

My flatmate didn't jump in with a suggestion like I'd hoped she would. Instead she dropped some sugar into her tea and stirred it, before taking a sip. Finally she said, 'Maybe you shouldn't be trying to get out of it. Maybe it's not such a bad idea for you to have a change of scene.'

I blinked, unable to believe what I was hearing. 'What're you saying?'

She just looked at me. 'Come on, Charlie. You're getting out of control. Even you must see that.'

I couldn't believe what I was hearing. Lindsay had always been my partner in crime. And now she was agreeing with Richard. 'Seriously? You're taking his side?'

'It's not about sides. For God's sake, you nearly died the other night! It's not funny any more ... As far as I'm concerned, anything that gets you off the scene for a while has my vote. And I'm not going to apologise for feeling that way.'

Her words shocked me into silence. I could see her eyes shining brightly, shimmering with unshed tears. I knew Lindsay was upset with me, but I hadn't realised she felt this strongly. A knot began to form in my stomach. I didn't need this. She was overreacting – making a bad situation worse. And suddenly it occurred to me why.

'This is about Adrian, isn't it?'

'What?'

I ignored the disbelief in her voice, and nodded slowly to myself. 'You've found yourself some conventional boyfriend, and you're changing yourself for him, and expecting everyone else to do the same.'

'Are you serious?'

'Well, let's face it. You haven't been as up for going out lately, have you? Even before all this happened.'

Lindsay didn't answer straight away. Instead, she gnawed at the inside of her mouth. 'I think you're seeing this the wrong way. I still like going out and drinking and clubbing with you, but I want to be doing other stuff, too. I want more from my life than pulling shifts at The Nick and getting wasted. All I'm saying is that this time at Richard's company may be your opportunity to change your life for the better, too.'

I could tell she was trying to be reasonable, but for some reason her words irritated me. I'd always thought I could count on Lindsay, and now it seemed like she was moving on, and becoming one more person rejecting me and telling me what to do. 'So does this have something to do with the interview you had the other day?'

A flash of guilt crossed her face. 'Richard mentioned that? Yeah, it was at a casting agency. Answering phones and general admin at first, but it's a foot in the door, and I'll be learning the ropes. The acting hasn't worked out, but I'd still like to stay in the business, and this seems like a good way to do that . . .'

This was all news to me. Lindsay had gone to drama school, and working at The Nick was meant to be her way of supporting herself between acting jobs. But somewhere along the way she'd stopped going for auditions, and bartending had become a full-time gig for her, like it was for me. Now it seemed she was looking at moving on. The unsettled feeling in my stomach began to grow.

'Right.' I snorted a laugh. 'So you start seeing Adrian and suddenly you stop going out and decide that you're too good for The Nick.'

Her cheeks flushed. 'That isn't it at all, and you know it! I'm genuinely worried about you, and you're trying to turn this into something it's not! I only want the best for you, and as my friend, I thought you'd be happy that I'd met a nice guy and that I was trying to start on a new career for myself.'

'It's hard to be happy for you when you're becoming as boring as the dullard that you're dating.' I knew I was going too far by attacking her boyfriend, but I didn't care.

'How dare you!' Lindsay's eyes flashed. 'Don't start slagging off Adrian because you're unhappy with your life!'

We glared at each other for a long moment. Neither of us were the type to back down. After a moment I stood up. 'I'm going to rest up before work tonight.'

'Yeah?' Lindsay got to her feet, too. 'That sounds like a good idea.'

We both turned away. I slammed my bedroom door on the way in, and a second later Lindsay did, too.

I wasn't looking forward to going into work at The Nick that evening, because I knew I'd have to hand in my notice. I decided it would be best to get it over with quickly, so the first thing I did was tell my boss, Malachi, that my last shift would be Saturday night, because I had a new job starting on Monday morning. I didn't go into the details of how I'd been forced into it, but I let him know that it would be an office job – the last thing I wanted was for him to think I was going to a competitor. He got funny about things like that.

In fact, for someone who worked in an industry that by its very nature employed transient workers, he could be surprisingly moody when anyone resigned. So I fully expected to get some grief from him about leaving on such short notice.

'So you're finally joining the nine-to-five grind?' He finished pulling a pint, and handed it to a customer, then turned back to me. 'I never thought I'd see the day.'

'I know, right? I can't see it lasting.'

'Well, I hope it does.'

I frowned. 'You do?'

'Yeah. I think it'll be good for you.'

'Really?' I couldn't help feeling a little hurt. I'd expected him to be furious about the short notice – to demand I stay for longer. I'd almost thought I could put Richard off for a month or so by saying I needed to stay until a replacement could be hired, and that he might forget the whole arrange-ment as time went on. But now it seemed Malachi was totally on board, and I was stung by his willingness to let me go. 'But you always said I was your best barmaid.'

He leaned up against the bar, stroking his goatee as he mused the point.

'Yeah,' he said. 'You working here is good for my busi-ness, but is it good for you? That little stunt you pulled on Sunday night?' I'd have loved to keep that from him, but unfortunately I'd had to explain why I couldn't work

Monday and Tuesday nights. 'I've been waiting for some-thing like that to happen.'

This was news to me. He must have seen the shock on my face, because he gave a little smile. 'It's a hazard of the trade – bar staff liking the sauce a bit too much. This is a breeding ground for alcoholics.' I was about to object, but he held up a hand to quiet me. 'But it's not like that with you. You drink, but it's not about the booze. You abuse alcohol, but you're not addicted to it – not yet anyway. There's a darkness in you that you're just trying to cover up. And that makes this the wrong place for you to be around. So I hope this new start works out for you. You're a good girl, and I'd hate to see you get dragged down to a place you can't come back from.'

Before I could even think about formulating a reply, he turned back to serve a customer. It was probably lucky that he did, because I had no idea what I'd say to him. That little speech was about the last thing I'd expected to hear from the usually taciturn Malachi. When did everyone turn into an amateur psychologist? And, more to the point, when had everyone decided I was a problem that needed to be solved, a victim who had to be saved? It seemed bizarre, given that out of everyone I knew, I was the one most able to take care of myself.

Needing a moment alone, I went through to the kitchen, and began to unpack clean glasses from the dishwasher.

Whatever anyone said, I wasn't keen on Richard's little plan to straighten me out. Unfortunately it seemed there was no way I was going to be able to get out of it. Malachi had been my last hope – and look how that had turned out.

And then it struck me – while I might not be able to convince Richard to release me from our deal, what if it was his idea? I couldn't outright play up – that would just make him call my parents – but if I made minimal effort at his office, then surely he'd get so fed up that he'd have no choice but to let me get back to my life with no more interference.

For the first time that day, I felt a surge of hope. This didn't need to be quite the disaster I'd feared. I just needed to bide my time, and play things the right way.

With my plan in place, I carried the glasses through to the bar, humming as I went.

Chapter 7

The following Monday morning, I emerged from Tottenham Court Road Tube station just before nine. It was a crisp, bright day, and as I joined the throngs of commuters hurrying towards Soho Square, I tilted my face towards the warm sun. But it was hard to enjoy the pleasant weather when all I could think about was what lay ahead – my first day at Richard's advertising firm, Davenport's.

I knew more than I wanted to about the business – and Richard's role in it – because of my mother's obsession with everything he did. I'd spent dozens of family dinners being bored to tears as she recounted his exploits and sang his praises.

Davenport's had been set up in the eighties by Richard's father, Oliver. It had quickly risen to become one of the most respected advertising firms in London, but his death had left a vacuum at management level. Bad decisions were made, and the company started to lose accounts and failed to win new business.

With his father's passing, Richard had become the majority shareholder in the firm, but at nineteen, he'd been far too young to do anything about it. So he'd left the day-to-day management of the business in the hands of the board, and he'd continued on the path that his parents had set him – finishing his degree in Politics, Philosophy and Economics at Christ Church, Oxford, just like his father before him. Then at twenty-one, instead of going to work at Davenport's, he'd gained a place on a graduate training scheme at a rival advertising firm, where he'd cut his teeth in the industry.

Once he'd firmly established himself as an advertising guru, he'd moved to Davenport's. By that point, the company was in a bad way. Richard had taken control and been instrumental in promoting fresh talent. Now it was known as one of the most cutting-edge firms in London.

Davenport's offices were based in Soho, which was pretty much London's equivalent to Madison Avenue for advertising firms. Soho, Covent Garden and Charlotte Street formed the heart of the industry – where there were plenty of cocktail bars and upscale restaurants for entertaining clients and celebrating account wins. As I walked along Dean Street with all the other commuters, I couldn't help thinking that this was the last place I should be. It might be the hub of the sought-after media and arts industries, but it was still too conventional for my liking.

I didn't bother to cover my mouth as I yawned. I was pissed off and tired. I'd been working in bars ever since I'd been kicked out of art school six years ago, so I hadn't been up this early for ages.

To get to Richard's office building, I had to walk through the maze of streets that made up Soho. As I passed a row of shops, I caught sight of my reflection in one of the windows. I hadn't made any effort to tone down my appearance for the office. I was wearing pretty much what I had on at the bar every night – thigh-high thick cotton stockings, a black miniskirt, white tank top and my favourite vintage leather jacket. My platinum-blonde hair hung wild around my shoulders, and I had on my heavy blue-black mascara and eyeliner. Usually I would have fitted right into the area, but at this time of the morning the commuters were out in force. The media types might not be suited and booted businessmen, but they were still well turned out, while I looked – to put it politely – scruffy. No wonder I could feel all the suits giving me sideways looks, wondering what I was doing here. I stuck out like a whore at a church fundraiser.

When I'd walked into the kitchen that morning, Lindsay had literally spat out her cornflakes when she saw me.

'You're not seriously going like that?' she'd said, not making any effort to hide her disbelief.

'Why?' I'd cast a glance down at my attire, as though I had no idea what she was talking about. 'What's wrong with how I look?'

She'd shaken her head, and held up her hands in defeat. 'It's none of my business what you do,' she'd said, and resumed eating her cereal.

The atmosphere between us had been tense since our bust-up a few days earlier. For the first time ever, we hadn't spent any of the weekend together. She'd texted to say that she was staying at Adrian's for a couple of nights, and to call if I needed anything. I hadn't bothered to phone, and she hadn't attempted to get in touch again. Right now, I think we both knew it was best if we stayed out of each other's way.

I tried not to be impressed as I arrived at Langley House, the building that housed Davenport's. It was one of those elegant Regency mansion blocks, crafted from beautiful white-grey Portland stone. But while the exterior retained its period feel, the interior had been thoroughly modernised, and was all glass staircases, minimalist furnishings and flat-screen TVs – reminding me of the Apple store on Regent Street, with its mix of classic exterior and modern interior.

As I walked into the shared marble lobby, I could feel everyone staring at me. I felt a bit like Julia Roberts' character in *Pretty Woman*, when she goes shopping. The only difference was, I didn't care what anyone thought of me. In fact, shock and disapproval were exactly the reactions I'd been looking for.

Langley House was home to dozens of different businesses – everything from hedge funds to advertising agencies. There was a bank of reception desks in the middle of the lobby, staffed by four well-dressed women. I went straight up to one of the receptionists, whose eyes widened in shock when she saw me.

She managed to collect herself in order to ask my name, and who I was here to see. She then called up to check that I was expected. I could see her scepticism fade, and be replaced by a bright smile, as she came off the phone and directed me up to Richard's offices.

As I walked away, I could see her lean over to whisper to the woman sitting next to her. I wondered if they were taking bets on who the hell I was, and why I was here.

Davenport's was located on the sixth floor, at the top of the building. I caught the glass elevator up, and presented myself at the advertising firm's reception. Two young, attractive women dressed in black were already busy answering phones. When one of them finally had a moment to take my name, I could see her eyes widen in disbelief when I said I was here to see Richard Davenport.

She put the call through, and told me to take a seat. Five minutes later, a neatly dressed woman in her fifties came to greet me, introducing herself as Jean Butler, Richard's PA. She was too professional to show any reaction to my outfit, and instead led me down the hallway to Richard's office.

His office was situated at the end of the building. I'd been expecting some glass-walled goldfish bowl, but instead his office had proper walls and a huge mahogany door, which Jean knocked on. Richard called out for her to come in.

He was on the phone when we walked in, pacing the room like a prowling panther, but beckoned me through, indicating for me to take a seat while he finished up. His PA closed the door quietly behind her. Richard was clearly bawling out the person on the other end of the phone – who, it sounded, had missed a deadline – but doing so in the most reasonable, restrained way possible. I took a look round the room as he spoke – it was neat and minimalist, with no hint of personality whatsoever – no pictures or knick-knacks. Just like his flat.

It was interesting for me to see Richard like this. To me, he was just uptight and annoying. Here, he was calm, commanding and in control. He had on a dark-grey suit, the jacket thrown over the back of the chair, making it feel like he'd already been here for a long time. In the corner, there was a sports bag. That explained how he stayed so athletic even though he spent fourteen hours a day at the office.

He slammed the phone down, and then switched his attention to me. His eyes ran over my outfit, and I saw his lips twist in disapproval. 'Seriously?'

'What?' I affected the same innocent look I'd given Lindsay that morning.

He shook his head. 'Look, wear what you want. It's no skin off my nose. You want to make life difficult for yourself, that's entirely up to you. But let me assure you, it's not going to make me get rid of you before the three months are up.'

I tried not to show my disappointment at him having guessed my plan.

'Come on.' Richard walked over to the door. 'Let me introduce you to your team.'

I followed him along the corridors. As we passed other employees, Richard greeted everyone by name – and they answered deferentially back. A couple of the girls were a bit more friendly than necessary, but Richard didn't seem to notice. Here, at work, he was all business.

'You're like God around here,' I observed.

'That's what happens when you sign the pay cheques.'

I had a feeling there was more to it than that.

'So we have three main departments here,' he said, as we walked. 'They're Account Management, Planning and Creative.'

I didn't say anything. I'd resolved this morning to display no interest or enthusiasm. It seemed the quickest way to get out of here. But Richard appeared not to notice. He was too caught up in what he was saying.

'So Account Management is the "suit" side of advertising,' he said. I imagined that was what he'd specialised in, but I held my tongue. I refused to ask any questions unless absolutely necessary. 'The Account Managers are the main point of contact for the client. Then there are the Planners, who are in touch with what the consumer wants. And lastly, you have the Creatives. They're the ideas people. The ones behind the words and pictures.' He paused and looked over at me. 'That's where you're going to be working.'

I had a feeling he was expecting to get a reaction from me – gratitude or excitement, maybe? – but I refused to give it to him. Instead I managed to keep looking bored and underwhelmed. 'And what'll I be doing?'

'Each of the Creative teams has an assistant. We usually assign one of the graduate trainees, as part of their six-month rotation, but you'll be going there instead. You'll mostly be doing admin tasks for the team at first, but there'll be the potential to learn about the business, and perhaps get involved in more interesting projects.'

I gave him a sidelong look. 'I'm not looking to learn or get involved. You're forcing me to come and work here for three months, so that's what I'll do. But after that, I'm out of here, and back to my normal life. That's our deal.'

Richard sighed. 'Fair enough. But do me a favour, will you?'

'What?'

'Try to remember this isn't meant to be a punishment, Charlotte. It's supposed to be an opportunity. It's just up to you what you get out of it.'

He didn't bother to wait for my response, but instead led me down to the Creative department. The centre of the floor was open plan – for the more junior employees – and then at the side the more senior ones had offices. The creative teams worked in twos – one Copywriter and one Art Director.

We reached one of the offices. There was a desk outside – which I assumed was going to be mine – and then inside there were two people, a man and a woman. They were caught up in a heated discussion. The door was open, but Richard gave a quick rap just to let them know we were there.

'Hey guys.' They stopped arguing and looked up. 'I wanted to introduce you to Charlotte Cranford, your new assistant. And Charlotte, this is your team – Helena Roberts, who's one of our Art Directors, and Rex Morris, Copywriter extraordinaire.'

They stood to shake my hand. To say that they made an odd pairing was something of an understatement. But then again, I imagined advertising didn't exactly attract anyone average. The Art Director, Helena, was a severe-looking woman, who I guessed was in her mid-thirties. She was model tall, and extremely thin, with a long, angular face.

Her hair was pulled back in a tight bun, and she wore John Lennon-style glasses. She was smartly dressed in navy 1940s swing trousers, with a fitted white shirt tucked into the high waist. She'd topped the outfit off with a paisley scarf, tied like a cravat.

'Charlotte.' Her voice was clipped and no-nonsense. 'Good to meet you.'

Then it was Rex Morris's turn. Again, he must have been in his mid-thirties, but physically, he was the opposite of Helena – he was small and rotund, with a round face. He was also completely bald. But while he might not be much to look at, he'd presented himself as well as possible, and was dapperly dressed in a natty royal-blue pinstriped suit, with raspberry-pink trimming, which came complete with a matching waistcoat and a raspberry-pink shirt and tie.

'Fresh blood! Just what we need!' Rex's voice was surprisingly high and camp. He grinned at me. 'Let's see how long it takes to corrupt you.'

My eyes travelled to the picture on his desk. It was of him embracing a tall, beautiful young man, who looked like a male model.

He followed my eye-line, and grimaced. 'My ex. Broke my heart six months ago, but I can't bear to take that picture down. He just looks too yummy in it.'

Helena rolled her eyes. 'After what he did to you, I'd be using that thing for target practice.'

'Really?' Rex arched an eyebrow. 'For someone who hasn't been on a date in over a year, I'm surprised you feel able to hand out love-life advice.'

'I told you before, I'm too busy for a man in my life right now.'

'Maybe that's why you're such a bitch all the time.'

Helena glared at him, and then gave up and shrugged. 'Yeah, you're probably right.'

Rex turned to me. 'So, as you can see, this is us. A workaholic career woman and a camp-as-Christmas gay man. And your first task can be getting Helena here laid.'

She elbowed him in his ample stomach, and they grinned at each other before looking over at me. I just stared back, refusing to crack a smile. This affectionate teasing between them was clearly their 'bit', and I got that I was supposed to laugh, but I refused to join in. I wanted to make it clear to everyone that I was here under sufferance.

Richard cleared his throat, to remind us he was there. When I looked over, his eyes were on me. 'So you'll be in good hands with these guys. Any problems, just let Jean know and she'll find a slot in my diary for you to come up.'

With that, he disappeared. Once he was gone, Helena sat down, while Rex perched on his desk. Their focus was on me.

'So what are you hoping to get out of this placement?' Helena said.

I thought about it for a moment and then shrugged. 'To learn how to make good coffee.'

Rex laughed a little at this, and Helena gave a brief, tight smile. I got the feeling a sense of humour was in short supply for her.

'No – seriously,' she said. 'What part of advertising interests you?'

'Well . . . none of it, really.' I decided it was best to be honest. They were probably used to keen bean graduates, who were looking to impress them. Hopefully if they saw how little interest I had, they might tell Richard they didn't want me working with them. 'Richard's an old family friend. He wants me to work here for three months. So here I am.'

There was silence. Helena and Rex exchanged looks, as though they were trying to work out how serious I was.

'Well, all right.' It was Helena who spoke again, and I got the feeling she generally took the lead. 'I'm guessing you don't know too much about advertising, then. So perhaps it'd be best if I explain a little about our role in the business. As you know, we're the Creative team, and our job is basically about storytelling—'

It was obvious she still wasn't getting it, so I cut her off. 'Look, honestly, you don't have to go into all this. Just let me make coffee, or do some filing or whatever.'

There was another silence. I could see the genuine disbelief on both Helena and Rex's faces. Helena studied me for a moment, and then her eyes narrowed.

'Fine.' Her voice was clipped, and I could tell she'd finally got it. 'If that's what you want, then I guess you can get us some coffee.' Rex looked like he wanted to say something more, but she silenced him with a look. 'Kitchen's down the corridor, fourth door on the right. I take my coffee black, no sugar. Rex is a tea drinker – Earl Grey in the morning, but after midday he won't go near caffeine, so he switches to Jasmine.'

She turned to Rex, and resumed whatever conversation they'd been having before I walked in the room. I was clearly dismissed.

I sloped off to the kitchen, and spent some time making their drinks. I wasn't in any rush to get back – after all, it wasn't like I was trying to impress them with the speed of my tea- and coffee-making abilities.

Ten minutes later, I set the drinks on their desks, and then stood awkwardly, waiting for instructions. This was what I hated most about starting new jobs – not knowing what I was doing or how the company worked. I felt a bit like a spare part.

'So is there anything else you want me to do?' I said.

I was hoping they'd say 'no', and that I could spend the day on the Internet or texting my friends. But Helena clearly had other ideas.

'I've got something you can help with,' she said. 'We've

been asked to pitch ideas for a new celebrity perfume. It's for Willow Wynter.' I tried not to roll my eyes as Helena named the latest manufactured Pop Princess. She had a pile of magazines on her desk, and now she nodded at them. 'I want an idea of what's out there already. So go through these and pick out anything you think might be relevant.'

I picked up the prototype of the perfume bottle – a pale-pink plastic container, shaped like a mini version of the singer, with WW engraved in raised silver lettering on the base. 'I never get what drives celebrities to launch these perfumes. Why don't they just stick to their music instead? It's not like she couldn't use the practice.'

Helena didn't crack so much as a smile. 'It's not up to us to judge. Whatever we may think of the product, our job is just to come up with the best way to sell it.'

With that she resumed talking to Rex. I was officially dismissed. So I picked up a handful of the magazines and headed outside to my desk to get started.

The day dragged by. There was a lot of laughter and debate coming from the office, but I wasn't involved. I sat outside at my little desk, like a mistress at a funeral. Everyone else seemed to be rushing round, busy and important. I couldn't help feeling isolated and alone.

At five on the dot, I couldn't stand it any longer. I poked my head into the office to ask if there was anything else I needed to do before I left.

Helena glanced up from some sketches she was working on. 'Have you finished going through those magazines?'

'About half of them. I thought I'd do the rest tomorrow.'

Rex looked up. 'Actually, Charlotte—'

'It's Charlie.'

I could see him take a breath, trying to be patient with me.

'Actually, Charlie, it would be good if you—'

'Did it first thing,' Helena broke in. It seemed like Rex was going to say something more, but a look from her silenced him. 'We'll see you tomorrow morning.'

I stood crushed between commuters on the Tube home, feeling fed up. The first day had been as bad as I'd anticipated, and I wanted someone to complain to. I knew it was Lindsay's night off, and I wondered if she'd be up for doing something. I missed my friend, and I suddenly longed for everything to go back to normal between us. While I still thought she was wrong for not supporting me, I wondered if it was time to forgive her. I just hoped she'd be at the flat when I got back.

I hurried home from the station, spurred on by the thought of making up with my friend. As I opened the front door, I was greeted with the sound of running water coming from the kitchen – a sure sign that Lindsay was home. My cheeks lifted into a smile, as I dropped my bag and jacket on the hallway floor.

'Hey, Linds!' I called out, as I made my way towards the sound. 'What do you think about heading out later—'

The words died on my lips as I walked into the kitchen and saw a big, hulking figure standing in front of the sink. My heart sank as I realised my mistake. It wasn't Lindsay I'd heard – it was Adrian.

He switched off the tap, and turned towards me. 'Hi, Charlie.' He smiled shyly at me. That was the funny thing about Adrian – his looks were completely at odds with his personality. He was about six foot six, solidly built, and sported a shaved head – courtesy of premature balding. The whole effect made him look like some kind of neo-Nazi skinhead, when in actual fact I'd have to grudgingly admit he was probably one of the nicest guys I'd met. He was the archetypal gentle giant.

'How are you?' he asked tentatively, wringing the dish-cloth between his hands.

'What're you doing here?' I demanded, ignoring his polite question.

He blinked, looking a little taken aback by the abruptness of my tone. 'I . . . uh . . . came over to cook dinner for Lindsay. I thought it might cheer her up . . .'

It was then I noticed that the worktops were covered with the makings of a romantic night in. On the counters were ingredients for a pasta dish: a packet of fusilli and a jar of tomato and garlic sauce – nothing fancy, but still . . . it was more cooking than either Lindsay or I ever did. My eyes lingered over a plate of grated cheese and a bottle of red wine. Adrian had obviously thought of everything. I felt a stab of irritation and something else – a feeling akin to envy mixed with wistfulness.

I swallowed hard, and focused back on the present. 'Cheer her up?' I seized on what he'd said. 'Why does Lindsay need cheering up?'

'Well, uh . . .'

'Because I didn't get that job I went for.'

We both looked over to see Lindsay standing in the door-way. She regarded me with cool eyes, and I drew back a little. Maybe I'd been willing to forgive and forget, but it seemed she was still annoyed.

'So how did your day go?' she asked.

I shrugged. 'Not great.'

She snorted. 'Well, that's hardly surprising.'

I guessed that she meant it wasn't surprising given the fact I'd gone in with such a poor attitude. I was going to retaliate, but Adrian cleared his throat, so we both looked over at him.

'I was just about to start cooking.' He was addressing his comments to me. 'There's loads of food, if you'd like to join us.'

I could tell Adrian's offer was genuine, and I had to commend him for playing the peacemaker. My gaze moved to Lindsay. She stared back at me, challenging me to swallow my pride and join them. Maybe I would have, but then my eyes alighted on something else resting on the kitchen counter – a bunch of flowers, that Adrian had obviously brought round for my friend. Suddenly I realised just how much I didn't belong here. This was going to be an evening of cosy conversations and sweet domesticity. I wanted to get wasted and laid.

'Thanks for the offer,' I said to Adrian. 'But I think I'll skip it.' I looked meaningfully at Lindsay. 'I'm going to head over to The Nick.'

'Of course you are.' I flashed her a glare, and headed out of the kitchen, leaving the two of them alone.

It didn't take me long to get ready. All I needed to do was quickly brush my teeth and touch up my make-up. There was no need to change, as the outfit I'd worn to the office was outrageous enough for a night at The Nick. I might not be working at the bar any more, but that wasn't going to stop me hanging out in the place. As I stood in the hallway, slipping on my jacket, I heard Lindsay and Adrian laughing together in the kitchen. I felt a flash of loneliness and regret, but I pushed it aside, and pulled open the door to head back out.

The usual crowd was at The Nick that night. As soon as I walked in I spotted Gavin. I headed over to where he was sitting, and slid into a seat next to him.

He did a theatrical double-take when he saw me. 'I didn't expect to catch you here, girl. I heard you'd gone all corporate on us.'

'Yeah, well. That's during the day. I can do what I like at night.' To prove my point, I grabbed the shot glass in front of Gavin, and downed the tequila.

He nodded approvingly. 'That's my girl.'

I felt a surge of power. I was so fed up with everyone criticising me – this was my way of flipping them all off. Richard might think he could control my life, but I was going to show him otherwise.

I pushed my glass forward. 'Line up another shot,' I said. 'Let's start the night as we mean to go on.'

Chapter 8

I got into work the next morning just after nine. I'd stayed out until nearly three, and I was feeling pretty hung-over. Once I'd settled at my desk, I looked for the magazines that I'd been going through yesterday. Someone had moved them. I wondered if it was the cleaners. Assuming that Helena and Rex would know, I went through to the office. They were already hard at work, and looked like they'd been there for hours.

'Morning, my lovely!' Rex sang out when he saw me, while Helena didn't even look up as she clipped out a greeting.

'I was just looking for those magazines you had me go through yesterday. I thought I'd finish finding the perfume ads.'

'No need. I've already done it.' Helena still didn't look up as she spoke.

I frowned. 'What?' I glanced over at Rex, who gave me a sheepish smile. 'Why didn't you wait for me to do it today?'

'Because we needed it done yesterday, so we could start brainstorming ideas for the advert.' Helena glanced up at me then and frowned. 'God, what happened to you last night?' Before I could answer, she held up a hand. 'On second thoughts, don't tell me. Look, I think you made it clear yesterday that you see this as a job rather than a career. That's fine. I'm not going to force you to do anything you don't want to. There's no point. It's a shame that you aren't interested in advertising, as there are a lot of people out there who'd have loved to have this opportunity. But obviously you're not one of them, am I right?'

Helena had got the measure of me very quickly, which was what I'd wanted. But somehow when she put it that baldly, it didn't make me sound so good. All I could do was nod.

'Fine,' she said brusquely. 'Now, between the hours of nine and five we will give you work to do, and I expect you to do it to the best of your ability, because that's what you're paid for. After that, you're free to do whatever you want.' She paused to let this sink in a moment, and then said, 'Do we understand each other?'

I nodded again.

'Excellent. Then your first task of the day is to go down

to the canteen and get us both breakfast. Neither of us has had time to eat yet, and we're starving.'

She reached into her handbag to get some money, as I dutifully took down their food orders. As I went down to the canteen, I realised this was the exact treatment I'd asked for. So why then did I have a strange nagging feeling in the pit of my stomach?

The rest of the week continued pretty much like that. I came in at nine on the dot, took an hour for lunch and left at five, and during that time I did exactly what was asked of me, but no more. Then as soon as the workday ended, I headed out to meet friends. I turned up at the office bleary-eyed and with a hangover each day, which I was sure the astute Helena knew. In short, I got through the week with doing the bare minimum, while not completely acting out.

The following Monday afternoon, I got a call from Richard's PA, Jean, saying that he wanted to see me in his office. It was hard to keep the smile off my face as I went up to see him. This was it – after a week of working with the sullen, lethargic me, I was sure Helena and Rex had told Richard that they wanted me gone.

Richard was on the phone again when I got to his office. He indicated for me to take a seat, while he finished his call.

Finally, he turned his attention to me. 'So, Charlotte.' He sat back in his chair. 'How are things going so far?'

It wasn't quite the opening I'd been expecting. I thought he'd tell me straight off that he wanted me out. Well, if he wanted to take his time, then I was happy to play along . . . I assumed a bored face, and studied my nails. 'All right, I suppose. Why? Has someone complained?'

'Why?' he fired back. 'Have you given them something to complain about?'

I shrugged. 'I suppose you could say that I'm probably not the most enthusiastic employee Helena and Rex have ever had. So I assumed they'd probably told you that, and you'd called me up here to say that you'd finally come to your senses, and realised what a stupid idea your little experiment is—'

'Oh, no,' he cut in. 'As I said before, you're not going to get out of it that easily.' He planted his forearms on the desk, and leaned forward, so I could see how serious he was. 'But I have to confess that I am a little disappointed that you haven't been making more of an effort. I had hoped that once you started working with Helena and Rex, you'd find what they did interesting.'

'And I'd hoped that you'd have decided by now that it was a waste of everyone's time having me work here. So I guess we're both coming away from this meeting feeling disappointed.' I made to stand up. 'Now if that's all, I should get going. I'm sure someone somewhere needs coffee fetched—'

'Not so fast,' he cut me off. I flopped back down in the chair. 'There's one more thing before you go.' He opened the top drawer of his desk, pulled out a business card and handed it to me. There was the name and address of a Dr Margaret Milton printed in black type.

'Who the hell's this?'

'Dr Milton is a highly recommended psychologist. I've made an appointment for you to meet with her this evening at six.'

I groaned. 'Are you serious? I thought you were joking about that!'

'Well, I wasn't. It's all part of our deal. And you should count yourself lucky. She's very good at what she does, and usually impossible to get an appointment with. It was just fortunate that she had a cancellation.'

'Lucky me,' I muttered.

I glared at the business card in my hand, as though it might disappear if I scowled at it hard enough. I hated that Richard had control over me like this. I wanted to pay him back, but at the moment he seemed to hold all the cards. Then an idea occurred to me. If he wanted to play games, then I was happy to oblige.

He was undoubtedly waiting for me to storm out of his office in a huff. Instead, I forced my body to relax. Pushing a lock of hair behind my ear, I looked up at him from beneath lowered lashes.

'You know,' I drawled softly, making my voice deliberately throaty, 'I've never seen much point in therapy.'

Richard's eyes narrowed, clearly catching the change in my tone. 'Oh?'

'No.' I ran my hands over the arms of the leather chair, as though I was massaging a lover. Then I rose from my seat, in one fluid move, and began to walk round Richard's desk, trailing my hand across the polished mahogany. 'All that talking about your feelings – it's just not for me.'

'I can't say I'm surprised.'

I came to a halt by Richard, perching on the desk right in front of him. As I crossed my legs, my skirt rode up, and I made no attempt to pull it down, instead enjoying the way Richard's gaze moved up my exposed thighs.

I leaned forward, deliberately giving him a view of my cleavage. 'Do you know what I've always thought the best therapy was?'

'I have a feeling you're going to tell me.'

'Sex.' I whispered the word, making it sound even more clandestine than it should. I watched as Richard swallowed, hard. He fingered his collar, as though he was hot.

'Is that so?' He seemed to struggle to get the words out. It was the first time ever I'd seen him anything other than completely in control, and it took me all of my strength not to smirk.

'So what do you say?' I bit down on my bottom lip, just like I'd seen actresses do in those old film noir movies when the femme fatale was trying to be sexy. 'You and me – right here, right now.'

Maybe it was a bit much, but I didn't care – subtlety had never been my strong point. And all I needed to do was reel Richard in, and make him sweat with the awkwardness of the situation – then let's see if he was in quite such a hurry to interfere in my life again.

And then I saw the way he was looking at me – not with confusion or embarrassment, but more with a raw hunger and intensity that I hadn't been expecting.

'God, Charlotte.' The words were no more than a groan. 'You don't know how long I've waited to hear you say that.'

He stood abruptly, and in one deft move had shrugged off his suit jacket, and tossed it onto the wingback chair behind him, as he began to move towards me. Suddenly I realised my mistake. I'd planned to toy with him, and inadvertently created a situation I couldn't handle. Instinctively I uncrossed my legs, perhaps planning to slip from the desk, but before I could, Richard had moved between my parted thighs, his hands setting down on the desk either side of me, so I was trapped by his large body.

He was standing dangerously near to me. We were as physically close as two people could be without actually touching. I could feel the heat from his body, the warmth of his breath on my face as he loomed over me. Given the position we were in, it would have been the easiest thing in the world for me to wrap my legs around his waist, and the knowledge made me feel exposed and vulnerable, two words that I never usually applied to myself. I swallowed, hard, and wetted my lips, knowing I needed to say something to put a stop to this madness.

'Richard,' I began.

'Yes, Charlotte.'

It was then that I saw it – the wicked glint in his eye. The penny suddenly dropped. I drew back, stunned.

'You're winding me up, aren't you?'

Richard grinned. 'Took you long enough to catch on.'

He lifted his hands up from the desk, straightening up a little so I was no longer physically trapped, but he was still close enough that I couldn't simply slip away.

He shook his head in mock disapproval. 'You seriously thought I'd fall for that old seduction routine?'

'Yeah, well.' I tried to shrug it off, not wanting him to realise how foolish I felt – along with something else, too . . . a sinking feeling, akin to disappointment. But disappointment at what? Being bested by him? 'It was just a joke.'

'One that happened to misfire.'

I didn't bother to answer, and instead slid from the desk, and busied myself straightening my clothes. I could feel Richard's eyes on me, and knew this wasn't over yet.

'You know what your problem is?' he said.

'No, but I have a feeling you're going to tell me,' I fired back, deliberately echoing his earlier words.

'I am.' He smiled coolly, maddeningly in control. 'You see, you think you're worldly and experienced, but in fact you're totally clueless. You're used to sleeping with worthless little boys, who don't present any challenge. But you'd have no idea how to handle a real man.'

'You mean someone like you?'

'Precisely.'

The word hung in the air between us. I felt suddenly acutely aware of just how close we were standing. Richard's dark eyes held mine, silently challenging me. I had a strange urge to look away, and it took all my strength to hold his gaze. This conversation . . . it was oddly unnerving, in a way I couldn't quite put my finger on. I just knew I wanted it to end.

'You're such a sanctimonious jerk.' It wasn't my best comeback, but it was all I had right now. Annoyingly, it just made Richard's smile widen, as if he sensed my frustration.

'Oh, don't be such a sore loser, Charlotte, *darling*.' He emphasised the final word, knowing how much it would irritate me. 'It doesn't suit you.'

With that, he finally stepped back, allowing me to escape. I ducked by him, and headed for the door, desperate to get away from this whole embarrassing episode. I was almost there, when Richard spoke.

'Oh, and Charlotte?' I came to a halt. I paused to take a deep, cleansing breath. Then I turned back to find him smiling sweetly at me.

'What?'

He held out his hand. 'Don't forget this.'

I saw then that he had the psychologist's card that I'd accidentally left on his desk. I stalked over and snatched it from him. Then with one final glare I swept from the room, pretending not to hear his laughter.

Chapter 9

The therapist's office was located on Harley Street, of course – only the best for Richard Davenport. It was within walking distance of the office, so after work, I headed along the back lanes of Oxford Street, to where the practice was located.

The fine Georgian terraces all looked alike, but I found the right number, and walked up the stone steps to the black double door. I was buzzed into a discreet reception area, where someone took my name.

I'd looked up the practice, and I knew that there were three psychologists working out of the lower floors of the building. As I sat in the waiting room, I cast a glance at the other people, wondering why exactly they were there. There was a middle-aged guy in a dark suit, who looked like he worked at a large investment bank, and a teenage girl in her school uniform. They looked normal enough – a regular cross-section of London residents – but who could tell?

At six on the dot, the receptionist directed me up to the first floor. Dr Margaret Milton's office was the second door down. I gave a brief knock, and a clear voice called out for me to come in.

As I went inside, a petite woman rose to greet me. The first thing that struck me was how attractive Dr Milton was. I knew from my research that she was in her mid-forties, but she looked a lot younger. Small and slender, with a perfectly symmetrical face framed by dark blonde hair, she wore a tailored black dress, with a black and white suit jacket on top. She was the kind of therapist who'd get invited onto the couches of the morning news as a guest expert, and end up with her own programme.

She smiled warmly at me. 'Make yourself comfortable, Charlotte.'

I glanced around her office. It had the grand academic feel of an Oxbridge don's set – mahogany furniture; crammed bookcases; and heavy velvet curtains hung from the bay window that overlooked the street below. Two comfy armchairs had been arranged by the fire. I sat on the one closest to the door, in case I wanted to make a quick escape, and Dr Milton took the other. Once we were settled, she smiled encouragingly at me.

'So why don't we begin with you telling me why you decided to start seeing me?'

'I didn't,' I said flatly.

'Oh.' She blinked a couple of times, clearly taken aback by my admission. But she seemed to quickly recover. 'Then why don't you tell me why you're here?'

My eyes went to the notebook resting on her knee. I chewed at my inner lip, trying to decide how to play this. On my way here, I'd resolved to keep mute – after all, Richard could insist on me coming to Dr Milton, but he wouldn't know what I did or didn't say during the session. But now I was here, it didn't really feel feasible to remain silent for the next hour.

'I'm only here because I'm being blackmailed into it,' I said after a moment.

I'd been hoping to shock her, but I guess her profession made that impossible. She regarded me with mild interest, nothing more.

'And how did that happen?'

Despite my resolution to say as little as possible, I found myself telling Dr Milton all about Richard and the events that had led me to end up in her office. She didn't make any comment as I talked, and only stopped me once or twice to clarify a point. Once I'd finished, I'd been expecting her to show some reaction – shock, surprise, a sense of 'wow, I've never heard anything like that in all my years'. But instead she remained impassive.

'So what you're saying is that this friend of your family, Richard, thinks you're engaging in self-destructive behaviour, and he believes coming here will help you with that. So he has – from what I understand – coerced you into it with this threat to reveal information to your parents. Is that right?'

'Pretty much.'

'And do you feel that your behaviour is a problem?'

'God, no. It's just . . . how I choose to live my life.'

'I see.' She made a little notation on a piece of paper, and then looked back up at me. 'Well, now I've heard a bit about you, why don't you let me tell you about how I work?'

'All right,' I said guardedly.

She sat back in her chair, and began what I guessed was her normal spiel. 'I presume this is your first time to see a therapist?'

'That's right.' And hopefully my last, I added silently.

'Well, my sessions run for fifty minutes, and I like to see my patients on a weekly basis. Usually we meet for at least twelve weeks, and then we can reassess what progress is being made, and whether we feel it's worth continuing. I'm not here to give you advice, or comment on how you live your life. My job is more to help you understand yourself and why you're making the decisions that you do, and whether you're happy with that – and if you're not, then to find a different approach. Does that make sense?'

I gave a nod.

'Good.' She regarded me for a moment. I sensed a 'but' coming up. 'Now, I'm happy to take you on as a client, but—' There it was. 'My one reservation is that I do feel it's most beneficial if these sessions are voluntary. I don't like the idea that you're being forced to come here. If you don't believe that you need to be here, then you're going to be hostile towards the whole process, and you won't get anything out of it.'

It took me a moment to work out what she was saying. She was giving me an out – a way to avoid therapy.

'So I don't have to come back next week?' I said.

She smiled a little. 'You don't have to do anything you don't want to. I think the question you need to go away and consider this week is whether you believe that coming here would benefit you in any way. If you can honestly answer no, then you really shouldn't come back.' I was too stunned to say anything. I hadn't thought it would be this easy to get out of. 'So what I'll do is keep your appointment for the same day and time next week, and it'll be up to you whether you come or not.'

I sat there for a moment, expecting her to say more. She didn't.

'Is that it?' I said eventually.

'Time's up for today.' She nodded over at the clock on the wall, and I saw that she was right – the fifty minutes had already passed.

I got to my feet, and she rose to see me out.

I paused at the door. I wasn't entirely sure what to say to her. 'Well . . . uh . . . thanks for everything.' I wasn't sure if it was appropriate to show gratitude, but if nothing else, the experience had been less painful than I'd imagined.

She gave a brief, professional smile. 'That's quite all right. Enjoy the rest of your evening, Charlotte.'

With that, she closed the door behind me.

I was left standing alone in the corridor, feeling confused. Was that really it? Somehow I'd been expecting her to give me the hard sell at the end – to tell me in a solemn tone that while it was my decision whether to be here or not, in her opinion it would be worth my while. But she seemed, well, really not bothered if I came back or not.

I should have felt relieved about that – after all, that was exactly what I'd wanted – but for some reason it left me feeling strangely empty.

The following morning, I made an appointment to see Richard, so I could give him the news that his therapist refused to see me because of his blackmail. I was still a little freaked out by the memory of what had happened between us last time; it had felt a bit too close to flirtation for my liking, so I was determined to keep things strictly business.

I'd worried about how he'd react to finding out that I wouldn't be seeing Dr Milton – after all, seeing a psychologist had been part of the deal for him not telling my parents. Would he view this as me breaking our pact?

But when I'd finished telling him what Margaret had said, he simply shrugged.

'Fair enough. I suppose you won't be able to do the therapy then.'

I blinked. '*Fair enough*?' I repeated. 'That's all you've got to say?'

'Well, how else should I react?'

'I thought you'd try to force me to go back. Or see someone else.'

'Like Margaret said, there's no point doing the therapy if you aren't open to the idea.'

'Well, then, why did you send me in the first place? You knew I didn't want to go. Wouldn't it have saved us all a lot of time and effort if you'd told me it was optional?'

'I suppose. But I had hoped that once you got there you might warm to the idea.' He paused to let this sink in. 'You don't seem to realise, Charlotte. I'm not doing this to inconvenience you. I'm doing this because I think it's in your best interests. I'm doing it because I care.'

His eyes held mine, his sincerity clear. The intensity of his gaze unnerved me, so I cut my eyes away.

'Yeah, well.' I cleared my throat, trying to think of a way to lighten the mood. 'Maybe next time you could show how much you care by letting me get on with my life. Or by sending me on an all-expenses trip to Thailand. Either works for me.' I stood abruptly. 'So, if there's nothing else, I better get going.'

With that, I hurried from the room.

Chapter 10

The next ten days dragged by with a routine predictability that made me want to scream. By the following Friday, I was feeling thoroughly fed up. As usual I collected Helena and Rex's lunch, and brought it to their office. Neither of them was at their desks as I came back in – with a sushi and sashimi selection for Rex, who was constantly on a diet, and a Big Mac meal for Helena, who seemed to eat loads and never put on an ounce of weight.

As I placed the burger, fries and large Coke on Helena's desk, I happened to glance down at what she'd been working on. It was the sketches for a print and TV campaign for the celebrity perfume that she'd had me leafing through magazines for. The perfume was called 'Star', and the advert featured an ordinary girl who turns into a rock star after she spritzes on the perfume, with the caption saying: 'So every girl can feel like a star.' It was cheesy, but that wasn't what was bothering me – the drawings themselves just weren't very good.

'Well, you don't look very impressed.' Helena's amused voice came from behind me. I looked up, embarrassed to have been caught going through her stuff. But luckily she didn't appear to mind. She walked over and slipped into her seat. 'So what's with the face? You don't like the idea? I know it probably seems simplistic, but those are often the most effective campaigns for a product like this.'

'It's not that . . . The idea's fine. Just the drawings are a bit . . . well . . .'

'Rudimentary?' Helena filled in.

'Yes.' I felt embarrassed admitting that that's what I'd thought. 'I thought you were the Art Director.'

She laughed a little. 'That doesn't mean I draw. My job is just to get something down that's good enough to communicate the basic idea. Then, once we have the agreement of the Creative Directors and Account Executives, we have a team of sketch artists who'll put together something more professional to present to the client.'

'What – like on storyboards?' For the first time, my interest was piqued.

'When I first started in the industry, it used to be just storyboards. But now we use other mediums as well – digital images, animation, that kind of thing.' Helena sat back, studying me. I could tell she was pleased that I'd shown an interest in something finally. 'Richard mentioned that you studied art. Do you draw?'

'Used to.' My answer was abrupt, my voice guarded. I didn't want to start sharing my life story. I was beginning to regret showing interest in her work, and giving her a chance to probe me. I'd unwittingly opened a door I hadn't wanted to.

'But not lately?' she prompted. I could sense she was watching me keenly.

'No.'

'How come?'

'Just lost interest, I suppose.' I started backing out of the room. 'Anyway, I'll leave you to your lunch.'

She looked like she was going to argue, but then she gave up.

'Sure,' she said, and began opening up her Big Mac.

I crept back to my desk, hoping the whole incident would be forgotten. But obviously it wasn't going to be that easy, because two hours later, as Helena and Rex emerged to go to a meeting, she stopped by my desk.

'We've got a briefing for a new product now. Why don't you come along?'

I sensed this was my reward for having shown some interest in her sketches. Great. This was precisely what I'd wanted to avoid. I was meant to be so uninterested that they'd ask Richard to get rid of me. 'Do I have to?'

Helena's smile dimmed a little. 'I just thought you might find it interesting. But if you don't want to—'

I was torn. It was tempting to decline simply out of stubbornness, but the fact of the matter was that I was quite curious to see what happened at these briefings – even though I'd die before admitting it. Plus, it sounded more interesting than sitting at my desk and browsing the Internet to kill time.

'Sure. Why not?'

We headed upstairs to Miles Fairfax's office. He was one of the Account Managers, which was, as I'd suspected, the job that Richard used to do – the more 'suit' end of the industry.

Miles came out to greet us. 'Helena, Rex – good to see you.' He shook both their hands, but ignored me.

That was typical of Miles. He was in his early thirties, and known round the office for being a charmer. He was always networking and had a permanent smile on his face for anyone he thought could help in his career – obviously I didn't fall into that category, which is why he didn't bother with me. He was terribly posh, and you could hear his plummy drawl booming out whenever he was anywhere near. He was very different to Richard, who was much more serious, but I could see how they were both good at their jobs, just in different ways – whereas Richard was the kind who would win a client's confidence with his seriousness, Miles was the type to charm them into a deal.

We went through to his office, and settled ourselves around the large conference table. Nathalie Drummond, Miles's assistant, also joined us. She was something of a legend around the office. One of the graduate trainees, she was clearly going places fast. She was neat and professional-looking, and I couldn't help feeling even more thrown together than normal as I took my seat next to her.

The briefing turned out to be for a potential new client called PURE, a charity that specialised in helping young drug addicts. They wanted to come up with a hard-hitting print and TV campaign, to dissuade youngsters from taking drugs at clubs, parties and festivals.

I tried to follow the discussion as best I could, but it wasn't always easy, as everyone was throwing around acronyms that I didn't understand. I jotted them down on my notepad with a big question mark, planning to look them up afterwards when I got back to my desk.

'Ranker and daypart.' I glanced up to see Nathalie studying my notepad. They were two of the words I wasn't sure of. Miles had gone outside to take a quick phone call, so there had been a brief lull in the meeting. She'd obviously decided it was a good opportunity to stick her nose into my business. 'Don't you know what they mean?'

Her voice was filled with disbelief and a hint of contempt. My instinct was to deny my ignorance, but I knew it would be even worse to be caught out in a lie.

'No. I don't.'

I kept my answer short, trying to sound as though admitting this didn't bother me. But I was all too aware of Rex and Helena looking at me with undisguised sympathy. Naturally Miles had taken that moment to reappear, and was regarding me with far less compassion.

'Well,' Nathalie said, ignoring my discomfort, 'a ranker is a report showing a selected demographic audience of each radio or TV station in a market, ranked from the highest to the lowest – for example, the number of women 18 to 35. And dayparts are time periods throughout the day in which radio and television stations sell ads.' She paused, with a meaningful look at my notepad. 'Got that?'

I was forced to jot down her explanation, the room silent apart from the sound of my pen scratching against the paper. I hated Nathalie in that moment for singling me out for the sole purpose of showing how accomplished she was – as though we weren't already aware of that.

Finally I looked up to see Nathalie smiling coolly at me. 'Anything else, just ask.'

Miles cleared his throat. 'Well, if we're quite finished with the lesson,' he said in his plummy drawl, 'let's get on with it.' He sat back to address Rex and Helena. 'Look, guys, the budget for this isn't huge. Frankly I wouldn't normally bother with such a piddly client, but the patron of the charity is Luke Ramsey, the property developer. His company commissions tens of millions of advertising each year. So I'm hoping if we do a good job here, we might win a slice of that action—'

'We'll do a good job because we've been asked to by a worthy cause,' Helena said, cutting him off. She was regarding him with the same distaste I felt. 'And not as part of some Machiavellian plan concocted by you.' I bit back a smile, as I watched his face redden. Helena was one of the few people who could put him in his place. 'Now, when are we presenting to the client?'

'I'm not sure of the exact deadline yet,' Miles said, recovering quickly. 'But they said it'll be tight. They're meant to be getting back to me ASAP, so I'll call down with the details when they're ready.'

'Fine.' Helena rose, and Rex and I followed suit. 'We'll be in touch when we have something.'

'Well done,' Rex whispered to Helena as we left the room. 'If you hadn't put that jerk down, then I would have.' He glanced over at me. 'And by the look on Charlie's face, I think she felt the same.'

'I was just planning on punching him. Or Nathalie. I hadn't quite made up my mind,' I deadpanned. Rex and Helena both laughed. I don't know why, but the fact that I'd amused them made me feel good. As much as I wanted to pretend otherwise, these guys really weren't that bad. And the project sounded interesting, too.

'Maybe you can help with the research on this,' Helena said as we made our way to the lift.

'I'd like that.' It was only when I heard the enthusiasm in my voice that I caught myself. I forced a nonchalant shrug. 'I mean, I'll do it if you want me to.'

Helena exchanged an amused look with Rex. I steeled myself for her to tease me about my eagerness, but she simply said, 'I think it'd be good for you to get involved.'

Fortunately she changed the subject then, and started talking to Rex about other clients. I stayed silent the rest of the way back to our office.

I'd only been at my desk for a couple of minutes when my phone rang. It was Miles's assistant, Nathalie. I'd know that haughty voice anywhere.

'The client called with details about the presentation date,' she said, without any preamble. 'It's on 2 November, at 12 p.m. And Miles wants to meet Helena and Rex the Monday before at 10 to go over their ideas—'

'Wait a sec—' I said as she rattled the details at me. I was searching around on my desk for a piece of paper and a pen, but couldn't see one. Just then my mobile rang. Along with the persistent sound of the ringtone, I could hear Nathalie on the other end of the landline, sighing deeply, as though I was invading her precious time. 'Hold on. I'm nearly with you . . .'

I found a pen, and scrawled down the important details of the meeting.

'Great. I've got it,' I said to Nathalie. 'Anything else?'

'That's all.'

I wasn't sure which of us slammed the receiver down first. My mobile was still ringing, so I snatched it up. It was Gavin, who I'd been hanging out with a lot lately since my falling out with Lindsay. I'd slept with him a couple of times, after some crazy nights out, but when he started thinking that made us a couple, I'd had to put a halt to it. Now we were just drinking buddies. He gave me the details of a party he was going to later that night. I told him I'd be there.

When I'd finally finished with the call, I went through to Helena. 'Nathalie phoned with details of the client meeting.'

'Oh, yes? When is it?'

I looked down at my pad. I'd scrawled down three key details — '2', 'Nov' and '12', in no discernible order. I frowned, trying to remember what Nathalie had told me — was it 2nd November at 12 p.m., or 12th November at 2 p.m.?

'Charlotte?' I looked up and saw Helena staring quizzically at me. 'Is there a problem?'

I briefly thought about saying I needed to check. But the last thing I wanted to do was speak to Nathalie again. I made a decision. 'It's 12 November, at 2 p.m. And Miles wants to go over the details on the previous Monday, at 10. So that'll be—' I quickly checked my calendar. 'The fifth.'

Yes. As soon as I said it, that sounded right.

'Oh.' Helena looked relieved, if a little confused. 'I thought Miles said it'd be a tight deadline? That doesn't sound too bad to me. Oh, well.' She glanced up at me. 'Put those dates in the diary, will you?'

'Sure.' I went back out to my desk, pulled up our team's calendar, and did just that – and then I forgot all about it.

Chapter 11

Ten days later, at 10 a.m. on a Monday morning, the phone went on my desk. I saw from the display that it was Nathalie, Miles Fairfax's assistant. I groaned to myself as I answered.

'Where are they?' she said without preamble.

'Who?'

She huffed a little. 'Helena and Rex, of course. They're due up here to go through their ideas for the PURE campaign.'

I frowned. I'd just checked the team's calendar, and there were no meetings scheduled for today. I pulled up Outlook and checked when it was written in for. 'That's not 'til next Monday.'

There was silence on the other end of the phone. 'No,' she said. 'It's today. The presentation to the client is on Friday. Next Monday will be too late.'

I sat up a little straighter, my heart beginning to beat faster. 'But the presentation is at 2 p.m. on Monday 12th November. I remember you telling me. And you said they were to present their ideas to Miles on the previous Monday. So that's the fifth—'

'Charlotte, I really hope this is one of your jokes.' Even she was beginning to sound panicked. 'I told you the client presentation is the 2nd November at 12 p.m. That's this Friday, so the previous Monday's meeting is—'

Now.

Suddenly all the elements fell into place, and I realised the mistake I'd made. I closed my eyes, hoping that this might just turn out to be some nightmare, and I was about to wake up.

I opened my eyes, but unfortunately I was still here, sitting at my desk. A cold, sick feeling began to form in my stomach.

'I'll call you right back,' I mumbled, and slammed the phone down.

I didn't want to start dealing with Miles until I'd had a chance to explain my mistake to the team. I looked into the office, where Helena and Rex were working on another campaign, happily oblivious to the disaster that was just about to unfold. I had no desire to go in and explain my mistake – in fact, I'd have done anything right then to leave the building and never come back. But unfortunately that wasn't an option. However unpleasant this was, I needed to face it head on.

Helena and Rex looked up as I walked into the office.

'Whatever it is, can it wait, Charlotte?' Helena said. 'We're working to a deadline—'

I swallowed. Oh, great. They were already busy and stressed, and now I was about to make things a hundred times worse. 'I'm sorry.' Somehow I forced myself to say the words. My voice sounded far away and detached. 'I need to talk to you now.'

The panic on my face must have been evident, as I watched them exchange concerned looks.

'Go ahead,' Rex said. 'Tell us what's going on.'

I quickly explained what I'd done, surprised at how calm and coherent I sounded, given that I felt like I was about to throw up. I could see the blood draining from Helena's face as I talked.

'What the hell, Charlotte?' she exploded once I'd finished. 'How could you do this?'

'I'm sorry. I really am—' I started, but I could tell she wasn't listening.

'You're sorry? Well, that's all right then, isn't it?' I quaked a little at the sarcasm in her voice. Usually Helena was so calm and reasonable. Seeing her lose it like this was unnerving me more than anything else. 'As long as Charlotte's sorry for screwing up, we should all just forgive her. Let me guess how this happened. Were you hung-over?'

'No—'

'Busy organising your social life?' I thought back to that afternoon when I was scheduling the meeting, and how I'd got a call from Gavin about going out that night. I dropped my eyes to the floor. The action didn't go unnoticed by Helena. 'Ah, so that's it, is it? Typical—'

'Helena,' Rex interrupted. 'I know how upsetting this is, but try to stay calm—'

She rounded on him. 'How can I? Do you know how bad this looks? We'll never have time to come up with anything decent now, so we'll have to ask for an extension, and it's not going to cut it to say that our lazy, apathetic assistant—' I winced at the description of me – 'who has no interest in being here, screwed us over. They're a small charity, who've come to us for help, and we're going to look like we don't give a damn about them.'

Before Rex could say anything to this, she turned back to me. Her eyes blazed with such fury and contempt that I automatically took a step back. 'Was this your ploy to get sacked from here? Well, congratulations. You're about to get your wish. Because I sure as hell don't want you on my team any longer. And I'm going to tell Richard that now.'

She got up and stormed out before I could say anything else.

There was silence after she'd gone.

I looked over at Rex. I hoped he couldn't see, but I was actually physically shaking.

'Overreact much?' I said, trying to turn it into a joke, even though I didn't feel much like laughing.

Rex didn't even crack a smile. He was the softer one, who never lost his cool. But even he looked faintly disapproving. 'It was just a project very close to her heart.'

I waited for a fuller explanation, but he just shook his head. That didn't make me feel any better. Even if I did think her reaction was a bit extreme, I hated the thought that I'd upset her like that, simply because of my carelessness.

'Look, don't worry about it,' Rex said, obviously seeing the look on my face. 'She'll calm down.'

Somehow that didn't make me feel any better. I crept back out to my desk, and tried to make myself as small as possible.

Half an hour later, Helena returned.

'Richard wants to see you in his office,' she said as she walked past my desk. She didn't even look in my direction.

I wanted to apologise again, but I could see there was no point – she wasn't in the mood to listen to me. And then I wondered, why did I feel so bad about this? When I'd first started at Davenport's, all I'd wanted to do was leave, and find a way to cut my three months short. Now that I'd inadvertently got my ticket out of here, I should be celebrating. Soon I wouldn't have to think about any of these people again.

I was still feeling defiant when I reached Richard's office. I walked in like I didn't give a damn and flopped into the chair opposite him.

'So,' I leaned back and stretched my hands over the armrests, regarding him with a deliberately bored, defiant expression. 'Can you do me a favour and skip the lecture? I know I made a mistake, but whatever Helena thinks, it wasn't deliberate.'

Richard wasn't exactly a shouter, but I'd perhaps expected him to raise his voice and bawl me out. Instead, he regarded me with grave eyes. 'There's going to be no lecture,' he said quietly.

That took the wind out of my sails. For a moment I didn't know what to say. I'd been geared up for a fight – I wasn't prepared to deal with anything else. Then I regained my composure. 'Oh, right. Then what am I doing here?'

He frowned, as though confused by my response, and I suddenly realised that I was meant to have already got this.

'I just wanted to tell you that you've got your wish – I'm going to release you from our deal.'

I blinked, momentarily stunned by his words. 'Oh, right.' My eyes narrowed suspiciously, certain there must be a catch. 'So what does that mean? That you're going to tell my parents about the hospital?'

He sighed. 'No, I'm not going to do that. I would never worry them like that.'

'You wouldn't? So – what? This whole thing was just a massive joke to you? Your way of wasting my time?'

'No, Charlotte. Of course not. I wanted you to work here because I hoped . . .' He stopped.

'What?' I prompted.

He studied me for a long moment, and then shook his head. 'It doesn't matter. You've made it clear that you don't want to be here, and it's obviously not working out. We're going to arrange for a temp to cover your role, but we can't get anyone until the start of next week, so if you could hang on until Friday, I'd be grateful.'

I waited, somehow expecting there to be more. And then I realised – this was it. There was nothing else to say. I was being dismissed. I got up to leave then, and Richard didn't stop me.

On the way back down to my desk, the significance of what had just happened finally sank in. I'd got my way. Richard was releasing me from our deal. So why didn't I feel happier about it?

I spent the rest of the day trying to be as inconspicuous as possible. I sat quietly at my desk, going through the routine tasks. The door to Helena and Rex's office remained firmly closed, and they were clearly locked in deep discussion – no doubt trying to find a way to come up with a campaign before they were due to present to the client on Friday. Helena didn't come anywhere near me, and I studiously avoided her.

Guilt was gnawing at me, and I didn't want to feel this way. After all, it wasn't my fault – the screw-up with the meeting hadn't been intentional. And even if I hadn't been the most dedicated employee, that was hardly a surprise, either, was it? After all, I'd never asked for this job. It was Richard who'd forced me to work here, despite my protests. That's who was to blame; not me.

'It's all Richard's fault,' I railed at Lindsay three hours later. I was sitting up at the bar in The Nick, having gone straight there from work. It was early and still quiet, so Lindsay – who was meant to be working – was able to sit and listen to me rant between serving the half dozen other customers. I knew we hadn't been close recently, and that she'd been spending more time with Adrian while I was out a lot with Gavin and anyone else who wanted to party with me. But still, she'd been my best friend for a long time, and I was sure she'd understand. Plus, I didn't exactly have anyone else to confide in.

I took a sip of my beer, and continued my rant against Richard. 'None of this would have happened if he hadn't forced me to work for him in the first place. I don't know why he had to stick his nose into my business.'

Lindsay didn't respond. In fact, I suddenly realised that she wasn't looking at me – instead she was busy ripping up a cardboard beer mat. My eyes narrowed as I watched her. 'You haven't said much.'

'Haven't I?' She continued tearing.

'Look, I know we had that argument a few weeks ago, but don't you think it's about time you got over it by now? I told you, I didn't mean to mess this meeting up at work. I don't understand why you aren't on my side over this—'

'You really want to know why?' she said suddenly. 'Because I'm sick of hearing you bitch about this!' I stared at her, too shocked to respond – which was just as well, because she didn't seem to have any intention of letting me get a word in edgeways. 'Even though I've been trying to stay out of your way, I've still had the misfortune of overhearing you drone on about how hard done by you are. It's driving me crazy! All the times you've moaned about Richard – has it never occurred to you that he's actually trying to do you a favour? He saw you were going off the rails, and he cared enough to try to intervene. God!' She shook her head in exasperation, her pink spikes moving with the force. 'Do you know how fortunate you are to have someone looking out for you the way he is? You're one lucky girl, yet all you can do is complain.'

'Yeah?' I said, once I'd finally recovered enough to respond. 'Well, I didn't ask for his help, and I don't remember asking for your opinion, either. I've had a shit day, and I came here for some sympathy tonight from the person who I thought was my best friend. But all you can do is attack me.'

I looked round the bar. My eyes settled on Gavin, who was there with a group of guys I vaguely knew. Without another word to Lindsay, I slid from the stool.

Lindsay had obviously guessed what I was planning. 'Charlie, don't do this—' she said as I walked over to where they were sitting, but I ignored her.

I dropped into a seat next to the guys. They turned to look at me, and I flashed a broad smile, ever the party girl. 'So what are we drinking, boys?'

'Drink! Drink! Drink!'

It was an hour later, and the group was chanting at a skinny guy, Joe, who had just lost out on the drinking game again. I joined in, but my heart wasn't in it. Even though I wanted to forget what Lindsay had said earlier, her words kept going through my mind. Was she right? All this time, I'd been obsessed with the idea that Richard was interfering in my life. I'd never really considered that he'd been trying to help me, at great expense to himself. The realisation left me feeling confused and disturbed.

Everyone drained their pints. 'Hey.' Gavin nudged me, and nodded down at my untouched drink. 'What's up with you?'

'I'm not feeling great.'

'Yeah?' He didn't look like he was about to ask more details. This wasn't the kind of relationship where you shared intimate details of your life. 'We're off to Inhibition. You coming?'

Inhibition was a nightclub I'd been meaning to get to. Usually, I'd have agreed without a second thought. But for the first time in a long while, I hesitated. I was always the party girl, the one who wanted to stay out longer, drink more. It had never occurred to me to feel guilty about it.

'Not this time. I've got an early morning.'

He just shrugged. 'Suit yourself.'

He rose with the others, and the guys headed off. I looked down at my half-finished beer. I really wasn't interested in drinking it. The mix-up today hadn't been deliberate, but I still felt guilty. Not just about that, but about the way I'd behaved since Richard had given me the job. Maybe his methods had been a bit barbaric, but now I could see that his heart had been in the right place.

Lindsay was still working at the bar, so I headed home on my own. I'd planned to go straight to bed, but the events of the day were still swirling around my head. So I made myself some tea, and brought it into my room, intending to read. But instead, as I sat up in bed, I took out a notepad and began to jot down everything I remembered about the

PURE client brief. I then thought back to the discussions I'd overheard between Helena and Rex, about the feel that they wanted for the campaign.

Half an hour of brainstorming later, I dug out an old sketchpad and began to draw.

Chapter 12

I worked through most of the night, sketching ideas for a print ad for the PURE campaign. By three in the morning, I had something that I was happy with, so I decided to get some sleep.

I set my alarm for six thirty, and was up, showered and dressed in twenty minutes. I didn't have time to think much about what I was wearing, so I grabbed a pair of fitted black trousers and a black t-shirt. I also didn't have time for make-up or to style my hair, so I went bare-faced for a change, and pulled my platinum frizz back into a ponytail. It was a much more conservative look than normal. I needed something to carry the storyboard in, so I rummaged in the back of my wardrobe and took out my black portfolio case – the one I'd used for my art lessons at school and when I went to college. I hadn't taken it out for nearly six years, since I'd dropped out of art school.

I got to my desk just before eight, the earliest I'd ever been in. Helena and Rex were already there. Even though the door to their office was firmly closed, I could hear them brainstorming inside. I dumped my bag on the floor, and slipped my coat off, playing for time.

I looked down at my black portfolio case. I'd been excited about showing them my work, but now I was here I suddenly felt nervous. Just because I thought I'd done a good job, it didn't mean they would. And Helena had been so furious with me last night – it suddenly occurred to me she might not even agree to look at my drawings. In some ways it would be easier just to stay quiet, and keep my head down, rather than putting myself out there and trying to make amends.

But that would be the coward's way out. I'd gone to the trouble of putting this together, I might as well show it to them.

I picked up my portfolio case, and walked over with a determination I didn't feel and knocked once on the door. Through the glass I saw both Helena and Rex look up. Neither of them seemed especially happy to see me. Helena said something I couldn't hear, but I presumed it was something derogatory about me. Rex allowed himself a smirk, and then he straightened his face, and called for me to come in.

'Whatever it is, can it wait?' Rex said brusquely as I

opened the door. They'd obviously decided it was best if he did the talking. 'We're in the middle of something.'

'Yes.' Helena's voice was like ice. 'We're trying to work out what the hell we're going to pitch to the client on Friday so we don't look like a couple of idiots. Because right now, we've got nothing.'

I flinched at that. I caught Rex shooting her a look, frowning at her and shaking his head a little. Obviously he'd suggested it was best not to engage with me. Helena just shrugged back – as if to say, I'm not pussy-footing around to make this idiot feel better. I can't say I blamed her.

I looked between them, shrinking a little under Helena's expression of contempt. Even the usually playful Rex seemed cool towards me. It would be easier just to turn and walk out of here, and keep a low profile until I finished up at the end of the week. And perhaps I would have done just that if all I wanted was their forgiveness, because I knew I didn't really deserve that. But I realised now, standing here, that forgiveness had never been the point. I had no chance of winning their respect, but I did feel what I had put together could help them with their campaign. Maybe it wasn't perfect, but I could always amend it for their suggestions. Perhaps they'd even reject my idea outright – but if I didn't show them now, then I'd never know. It would be better to risk the rejection. After all, at this stage, what did I have to lose?

So I took a deep breath, and started to speak. 'Look, I appreciate you're busy. But this won't take long, I promise—'

Rex flashed a worried look at Helena. 'Charlotte, this really isn't a good time—'

'I know that. But I just had something I wanted to show you.' I lifted up my portfolio. 'It honestly won't take a moment.'

'Maybe later—' Rex began, but Helena cut him off.

'Actually, why don't you show us what you've got there?' She leant back in her chair and folded her arms. 'I, for one, wouldn't mind seeing what you think is so important that you need to disturb us.'

I could tell she wasn't expecting much, and that she was primed to rubbish whatever I showed them. But I tried to block that out. I looked around the room. I needed some- where to rest my portfolio, so I could unzip it and take the storyboard out. One of their desks would have been an obvious place, but I didn't think either of them would take kindly to that. The couch caught my eye. So I rested the portfolio on the spare chair, and started to unzip. As I did so, I talked.

'Look, I know you guys think I haven't been paying attention.' Helena snorted at this. I ignored her, and ploughed on. 'But I did hear you brainstorming over this anti-drugs advert.'

'Charlotte, please—' Rex said warningly. But I ignored him, and carried on.

'So I went home last night, and jotted down everything I remembered you saying.' I took out the storyboard, and straightened up. I was standing in the centre of the room, with them both facing me – Helena staring at me with a bored, contemptuous look, while Rex was shooting her worried glances, as if he expected her to explode at any minute. 'And I wondered – what about something like this?'

I turned the storyboard around, so that they could both see it.

I'd spent the night focusing on the print ad. The picture showed a family huddled together by a graveside, sobbing softly. To the side, stood the ghostly figure of a teenage girl. On the headstone, I'd written the words: 'It's Your Funeral', and then at the bottom ran the line: 'Think Before You Take Drugs'. I'd kept the colour scheme simple – black, white and grey – to suit the sombre tone of the message.

My eyes were focused on Helena, wanting to gauge her reaction. At first, she sat with her arms folded, looking bored. But as she took in what I'd drawn, I saw interest flicker across her face, and then she leaned forward, wanting to get a better look. Her forehead creased a little. She didn't say anything, but she held out her hands for the picture.

I guessed there was a chance that she might just want to rip it up, as a way to get me back for yesterday. But somehow I sensed that wasn't the case. I walked over, and gave her the drawing.

She shook a little as she took it. Her eyes roamed the scene, taking every detail in. I watched her mouth soften and her eyes begin to water.

Without warning, she let the drawing slip from her hands onto her desk.

'I'm sorry,' she murmured.

Before I could say anything, she got up and hurried from the room. I stared after her, completely stunned. Of all the reactions I'd anticipated, I certainly hadn't expected that one – particularly not from her. I knew people who cried at the drop of a hat, to the point where it became meaningless – but with someone like Helena, you had to take a breakdown like this seriously, because she was one of those people who no doubt only cried once every few years, if something really deserved it. What had I done now?

I turned to Rex. 'What the hell was that all about?'

He hesitated for a second; I could tell he was debating whether to tell me or not. But then he obviously decided that Helena's behaviour needed some kind of explanation. 'It's to do with her older sister. She died fifteen years ago, after taking ecstasy at a rave.'

Suddenly I understood why Helena had had such an extreme reaction yesterday. Even though I'd appreciated that I'd messed up, I'd also felt she'd overreacted a little. Now I knew why. This was a campaign close to her heart. She hadn't been upset for professional reasons – it had been more personal than that.

'The loss devastated Helena's family,' Rex went on. 'Her mum fell into a depression, and her father couldn't cope and eventually left. I think that's why Helena's so straight-laced. She ended up becoming this perfect person, because she didn't want to cause her family any more distress.'

I suddenly understood why she'd been so unimpressed with my slacker ways when I'd first started working with her and Rex. I'd felt irritated with her for giving me a hard time, without considering the reason she'd reacted that way – that there was something so awful in her past that she was just trying to compensate for it through her behaviour.

I swore under my breath. 'I shouldn't have done this.' I picked up my storyboard and walked back to where my portfolio lay open on the couch. 'I was trying to put things right, and instead I've just made them worse—'

Suddenly Rex was by my side, his hand on my shoulder, stopping me from putting my picture away.

'It was a good thing that you did. And your picture was great – making someone cry . . . that's the ultimate. It's exactly what we're aiming for in advertising – to create a strong reaction through our storytelling.'

'Yeah, well, I'm not sure Helena will see it that way.'

'Actually,' Helena said, 'that's exactly how I see it.'

We whirled round to see Helena standing in the doorway. She was back to her usual composed self – and there was no evidence of her breakdown a few minutes earlier.

She walked over and took the drawing from me, studying it again, more clinically this time.

'As Rex said, this really evokes a reaction. You've managed to capture everything that we talked about. It's not perfect, by any means – but it's the kind of quality that we could easily present to the client to get our ideas across.'

Relief coursed through me. But I didn't feel I was out of the woods yet. 'Look, I really am sorry about yesterday. I know you thought I did it on purpose, but I didn't. It was an honest mistake.'

Helena stared at me for a long moment, clearly weighing up whether to trust me or not. 'Tell you what,' she said finally. 'If you manage to put together more storyboards like this for the TV advert, then I'll forgive you.'

I smiled. 'I think that sounds like a fair deal.'

'Good. Well, you better get on with it then, because the one thing we don't have is a lot of time to waste.'

I spent the next few days putting together the storyboards for the TV advert. It was an extension of the print ad I'd come up with – the teenage girl getting ready for her night out; saying goodbye to her parents; and then hitting the club and enjoying her evening, before accepting drugs. Then there were scenes of her collapsing, and paramedics working to revive her. This was all in colour, and intercut with scenes of the family getting ready for the funeral, all sketched – and to be filmed – in black and white. The final shot, by the grave, was the same scene as the print ad – the family all huddled together, while the ghostly figure looked on.

It was a lot of work, but I enjoyed it. The sketches were easy enough for me. I worked late each night, and came in early every morning to get it finished. While I was doing that, Helena and Rex worked on their presentation.

By Friday, everything was ready. The pitch had been moved at the request of the client, from midday to three in the afternoon, which meant more waiting around.

At two, I stood to say goodbye to Helena and Rex. 'Thanks for everything you did for us this week,' Helena said.

'We would invite you along, sweetie, but there's already going to be a lot of people there,' Rex added.

'Of course. I understand.'

It was only once they'd gone that I realised how exhausted I was. I'd been working flat out for the past three days, and I'd been running on adrenaline. Now that my purpose for working had been taken away, I just wanted to sleep. That wasn't an option though, so I busied myself for the rest of the afternoon, catching up on the mundane tasks that I'd put to one side over the past few days.

I tried to keep myself distracted, but my mind kept wandering to the pitch. I was surprised at just how desperate I was to find out how it had gone. I wasn't sure how long it would take, but by five I was certain that it should be over. I doubted that Helena and Rex would come back to the office – they'd both worked their butts off as well, and no doubt wanted to head home and relax – but I thought they'd probably call to let me know how it went. After all, whatever had happened earlier this week, we'd worked as a team on this.

But over the next hour, I still didn't hear anything. Whenever my phone went, I'd snatch it up, hoping it was going to be one of them, but it never was. Gradually I began to feel deflated. Either the pitch hadn't gone well, or they hadn't ever seen me as part of the project. Either way, I couldn't help feeling disappointed. I'd put myself out there, but clearly it still hadn't been enough.

By half six, I decided to leave. I was just sending off a last email when I heard a man clearing his throat above me. I looked up to see Richard, looking impressive as usual in a well-cut suit. I felt my heartbeat speed up a little at the sight of him. It was strange, the effect he'd had on me ever since I'd started working here. I put it down to the fact that he obviously commanded so much respect around the office – I suppose anyone would feel a bit intimidated by him.

He was smiling down at me, and looked a lot more relaxed than he had the last time I'd seen him.

'Charlotte, I'm glad I caught you. I wanted to let you know – we heard back from the client, and they loved the concept. It looks like we're going to get the whole account.'

'Really?' I couldn't keep the delight out of my voice. 'That's amazing! Helena and Rex are going to be so pleased.' I started to reach for the phone. 'I should let them know—'

'There's no need for that.' Richard's voice stopped me. 'I've already called Helena and Rex to tell them the good news. In fact, it was them who asked me to stop by to let you know the outcome – which I have to admit was something of a surprise. But then Helena explained you'd actually ended up putting the visuals for the campaign together for them. They said you saved the day.'

There was a question in his voice that couldn't be ignored. 'I just took their ideas and brought them to life.' I wasn't sure it was fair to take the credit, when it was my mistake that had caused all the problems in the first place. 'It wasn't a big deal.'

'Still, you could have walked away and not bothered. Instead you pulled through for them. That's all I wanted from you, Charlotte – for you to do your best.'

'Yeah?' I grinned. 'And I thought you just enjoyed being a controlling asshole.'

He laughed. 'Trust me – I have far better things to do with my time than interfere with your life. I wouldn't have bothered if I didn't think you were worth it.' He grew serious. 'You're extremely talented, Charlotte. I hate seeing you throw your life away.'

His dark eyes held mine for a moment. Feeling flustered by the intensity of his gaze, I glanced away, picking up some papers on my desk, and straightening them, to give me something to do.

'Yeah, well. It was pretty simple stuff. I'm just glad it all worked out.'

I snuck a glance up at him. Whatever had been there before – that soul-searching stare of his – had disappeared. I didn't know whether to feel relieved or sad.

'Anyway,' he said briskly, as though he wanted to put our relationship back on a more familiar footing. 'I just wanted to pop by and let you know that everything worked out. And that you did a good job.'

I smiled up at him, unexpectedly warmed by his praise. 'Thanks,' I said softly.

'And I also hope that you'll consider staying on now. At least until the three months are up.' He held up his hands. 'But it's entirely up to you. I'm not making any threats or bargains. This time I want it to be your decision.'

It hadn't even occurred to me that this offer might be forthcoming. Earlier in the week, I would have expected to run in the opposite direction, but now I wondered what would be the point of that. So I could go back to pulling pints in The Nick? This week had been the first time in ages that I'd felt good about myself. Maybe Richard knew me better than I realised. 'If it's all right with Helena and Rex, I'd like to stay on.'

Richard looked like he was about to say something else, but instead he gave a brief, satisfied nod. 'I'm glad to hear that.'

There was a silence then. We both stared at each other, as though waiting for something to happen, though I had a feeling neither of us were entirely sure what. I felt a little awkward, like an actor who'd forgotten their words in the middle of a play.

It was Richard who recovered first. 'Now, get out of here,' he said, backing away. 'And enjoy your weekend. You deserve it.'

He turned away without another word.

By then it was coming up for seven, and I felt keyed up. I had a message on my phone. It was from Gavin, asking me if I was coming out that night. I sent him a quick text saying I couldn't make it, and headed home instead.

Lindsay was working, so I had the flat to myself. I made a quick dinner of pasta and pesto, and then collapsed on the sofa in our sitting room, wondering what to do with the rest of my night. My eyes went to the mezzanine, built into the eaves, where I'd stored the half-finished paintings from my college course. I hadn't been up there since we'd moved in, but tonight I wanted to.

I walked up the metal spiral staircase. At the top, I saw my canvases were where I'd left them, piled up in a corner, with a big plastic sheet covering them. Before we'd moved in here, I'd thought about throwing them out, to save space, but Lindsay had convinced me to keep them. I hadn't looked at them for years, and frankly hadn't expected to again. But now something was drawing me to them.

I ducked my head under the low, slanted ceiling, and went over to where they lay propped against the brick wall. I removed the plastic sheet, and knelt down and started to flip through the canvases. Looking through them, remembering how long I'd spent on each one, unsettled me – it was hard to imagine that one time I'd loved painting so much. I hadn't done it for so long.

It took an hour for me to go through them. When I was finished with my trip down memory lane, I went back downstairs, and curled up on the couch. But instead of switching on the TV, I opened up my sketchpad and started to draw.

Chapter 13

'So tell me – when did you embark on your current lifestyle?'

I smiled at the psychologist's polite euphemism. 'You mean when did I start drinking and screwing around?' But my blunt words didn't even elicit so much as a smile. My attempts to provoke a reaction from Margaret Milton weren't working.

She gave a brief nod. 'Yes. When do you last remember trying to get your parents' approval?'

I sat back and thought about it.

I hadn't been back here since my first session a few weeks earlier. Once Dr Milton had said that there was no point in me seeing her if it wasn't voluntary, I'd taken the easy route and not bothered coming back. But now that I was staying on at Davenport's, it seemed only fair to give it a go like Richard had wanted. After all, he'd been right about working with Helena and Rex, so maybe he was on to something with seeing Dr Milton. And at least if it didn't work out, I'd know that I hadn't missed out on any opportunity.

So far my second session seemed much the same as the first. We were in Dr Milton's office, sitting across from each other in the huge leather armchairs, like last time. Dr Milton – or Margaret, as she'd invited me to call her – looked as neat and professional as before, her legs demurely crossed, a notepad resting on her knee, and an expensive-looking fountain pen in her right hand. Every now and then she'd jot down a couple of details in her elegant handwriting. I presumed that she then typed the notes up on her computer once I'd gone – filling up the last ten minutes of our fifty-minute hour.

I'd come straight from work, and I could sense her assessing me as soon as I walked in. I knew I looked more conventional than last time we'd met. I had on my now standard uniform of black skinny trousers and a round-neck black t-shirt, which I'd teamed with black pumps. My white-blonde hair was tied back from my face. I'd been opting for the more conventional items in my wardrobe lately. It was a clean-cut yet artistic look – more toned-down than my usual Gothic Barbie style, but still true enough to me not to feel completely out of character. I glanced down at myself self-consciously. God, now I remembered why I was so reluctant to come here – I didn't want to feel like every little thing I did was being analysed.

'So you want to know when I stopped being a good little girl,' I said, drawing myself back to the present. It wasn't something I gave much thought to these days. The way I behaved was so ingrained that it felt like I'd been this way forever. 'I suppose it was the summer I turned eighteen.'

I saw the barest hint of a frown between her eyes. It was the first reaction I'd got from her, and the only sign that the answer had taken her by surprise. 'So, not the year of your brother's death?'

That was the assumption everyone always made – that I'd gone off the rails because of what happened to Kit. 'Actually, it was the year after he died.'

She nodded a little, and scratched a brief note on her pad, before looking back up at me. 'Why don't you tell me about it? That summer, the last time you remember being your old self.'

'What about it?'

'Whatever you think seems important.'

She settled back into her armchair, a sure sign she wasn't going to give me any help or point me in the right direction for what she wanted. I scrunched up my forehead. God, this was irritating. I had a feeling she wanted something specific from me but I had no idea what.

'Don't think about it too much,' she said, obviously aware of my irritation. 'Just say whatever comes into your head first.'

Fair enough. If she really wanted to be bored out of her mind . . .

'Well, I came home from boarding school for the summer . . .'

Seven years ago

It was mid-afternoon by the time my father drove through the gates of Claylands. The familiar crunch of gravel under the tyres of the car signalled to me that I was home. It was one of those perfect, hazy summer days, when everyone seems to be out enjoying themselves. A few minutes earlier we'd passed the local cricket team on the nearby village green, and seen a newly married couple emerging from the local church to the sound of bells pealing, a shower of confetti falling over them as the photographer snapped away. I'd just finished my A-level exams and it felt good to be getting away from all that stress and embarking on a summer of total relaxation.

I'd called ahead to tell my mother that we were nearly there, and she'd clearly been listening out for us, because seconds after we parked, she appeared on the stone steps of the front entrance, looking her usual perfect, together self, in cream capri trousers and a light-blue linen shirt. While Dad unpacked the car, she came over to embrace me.

'Darling! Don't you look well!' She held me away from her, giving me a critical once-over. 'Your skin's a lot clearer, and I think you've lost some weight.'

I knew she meant well, but somehow when she said those things it just made me feel worse about myself – had my spots been that noticeable? My puppy fat that bad? If my own mother felt the need to point these things out, that couldn't be great.

But as usual, she seemed oblivious to my insecurities. She put an arm around my shoulder as we walked into the house. 'Now I'm sure you're exhausted after that long journey, so why don't you go up and rest, so you'll be ready for dinner? Your sister will be here later, and she's bringing her new boyfriend with her.'

'I didn't know she was seeing anyone.' Not that it was a surprise. My beautiful, charming older sister had always had a knack for attracting the opposite sex. 'Is it someone from King's?' My sister was studying medicine at King's College, in London.

'That's right. His name's Toby. He's a medic, too. The year above her, and top of his class, apparently. Wants to be a surgeon.'

Well, of course he did. It wasn't like Kate would ever date anyone other than the best. Unlike me, she'd had several boyfriends. I blamed it on the fact that my boarding school was single sex, although that wasn't the full story. Some of the girls would sneak out into town, and looked forward to the dances we had with the local boys' school. But I wasn't one of them. Perhaps if I'd looked like one of the beautiful girls in our year – with their long, silky hair, clear complexions and svelte bodies – then I'd have gone. But I knew instinctively there was no point for me – that boys wouldn't like my boring brown hair, spots and heavy physique. It seemed easiest to pretend I wasn't interested, either.

That's why I couldn't get excited about meeting another one of Kate's boyfriends. I knew the drill by now. The guys she brought home never showed any interest in her mousey little sister.

'I'm going to put him in the room next to Kit's.' My mother's voice maintained its normal tone as she said my dead brother's name. It was only the over-brightness of her eyes that let me know it was a strain for her to talk about him.

She'd given herself precisely two weeks to mourn my brother's death. Then, once the funeral was over, it was back to business as usual for her. She resumed her normal routine, and urged us all to do the same. Keeping busy was the best way to deal with things, she'd always said. Friends of the family would often talk about how well she'd dealt with Kit's death – although I sensed that secretly they thought she was a little cold and robotic.

To be honest, even I'd found her lack of outward mourning a hard thing to process. I knew how much she'd adored my brother, her eldest child and only son. I couldn't understand how she'd whipped herself back into shape so soon afterwards. I'd once asked her, a month or so after the funeral, why she didn't cry more. She'd frowned, as though she couldn't quite understand why I was asking such a question.

'What's crying going to accomplish?' she'd said, after a moment. 'If it would bring him back, I would cry and scream and rip my own hair out. But he's dead. He's gone. No amount of regret or mourning will ever change that.'

That logical approach was typical of my mother.

'Richard can't make it, unfortunately,' she said now, as we reached my room. 'He's working so hard. Every time I talk to him he's calling from work.' My mother said that last part with undisguised pride. She valued hard work more than anything. And now that Kit was gone, she channelled everything into Richard, her dead son's best friend. I couldn't help feeling a pang of resentment. My sister and Richard were the type of people who would always effortlessly achieve academically and professionally, which were areas that my mother valued. Unfortunately, I was not built that way.

I felt a little better as we went into my bedroom. It was just as I remembered it – the cream walls and carpet, with the pale pink curtains and linens. There was something so comforting about coming home – that feeling of familiarity and belonging.

I sat down on the edge of my bed, as my mother hovered in the doorway.

'So did you think any more about having someone to stay this summer?'

My shoulders sagged. It seemed all her pet jibes were coming out today. She hated the fact that I was a loner, and was always making me feel bad for not having a gang of friends to stay at the house – which is what Kate used to do when she was at school.

'I told you before, Mum. Northridge isn't that kind of place.'

My boarding school was very small and cosy, with only two hundred pupils. My parents had originally wanted to send me to the same school as my sister, but the year that I was meant to apply, my prep school head had told them that it was a bad idea – I wasn't academic enough to handle the competitive intellectual environment. She'd suggested Northridge would suit me better.

It was one of those Enid Blyton-style boarding schools, where everyone is *jolly* nice. It was all girls, and most of the other pupils had been sent from overseas. That meant it was hard to keep in touch during the holidays, and there was always a sense that they wouldn't be staying in England for good. The upshot was that while I got on with everyone at school, I didn't have any close friends. I kept telling my mother that, but somehow she still thought it was my fault.

She pursed her lips now. 'That's such a shame. I just hope you'll fit in a bit more at university.' She came over to smooth the hair from my face. 'After all, you have such a lovely little personality.'

And with that parting blow, she left.

Just before seven, I heard a car pulling along the gravel driveway. A moment later, my mother called out, 'Kate's here!'

I ran downstairs to greet my sister and her new boyfriend. I was just in time to see them pull up, in what I assumed was her boyfriend's car, a silver Audi TT – a nice ride for a student, and a sure sign that his family were pretty well-off. As usual, my sister looked clear-eyed and fresh-faced, her dark brown hair falling impeccably around her shoulders. Given that they'd driven with the top down, how hadn't her hair got blown around? My mousey brown curls would have been a ball of frizz by now.

She got out of the car and ran over to me, all coltish limbs and shiny, swishing hair, making me feel even more self-conscious of my thick, lumbering frame.

'Hello there, Mouse,' she said, using the nickname she and my brother had been calling me since we were children. 'You look well.'

My parents emerged then, and as she greeted them, I turned my attention to her boyfriend, Toby. He was gorgeous, of course. I wouldn't have expected anything less from my sister. He was blond, blue-eyed and tanned, another preppy golden boy, like Richard, wearing chinos and a light-blue polo shirt. But unlike Richard, who was dark and serious, Toby seemed more at ease as he took their bags from the boot and strolled over.

Kate quickly introduced him to our parents, and then he turned his attention to me. 'So, you must be Charlotte?' He grinned down at me, his cheeks dimpling as he flashed a set of perfectly straight, white teeth. I felt my stomach flutter a little. 'Lovely to meet you.'

Before I could say anything, he bent to kiss me on both cheeks, greeting me in what seemed at the time a very grown-up, sophisticated way. I felt my face heating up, and looked away before anyone noticed.

'Well.' My mother beamed at Kate and Toby. 'Let's get you two settled, and then we'll sit down for dinner.'

I followed everyone through, my eyes moving to Toby. I could still feel where his lips had brushed my skin. I sighed deeply, wistfully. Kate had all the luck.

Dinner was served on the patio. Because of my mother's love of her garden, she liked to eat outside whenever she could. My childhood memories often revolved around family meals, sitting and talking for hours as the sunlight faded, our laughter and chatter filling the warm night air.

The meal passed easily enough. My mother dominated the conversation as usual. She wanted to hear all about Kate's course, and Toby's plans to become a surgeon, and then spent a long time telling him about her job. My father interjected with his own comments now and again, but I said little, content to just listen to the conversation flowing around me.

It was only once the main course was finished, that Toby turned to me. 'So, which are you going to be, Charlotte? A doctor or a lawyer?'

I opened my mouth to answer, but my mother got there first. 'Neither. Charlotte's the artistic one in the family.' She flashed what I could only assume was her best impression of a proud smile at me. 'She's going to do a Fine Art degree at Central Saint Martins. It's apparently terribly competitive to get in. Charlotte was very lucky to be accepted.'

She beamed across at me, a big, forced smile, and I cringed. Somehow my mother's attempts to sound supportive were worse than if she'd said outright that she didn't approve of the choices I was making.

But Toby appeared not to have noticed my mother's fake enthusiasm. His eyes were on me as he said, 'A Fine Art degree, huh? But I thought you'd just finished school. I remember a friend of mine applying, but he had to do a foundation course first. How come you didn't have to?'

I didn't answer at first. I was too stunned that someone was showing interest in me.

'Charlotte?' my mother prompted, with a touch of exasperation. She always found my shyness slightly irritating. 'Toby asked you a question.'

I felt a blush stain my cheeks. Why did she have to embarrass me like that?

'Usually you have to complete a foundation course, but in some cases an exception can be made.' All eyes around the table were on me, but I addressed my answer to Toby. He seemed genuinely interested in what I had to say, which was a nice change for one of my sister's boyfriends. I could tell I hadn't quite answered his question, but I didn't want to sound like I was bragging. Luckily my father stepped in.

'If the candidate's portfolio is considered strong enough, then they can be admitted straight onto the course.' My father smiled at me. 'Charlotte's art teacher encouraged her to apply directly, and the staff were so impressed with her work, that they gave her a place.'

Toby's eyes widened in admiration. 'Wow! You must be really talented. I know how hard it is to get into St Martins.'

I opened my mouth to say something self-deprecating, but my mother beat me to it.

'Yes, it is wonderful,' she said. 'I just hope Charlotte isn't being too ambitious. But if it turns out to be too much, you can always rethink and go back to do a foundation course, can't you, darling?'

I dropped my eyes to the table. There it was. Maybe her assurances that it wouldn't matter whether or not I got in, were meant to be reassuring and supportive, but instead they felt like she was already assuming I was going to fail.

'Well, I think it sounds wonderful.' Hearing Toby's voice, I looked up. He was smiling kindly at me. 'Fine Art is bound to be a lot more interesting than law or medicine. You'll have to invite me to one of your shows when you're a famous artist. Add a little excitement into my conventional life.' He gave me a wink then, and I felt an unexpected fluttering in my stomach.

My mother took charge of the conversation then, changing the subject to current affairs. I picked at my food, pushing it around my plate. For some reason, my appetite had deserted me. Every now and then, I would catch myself sneaking a look at Toby. I couldn't help hoping that he'd be coming to visit a lot this summer.

Back in the psychologist's office, I finished speaking, and looked over at Dr Milton. 'So what else do you want to know?'

She glanced down at her wristwatch. 'Actually, that brings us nicely up to time for today.'

I checked the clock across the room, and was surprised to find that she was right – fifty minutes had passed. I couldn't believe I'd been talking for that long. 'Is that it?'

'For today, yes.'

'And what's your big conclusion?'

'What do you mean?'

'Well, aren't you going to tell me what's wrong with me?'

She closed her notebook. 'It doesn't work like that, Charlie. I'm not going to be able to help you after just one session. And I'm certainly never going to tell you that anything's "wrong" with you. That's not my job.'

'So what is it then? Your job?' I didn't mean to sound combative, but something about these past fifty minutes had made me feel uncomfortable. I didn't want to remember that summer – when I'd been so preoccupied with feeling inadequate. 'Because I really don't understand what we're doing here.'

'My purpose in these meetings is to guide you to important events in your past, and help you understand how they influence you today. You've come to me because you – or people in your life – are concerned about your behaviour. At the moment, I want to understand – and help you understand – why you behave the way you do. After that, if you want, we can look at ways to modify your ingrained behaviour patterns.'

'Well, as long as there's a plan,' I said, sarcasm dripping from my voice.

Dr Milton smiled sympathetically at me. 'I know you're a sceptic, but just try to give the process a chance. I think in the long run you'll be pleased with the results.'

'Whatever you say, Doctor.'

Chapter 14

I stood outside of the door to my flat, holding my keys. I'd been there for at least five minutes, trying to work up the courage to go in. I'd come straight home after my appointment with Dr Milton, and the events of our session were still on my mind. I didn't like thinking back to that summer, and what had happened with Toby. It felt like a lifetime ago now, when I'd been another person, and there seemed no point in dredging it all up. Plus, I had a more immediate problem right now – and that was going into my flat and apologising to Lindsay.

I hadn't seen her properly since she'd given me a piece of her mind that night in The Nick. I'd been working long days at Davenport's, and her nights were either spent at the bar or staying at Adrian's, I presumed. But I'd texted her earlier to check that she'd be home tonight, and she'd confirmed – very briefly – that she would be.

Inhaling deeply, I finally opened the door.

I heard the sound of the television as soon as I stepped inside. I slowly removed my jacket and shoes, and headed towards the sitting room. Sure enough, Lindsay was lying on the sofa, watching some animal rescue programme. She looked up as I walked in, her expression guarded. I had a feeling this wasn't going to be easy.

She sat up, and switched off the TV. 'So you said you wanted to talk?'

'I did.' I moved into the centre of the room, feeling suddenly nervous. I perched on one of the chairs opposite her, my eyes fixed on the ground, unable to meet her gaze. 'Look, I wanted to say I was sorry.'

'Oh?' Her voice gave nothing away.

I folded my arms across my stomach. 'Yeah. I mean, I think maybe I overreacted to some of the stuff you were saying.' I paused, and again she said nothing. Why was she making this so hard for me? 'I guess I can see now that you were trying to look out for me.'

I fell into silence. Maybe it wasn't the best speech, but it was hard to admit that I'd been wrong. When Lindsay still hadn't said anything, I raised my eyes to look at her. To my surprise, she was trying hard not to laugh.

'Well, that has to be pretty much the lamest apology I've ever heard.'

I pulled a face. 'I know. But it's about the best I can do.'

'Fair enough. I suppose I've got no choice but to forgive you, then.'

I sat back in the chair, and pretended to wipe sweat from my brow. 'Phew. You really made me work for it, you know?'

We grinned at each other. Other female friends in this position would probably embrace, but as Lindsay knew, I wasn't a hugger. She often joked that I was more comfortable getting naked with a stranger than putting my arms around my own family.

'So what do you fancy doing tonight?' she asked, letting me know everything was back to normal.

'I thought maybe we could grab some dinner. My treat.'

'That sounds good. Just let me get my jacket.'

She got to her feet, and was halfway to her room when I said, 'Oh, Lindsay?' She stopped, and turned back. There was one last thing I needed to do to resolve all of this – I just hoped it wasn't too late. I tried to look nonchalant. 'And I wondered if Adrian might like to come out with us, too.'

A slow smile spread across her face. 'I reckon he'd love that.'

Lindsay called Adrian, and we arranged to meet him at a Thai restaurant near us. We called it a restaurant, but it was more like a small, dingy canteen. Fortunately the food was excellent and also cheap, so we were able to ignore the surroundings.

I'd planned to apologise to Adrian, too – I hadn't exactly been particularly friendly towards him since he'd started seeing my friend. But as soon as he arrived, he greeted me with a big hug, as if to let me know that everything was all right between us. Even though I wasn't usually the hugging kind, I fought my instinct to push him away – after all, I felt it was the least I could do.

'I'm glad you two made up,' he whispered in my ear as his meaty arms squeezed my middle. 'Lindsay was miserable without you.'

For the first time I could appreciate how lucky my friend was to have such a nice boyfriend. I'd heard so many tales of girls seeing possessive guys, who hated them going out with their friends. I was glad Lindsay had found one of the good ones.

We took our place at a round plastic table, and ordered off the scruffy menus. Then we sipped at bottles of beer as we caught up. Lindsay was still trying to get a job, but she was going for a second interview at a talent agency, which represented actors, directors and writers, and she was hopeful that she'd get it.

'And what have you been up to?' Lindsay asked, as our food finally arrived. 'Did you manage to sort out your crisis the other week?'

As we ate, I told her what had happened with the PURE campaign. I was surprised at how enthusiastic I sounded as I spoke.

'Richard seemed really pleased with the sketches, and that we won the client,' I concluded twenty minutes later. 'It's really weird seeing him at the office, to be honest. Everyone looks up to him, and he's totally in charge—'

I suddenly stopped, noticing that Lindsay and Adrian were exchanging amused glances. 'What's up with you two?'

Lindsay held up her hands. 'Nothing. Just surprised to hear you saying anything nice about Richard, that's all.'

'Yeah, well . . .' I felt suddenly embarrassed. I must sound like a total hypocrite, talking about how great Richard was, after I'd bad-mouthed him so much. 'I guess maybe I was being a bit hard on him.'

I changed the subject then, wanting to move the spotlight off me, and asked Adrian about his work instead. The rest of the evening flew by, and I couldn't believe it when I looked at my watch and saw that it was after eleven.

'We should get the bill.' I looked round for a waitress. 'I've got a meeting at eight tomorrow morning, and I need to get a decent night's sleep.'

Lindsay happened to be drinking her beer as I spoke. She snorted a laugh, sending liquid flying all over the table as she started to cough. Once she'd finally recovered, she shook her head.

'It's going to take me a long time to get used to hearing you say stuff like that.'

*   *   *

Over the next couple of weeks, my life settled into a routine. Since the PURE campaign, I'd started to spend more time at the office. And as I began to take more interest in my work, the work itself became more interesting.

While I still had to do mundane tasks – typing letters, making coffee, photocopying, filing and scheduling meetings – none of it seemed so tedious now that I could see how it contributed to the larger picture. I also began to get assigned more interesting tasks. When it came down to it, Helena and Rex's job was about storytelling, which was why I'd always loved art. Now I started sitting in on Rex and Helena's meetings, listening to their ideas, and then translating them onto paper. This saved Helena time, and I was often able to bring to life concepts in a more polished way than she could. I'd also liaise directly with the art department, to make sure they knew exactly how to execute the concepts. To my surprise, I enjoyed having more responsibility. It was rewarding to see something I'd overseen being brought to life.

I also had a couple of more sessions with Dr Milton. It was much like the last time I'd been there. She seemed fixated on that summer I'd turned eighteen, just before I went off the rails and became 'Charlie' instead of 'Charlotte', so I continued to reminisce for her. I had a feeling she felt this period in my life was important, but I had no idea why. Our meetings weren't unpleasant, but I wasn't sure I was getting much out of them. I also wasn't sure why she seemed to think there'd be some big revelation about why I acted the way I did – surely a lot of youngsters turned eighteen and drew away from their families and changed significantly, started drinking and having sex. I thought that was called growing up.

Between work and seeing Dr Milton, my social life wasn't as big as it used to be. I still went out, but I kept it to the weekends. I was at work from half eight in the morning to seven at night most days, and by the time I finished, I was too tired to go out, and I didn't like the fuzzy way my head felt after an evening of drinking. For the first time in a while, I hadn't brought any guys home – a fact that didn't go unnoticed by Lindsay.

It was good to have my friend back again. Of course we weren't going out as much as before, because of my job and her hanging out with Adrian. But it suited us both, and I was pleased the tension between us had gone.

A fortnight after we'd secured the commission for the anti-drugs advert, we received a brief to pitch on a new tooth-paste, called Brite, that had been designed by a mid-range cosmetics company. It was unusual, because typically it was consumer goods companies like Unilever that produced toothpaste. But this felt more like a gimmicky product – one that was a mix of a teeth-whitening product and a toothpaste.

That was the USP that the client wanted to get across in the advert – the idea that this was the strongest whitening toothpaste on the market, and that it would lighten teeth fifteen shades whiter than any other brand. They liked the idea of going with a glamorous campaign, rather than the functionality usually associated with toothpaste adverts.

After the meeting with the account manager, Helena, Rex and I went back to their office to brainstorm.

'Ugh.' Rex pulled a face, as he dropped into his chair. 'How the hell are we meant to make this glamorous? Toothpaste isn't exactly the sexiest of items, is it?'

Helena pulled out a new pad, and drummed her pen against the paper. She always thought best when she was jotting down words or images. 'Let's think – what are we trying to say here?' This was typical of her thought process – other than my mother, she had one of the most logical brains I'd ever encountered, and always boiled projects down to their simplest concept and then built up from there. 'We basically want something that says it's going to whiten your teeth, but also keep them strong. Now what has strong teeth? Maybe an animal of some kind . . .'

Her pen was moving across the page already, as she started running through ideas. Then something popped into my head.

'What about a vampire?' I said it without thinking whether they wanted to hear from me. Up until now, I hadn't put any suggestions of my own forward, but instead had just carried out the ideas that Helena and Rex gave me. They both turned to stare at me, surprise written across their faces. Maybe it wasn't appropriate, but I ploughed on regardless. 'Vampires use their teeth all the time, to bite their victims, which means they have to be strong. And they're alive for ages, so that gives the suggestion that the toothpaste helps your teeth last. And vampires – well, everyone thinks of them as sexy and glamorous, don't they?'

Neither of them spoke for a moment. I wondered if they were going to tell me what a ridiculous idea it was, but then Rex broke into a smile.

'I like the way you think, girl.'

'Not bad.' Helena was nodding thoughtfully. 'That's not bad at all.'

Rex began jotting some words onto a page. 'And how does this grab you for a caption: "For strong, white teeth, that will last several lifetimes."'

Helena held up the package of Brite toothpaste. 'And instead of "Bite Me", we could say "Brite Me".'

Rex chuckled. 'That's just cheesy enough to work.' He looked over at me. 'Congratulations, darling. It looks like you've just come up with your first creative concept.'

The rest of the day was spent refining and honing the idea, and then it was left to me to put together the storyboards. It was a Friday, and Rex and Helena were both leaving early – he was going home to see his family in Cornwall, and she was heading to Paris for a friend's hen do. Before they went, they both looked over my work, and gave me a couple of small changes to put through.

'There's no rush on it, though,' Rex said as he was leaving. 'You can make the changes on Monday, if you want.'

'I might stay and get it out of the way, rather than have it hanging over the weekend.'

'Whatever works for you.'

It took longer than I'd imagined to make all the amendments. When I was finally happy with what I'd done, I straightened up, stretching my back, suddenly aware of just how stiff I was from hunching over my sketchpad. I looked up at the clock, and saw that it was just after eight. The night cleaners had arrived, and I could hear the distant hum of a vacuum cleaner down the hallway.

Helena had asked me to put the sketches on Richard's desk when I'd finished them. He liked to cast his eye over all the campaigns before they went out. So I put on my coat, and got my bag together, planning to drop them off on my way out. He wouldn't be around at this time, but at least the sketches would be there for when he came in on Monday morning. Although knowing Richard, he'd be in at some point over the weekend anyway.

The offices were pretty much deserted at this time on a Friday night. There was only a handful of people still around, and they were on deadline, so no one stopped me to talk. They didn't have time for idle chitchat.

The executive offices were all shut up, and the secretaries' desks empty, their computers powered down. The door to Richard's office was closed, but I didn't even think about knocking. I just turned the handle and walked straight in – which was unfortunate, because at that exact moment, he strolled out of the ensuite bathroom, wearing nothing but a pair of jeans.

I could feel my mouth forming a cartoon-like 'o', as my eyes ran over his bare chest. He had a towel thrown round his shoulders, but it did little to cover him. He was seriously ripped, with an actual six-pack, every muscle perfectly defined, like an underwear model.

I wasn't sure why his perfectly sculpted physique surprised me so much. I knew he worked out a lot and did a lot of sport. But somehow seeing him semi-naked like that had shaken me. I was so used to seeing him in suits, looking smart and commanding, I'd forgotten what existed beneath. I also had to admit that for all the naked male bodies I'd seen in the last few years, I'd never come across such a perfect male specimen in the flesh before. I was used to guys who drank and smoked too much, and would have to sit down after running twenty metres.

'Can I help you with something?' Richard's amused voice jolted me out of my daydream.

'S—sorry.' I stuttered a little, feeling flustered that he'd caught me staring at him with such blatant approval. It was so unlike me – where were the smart remarks and general air of nonchalance that usually came so easily? 'I wasn't expecting to see you here – and not like, well . . .'

I didn't want to look, but my eyes seemed to have a life of their own, and I found my gaze running over his naked torso again.

'I've just been to the gym,' he said to my unvoiced question of what the hell he was doing strolling round like this. 'And I prefer to shower up here.'

'Oh, right. Of course.'

A fresh shirt hung on the handle of one of the filing cabinets. It looked like it had just been picked up from the dry-cleaners given the plastic cover on it. Richard walked over and, turning his back to me, slipped the towel from his shoulders, and shrugged the shirt on. 'So what can I do for you?' he asked, turning back to face me, as he buttoned up. 'Or did you just stop by in the hope of ogling me?'

Usually I'd fire off a witty comeback, but for the first time ever my mind was blank. I cleared my throat, trying to pull myself together and focus. I nodded down at the storyboards in my hand. 'I've got some sketches with our ideas for the Brite campaign.'

Richard's eyes brightened with interest. 'Great. Bring them over. I'd love to see them.'

'What – now?'

'No time like the present, is there? Unless you need to rush off?'

'No, not at all.'

I walked over and laid my drawings on his desk. He came to stand by my side, and I tensed a little. I could smell the musky, masculine scent of his shower gel, and somehow I felt suddenly aware of him as a man – something I'd never felt before.

He appeared completely oblivious to how I was feeling, as he stood there flicking through my work. 'These drawings are great,' he said finally. 'I'd forgotten how talented you are.'

'Thanks,' I mumbled, both pleased and embarrassed by his praise.

'And Helena told me this was all your idea?'

'It was a team effort.'

He looked up and smiled at me. 'I'm glad to hear all the praise hasn't gone to your head.' He perched on his desk, growing serious. 'But honestly, I'm really pleased with how everything's worked out. You're doing a great job.'

'I'm enjoying it. More than I thought I would.' I glanced away, knowing that there was something I needed to say, but not wanting to put it into words – to admit it to him, or to myself. I cleared my throat. 'You were right,' I said finally. I forced myself to raise my gaze to meet his. 'Working here has been good for me.'

His eyes glinted. 'Do I get to say I told you so?'

'Not if you value your front teeth.'

Richard laughed. It was a rare sight, seeing him relaxed like that. His eyes crinkled and his strong cheekbones seemed more pronounced. It suddenly struck me how good-looking he was. I wondered why it hadn't occurred to me before.

His eyes dropped to the TAG Heuer watch on his wrist. 'Look, I was heading off now. Do you want to walk out together?'

To my surprise, I couldn't think of anything I'd rather do. 'Sure. Why not?'

He grabbed his gym bag, and we headed towards the lift. We walked in silence, which was unusual for us. Usually we were bantering about something or other. But tonight I felt strangely shy around Richard. I guessed it must have been the shock of seeing him half naked.

'So what're you up to this weekend?' Richard said as we stepped into the lift. He gave me a sideways glance. 'Or is it best if I don't know?'

'What do you mean by that?' The teasing about my excessive lifestyle was standard for us, but for the first time ever it bothered me. 'Oh, right, I get it. You don't want to know because I must be up to something debauched?'

He looked a little taken aback by my snappiness. 'Sorry . . . I didn't mean anything by it. I just know you like to go out a lot, and I assumed you'd have plans tonight.'

'Well, I don't.' I sounded prissier than I'd intended. I couldn't understand why I was feeling so defensive. And then an idea entered my head. 'In fact, do you want to grab a drink?' I said abruptly. The words were out of my mouth before I was even aware of what I was doing. 'Maybe even dinner? My treat. To say thank you for everything you've done for me.' I wasn't entirely sure that had anything to do with why I wanted to take him for dinner, but I didn't want to examine my motives too closely yet.

Richard's eyes flicked over to me. I saw a hint of surprise there, and then it was gone. 'I'd love to.' His words were clipped. 'But I've got plans tonight.'

I was surprised by just how disappointed I felt. 'Oh, right. Of course.' I forced my voice to sound bright. 'Another time perhaps . . .'

He didn't respond.

I stared at my feet, feeling a little awkward and embarrassed. Fortunately the elevator door pinged then, alerting us to the fact we had reached the ground floor. But any relief I felt at the chance of making a quick getaway evaporated as the doors pulled open, and I saw Petra sitting on one of the couches in reception.

She looked up as the lift doors opened, and when she saw it was Richard, she got to her feet, reminding me just how annoyingly tall, slim and elegant she was.

'So I take it you two made up?' I said to Richard, as we crossed the reception floor.

He didn't bother to reply, and there was no more opportunity to ask questions, because we'd already reached Petra. I stood by as she exchanged a quick kiss hello with Richard. I felt small and scruffy next to her, like I'd been thrown together. I caught a glance of myself in the glass frontage of the building. Even in my more sober clothes, I still looked cheap and trashy. Not smooth and classy like her. I blamed my hair. The bleach was just too much . . .

Richard turned to me. 'Petra, you remember Charlotte?'

Petra's smile dimmed a little. 'How could I forget her? Richard mentioned he'd found you a job here. He said it was difficult for you at first, but that you'd settled in now.'

'He did?' I couldn't help feeling a little betrayed that he'd been talking about me with her.

Petra must have sensed my discomfort, because I saw a small smile playing on her lips as she ploughed on. 'He's so sweet to you, isn't he? Talks about you all the time, like he's a concerned big brother.'

I'd heard this said before, but for the first time it annoyed me.

'Really? He talks about me all the time?' I smiled pleas-antly, to take the sting out of my next words. 'That's funny – because he never mentions you.'

Petra blinked in surprise, and then her green eyes narrowed a little, as she studied me more carefully. Richard frowned at me, looking perplexed.

'I hate to be rude,' Petra slipped her arm through Richard's. The knife twisted further in my gut. 'But we really should be going. We're already late for our reservation, darling.'

'Sure. Let's grab a cab.' Richard looked over at me. 'Can we drop you somewhere?'

The look of horror on Petra's face at the prospect of me crashing their evening was almost enough to make me take him up on his offer, but I had no desire to play third wheel. 'Thanks, but I'm fine.'

They bid me goodnight, and hurried outside to hail a cab. I followed them, but turned in the direction of the Tube station. I glanced back in time to watch Richard open-ing the car door for Petra. She paused as she was getting in, to say something to him, and he threw back his head and laughed. I hadn't seen him so relaxed for ages. But it wasn't the sight of Richard looking happy with Petra that took me by surprise – it was the flash of jealousy that ripped through me.

Chapter 15

'Earth to Charlotte,' Rex said. 'Is anyone in there?'

He waved a hand in front of my face. I blinked a few times, as I came out of my daydream. I looked up to see Rex standing above my desk and staring at me with a quizzical look on his face. 'Sorry. What did you say?'

'Forget about that.' He perched on my desk. 'I want to know what the hell was going on in that head of yours just now? You looked miles away.'

I felt my cheeks heating up a little. Although I'd never admit it, I'd been thinking about Richard. It was strange, since walking in on him half naked the previous Friday, he'd been on my mind. Whereas before I'd go out of my way to ignore him at work, this week I'd found myself looking out for him all the time, hoping that I might run into him or find an excuse to talk to him. I'd even caught myself spending more time over my appearance in the morning, thinking about what I was wearing and how my hair and make-up looked.

I hadn't really understood why at first. Then the truth had hit me like a ten-tonne truck. I had a crush on Richard.

It was as if I was seeing him for the first time. I'd previously found his seriousness irritating, thinking he was just uptight – but now I could see that made him commanding. His passion for his work and his single-mindedness – how had I never appreciated those qualities before? And maybe I didn't usually go for conventional good looks, but it was amazing how they grew on you – the strong jaw and nose; the perfectly proportioned, clean-shaven face; the athletic build . . . Suddenly rocker boys who shunned showers and razors seemed far less appealing.

Rex must have noticed the blush on my cheeks, because he gave me a knowing smile. 'Oh, so that's it. Someone likes a boy,' he said in a sing-song voice.

'What?' I tried to convey just how ridiculous that was. 'Please. I'm just tired, that's all.'

'Oh, don't give me that. You can't fool me. I know that look.' He turned to Helena. 'Hey, Hel,' he called in to her. 'Charlotte fancies someone.'

'Good for her.' She didn't bother glancing up from her desk.

'Ugh,' he tutted. Unable to evoke any interest from her, he turned his attention back to me. He leaned over my desk, lowering his voice in a conspiratorial manner. 'So just between us girls, who is it? You can tell me.' He pretended to zip his lips shut. 'I won't tell a soul. I swear. I'm very discreet.'

As much as I adored Rex, I also knew what a gossip he was. Whatever he said, if I told him anything, it would be all round the office in an hour.

'I told you before. You've got it all wrong. There's no one I like.' The last thing I needed was this getting out. The teasing would be merciless. I wouldn't be able to show my face. Not to mention the awkwardness it would cause with Richard . . .

'Hmmm.' He gave me a disappointed look. 'You know I don't believe you for a moment, right? But don't you worry, I'll get it out of you in the end. No one can keep a secret from me.'

I hoped he was wrong about that, because I didn't relish anyone finding out I had romantic feelings for Richard. Especially not the man concerned. For one thing, he had a girlfriend. And as much as I didn't like Petra, I wasn't the type to start trying to steal another woman's guy. I had a lot of flaws, but that wasn't one of them.

I managed to avoid any more awkward questions from Rex for the rest of the day. I threw myself into my work, which helped to put Richard from my mind, too.

I got home that night to find a message on my answering machine from my mother. It was the sixth message that she'd left, and I could hear from her tone that she wasn't going to tolerate much more of me avoiding her, so I had no choice but to call back.

I sat curled up on the couch, half listening and saying uh-huh in what I hoped were the appropriate places, as she caught me up on what she had been doing. Then she hit me with it – the real reason she'd phoned.

'I was hoping you might be free to come down to Claylands this Sunday.' Hearing that, my shoulders slumped. 'We haven't seen you since our anniversary.' When I didn't answer straight away, she added, 'And I know your father would love to see you.'

I'd already been formulating my excuse, but hearing that I knew there was no way I could get out of it. It was the only way I got to see my father, so I would have to go.

I was going to accept the invitation, but my mother was still speaking. 'Unfortunately your sister and Toby won't be able to make it.'

'Shame,' I muttered. Well, that was one small mercy at least.

My mother appeared not to catch my sarcasm. 'Although just to warn you, Richard will be here.'

Hearing that, I sat up straighter. 'Richard's going?' Suddenly the prospect of lunch didn't seem so bad after all.

'Yes.' My mother sighed. 'I know you get irritated with him "interfering" in your life, but I like to see him. It makes me feel closer to – well, to your brother.'

Hearing her speak about Kit, I felt bad then. We spent so much time bickering that sometimes I forgot how hard it was for her to lose her son.

'I know that, Mum.' For once my voice was soft, understanding. 'And don't worry, I'll be there.'

'You will?' She couldn't keep the surprise out of her voice. It must have been the first time she'd got me down to the house without a battle for years. 'That's wonderful news, Charlotte.' She sounded so pleased at the thought of seeing me that I almost felt guilty for demonising her all the time. Then she said: 'So we'll see you around midday? Try not to be late this time, though. I don't want to hold everything up for you again.'

And there it was. The reason we would never get on.

We said our goodbyes, and I lay back on my bed, hands behind my head, staring up at the ceiling.

She was right – I hadn't seen my parents since my performance at their anniversary lunch. I also still hadn't told my mum that I was working at Davenport's. I'd asked Richard to leave it to me to break the news. My dad wouldn't pass much comment, but my mother was bound to have an opinion – and one that was inevitably going to annoy me, I would put good money on it.

215

But right now, none of that was of any importance. All I cared about was that it would give me an opportunity to spend some time with Richard, so I could try to figure out what the hell I was feeling for him.

I dressed carefully for work the next day. I chose a cute, flirty dress, with an A-line skirt, in a rich royal blue. I washed and dried my hair smooth, and kept my make-up to a minimum. It was still me, but a fresher, softer version.

Unfortunately my efforts with my appearance didn't go unnoticed. Rex commented on how nice I looked with a knowing smile – he clearly suspected my crush was on someone in the office. I made a mental note that I had to be careful of that. The last thing I needed was for him to figure out the truth.

I waited until he went out for lunch, and then headed up to Richard's office.

Outside his door, I hesitated. His PA wasn't around, which meant I couldn't check if he was free to see me. But that was the least of my worries. Before, I'd have had no qualms about talking to him – I wouldn't have given it a second thought. But now I felt unsure of myself and worried about saying the wrong thing. It was strange. I wasn't used to feeling nervous around him.

I took a deep breath and knocked.

'Come in,' he called out.

Trying to ignore the squirming in my stomach, I pushed the heavy mahogany door open.

He didn't even look up as I walked in. He was too engrossed in typing something on the keyboard of his computer.

'Just give me a second . . .' His eyes trawled the screen – I presume he'd just written an email – and then he clicked, no doubt to send. Finally he turned his attention to me. 'Charlotte.' He seemed surprised to see me. 'What brings you to my office?' He leaned back in his chair, contemplating me. 'In fact, let me guess. You were hoping to catch me coming out of the shower again.'

I knew he was teasing, but it was too close to the truth to raise so much as a smile from me. Not trusting myself to answer, I simply ignored the question, and walked over to slip into the seat opposite him.

'So I heard my mum roped you into Sunday lunch?'

'That's right.' His eyes narrowed. 'Why're you asking?' Then his expression cleared, and he chuckled. 'Don't tell me – you want a lift down there?'

That was exactly what I wanted – a chance to spend some time together. I knew he wouldn't suspect anything, because I was always blagging lifts off him. 'Well, since you're offering . . .'

'You never change, do you, Charlotte?' He shook his head, in a slightly exasperated way. 'I'll come over about half ten.'

'Great. I'll be ready.'

I got up to leave, but I was halfway to the door when he said, 'Just one thing.' I turned back to see him regarding me with an amused look in his eyes. 'This time I don't want to have to see any naked men in your bed. That's all I ask of you.'

Vivid images flashed through my head – of Richard finding Gavin in my bed, the used condoms on the bedside table, and then of me parading naked in front of him. I flushed at the memory.

My reaction didn't go unnoticed by Richard. 'Oh, Charlotte.' He peered at me as though he couldn't quite believe what he was seeing. 'Don't tell me that you're blushing.'

I gave a haughty sniff. 'I just don't think there's any need to bring that up.' I knew I sounded a bit prissy, but I felt ashamed at the memory. I'd never cared what Richard thought of me before, but now I did. I didn't want him to think of me that way any more.

He looked taken aback by my reaction. 'Sorry, I didn't realise you were so touchy about it.' He frowned. 'You've always made a joke about that stuff in the past. And you never seemed to mind if other people did the same.'

'Well, now I do.'

He stared at me for a long moment, and then finally nodded. 'Fair enough. I'm sorry I brought it up, and I won't mention it again. You have my word.'

I could see he meant it. But that wasn't the point. Bringing that up about Gavin had soured the meeting for me.

'Good.' My tone was brusque, standoffish. 'I'll see you Sunday then.'

I walked out of the office, trying to ignore the confused look on his face. Damn. If I was hoping to get him to see me in a new light, it didn't seem like I was doing a particularly good job of it. I'd just have to hope to do better on Sunday.

Chapter 16

The following Sunday morning, I stood in front of the full-length mirror that hung on the back of my bedroom door, casting a critical eye over my appearance. I couldn't make up my mind if I liked what I saw. I'd ditched my usual black, scruffy rebel look, and in my place stood a much softer, more conservative version of myself. I had on a grey woollen skirt, which stopped just above my knee, and a baby-blue cashmere jumper, with elegant knee-high boots in brown leather.

That wasn't my only change. Along with shopping for a new outfit yesterday, I'd also booked an appointment with a hairdresser. After a lot of headshaking and disapproval about the damage that the home bleaching had done, she'd shown me swatches of colours to add in low-lights. She'd warned that the shade might not turn out exactly perfect, but it was much better than we'd both feared — now, the unnatural whiteness was gone, and had been replaced with shades of dark blonde, warm auburn and chestnut brown. The dry split ends had been ruthlessly cut away too, so my hair fell softly around my shoulders, like a long-layered, grown-out bob.

I nervously fiddled with the ends of my hair. The hairdresser had kept telling me how great the new style looked – well, what else was she going to say? – but I couldn't decide whether I agreed. My over-the-top clothes, makeup and hair had been my armour for the past seven years – my way of hiding from the world. Looking like this, I felt strangely vulnerable.

I glanced at my watch, eager to get on with the day. Unlike the last time Richard had picked me up, for my parents' anniversary lunch, I was ready twenty minutes early. It was giving me far too much time to think, so I decided to head out to the sitting room to watch some TV. At least it would distract me from fretting about the day ahead. I'd been there for a few minutes, mindlessly channel surfing, when Lindsay stumbled out of her room, in her usual nightwear of shorts and an old t-shirt.

'Hey,' she mumbled, bleary eyed, throwing a glance in my direction as she headed to the bathroom. She'd made it just a few steps past me when she stopped, turned and did a double-take.

'What the hell happened to you?' She was suddenly fully alert. She rubbed her eyes with her palms, in a theatrical gesture. 'It looks like Doris Day gave you a makeover!'

I groaned inwardly. That was the last thing I needed to hear. 'Is it that bad?' I glanced down worriedly at myself. 'Should I change?'

'No!' Lindsay's response was so vehement the walls practically shook. 'I'm only teasing. You look good – really good.' Then she raised one eyebrow suggestively. 'Much more Richard's type.'

'What?' Lindsay recoiled as I screeched the word. 'This—' I indicated my outfit – 'has nothing to do with him.'

'Whatever you say,' she said, in a voice that suggested she believed otherwise.

I groaned. 'Oh, no. If you think that, he's going to as well. I had better go and change . . .'

I stood, to go to my room, but before I could make it two paces, the intercom sounded. I looked desperately at Lindsay, but she just shrugged – as if to say, that's your problem – and headed to the bathroom. I stood frozen for a second, but the intercom sounded again, more demanding this time. Remembering my promise to be on time, I ran over to answer it.

'I'll be right down,' I said. Well, it looked like I had no other choice than to go like this. The only other option was to keep him waiting – and I couldn't do that.

I tried not to think about what he'd make of my new look. Instead I shrugged on my royal blue suede jacket – a vintage item I'd already had in my wardrobe, which had seemed to suit my outfit – grabbed my bag and ran down the stairs.

Richard was sitting in the lobby of our building, looking at something on his iPhone, when I got downstairs. He only gave me the briefest of glances, and then resumed what he was doing. I stood there for a moment, before I realised what was going on – he simply hadn't recognised me.

'Richard?' My voice was tentative, but unmistakable.

He looked up then, his gaze running over me as he frowned in confusion, trying to link my voice to my appearance. Then everything must have clicked into place, and like Lindsay, he did a double-take.

'Charlotte?' He stood, his eyes not leaving me as he tucked his phone away. 'What the hell?'

It wasn't quite the response I'd been looking for. 'What's that supposed to mean?' I said guardedly, sticking my hands into my jacket pockets.

He must have sensed my defensiveness, because his eyes, which had been scanning me, came to rest on my face. 'What I mean by that is – wow.'

With that one word, my confidence lifted. 'Really?' My hands came out of my pockets, and lightly touched my hair. 'Because I'm on time; not hung-over; and looking more preppy than I'd ever have thought possible.' My voice took on a light, flirtatious tone. 'You like the new me?'

He gave me a strange look. 'I always liked you, Charlotte. Whatever crazy clothes you wore, or whatever strange antics you got up to. I just wasn't sure if you always liked yourself.'

The seriousness of his answer threw me. I wasn't exactly sure how to respond, so I searched for a way to lighten the conversation. 'Are you psychoanalysing me now? I thought that was Dr Milton's job?'

He regarded me for a long moment. I felt a flutter of anticipation, wondering what he was about to say. But then he seemed to change his mind. 'We should get going,' he said. 'I promised your mother we'd be on time.'

Trying to ignore my disappointment, I followed him out to his car. To my relief, the front seat was empty.

'No Petra?' I said, as I got in. It had crossed my mind that he might bring her along, which would have scuppered my plans for the day.

'Not today.' I waited, clearly wanting a fuller explanation. He hesitated, and then said, 'We broke up.'

I tried not to show how pleased I was to hear this. With her out of the picture, I was free to make my move, if that's what I wanted to do.

'So how come you split?'

He flicked a look over at me. 'You know the answer to that.'

'Yeah, but I still want to hear you say it.'

'Well, turns out you were right – she was looking for something more serious than I was. She told me that she wanted us to move in together. I told her I wasn't ready. So she ended it.'

I could imagine how that conversation had gone. She'd probably hoped that giving him an ultimatum – we either move forward or end it – would press him into doing what she wanted, when instead he called her bluff and held firm.

It would have been easy to let the subject rest there, but my curiosity had been piqued. I'd never paid much attention to Richard's love life before, but now I had a vested interest in finding out what made him tick. 'So why didn't you want to settle down with her?'

'I told you before – I'm busy with work.'

I thought about this for a moment, and then shook my head. 'No, it's more than that. You've always been this way. You're a serial monogamist. You've brought how many girls home to meet my parents over the years? And they're all perfectly nice and presentable – good catches each and every one of them – attractive, intelligent, beautifully presented. But after a while you drop whomever you've been seeing, and move on to the next. Which always seems somewhat pointless,' I said thoughtfully, 'as they're pretty much interchangeable. It's almost as if—'

'As if what?' Richard kept his eyes fixed firmly on the road.

I considered my chain of thought for a second. 'You don't want to go out with someone who you're really serious about. You'd rather date girls who you know aren't right for you, so that you can keep your distance, rather than risk getting close to someone and getting hurt.'

Richard snorted a laugh. 'So you're the one psychoanalysing me now?' he said lightly. 'I think you've been spending too much time with Dr Milton.'

I snuck a look over at him. I might have bought his blasé reaction if I hadn't noticed how tightly he was gripping the steering wheel. 'Perhaps you're right,' I murmured, deciding it was easiest to let it go.

But I had a feeling I'd struck a nerve with him.

After that, I changed the conversation to the less controversial topic of work. There was a lot of office gossip – who was dating whom – which I got from Rex. Richard tried to stay above it, but now I happily filled him in. We also talked about the forthcoming Christmas party, which was the Friday after next.

I was in a surprisingly good mood when I reached my parents' house. My mother was so shocked that we'd arrived on time, and that I wasn't looking as trashy as normal, that she didn't have time to formulate her normal passive-aggressive criticisms of me.

We ate in the formal dining room, as was traditional in our household for Sunday lunch, seated at the oval mahogany table that my parents had bought when they were first married. It was one of the most relaxed times I'd had with my parents in a while. I stuck to drinking water, which I think helped. It was only once the main course was finished, and the dishes cleared, that my mother finally turned her attention on me.

'So, Charlotte.' She sat back in her chair and smiled at me. A casual observer might assume it was a genuine smile, but I knew better – it was her way of disarming you before an attack. 'How are things at that bar you work at?'

Here we go, I thought. However hard she tried to pretend otherwise, it was always clear that she hated the idea of her daughter working in a bar. I wasn't sure how she'd react to the news of my new job – in some ways, she'd see it as an upgrade on pulling pints, but given that it was my mother, she'd inevitably find some way to criticise me.

But there was no way I was getting out of this. It was the moment of truth. I set down my glass. 'Actually,' I said carefully, 'I'm not working at The Nick any more.'

My mother's sharp eyes narrowed. 'Oh? What happened?'

I could tell what she was thinking – that I must have done something to get sacked. She always liked to assume the worst about me. Having the opportunity to prove her wrong was too good to miss.

'Nothing "happened", I just got a new job . . .' I nodded over at Richard. 'Working at Davenport's.'

I'd timed my announcement well. My mother had just been sipping her wine, and the shock of my news must have made her swallow it down the wrong way, because she started to cough. I bit back a smile.

'When did this happen?' she said, once she'd regained her composure.

'About eight weeks ago.'

'And you didn't think to tell me before now?' She looked hurt. So that was going to be the angle this time – that I'd kept things from her.

'I didn't want to say anything until I knew how it was working out.'

She turned to Richard. 'And how is it? Working out?'

I tried not to feel annoyed that she hadn't asked me. It had always been this way – she still saw me as a child, while Richard was a grown-up. But there was no point getting upset about it, so I turned to Richard, too. I wondered what exactly he was going to say. He could quite rightly bring up my early petulance, confirming my mother's opinion of me as irresponsible. But instead he smiled at me.

'Charlotte's doing an excellent job. She's been a real asset to the team she's working in.'

'Really?' My mother made no effort to keep the surprise out of her voice.

'No need to sound quite so shocked,' I muttered.

'I'm not,' she said defensively. 'I've always said you had a good brain, Charlotte. I just worried that you had no intention of using it.'

'Thanks for the vote of confidence.'

I could feel irritation building up inside me. My mother opened her mouth to say something back, and I could see the argument escalating and fast spinning out of control – it had happened so many times before. But before it could, my father reached out across the table and caught my mother's hand. 'Eleanor. Please.'

She looked at my father and then at me. 'I was just trying to show some interest in Charlotte's life.' She sniffed. 'It doesn't matter what I do or say, I'm always the bad guy.' She pushed her chair back from the table, and stood up. 'I'm going to get dessert.'

She swept from the room. There was silence after she left. Richard waited a beat, and then said, 'I'll make sure she's all right.'

He got up and followed my mother out to the kitchen.

After they'd gone, my father and I just looked at each other.

'We almost made it two hours without an argument,' I said. 'That must be some kind of record.'

My father couldn't help smiling. Then he grew serious. 'You know, it may not seem like it, but your mother just wants you to be happy.'

'Then maybe she could lay off criticising me every time I come down here.'

'And maybe you could be less sensitive,' he said mildly. 'She may not always say the right thing, but none of us are perfect. And remember, above all, she loves you and wants only the best for you.'

I had no reply to that. Luckily, my mother chose that moment to reappear, carrying an apple crumble. Richard followed behind, with a jug of cream in one hand and a tub of ice cream in the other.

'Here we go.' My mother set the still sizzling dish in the middle of the table. 'Be careful – it's hot.'

I'd expected her to resume our argument after coming back from the kitchen, but instead she began to chatter on about making the crumble, as she started to dish up. I snuck a look over at Richard, wondering what he'd said to her in there. He'd always been able to handle my mother.

I waited until my parents bent their heads to start eating their pudding.

'Thank you,' I mouthed at Richard.

'You're welcome,' he mouthed back.

We grinned at each other across the table. Our eyes held for a moment longer than was necessary, and I felt that strange fluttering in my stomach again. I looked away, worried that he might see my feelings written across my face. I glanced at my watch, wondering how long it would be until we could get out of here, so I could finally have Richard to myself.

Chapter 17

It was nearly six by the time we left my parents' house. The rest of the afternoon had passed pleasantly enough, and my mother and I had miraculously managed to avoid any more snippiness between us.

Richard and I chatted easily on the drive back. But as we got closer to London, I grew quieter. We'd be back at my flat soon, and I wasn't ready for the day to end. It was hard to know when I might get another opportunity to be alone with him, and if I was going to make a move, it needed to be now.

'So, any plans for tonight?' I asked casually, as he drove towards my flat.

'Just getting an early night. It's been a long week.' He waited a beat and then said, 'How about you?'

'Probably just watch a movie, something like that.' I saw a hint of surprise in his eyes at my response, but he didn't push it. I guess he'd remembered my sense of humour failure from the last time he referred to my wild lifestyle.

I waited, hoping he might take the bait, and suggest that we spend the evening together. But he said nothing, and we lapsed into silence.

Finally he drew up outside my building. 'Well, here you go. Home sweet home.'

I forced a smile. 'Thanks,' I managed, but my mind was racing. I couldn't let him go now. If I did, I was sure nothing would ever happen between us.

I unclicked my seatbelt and gathered up my bag. Then, just as I reached for the handle to open the car door, I turned back to him.

'Hey,' I said, as though a thought had just struck me. 'Why don't you come up for a bit?' He frowned, obviously taken aback by the invitation. 'I mean, you said how tired you are,' I rushed on. 'And it's been a long journey back. Why don't I make you some coffee before you drive home? Wake you up a bit.' I could see him hesitate, and I didn't blame him. It was hardly a long way back to his apartment in Canary Wharf – it would clearly be most logical for him just to continue on. But I didn't want to give him a chance to think about that. Instead, I gave him what I hoped was an enticing smile. 'If it makes any difference, the flat's actually tidy for once.'

He laughed, and to my relief, switched off the engine. 'Now that I have to see.'

We went up to my flat, and I left him in the sitting room, while I went to the kitchen. Once I was away from him, I leaned up against the countertop, and ran a hand through my hair. Now I had Richard here, I was beginning to realise that I really hadn't thought this through very well. This kind of situation was new to me. Usually if I wanted to get a guy into bed, it was just a case of getting drunk, doing some clumsy flirting, and that was it. All I needed to do was throw myself at them. Richard, I suspected, was used to a more sophisticated seduction technique.

'Is everything okay in there?' Richard called through.

Damn. I needed a plan of action fast. 'Yeah. I'll be right back.'

I cast my eyes round the kitchen, desperately looking for inspiration. The wooden wine rack on the opposite counter caught my eye. There were twelve bottles stacked in it, and they all belonged to Lindsay. She had taken a wine course the previous year, and had started developing a small collection whenever she had spare money. It seemed like a good place to start.

I walked over and selected a bottle of red, and mentally crossed my fingers that Lindsay wouldn't be too mad at me for opening it. I popped the cork, and poured two large glasses. I downed one for Dutch courage, topped it back up, and then carried the glasses through to Richard.

I walked into the room to find it empty. For one heart-crushing moment, I thought Richard had got bored and left. But then I heard him say, 'Up here.'

I looked up and saw him standing on the mezzanine level, where I'd been doing my painting. He had his back to me, and was studying the canvas I was working on. It was a recreation of the view across the rooftops from our flat at dusk, a typical London scene, rendered in oils.

Looking up at him, I felt the alcohol start to hit me. It was strong wine, and it had gone straight to my head, emboldening me to make my move.

Being careful not to spill any wine I slowly manoeuvred my way up the little spiral staircase that led to the mezzanine level. It was a bit of a struggle, but when I got to the top, I felt secretly pleased that Richard had come up here. In a lot of ways, it was a much more romantic setting than the sitting room. I'd kept the lights deliberately low – 'seduction lighting,' as Lindsay called it – and the pale moonlight filtered in through the skylights that took up one side of the ceiling, casting a soft glow over the space, so it was bright enough to see without being overpowering.

Richard was still studying my canvas. I'd painted the scene in shades of dark purples, which gave it a sinister feel – almost like something out of a Victorian steampunk story. I stood by, waiting for him to finish. I sipped at my wine, a way to stop myself from disturbing him. As the silence grew, my heart-rate sped up. I always found it nerve-wracking, having someone inspect my artwork, and combined with my other fears about making a move on him, I was beginning to feel like a full-blown panic attack was about to hit.

Finally he turned to me. His eyes were solemn, the way they always were when he had something serious to say. 'You're very talented, Charlotte.'

I looked away. I never knew how to take a compliment. It always embarrassed me. 'It's not finished yet.'

'Still, have you thought about going back to art school? I never really understood how you ended up getting kicked out.'

There was an unsaid question in his words, but it was one I didn't want to get into right now. I'd been drinking and partying too much, and kept missing deadlines for submitting coursework. Artists might be known for being temperamental, but it seemed there was only so much that the faculty at Saint Martins were prepared to put up with. To be fair, I'd been given several warnings, each of which I'd chosen to ignore. Did I regret it? Perhaps. Should I go back? Maybe. But I had no desire for this evening to turn into a discussion of my career plans. I had another agenda.

'Here.' I held out a glass of wine to him. 'This is for you.'

Richard looked down at the glass in my hand, and then up at me, frowning a little. 'What happened to the coffee?'

I gave a little shrug. 'I thought this might be more fun.' I stretched my arm out further, so the glass was closer to him, but he still didn't take it from me. I could see the wariness in his dark eyes as he studied me, trying to work out what I was up to.

'Can't,' he said shortly. 'I'm driving. You know that.'

I took a step towards him. 'I thought you could leave your car here, get a cab.' I looked up at him from beneath lowered lashes. 'Or you could always stay the night.'

He went very still. If he'd been in any doubt before, there was no mistaking my intention now. I took a long sip of wine, and then put both of the glasses down.

My heart was beating even faster now. Richard still hadn't moved, so I took that as an invitation. I stepped forward again, so I was only an inch or so away from him, and then, placing my hands on either side of his face, I stood on my tiptoes and kissed him full on the mouth.

For a moment he resisted, and I half expected him to push me away. But then something seemed to shift within him. His head tilted down and his mouth softened, as he began to kiss me back.

I felt a surge of triumph, and something else, too . . . a tightening in my groin, that took me by surprise. I'd never been particularly into kissing. For me, it was just a means of getting to the main event. The guys I was usually with were always drunk and sloppy, their technique more of an assault than a seduction. But Richard kissed with an expertise that left me breathless. His mouth brushed back and forth against mine, feather-light and teasing, as though he had all the time in the world. The tip of his tongue swept gently across my lower lip, igniting a million nerve-endings I hadn't even known were there. I considered myself to have a lot of experience, but this was a first for me. I might have been the one who initiated this between us, but there was no mistaking that Richard was firmly in control.

As his lips parted mine, deepening our kiss, a shiver of desire ran through me, something new and unexpected. Richard must have sensed my reaction, because his hands went to my waist, drawing me in to his solid body. I could feel how turned on he was, and I pressed against him, urging him to take this to the next level. But instead of giving in like I'd hoped, his fingers tightened on me, holding me fast, a silent signal that he wasn't going to be hurried.

Irritation coursed through me. It was the usual battle of wills between us, and yet again I seemed to be losing. Most girls probably would have liked the fact that he was determined to take it slow, but this didn't suit me at all. I just wanted to seal the deal already. And I knew just how to do that. Slowly, carefully, so as not to alert him to my plan, I let my palms slide over his buttocks, and then before he could stop me, I snuck one hand between us and grabbed his crotch.

I felt Richard freeze, and then a split second later his hand snapped around my wrist, and he jerked away from me so abruptly that I stumbled backwards.

'Jesus, Charlotte.' I looked up, and saw his expression, a mix of horror and confusion. Instead of moving things on between us, my crude overture appeared to have snapped him back to reality. 'What the hell are you playing at? That's the last thing I wanted.'

'Really?' I felt my cheeks flush. 'Because you seemed pretty into it a second ago.'

'Is that any surprise?' He ran a hand through his hair. 'Christ, I'm only human! I'm a thirty-year-old, red-blooded male, and you're an attractive woman. Of course I responded. But that doesn't mean I want anything to happen between us.'

I sucked in a breath. It felt like he'd slapped me.

Richard obviously realised then what he'd said, and how it had sounded. He took a step forward. 'Oh no, Charlotte. I didn't mean it like that—'

This time it was me who backed away. 'Hey, don't worry about it.' I affected a casual shrug. 'It's no big deal. I felt horny, and you were here. There was nothing more to it.' The words were pouring out of me. I didn't care how I sounded – I just didn't want him to know how hurt and rejected I felt. 'Don't for one minute assume you're special. I can get out my little black book and have a dozen guys round here in the time it takes to get a pizza delivered.'

Richard winced at my words, and I couldn't blame him. I'd wanted to defuse the situation, but unfortunately I hadn't been able to carry off the reference to my casual sleeping around. I think it had something to do with my new image – in my usual rock chick attire, I could face down anyone; no one could shame me. But the new, preppy me was a lot more sensitive. I had nowhere to hide.

I picked up my glass and took a slug of wine. 'So?' I looked pointedly at my watch. 'Am I getting rid of you any time soon? Because I'd like to get on with my night.'

His eyes went to the alcohol. 'I'm not leaving you like this.'

Oh, great. This situation was going from bad to worse. The last thing I wanted was for him to be staying with me out of pity. Luckily, before I had a chance to argue back, we both started at the sound of a key in the lock. A second later Lindsay's voice rang out. I breathed a sigh of relief that we'd been interrupted. I don't think I'd ever been so pleased to hear from anyone in my life.

'We're up here,' I called down to my friend. Then I re-focused on Richard. 'See? Lindsay's home. You don't need to stay and babysit.'

'If that's what you want—' Richard said, unsure.

'It is.' I hoped he couldn't hear how over-bright my voice was, or see my eyes beginning to water. 'You can see your-self out, right?'

He hesitated for a moment. I could tell he wanted to say something, to make sure I was all right, or – worse still – to talk through what had happened. But I wasn't in the mood for platitudes.

'Please.' My voice cracked a little, my eyes pleading with him to listen. 'Just go.'

He must have finally got the message that his presence was making this worse, because he said, 'Sure.' He put a hand out and squeezed my arm a little. 'Goodnight, Charlotte. And take care of yourself.'

I watched as he headed back downstairs, trying to ignore the feeling of emptiness spreading through the pit of my stomach. I'd been rejected before, but this was the first time that it had hurt.

Chapter 18

'So what do you want to hear about today?

I looked across at Dr Milton, surprised at how comfortable I felt with her now. It was our sixth session, and from dreading coming here, I now found it one of the most relaxing parts of my week. The seasons had changed since my first appointment. From the early autumn brightness, we were now in the dead of winter. It was six in the evening, but it had already been dark since mid-afternoon. Outside the wind howled, and the bare branches of a tree kept tap-tapping against the window pane, as if they were trying to get through. As usual, we sat facing each other in burgundy leather armchairs. She'd lit the real fire, and I could feel the warmth of the embers emanating from it. My hands were still red from the cold outside.

I was especially pleased to have this session tonight, because it took my mind off what had happened with Richard on Sunday night.

After he'd left, I'd gone downstairs to join Lindsay, hoping to take my mind off what had happened. But she'd sensed that something wasn't right, and kept asking me what had put me in such a bad mood. I refused to tell her. I was supposed to be the liberated woman; the girl who didn't need a man – who hooked up with guys casually, and never expected them to call. How could I now admit to being hopelessly obsessed with someone who I couldn't have? Especially after everything I'd said about Richard in the past – how I'd called him uptight and annoying.

I'd been dreading running into him at Davenport's that week, until I remembered that that he was away visiting the New York office. At least that gave me a reprieve from the inevitable post-kiss diagnosis Richard was going to force us to have. With any luck, he might have forgotten the whole sorry incident by the time he got back.

'Why don't we just pick up where we left off?' Dr Milton said now, bringing me back to the present. 'You were telling me about your family holiday?'

So far, this had been all we'd covered in the sessions. Each week, I'd talked her through various moments from that same summer we spoke about the first time – the summer I'd turned eighteen, when I was still the good girl Charlotte, and hadn't yet become Charlie. To be quite honest, I really didn't feel like we were getting anywhere. But Dr Milton seemed to feel that these reminiscences had a purpose, so I just went along with her.

'Oh, right. Yes. Our holiday in France.' I thought back. 'The first week was fairly uneventful. But then my sister and her boyfriend turned up . . .'

Seven years ago

It was the pain that woke me. A throbbing in my ankle, where I'd fractured it running down the marble staircase of our villa yesterday. I'd fallen awkwardly in a heap, and had to be taken to the local hospital, and now – as my mother kept telling me – my clumsiness had ruined everyone's holiday.

I lay awake for a moment, listening to the sounds of the night. I could hear the cicadas, along with the sound of the waves rushing the shore. The place was so familiar to me. My parents had rented the same villa in the South of France ever since I was a child. We went there the first two weeks of August, every year. It had become a family tradition.

This year it had been just them and me for the first week. Toby and Kate had been away in Thailand, on a diving holiday. It was the first time ever that it had just been me alone with my parents, and I'd been surprised by how much I resented it. It had made me more conscious of my lack of friends, and it felt like there was something wrong with me, an eighteen-year-old hanging out with my parents alone like this. I'd spent most of my time drawing and painting, and preparing for my art degree. My sister had joined us that morning, with Toby, but I hadn't seen much of them. With my ankle like this, I hadn't been able to go out and frolic in the pool with them, or go on their long early-evening walk.

The pain wasn't easing, and I knew I'd have to go downstairs and get the medication that the doctor had prescribed. My mother wouldn't leave the tablets by my bed, in case I took too many. Her reasoning was logical enough, although she'd failed to take into account that someone with a fractured ankle might not want to have to traipse down a huge flight of stairs to get pain relief – especially when those stairs were the reason she was in pain in the first place.

I managed to hobble downstairs, and made my way to the kitchen. I balanced on one foot as I got myself a glass of water, and took two of the painkillers that the doctor had prescribed. I was on my way back to bed when I heard a sound coming from the room that my mother used as a study, like a fox howling. At first I assumed that we'd accidentally left a window open, but as I got closer, I saw through the crack of the half-open door that it was my mother, sobbing as though she wouldn't ever stop.

I stood, unsure what to do. She was curled foetal-like on the floor, her knees pulled up to her chest. On the floor in front of her, there was an old family album, with pictures of us all enjoying holidays out here. It was lying open at a photo of my brother, Kit, back when he must have been only eight years old, smiling a toothy grin as he jumped into the swimming pool.

Seeing her like this, keening for her lost child, my heart contracted. We'd all cried for Kit over the years – even my huge bear of a father. But somehow seeing my usually controlled, collected mother like this, in the pit of despair, was worse than anything I'd experienced before. I wanted to go and try to comfort her, but somehow I sensed that she didn't want anyone to see her this way; that it was easier for her to keep up the pretence that she had dealt with her grief. But how could I just walk away and leave her like this?

A cool hand rested on my shoulder and I jumped, barely managing to stifle a yelp. I turned to see Toby standing there, concern written across his handsome face. He put a finger to his lips.

'Come on,' he whispered. 'Let's leave her in peace.' I opened my mouth to object, but he shook his head. 'Trust me, it's the right thing to do.'

Hearing that from someone I trusted helped me finally make up my mind. I didn't object as Toby took me by the arm, and led me to the kitchen. Once we were there, he turned to me, his face full of concern.

'That can't have been much fun to see.'

'No.' My voice shook more than I'd been expecting. I had no qualms about opening up to Toby. Over the summer, ever since Kate had first brought her boyfriend home, I'd seen him about a dozen times. Usually I didn't get along with Kate's boyfriends, but Toby always seemed interested in what I had to say. 'I just don't know how to help her.'

'I don't think you can. To be honest, I know maybe it sounds odd . . . but the best you can probably do is let her get on with it. This is her way of coping with what happened to your brother. It's something very private and personal to her.'

'But she never says anything.'

'She's trying to be strong for you all. And she probably knows, if she does start crying in front of you, she won't be able to stop. This is her way of compartmentalising. She only lets herself cry when you guys aren't around.'

I paused to turn what he'd said over in my mind. It made sense, and now I felt bad. I'd always thought of her as being so cold, but she was clearly mourning, too.

Toby must have sensed my inner turmoil, because he took a step towards me, putting a hand on my shoulder. 'Are you all right, Mouse?'

Hearing the nickname, I pulled a face. Thoughts of my mother were temporarily forgotten. 'Don't call me that.'

'What – Mouse? Why not?'

'Mice are small and weak. I don't want to be like that.'

He grinned. 'They're also quick and agile, and—' he tweaked my nose – 'very cute.'

I managed a weak smile.

'That's more like it,' he said. 'I knew there was a smile in there somewhere.'

It was only now that I'd calmed down that I finally realised he just had on boxer shorts and a t-shirt. It was the first time I'd been so close to a half-clothed member of the opposite sex. In my thin white cotton nightdress, I wasn't much more covered up. I felt my cheeks heating up.

'Well . . . I should be going back upstairs,' I said, to cover my embarrassment.

'Let me just get some water, and then I'll help you—'

'Oh, no,' I started protesting, as he poured himself a glass. 'I'll be fine on my own. If I could get down all right, then I can get back up again, too . . .'

While I was still rambling on, he'd finished drinking the water down, and was over by my side. He didn't bother to argue back with me – instead, before I knew what he was doing, he scooped me up in his arms, as though I weighed nothing.

'Put me down!' I squealed. 'I'm too heavy.'

'You're fine,' he said. 'As long as you stop squirming.'

He gave me no more chance to argue, and instead started up the stairs. My arms instinctively snaked around his neck, and I rested my head against his chest, secretly thrilled to be treated in such a romantic way.

Outside my bedroom door, he lowered me gently to the ground.

'Thank you for that,' I managed to whisper, still feeling overwhelmed.

He tweaked my nose. 'That's quite all right . . . Mouse. See you tomorrow.'

I watched as he sauntered down the hall, and disappeared into his room. Once I was back in bed, I hugged the event to myself. As much as I told myself that Toby was my sister's boyfriend, I couldn't deny that there was something between us. And I was sure he felt it, too.

The next morning, the whole family gathered in the dining room for breakfast. My mother was back to her usual self, totally composed. I kept sneaking glances at Toby, unable to forget the previous night.

'We ran into Sebastian yesterday, Kate,' my mother was saying. 'You know – the Mortimers' boy. He was asking after you. We had to break his heart, and tell him you were bringing someone out with you this year.'

'And not just him, Jean-Luc, too.' My mum turned to Toby. 'His family live in Paris but they have a place down here. We're here at the same time as them every year. The children all played together when they were young, but

once they got into their teens, the boys were more interested in running after Kate. I think Seb and Jean actually
came to blows one year, didn't they?'

'Oh, Mummy.' Kate blushed modestly. 'Don't be so
ridiculous.'

In fact, what my mother was saying was perfectly true.
Once adolescence had set in, and my sister had discovered
bikinis, all the boys had gone crazy for her.

Toby turned to me, smiling. 'And what about you,
Charlotte? Have you been out at any wild parties this year,
chatting up the local French boys?' He winked at me, and I
blushed. My dad gave a snort of disapproval – however liberal
he was, what father ever likes to think of their daughter with
the opposite sex? – while I saw my sister bite back a smile, no
doubt at the sheer ridiculousness of the suggestion. I knew
she didn't mean anything by it. Kate wouldn't ever be deliberately cruel – but still . . . it didn't do much for my ego.

'Charlotte isn't one for parties, are you darling?' my
mother said. My body tensed. 'She's never been much of a
mixer. You prefer your own company, don't you?'

She graced me with a warm, indulgent smile, sending my
blood pressure sky-high. I could feel the vein in my forehead begin to beat like a pulse.

I was trying to conjure up an appropriate answer, when
Toby jumped in. 'I'm sure she's just too good for them,' he
said smoothly.

I flashed him a grateful smile.

Thankfully the talk turned from me, and towards how everyone planned to spend the day. My family always liked active holidays, and they'd arranged to go white-water rafting. I'd been looking forward to it, but there was no way I could go with my ankle like this.

'So what's the plan?' my sister asked. 'Are we still going rafting?'

'It's booked, but Charlotte won't be able to come. Not with her foot like that.' My dad looked at me sympathetically. 'I tried to change the date, but they're all booked up for the next ten days. It's today or wait until next year, I'm afraid.'

I felt a pang of disappointment. 'You lot go without me. I'll be fine here on my own. I wasn't that bothered about going anyway,' I lied.

My parents looked between each other. 'It feels a bit miserable leaving you here alone,' my father said. 'One of us should stay to entertain you.'

'But who?' my mother said, looking between my father and sister.

'I'll stay,' Toby said suddenly.

We all turned to him.

Kate covered his hand with her own. 'You don't have to miss out because of Charlotte.'

'I'm really not bothered. I've been loads of times before. And anyway, I won't be missing out.' He looked over at me and grinned. 'Charlotte and I will have a great time, won't we?'

And just like that, the decision was made. Within half an hour, my parents and sister had gone for the day, and I was left alone with Toby.

I looked at him shyly.

'What do you feel like doing?'

'Well, what were you planning on doing if you'd been left here alone?' I hesitated, reluctant to tell him. 'Go on. Just tell me. It can't be that bad.'

'I bought the box set of *Dexter*. I was planning to work my way through the entire first season.'

After I said it, I could have kicked myself. My sister and Toby weren't the kind of people to sit round watching TV. They were active people, who believed in socialising and sport, not sitting in front of a television screen. I'd just confirmed myself as the biggest geek. I don't know what kind of reaction I'd expected from him. He was nothing if not polite, so I knew he wouldn't ridicule me – but I'd expected him to perhaps look a little surprised, and then maybe make some polite excuse to go off on his own. But instead his eyes widened a little.

'Are you kidding me?' he said.

'What?'

'I've been dying to watch *Dexter* for ages.'

'You have? Then why haven't you?' For me, it was impossible at boarding school, especially with A-levels to study for. But I imagined he'd have a lot more freedom to do whatever he wanted.

He pulled a face. 'Put it this way – it's not really your sister's thing. I think her exact words were, "why would I want to watch something involving a serial killer?"'

I laughed at this. My family were far more focused on fact than fiction. 'That sounds like Kate.'

He smiled. 'Just don't tell her I said so, all right?'

'I promise.'

We grinned at each other, bonded by our conspiracy.

I went to sit on the couch.

Toby pulled the blinds against the already blazing sun. 'That makes it feel more like night time, doesn't it?'

Although it was warm outside, my mother always kept the air conditioning in the villa at a very cool eighteen degrees. That meant we were always freezing. A blanket lay on the nearby couch. Toby picked it up and brought it over with him. Before I knew what he was doing, he'd sat down next to me, and shaken the blanket out, spreading it, so that it was covering both of us.

I stiffened, feeling somewhat odd about the idea of us both being under the same blanket. I wasn't sure why, but it felt like we shouldn't be doing it. Toby must have sensed my concerns, because he glanced over at me.

'Is that all right? I can move if you want.'

I hesitated for a second, and then felt stupid for making such a big deal about nothing. 'No. It's fine.'

We'd just started on the second episode, when behind us, the door opened. We jumped and looked round. It was our housekeeper, Sophia.

She glanced suspiciously between us. 'What's going on in here?'

'Oh, nothing. We're just watching a programme.'

She gave us a disapproving look and then disappeared into the hallway, grumbling beneath her breath.

'What's her problem?' I said.

'No idea.'

Toby put his arm around me, and I snuggled up into him. But even though I was enjoying myself, something was niggling at me – a sense that this wasn't quite right. For some reason it felt like a betrayal of my sister. But then that was stupid. Nothing was going on between us. Maybe I had a little crush on Toby, but that's all it was. There was no way he was ever going to feel anything for me. I should just enjoy the novelty of having a good-looking guy spend time around me. There was no harm in that, right?

'So you developed a crush on Toby that summer?' Dr Milton said, once I'd finished.

'I suppose,' I admitted reluctantly. Then she fixed me with that penetrating stare of hers, and I had to give in. 'Well, all right then, yes. I did have a crush on Toby.'

'And how did you feel about that?'

'How do you think? Guilty, mostly. He was my sister's boyfriend.'

'And did you believe he reciprocated your feelings?

This time, I snorted. 'Why would he? My sister's beautiful and charming, and I'm—' I shut up, not wanting to finish the sentence.

'You're what?' Dr Milton prompted.

This time, I just shook my head, and no amount of her penetrating gaze would make me say more than I already had.

'All right then,' she sighed, making a quick note on her pad. 'We'll pick up the story next time.'

For some reason, hearing that, I felt a prickle of unease – something that I hadn't experienced since we'd first started these sessions. I'd never told anyone the next part of the story – I'd always been far too ashamed. And the prospect of sharing it with Dr Milton filled me with dread.

Chapter 19

I'd spent so much time preparing for my first encounter with Richard, imagining what I'd say and do. But unfortunately it happened when I least expected it, rendering all my plans irrelevant.

It was the following Monday morning, and I was on my way back from the art department with some finished storyboards for Helena to review. As I rounded a corner, I collided with someone. I took a step back, forming an apology, but when I looked up and saw that it was Richard, the words died.

'Charlotte!' The usually unflappable Richard looked as stunned as I felt.

I blinked a couple of times, making sure that this wasn't some elaborate daydream, and then I gathered my wits. 'I thought you weren't back until the end of the week.'

'A meeting came up that I needed to be here for.'

We lapsed into silence, the awkwardness settling between us. A couple of colleagues brushed past, nodding greetings at us. I could see Richard frowning with frustration. It was such a public place – hardly the time for a heart-to-heart. But that suited me just fine. As far as I was concerned, we'd both said everything we needed to that night in my apartment.

I held up the prints. 'I should get these back to Helena.'

I made to walk past, but Richard caught me by the arm. 'Wait.' Reluctantly I turned back to face him. He glanced around to make sure no one was listening, and then said, 'Look, Charlotte, I think we should talk about the other night.'

This was exactly what I'd been dreading. I forced myself to give a casual shrug. 'Why? Nothing happened, so there's nothing to talk about, is there?'

He frowned, and I could tell he was thrown by my nonchalance. That was fine with me – the last thing I wanted was for him to think that his rejection had hurt or affected me in any way.

'Come on, Charlotte.' He lowered his voice. 'I know you're upset, and I just think it would help if you gave me a chance to explain myself—'

I forced a laugh. 'Don't flatter yourself. I couldn't care less about that night. I just had an itch that needed scratching, and you were the closest man around.'

257

Richard's jaw tightened, and the vein in his neck began to throb. It was worth remembering that this was all it took to annoy him.

'All right, if that's how you want it,' he said finally. I made to walk away again, but then I heard him say, 'Are you still coming to the party on Friday night?'

It took me a second to remember – it was the firm's Christmas party. I'd been looking forward to it before, but now that I'd thrown myself at him, I couldn't think of anywhere I'd less like to be going. Unfortunately if I tried to back out, he'd assume that it was because of him, and I didn't want him to think that – even if it was true.

I looked back, forcing a bright smile. 'Of course I'll be there. You know me – can't keep away from a good party.'

With that, I finally managed to escape. But as I made my way back to my desk, I couldn't help wondering how I was ever going to get through the evening.

That Friday night, I sat in the back of a black cab, nervously picking at the beading on my dress. I was on my way to Vinopolis, the elegant events venue in Southbank where Davenport's Christmas party was being held. Luckily my flat was close enough to the office to allow me to go home to change for the party, and I'd decided to make use of the advantage. A lot of the other staff members weren't so lucky, and had to get ready in the company loos, which meant that by five that evening the ladies' room reeked of hairspray and was full of women jostling for a place in front of the mirror.

I'd picked out my gown two Saturdays ago, when I'd had my hair done. It was a strapless red velvet dress, with a full ballerina skirt, and I'd managed to find heels in the same shade. The dress had a proper bodice, which cinched in my waist and pushed up my bosom, in a flattering but not indecent way. Even though I was dressing more conservatively for work, I still hadn't completely abandoned my unique style – I was just trying to save it for more appropriate occasions. Tonight's dress was the kind of outfit you wore to be noticed.

Even after what had happened with Richard, I'd gone through with my plans to look as spectacular as possible this evening. If nothing else, I was determined to show him what he was missing. I'd planned out every detail. Along with wearing the stunning red dress, I'd borrowed Lindsay's curling wand, and after burning myself a few times, I'd eventually managed to style my hair in loose curls. I'd applied my make-up carefully – losing the heavy eyeliner in favour of just a lick of mascara along with a rose lip gloss – and finished off with a dusting of silver glitter across my shoulders and on my cheeks. Richard might not want me, but I was going to make sure I still had a good time.

It wasn't like me to splash out on a taxi, but with these heels there was no way I was going to be able to walk, so I'd gone ahead and ordered a minicab. Twenty minutes later, the driver pulled along a cobbled street, which led to the private entrance to Vinopolis' Great Hall, where the party was being held. The venue was close to Borough Market, and the whole area had a Dickensian feel. I paid the driver and stepped out into a swirl of women in evening gowns and men in black tie. It was Friday night, two weeks before Christmas, and it seemed everyone in London was out celebrating.

Bouncers stood outside an arched doorway, checking names off a list to keep out gatecrashers. Inside, signs directed me up a huge stone staircase. I dumped my coat in the cloakroom, and then followed the stream of people and thump of the music to the Great Hall.

When I got there, the party was already in full swing. I stood at the entrance for a moment, drinking in the scene. The Great Hall continued the Victorian London theme – it was a vast room, with magnificent high-vaulted ceilings, oak-wood flooring and exposed brickwork. Practically the whole of the London office must have been crammed in – all four hundred of us. But the historic setting contrasted with the modern nightclub feel. Waiters circulated with trays of champagne and canapés, and the lights were low, the music blaring out. A DJ was up on the stage at one end of the room. There were chairs and tables around the outside, surrounding a huge dance floor. The throb of the bass shook the floor. The strobe lights flashed pink and blue, merging into purple.

My eyes searched the sea of people, trying to pick out a familiar face. I couldn't see anyone I knew, so I decided to make my way through the crowd until I stumbled across someone to talk to.

I began to fight my way through, with no luck, until I heard: 'Hello, luvie.' Rex's camp voice rose about the music. I turned to see him elbowing his way towards me. He'd gone all out for the occasion, looking even more flamboyant than usual in an electric-blue velvet suit. The pink cocktail in his hand finished off the look. He kissed me on each cheek, and then held me away from him, his eyes sweeping over me, to take in my outfit. 'Now don't you look a treat?' He nodded approvingly. 'So who are you trying to impress tonight? Come on, don't be shy, you can tell Uncle Rexie.'

I was pleased that with this lighting he couldn't see my cheeks flush red. 'I told you before, I'm not interested in anyone.'

He folded his arms, and pouted. 'Oh, don't play dumb with me. No one comes dressed like that if they're not hoping to catch someone's eye.'

'Oh, leave the poor girl alone.' Helena appeared. I wouldn't have recognised her if it hadn't been for her trademark steely voice. She'd lost the severe glasses, and her hair had been released from its tight bun for the first time since

I'd met her, floating like silk around her shoulders. She had on a black fitted dress, which showed off her slim figure perfectly. 'After all, from what I understand she's not the only one with her eye on someone this evening.' She gave a pointed glance towards Tristan Thorne, an Account Executive who Rex had been nursing a crush on for ages.

'And I have no problem admitting it,' he said. 'In fact, on that note—' He raised his cocktail glass, swallowed down the last of his drink and headed off through the throng, cutting his way towards the unsuspecting Tristan.

Right then, the DJ began to blend into another song, something more familiar. It took me a moment to recognise the opening refrain of Beyoncé's 'Crazy in Love'.

'Oh, I love this!' Helena cried. She cocked an eyebrow. 'Fancy hitting the dance floor?'

To my surprise, she looked deadly serious. It seemed the Christmas Party was bringing out a new side in her tonight. The more pop-y beat had everyone flooding onto the dance floor, but it was too early in the evening for me – I needed some food first. I was about to refuse, but the words stuck in my throat as another familiar face caught my eye – it was Richard, standing a few metres away. He looked tall and dignified in black tie, and I felt the slow flip of my stomach that seemed to be happening whenever he was around lately.

He hadn't spotted me yet, which gave me a chance to stare. He was deep in conversation with Davenport's Managing

Director, Chris Lamb, and a petite redhead, who I assumed was his wife. There was another woman in the group, tall and elegant in a bias-cut white satin evening gown, with silky dark hair falling like a ribbon down her bare back. She was facing away from me at first, and so I simply assumed she was someone from the firm who I didn't recognise. But then Richard must have said something funny, because she turned to laugh, laying a manicured hand on his arm – and that's when I saw her high cheekbones, English rose complexion and green cat's eyes, and realised who she was: Petra Hawthorne.

I instinctively took a step backwards; the shock of her being there was like a physical blow. I thought back to what Richard had told me when we went down to my parents' – he'd said that they were over. Had he lied? Or had my clumsy attempt at making a pass at him driven him back into her arms?

'Are you all right?' Helena touched me lightly on the shoulders. I tore my eyes away and focused instead on my boss. Her look of concern told me just how much seeing Petra with Richard had shaken me.

Somehow I managed a smile. 'I'm fine.'

'You sure?' Her eyes flicked over in Richard's direction, and I wondered how much she'd figured out. She was, after all, pretty shrewd. And she was also, unlike Rex, entirely discreet. If she did suspect anything, she'd never mention it unless I brought it up.

I threaded my arm through hers and forced a bright smile. 'Just desperate to get out there and dance!'

I pulled her over to the dance floor, and concentrated on looking like I was having the time of my life.

We spent the next couple of hours dancing. Helena was a surprisingly good dancer – was there anything she couldn't do? – and moved with a natural rhythm that had everyone looking on. Luckily, we joined up with another group from the creative department, so I was able to bop around with them. It was a typical Christmas party – everyone taking the opportunity to let their hair down after a hard year.

Around ten, the DJ took a break, and the Master of Ceremonies came onto the stage to get the room's attention. 'I understand that your CEO, Richard Davenport, wants to say a few words.'

The waiters were coming round with more champagne, in preparation for what I assumed would be a toast.

Richard took to the stage, and I felt my heart do a little flip. He looked like he'd been born to wear a tux, reminding me of a young James Bond. As he began to speak, the crowd surged forward, towards the stage, but I moved to the side, taking refuge in one of the brick archways. I wanted to be out of sight, so I didn't give my feelings away. I took a sip of champagne, trying to calm myself, but my gaze was drawn back to Richard. I knew I was staring, but fortunately everyone else was looking at him too, so it wouldn't be noticeable. I decided to make the most of the opportunity.

'You're in love with him, aren't you?'

The voice made me jump. I turned to find Petra standing behind me. Close up, I could see just how stunning she looked tonight. She wore a floor-length white satin sheath – a simple, classic look. Next to her, in my clinging red velvet, I felt tacky and obvious.

But her eyes weren't on me – she was looking across the room at Richard.

'I'm referring to Richard, by the way,' she said, finally shifting her attention to me. 'You're in love with him, aren't you?'

My arms folded protectively over my chest, an instinctive move. 'I don't know what you mean—' I started, but she waved a hand, cutting me off.

'Oh, don't bother lying to me.' Her eyes were narrow like a cat's, and suddenly the nice girl act was dropped. 'I never liked the two of you spending time together, but at least at first neither of you wanted to see the other in a romantic way. Then that last time I met you, it was written all over your face.'

I thought back to the time she was referring to – that night we'd run into her in Davenport's reception. It was about the time I'd realised I had a crush on Richard. But that's all it was, surely? How could she think I was in love with him?

'You're wrong—'

Petra gave a light chuckle. 'Am I? Well, I can understand why you couldn't admit it to yourself. You honestly think he's going to want anything to do with a whore like you?' She shook her head, as though she'd never heard anything so ridiculous. 'I mean, exactly how many guys have you slept with? Do you even know? And you think a sought-after man like Richard, who could have his pick of women, is going to so much as look at you?'

'Maybe not,' I fired back, refusing to let her see that she'd hurt me. 'But from what I heard, he isn't particularly inter-ested in an uptight bitch like you, either. Didn't he dump your over-primed arse?'

But instead of looking phased by my attack, Petra simply shrugged. 'That's right. We did break up. But we're here together now.' A little smile played around her mouth. 'And even if it doesn't ultimately work out between us, let's face it – when he does settle down, I can guarantee that it'll be with someone who's more like me than you.'

I wanted to cut her down with a sharp retort – I really did. But there was nothing I could say to that, because honestly, deep down I knew she was right.

Petra could obviously see that she'd got the reaction she'd wanted, so she raised her glass to me. 'Enjoy your evening, Charlotte.'

Then she picked up the skirt of her gown, and swept off, leaving me standing alone.

I looked back over at Richard, who was concluding his speech, to a round of applause. What had I been thinking? That I could change my hair and put on a pretty dress and somehow make him want me? Whatever I did, he'd never see me as anything other than the immature party girl, who slept her way through London.

I tore my eyes away from him, and swept the room. My gaze finally settled on Miles Fairfax, the obnoxious Account Manager who had briefed us on PURE before I screwed up. He was sitting up at the bar, not even bothering to pretend he was listening to Richard's speech.

I walked over and slid onto the stool next to him. He swivelled round to face me. If he was surprised to see me there, he didn't show it. His eyes swept over me, spending far too long on my cleavage, and I could see a spark of interest. Miles had never once acknowledged me in the office – I was of no use to him there – but it was clearly going to be a different matter tonight.

'Hey . . . you.' I could see him searching for my name, and failing to recall it. I didn't give a damn. All that I cared about right now were the endless stories I'd heard of him bedding half the ladies at Davenport's. He fixed me with what he no doubt considered to be his most winning smile. 'You're looking stunning tonight, if you don't mind me saying.'

'You scrubbed up pretty well yourself.' I signalled for the bartender, and flashed Miles my party-girl grin. 'So – what're we drinking?'

Chapter 20

'Another one?' Miles held up the tequila bottle for my perusal. He had to shout to be heard over the music. I knew the answer he was looking for, but I couldn't find it in me to give it to him. The thought of getting wasted with him made me feel nothing except exhaustion.

Miles and I were three shots in, but unfortunately the alcohol hadn't made him seem any more appealing. He'd spent most of the past half hour telling me how great he was at his job, which was true, but also frankly boring. But that had never been a deal-breaker for me before. A few months back, I'd routinely taken guys to bed who were much bigger jackasses than him. When had I become so discerning?

'I'll skip this round,' I said.

He gave a 'suit yourself' shrug, and poured another shot for himself. As he downed it, I swivelled my bar stool so I was facing away from him, and looking out into the crowd of partygoers. I wasn't even aware of what I was looking for at first, and then my eyes found Richard.

He was standing in a group, chatting, but his gaze kept flicking over to me – and Miles. Knowing Richard was watching us suddenly made me reassess the whole situation. I wanted to show him that he was nothing to me – that when I'd kissed him it had meant as little to me as it apparently had to him. And I knew exactly how to do that.

I turned my attention back to Miles. He'd just poured himself another shot. It was halfway to his lips, when I caught hold of his hand. Looking up at him beneath lowered lashes, I took the glass from him, and downed the shot.

'What do you think about getting out of here?' I drawled.

Miles blinked a couple of times, obviously confused by my sudden about-face and wondering if I was being serious. 'You what?'

'You heard me.' I slid from the stool and took him by the hand. 'Come on. Let's find somewhere that we can be alone.'

A slow grin spread over Miles's face. 'Why not?'

I flicked a look over at Richard, just to make sure he was still watching. His eyes were narrow, his jaw tight. Then I tossed my head back and started to lead Miles towards the exit.

We were almost at the door when Richard materialised in front of us. He ignored Miles, and fixed his gaze on me.

'Charlotte.' He spoke my name with a quiet fury. His eyes glittered with anger, and I could see it was taking all his self-control not to explode. 'Can you come with me for a moment please?'

Before I had a chance to object, he took me by the elbow, and began to usher me outside. I could guess that as much as he wanted to talk to me, he also didn't want to create a scene when everyone who worked for him could see. It crossed my mind to refuse to go with him, but deep down I knew that this was what I'd wanted all along – to get his attention.

'Hey—' Miles began to object, but a look from Richard silenced him and he held up his hands and backed off.

My heart was hammering hard in my chest as Richard led me outside into a large, empty hallway. I had no idea what he was planning to say or do, but I sensed that we were at a turning point, and all I could do was wait to see how it played out. The doors to the Great Hall slammed shut behind us, so all we could hear out there were the muffled sounds of the party. Richard looked around. His eyes settled on a side room. He walked over, and checked that there was no one inside.

'In here,' he commanded. I did as he said and went in. It was a small conference room, with an oval table in the middle that could accommodate twelve people. It must have been where the Vinopolis staff held their meetings.

As soon as the door was closed, Richard rounded on me. 'What the hell were you playing at in there?'

I leaned back against the table, affecting boredom. 'What did it look like? I was trying to get laid.'

His mouth twisted in disgust. 'Jesus, Charlotte—'

'What?' I challenged. 'You don't like that I sleep around?'

Petra's words were still ringing in my head. I hated that her slut-shaming had bothered me so much. And I was determined to defend myself. If Richard didn't want me because I slept around, then that was his problem. But I refused to feel bad about this a second longer.

'What is it with men and their double standards?' I shook my head in disgust. 'If I was a guy, you'd be slapping me on the back and congratulating me. Instead, because I'm female, you act like there's something wrong with me because I enjoy sex. Like I'm damaged goods, or something.'

Richard's eyes widened. 'Is that seriously what you think? Because trust me, nothing could be further from the truth. I have no problem with a woman enjoying sex, or having as many partners as she wants. But what I hate is seeing you lowering yourself to sleeping with men who are beneath you. Men like that scum—' he spat out the word – 'Because I know you're better than that. And I just want you to realise it.'

Now I was confused. 'If that's the case, then why did you push me away that night in my flat?' A horrible thought occurred to me. 'Oh, God. Do you really find me that repulsive?'

He rolled his eyes in exasperation. 'No. It wasn't that.'

'Then what was it? Why don't you want me?'

He turned away. 'Just leave it, Charlotte—'

'I can't! I need to know—'

'Because I was scared!' He whirled round, his eyes flashing with pent up anger. 'Because I was scared of how I felt about you!'

It took me a moment to work out what he was saying. Had I heard him right? Because if I had, then it sounded like he had feelings for me.

Anticipation reared inside me. I was suddenly completely sober.

'I don't understand.' My eyes searched his. 'What exactly are you saying?'

He turned away and walked towards the window that looked out on the street below. In the reflection, I could see him sigh, and run a hand across his face. For a moment, I thought he wasn't going to answer, but then he started to speak, in a hollow, almost distant voice.

'Hasn't it ever occurred to you that every person I've cared about has died? First my parents, which was bad enough, and then your brother. Do you know what it's like to recover from losses like that? How hard it is not to let the grief consume you? It's one of the reasons I haven't wanted

273

to get close to any woman over the years. And up until now, it's worked for me. Because I'd never met anyone who I felt strongly enough about to want to let in.'

He paused, and turned to face me. 'And then I find myself developing feelings for you, of all people. I've always cared about you, about your family, but lately . . . it's been different. Something changed between us.'

I could see the confusion on his face, and understood it – because I'd felt it, too. That odd sensation of being around someone for so long, but only just feeling like you were getting to know them.

'So I find myself falling for you . . . this person who's living their life on self-destruct.' He shook his head in disbelief. 'Do you know how terrifying that is? That night in your flat, when you kissed me, all I could think was: how can I be with someone who seems to have a death wish? Who has so little regard for their life?' There was a catch in his throat, the sound of real agony. 'Because I couldn't stand to lose anyone else. And I'm not sure you can promise to keep yourself safe.

'So that's why I pulled away that night – because I didn't want to get close to you. Because if I do – if I allow myself to feel what I'm feeling – I also open myself up to all the pain that would come with losing you.'

I stood, stunned. It had never occurred to me before that Richard had been so deeply affected by what had happened. I knew of course that he'd grieved for his parents and for Kit

– I appreciated that they were both devastating moments in his life. But he'd always seemed so together, as though he could cope with anything. It was a shock to find that he was frightened, too.

'Then why are you here?' I said finally. 'If you're scared to be with me?'

His face softened. 'Because I realised tonight that I'm more scared to be without you.' He took a step forward, towards me. 'Seeing you with Miles . . . I couldn't stand the thought of you being with him. And that's when I knew, however much I might want to deny it, I'm falling for you.'

I felt happiness surge up inside me. Part of me just wanted to end the conversation there, and let him kiss me, but there was something that was still bothering me. I stepped back away from him, so I could keep my head clear. For once, I wanted to think before I acted. 'But I don't understand. If that's how you feel about me, then why did you bring Petra tonight?'

'Petra?' He looked genuinely confused. 'I didn't.'

'Oh, please. I saw her talking to you earlier.' Not to mention what she said to me, I wanted to add.

His face cleared. 'Yes, she's here tonight, but not as my date. She started seeing Carl Wilcox, one of the art directors, after they worked on a shoot together. She's with him.'

The events of the evening clicked into place. How naïve guys could be. Petra might be here with Carl, but she was still clearly after Richard. But I suppose as long as he wasn't interested back, then there was no harm.

'I guess I got it wrong,' I said. I could have told him about what Petra had said, but somehow I didn't feel inclined to now. Knowing she was still hung up on Richard, and yet he was here with me, I couldn't help feeling sorry for her.

'I guess you did.' He smiled a little. 'But it's nice to see you jealous. Now,' he said, drawing closer to me. 'Have I answered every question to your satisfaction?'

Before I had a chance to respond, he kissed me.

Unlike last time, in my flat, there was no sense of him holding back and taking things slow. His mouth was firm and demanding against mine, his hands in my hair, as he kissed me like his life depended on it. The control he usually displayed seemed to have deserted him. He couldn't seem to get enough of me, and before I knew what was happening, he was backing me up against the table, lifting me in one deft move so I was sitting on top of it. My legs instinctively wrapped around his waist. As his erection rubbed against the gusset of my underwear, I felt myself moisten. It reminded me of how I'd reacted that night we'd kissed in my flat. My body seemed to respond to him in ways I never remembered experiencing before.

But I didn't want to start analysing that now. Instead I tugged out his shirt, my hands smoothing over the warm flesh of his back. His lips were on my neck, and my head dropped back. It was only when I reached for the zipper of his trousers that I felt Richard tense. His hands came down to stop me, and with a groan of frustration, he pulled away.

From where I was perched on the table, I frowned up at him. 'What now?'

'This isn't right.' He ran a hand through his hair, clearly trying to get himself under control. 'We're not doing it here, like this. As much as I may want to.'

'Are you serious——?'

'Deadly.' He took a step forward, closing the gap between us. His gaze fixed on me, dark and intense, like he was hypnotising me. 'That night at your flat, when you kissed me? I wanted you so badly. Do you know the willpower it took to walk away from you then?' He reached out, his right hand cupping my face. I was looking directly into his eyes, so I could see the sincerity there, as his words rolled over me like silk. 'I don't want to be just another one-night stand to you – a quick roll in the sack. When we sleep together, I want it to mean something. I want you to feel every moment – not to be so drunk you can't remember what happened or enjoy the way I touch you.'

I felt warm desire spread through my belly. For so long, sex had meant nothing to me. Richard was right – I'd had so many sexual encounters, and yet I wasn't sure if I'd ever enjoyed any of them. I knew instinctively that it would be different with him.

He bent his head so his mouth was close to mine. 'When we sleep together, I want every second to be exquisite pleasure.'

I gasped as he drew his thumb across my bottom lip. How was it that such a simple gesture was more erotic than all the one-night stands I'd had?

'I want to wine you and dine you,' he went on. 'Treat you properly.' His eyes twinkled wickedly. 'And then, at the end of it all, seduce you.'

The thought sent shivers through me. 'How very old-fashioned of you.'

Even though I felt a bit frustrated, I had to admit that I secretly liked the way he was thinking – it would make a change to go on a proper date.

'So when are we going to do this dinner?'

'How does tomorrow night sound?'

'Perfect.' Our gaze held for a moment, and I felt my breath catch. It was going to take all my willpower to make it through to tomorrow night. 'Well, I suppose we better get back to the party,' I said reluctantly.

'I suppose we should.' He held out a hand, and I hopped down from the table. We walked hand in hand towards the door. When we got there, Richard stopped, and turned back to me. 'I'll text you details about our date tomorrow.'

His head dipped down to murmur in my ear. 'And trust me when I say – I can't wait.'

His throaty voice was full of promise. Before I could respond, he opened the door for me. I floated back to the party, already feeling impatient for it to be tomorrow night.

Chapter 21

'What the hell—?' Lindsay sat up from where she'd been stretched out on the sofa watching Saturday night TV, and stared at me bug-eyed from across the back of the chair.

I glanced down at myself, chewing at the inside of my mouth. 'Is it really that bad?'

After the excitement of arranging my date with Richard last night, I'd come crashing back down to earth over the course of today. It hadn't helped that he'd been cagey about where we were going tonight. He'd texted me that morning to say that he was sending a car for me at seven thirty, to take me for dinner. But he wanted to keep the destination a surprise. I'd asked him what I should wear, and he'd told me 'whatever you feel comfortable in'. But I wasn't stupid enough to fall for that. Richard was used to frequenting the best restaurants in London, and I imagined wherever we went, it was going to be somewhere upmarket, which meant trying to look glamorous and sophisticated.

At the back of my wardrobe, I'd found a strapless black cocktail dress, and teamed it with a pair of black heels and a fitted jacket – a simple, classic look. I'd kept my make-up light, like I had the previous evening, and found a YouTube video to teach me how to fashion my hair into an elegant chignon. It took a few tries, but eventually I'd got it – or so I thought. My final test had been coming out here, to see what Lindsay thought. And she obviously wasn't impressed.

I wiped a hand over my face, inadvertently pulling some strands of hair, and disturbing the style I'd spent hours perfecting. 'Maybe I should just cancel this whole thing.' I spoke almost to myself. 'I don't know what I was thinking . . .'

This felt even more nerve-wracking than the time we'd been going for lunch with my parents a couple of weeks ago. I was so used to wearing what I wanted and not giving a damn – caring about what I looked like was a whole new experience for me.

Lindsay jumped up. 'What? You want to cancel? No way!'

Now I was confused. 'But you seemed so shocked—'

'Because you look so *different*.' She came to stand in front of me. 'All dressed up like that.' She gave a soft, proud smile. 'You look amazing.'

Relief flooded through me. 'Really?'

'Richard won't know what hit him.' I felt a blush rising in my cheeks, and Lindsay peered at me closely. 'God, you really like him, don't you? I've never seen you care what a guy thinks before.'

Thankfully before I had a chance to respond, the intercom sounded, making us both jump. It was Richard's driver, here to take me to him. I felt my stomach start to churn again.

Lindsay must have seen the worry on my face, because she wrapped me in her arms. 'Now forget all your worries, and just go and have a wonderful time.' She pulled away a little and gave me a suggestive wink. 'And I better not see you back here before lunchtime tomorrow at the earliest!'

I turned away then, not wanting her to see that the last comment had made my cheeks turn an even deeper shade of red. I didn't understand what was happening to me. Usually I had no problem telling my best friend the most intimate details of my sex life, and now I was blushing at even the suggestion of physical contact.

Downstairs, I found the chauffeur-driven black Mercedes that Richard had sent to pick me up. The driver – a young, good-looking man in a dark suit – got out to open the door for me.

'So where are you taking me?' I asked straight off.

'Sorry, can't tell you,' he said with a smile. 'I'm under strict instructions not to reveal the location.'

I thought about refusing to go anywhere until I knew more, but it seemed a bit immature, so I got into the car, and settled against the buttery leather seats.

I watched out of the window as we drove through the streets of London, trying to figure out our destination. As we drove east, I realised we were heading towards Canary Wharf, which surprised me. I would have thought we'd be going out in the West End. I then started to suspect we were heading to a restaurant near to where Richard lived – that is, until we pulled up outside his apartment building.

I waited until the driver switched off the ignition. 'This is where you were told to drop me?'

'That's right.' From the amused look on his face, I guessed that he'd been primed to expect my surprise. He got out and came round to open the car door for me. 'Mr Davenport said that you're to go straight up to his apartment.'

The porter on the front desk took my name, and let Richard know I was on my way. As I waited for the lift, I wondered what the hell Richard was playing at. All I could imagine was that he'd got held up, and had decided it would be easier for me to meet him here, and that we'd then go on somewhere together.

The lift reached the top floor, where Richard's apartment was located. As I stepped out, I felt the flutter of nerves return. I walked down the long carpeted corridor, and when I rounded the corner, my heart turned over as I saw Richard standing in the doorway, looking tall and strong in faded blue jeans and a Diesel t-shirt. His feet were bare, and his usually slicked back hair was wet and mussed up, like he'd just got out of the shower. It was the most casually dressed I'd seen him for years, and he looked far younger than usual.

As I drank him in, his eyes ran over me too, taking in the curve of my breasts and hips. It was strange, having him appraise me in that sexual way.

He took a step forward to meet me as I drew near. 'It feels almost too obvious to point out – but you look absolutely beautiful tonight.' He rested his arms lightly on my upper arms, as he bent to kiss me on both cheeks, his lips lingering a little longer than necessary. I breathed in the masculine scent of his body wash. He drew away a little, and looked down at his t-shirt and jeans. 'I'm beginning to wish I'd made more of an effort now.'

I frowned a little at that, still confused about what was going on. I'd been expecting him to say he needed to change. 'So we're going somewhere casual?'

He stepped back, to allow me into the hallway of his flat. 'Actually, I thought we'd eat here.'

I could feel my eyes widening in surprise. 'You're cooking?'

He grinned. 'No need to sound quite so horrified.'

'Not horrified. Surprised.' He looked at me quizzically. 'I expected you to take me to some swanky restaurant.' As he helped me out of my jacket, I had a thought. 'Or were you worried I wouldn't behave myself in public? I guess you'd rather save the fancy restaurants for the likes of Petra.' I said it jokingly, but to be honest part of me wondered if perhaps I'd hit the nail on the head.

'Is that really what you think?' He hung my jacket up, and then indicated for me to follow him along the hallway. 'Because if you don't want to eat here, I'm sure I can get a reservation elsewhere—'

As Richard finished speaking, he pushed open the door to the entertaining area. I gasped as I stepped inside. Before, I'd only ever seen the place in the harsh light of day, and thought of it as a cold, sterile place. But tonight it had been transformed into the perfect romantic setting. The lights had been dimmed, and instead there was a soft, warm glow from the flames of dozens of candles placed around the room. Jazz music played softly in the background. The dark oak table had been beautifully set for two. The smell of garlic and onions and a rich, creamy sauce wafted over, reminding me of a French restaurant.

It struck me then how much effort Richard had gone to in order to make tonight special. And I'd accused him of wanting to stay in because he was too ashamed to be seen with me . . .

Richard materialised in front of me, a small smile playing on his lips. He'd obviously guessed what was going through my mind. 'Going out to a top London restaurant – I do that all the time. It means nothing to me. It's just . . . an ordinary day. And I wanted tonight to be special.' He waited a beat. 'So it's up to you. We can stay here, or I can take you to a Michelin-starred restaurant . . .'

'Staying in sounds good,' I said softly. I glanced down at myself. 'Only I wish you'd told me what we were doing. Then I would have worn something a bit more comfortable.'

'I did say to wear what you wanted.'

'But I didn't think you meant it!'

'Well, I can't say I'm sorry for the confusion.' His eyes swept over me again, and he looked up at me from lowered lids. 'I think it worked out rather well. For me at least.'

Unbelievably, I felt myself starting to blush again. I really hoped this wasn't going to turn into a habit.

'Anyway.' Richard held out his hand, as though he was inviting me to dance. 'Why don't you come this way?'

I put my hand in his, and he led me over to the kitchen. There were stools tucked under the central island. He pulled one out and gestured for me to sit down.

'Would you like something to drink?' He went over to his wine fridge, and after a second pulled out a bottle. 'Champagne perhaps?'

'I didn't think you liked me drinking,' I teased.

'I don't like you so drunk that you can't stand up. There's a difference. A big difference.'

He poured me a glass of Taittinger, and then turned his attention back to cooking. I watched as he laid out pieces of pancetta on a baking tray and put them in the oven.

'I'd offer to help, but frankly my culinary skills aren't up to much.'

'Yeah, I guessed from the state of your flat that you weren't exactly a domestic goddess. But don't worry. I have it all under control. The first course should be ready soon.'

'First course?' I raised an eyebrow. 'Don't tell me you're good at cooking, too?'

He half turned and grinned. 'I'll let you be the judge of that.'

Ten minutes later, the starter was ready – pan-fried scallops with cauliflower purée.

He carried the plates over to the dining table, which had been set at one end, with us on corners next to each other.

'This looks fabulous,' I said, as he placed the food in front of me.

He topped up our champagne, and I raised a glass. 'To a wonderful cook.'

His eyes fixed on mine. 'And a wonderful evening.'

We clinked glasses. Richard held my gaze as we drank, and I felt a shiver of anticipation run through me.

'No wonder you have so many girlfriends,' I said, sitting back in my chair an hour later. We'd just finished the main course – rack of lamb, cooked perfectly pink, drizzled with red wine and shallot jus, and served with rosemary roasted potatoes and crisp green beans. It had been just as exquisite as the starter. 'If I'd known you could cook like this, I'd have gone out with you a damned sight sooner.'

Richard picked up the plates and carried them to the kitchen. 'Actually, I've never cooked for anyone else before.'

'Seriously? Why not?'

He shrugged. 'I just like to keep my home life separate.'

'What – from your personal life?'

He didn't answer – perhaps sensing how odd that sounded. Instead he picked up the wine bottle, and brought it over to top up our glasses. It was a rich, fruity red, to complement the lamb. He'd obviously put as much thought into the wine as the food, and I couldn't help feeling flattered. After all, I was used to guys trying to get *me* to pay for *their* drinks.

I sipped at my wine, and thought about what he'd just said, the alcohol emboldening me to pry deeper. 'So, why did you cook for me then?'

'Because I wanted tonight to be different . . . to be special.'

It was my turn to go quiet. I had no idea how to respond. This was so far out of my comfort zone.

'Anyway,' Richard said, saving me from answering. 'That's enough confessions for now. How about some dessert?'

Part of me wanted to dig deeper, but there'd be time for that later. So instead, I decided to go along with him.

'Dessert?' My hand went instinctively to my stomach. 'I'm not sure I can manage anything else.'

'Trust me. You'll want to make room for this.'

As he headed back to the kitchen and turned on the oven, I studied him through narrowed eyes. It was strange – I felt almost shy around him. It was ridiculous of course, given that we'd known each other for so long, plus I wasn't exactly the kind of girl who got shy around guys. But that was how he made me feel. Then it suddenly struck me why I felt that way – I cared about how tonight turned out. Usually I didn't give a damn if I saw the guy again. But with Richard, I wanted this to work, and the pressure was making me nervous.

'Charlotte?' The sound of my name snapped me out of my reverie. I looked up to see Richard frowning at me in concern. 'Are you all right?'

'I'm fine.' And then I wondered why I was being so damned polite. If we were going to make this work, we both needed to stop being on our best behaviour. 'As long as you stop calling me that.'

'What?'

'Charlotte. I keep telling you it's Charlie, but you always insist on Charlotte. Why is that? Just to piss me off?'

'Not at all!' he protested, and then his face relaxed a little. 'Well, maybe sometimes I do it to annoy you. But mostly it's just because I think Charlotte suits you better.'

'How come?'

He thought about it for a moment. 'Charlie sounds like a goofy little boy – it makes me think of Charlie and the Chocolate Factory. Charlotte suits you better. It's a prettier name, more grown up, I suppose.' I liked the sound of that. 'But if it really bothers you, I'll switch to Charlie.'

When he put it like that, there wasn't much of a contest. Suddenly the name Charlotte had never sounded more desirable to me. 'No. Charlotte's fine.'

'Good.' He raised an eyebrow. 'So . . . what do you think about having that dessert, *Charlotte*?'

'That sounds lovely, *Richard*.'

Laughing, he headed to the oven. I watched as he plated up a perfectly round chocolate fondant, and added a scoop of vanilla ice cream and decorated it with a raspberry.

'You made that too?' I said, as he took a sieve, and covered the top of the fondant with a dusting of icing sugar. 'I'm impressed. Although you do know that you can save yourself a lot of trouble and just buy ready-made ones from the supermarket.'

Richard rolled his eyes. 'Ungrateful wretch.'

He carried over the plate and placed it in front of me. I frowned. 'You're not having anything?'

A slow grin spread over Richard's face. 'I thought we

could share. As long as you don't have any objections, that is?'

I shook my head, because I couldn't trust myself to speak. I was frozen, immobilised by the moment, and where it was going to lead. Seeming to sense my hesitation, Richard picked up a spoon and plunged it into the dessert. Hot chocolate goo oozed out. He added some ice cream, and then held the spoon out for me to try.

It was a deliberately intimate move. As I took a bite of the sweet, warm chocolate, our eyes locked, and I felt the last of my appetite vanish. It took all my effort to chew and swallow the dessert down.

'That was pretty spectacular,' I said finally, even though I'd hardly been able to taste anything.

'I'm glad you liked it. Do you want some more?'

I had a feeling he already knew the answer, but I shook my head anyway. I heard the clink of the spoon as he placed it on the plate. He leaned in towards me. My lips parted and I felt my heartbeat speed up with the anticipation. But before anything could happen, the music abruptly cut out, causing us both to pull back, startled.

Richard groaned. 'Great timing.' He got to his feet. 'I'll sort that out and be right back.'

As he disappeared off to fix the sound system, I took the opportunity to wipe my sweaty palms on my dress. I couldn't understand what was wrong with me. We were clearly at the seduction part of the evening, which was meant to be my area of expertise. But then why was my skin suddenly hot, and my stomach churning with nerves? I reached for my wine glass, gulping down the last of the alcohol, but that didn't seem to help. If anything, my breathing seemed more uneven, like I was heading for a panic attack.

I glanced wildly around the room, searching for something to help me out. My eyes settled on the half-finished wine bottle in the middle of the table. I snatched it up, and then headed over to the nearby couch. If we were going to do this, we needed to be somewhere more comfortable.

I'd just settled myself on the sofa when the music started up again. I looked up to see Richard coming over to join me. He watched me through narrowed eyes as I downed the last mouthful of wine. When I reached for the bottle, he put his hand out to stop me.

'Oh no you don't.' He took the glass from me, and set it down on the side table.

'Hey!' I protested.

'I told you before, Charlotte – I want you to remember every moment of tonight.' He cupped my face with one strong hand, his thumb slowly caressing my cheek. 'Every. Single. Moment.' He inched forward, his mouth moving towards me. 'Do you think you can do that?'

My breath hitched in my throat, and all I could do was nod.

Any objections I felt slipped away, as he bent his head and kissed me.

Chapter 22

I'd braced myself for the kiss, but I still wasn't fully prepared for the intensity of it. Richard's mouth was hot and hungry against mine, eager to finally experience what we'd been denying ourselves for so long.

I closed my eyes tighter, and tried to relax, as his hands began to roam my body. But I was too present, too in the moment. There was a reason I'd wanted the alcohol. It was to numb me, to make this easier. Last night, when he'd touched me, I'd been anaesthetised by tequila. Drunk, I could handle this. Sober, I wasn't so sure. I wanted to. God, how I wanted to . . .

Then his lips parted mine, and something clicked in me. I could feel myself closing off, my defences rising, my body going still and cold. I couldn't understand why this felt so uncomfortable. After all the guys I'd slept with – who I'd never given a damn about – why was it now, when I was finally with someone decent, that I was freezing up?

Richard's mouth was on my neck. As he reached for my breasts, my hands closed into fists. I tried to keep my breathing steady. If I could just stay focused on the moment, and not let the dark thoughts in, then maybe I could get through this.

If I could just get through tonight . . . Perhaps after this first time, it wouldn't be so bad. I reached for his t-shirt, pulling it up, wanting to get things moving. But he broke away a little, stilling me.

'Not so fast,' he murmured. 'There's no rush. We've got all night.'

His patience surprised me. Every other guy I'd been with had just wanted it over with – wham bam, thank you, mam – which had suited me just fine. But Richard was different. I could already see how he wanted this to play out – a slow build-up on the couch; an eventual adjournment to the bedroom. Agonisingly slow. He didn't seem to get it. He wanted this to be a long seduction, and I just wanted it over with.

He needed me to enjoy this, but I knew there was no way I could ever relax enough. The knowledge brought a rush of tears. He didn't deserve this, and neither did I. My heart was galloping, the breath catching in my chest. I was struggling not to crack. And Richard was completely unaware of it.

As if to prove my point, he chose that moment to draw away a little, tipping my chin up so he could look deep in my eyes.

'You're so beautiful, Charlotte.'

They were the words that every girl wanted to hear, spoken with such sincerity from someone who they felt deeply for. But for me, they were the final straw. I couldn't stand it another moment. As he went to take me in his arms again, I reared back, my hands hitting his hard chest and pushing him away so abruptly that he fell backwards against the cushions.

'For fuck's sake, just stop it, will you?'

My shrill words tore through the moment, leaving it in ruins.

Before Richard could react, I was already off the sofa and on my feet, putting distance between us. It might have seemed brutal, but I was closing myself off from him in the only way I knew how.

It was only when I felt far away enough that I dared to sneak a look at Richard, who was still over on the couch. I watched him sit up slowly. His dark hair was tousled, his clothes dishevelled. He'd never looked better.

'What is it?' The concern and confusion on his face made my heart ache. He stood, his natural reaction being to come and comfort me. But then he saw me take another step back and he froze, frowning. 'What did I do?'

I knew why he didn't understand. It wasn't like he'd caught my wrists in his hands or held me down. But that was the problem. That I could deal with. It was the tenderness that did me in.

'You were being nice, okay? Just so fucking *nice* that I couldn't stand it.'

He stared at me for a long moment, digesting my words. 'Are you being serious?'

I could see him turning over what I'd said in his mind, trying to make sense of it. Then finally he shook his head. 'I'm sorry. I just don't get it.'

'Come on,' I scoffed. 'All this romance, the big seduction.' I gestured round the room at the remnants of our evening. 'It's all an act, isn't it? You might light a few candles and cook a nice meal, but when it comes down to it, all you want to do is fuck me, like every other guy.' I took a step forward, feeling bolder now that I was back to my old self. 'So let's cut the crap. There's no need for flowery words and compliments. I'm a sure thing, so can we just get this done already?'

The confusion was clear on Richard's face. 'You're saying you didn't enjoy this evening?'

He didn't seem to get it. I didn't want love. I didn't want romance. This for me was never about feelings. It was about fucking – nothing more. And him trying to pretend otherwise was making it worse.

'I'm just saying it's all pretty meaningless. Seriously, have you ever asked yourself why you even make all of these romantic gestures? I bet deep down it's because it makes you feel better about yourself. You come away from the night feeling like less of a dick, right? You buy a girl dinner, open a few doors, and you think you're Prince fucking Charming. You look down on guys like Gavin, call them scum, but when it comes down to it, you're no better than them. You both want the same thing – a quick roll in the sack. They're just more honest about it. And I'm saying with me, you don't need to pretend.'

I reached round and unzipped my dress. The material fell from me, pooling in a heap on the floor by my feet, and leaving me standing in nothing but my underwear – a black, lacy push-up bra and matching low-rise shorts, put on with such hope earlier tonight, and now just a tool to torture a man who could have meant so much to me.

Richard took a step back, even as his eyes moved over me. 'Don't do this, Charlotte . . .'

'Why not?' My voice was low and throaty. Like this, I was in control. 'You don't have to pretend with me. I'm not looking for a gentleman.'

His jaw clenched. I could tell I was on the verge of pushing him too far, but I didn't care. I might not understand why I was reacting this way, but I knew he was to blame. He was the one who wouldn't let me get drunk. He was the one who'd insisted on trying to make this something I hadn't wanted. He'd pushed me to be Charlotte, when I was happier as Charlie. And now I planned to punish him; to hurt him the same way he'd hurt me.

I walked towards him slowly. Despite his best intentions, I saw the way his gaze drifted over my body. How much did he hate himself right now? I reached round to unclasp my bra.

'Just tell me what you want,' I murmured. 'I bet you like to get nasty, huh? All those hours in the office, pretending to be so perfect. Now it's time to unleash.'

My bra fell to the floor, and Richard drew a sharp intake of breath. As I drew level with him, he caught my shoulders in a tight grip, no doubt intending to push me away, but somehow he couldn't bring himself to do it. So I bit my lower lip and pressed my body against his, feeling a surge of triumph as his erection twitched against me.

'Fuck me, Davenport.' I looked up at him from lowered lashes. 'Right here. Right now.'

I was deliberately baiting him, and I'd expected him to react angrily. But instead he held his ground, refusing to let me chase him away. 'What the hell happened to you, Charlotte?' he said softly. 'What happened to make you this way?'

I went very still, unnerved by the shift in the conversation. 'I don't know what you're talking about.'

'Cut the crap. You don't need to pretend with me.'

I saw the resolve in his eyes. He was calling me out, refusing to let me hide behind my bravado any longer. The realisation sent a fresh wave of panic through me. I suddenly felt ridiculous, standing here half naked. I dropped to the floor, scooping up my bra, fumbling as I put it on. I didn't like the turn of this conversation. Not one little bit. There was nothing for it but distraction.

'You know, if you weren't up to it, you could've just said.' I kept my voice light, as I picked up my dress. 'Performance anxiety's nothing to be ashamed of.'

But Richard wasn't going to be put off that easily. 'Charlotte, what happened?'

I started to back away. This was getting too deep. 'So I'm guessing I should be on my way.' I made a point of glancing at my watch. 'And don't worry – I never kiss and tell. This'll stay just between us.'

'It was a long time ago, wasn't it?' he persisted. 'But still not long enough for you to move on.'

What was he saying? What was he implying? Deep in my subconscious, I felt a flicker of recognition, but I didn't want to think about that now.

'What can I say?' I said instead. 'It's been a fun night, but I guess we weren't meant to be. Let's put this down to experience.'

'Charlotte—'

'Just drop it, will you?' My eyes unexpectedly filled with tears. Even I was surprised by the anguish in my voice. 'Why can't you just drop this already?'

'Because I care about you!' he exploded, dark eyes glittering with anger. 'Because I hate to see you hurting like this! I'm tired of seeing you trying to self-destruct. And I think you're tired of it, too. So talk to me.' His voice was gentler now. 'Tell me what happened to you. And maybe you and I can sort this out once and for all.'

I stared at him for a long moment. 'You really want to know what happened to me?' I said finally.

His eyes were solemn, as he said, 'I do.'

'Then here it is. My big, dark secret.' I paused dramatically, and then allowed a smirk to cross my face. 'I failed to get laid tonight.'

I could see Richard's disappointment with my answer, but I didn't care.

'Now, if that's the end of amateur psychology hour, I'm going home.' I strode for the door.

'At least let me call you a car.'

His voice was so filled with defeat that it made my heart contract. Richard was usually so strong. But I had done this to him. I had broken him.

And yet still I wouldn't relent. I grabbed my jacket from the hallway cupboard, and yanked the door open. 'Don't bother. I can get home fine on my own.'

'Charlotte, please!' His hand was on the door, holding it closed. 'However angry you are at me right now, I want to make sure that you get home safely.'

His eyes were pleading with me. Suddenly I remembered his confession about his fear of losing people he loved – a fear that had come from the death of his parents and my brother.

'Why? Because you're worried something might happen to me?' My lips twisted into a nasty grin. Before, the knowledge had made me feel for him. Now, it was just another way to wound him. 'That's your demon, not mine.'

The shock of my cruelty made him loosen his grip, and gave me the opportunity I was looking for. I got the door open. And then I was out in the hallway, shrugging my coat on as I headed for the lift.

Moments later, I stumbled from the apartment block. The bitter night air was like ice against my bare face, freezing the tears to my cheeks. I hadn't dressed for the weather, and would have been better off waiting in reception for a cab. But I just wanted to be gone now, away from this place. So I stuffed my hands into the pockets of my thin jacket, and concentrated on just putting one foot in front of the other. Keep walking, keep moving, and eventually everything will be all right.

I headed towards the Tube station. At the end of the street, I paused and looked back into the still, silent night. No Richard. And even though I didn't blame him, I still couldn't help feeling disappointed.

I turned the corner, and made my way home.

Chapter 23

I was hardly aware of how I got home that night. Luckily the lift was available, because there was no way I could have dragged myself up the stairs. As if on autopilot, I managed to get my keys out of my bag, and opened the door. I walked into the sitting room, hoping to lose myself in some mindless television, and froze as I saw Lindsay and Adrian making out on the couch. Damn. In the turmoil of the evening, I'd completely forgotten that they'd be here tonight.

Luckily they were so engrossed with what they were doing that neither of them had noticed me, so I tried to back out of the room without alerting them to my presence. I was nearly at the door when a floorboard creaked under my weight. Their eyes flew open, and they broke their kiss to turn to look at me. Within seconds, they were sitting up and straightening their clothes.

'What're you doing back?' Lindsay was off the couch. 'I didn't expect you to surface until late tomorrow.'

'Yeah? You and me both.' It was hard to keep the bitterness out of my voice. 'Look, I didn't mean to disturb you. So I'll go, and you . . . well, just get back to what you were doing.'

I headed for my room, but not before I saw Lindsay give Adrian a look that said: I have to sort my friend out.

Great. That was all I needed.

She was right behind me as I stepped into my room. I walked over and crashed face down onto my bed. Even though I was in the warmth of my flat, I was still shaking. I'd blown it with Richard tonight. There would be no coming back from this, and with that realisation, I felt a tremendous sadness envelope me. I gripped my pillow harder, burying my head into its softness, as though it might somehow help to block the events of tonight.

'What happened?' Lindsay asked, closing the door over.

'I don't know.' My voice was muffled against the pillow. With a last show of strength I flipped onto my back, so I could look over at her, perched on my desk. 'I honestly don't know.'

She nibbled at the nails on her right hand. 'Do you want to talk about it?'

I knew an outright 'no' would begin a back-and-forth of her insisting I coughed up about the evening. So I decided to be a bit more calculating. 'Not right now. But tomorrow, maybe.' I gave a weak smile, and nodded towards the sitting room. 'If lover boy's not around, that is.'

I could see Lindsay hesitating, obviously keen to get back to her date, but also not wanting to be a bad friend.

'Do you want to come and join us? Adrian won't mind, I promise.'

I thought of what I'd just walked in on. Even if I had fancied some company – which I really didn't – I knew when I wasn't wanted. 'Thanks, but I'd rather just sleep.'

'All right, then. I'll leave you to it.'

She closed the door softly behind her.

Somehow I managed to get up to prepare for bed. As I removed my make-up and took off my dress, I was aware that I was slowly stripping away the remains of the evening. It was hard to believe that a few hours ago I'd got ready with such hope and excitement.

I'd just got into bed when my phone rang. I looked at the display, and saw that it was Richard. I sat watching my phone ring, waiting for it to go to voicemail, because I was too much of a coward to speak to him directly. The message he left was mature but pointed: he wanted to try to sort things out, but he was going to leave it to me to decide the right time to do that. He would be away on business until the end of the week, coming back on Friday, my twenty-sixth birthday. Maybe we could talk then . . .

Oh, and he'd also like me to let him know I'd got home safely.

I sent him a quick text saying I was fine – now I'd calmed down, I felt I owed him that at least. Then I switched my phone off, and burrowed down into the duvet. It was a relief to know he was going away. At least I'd have a few days' reprieve before I had to face him. I closed my eyes, and hoped that sleep would come soon.

I managed to avoid explaining to Lindsay what had happened at Richard's. When she asked me the next day, I just told her we'd got into an argument over something stupid, and that it was no big deal. I could tell she didn't believe me, but she also didn't pry. She knew me well enough to sense when I didn't want to share.

Chapter 24

'Something happened this week, didn't it?' Dr Milton asked, almost as soon as I'd sat down in the burgundy leather chair.

I looked up in surprise. It was true that Saturday night was still on my mind, but I hadn't realised it was quite that obvious. But then I suppose it was her job to sense the nuances of her patients' moods.

'Yeah . . . I guess you could say that.'

'Do you want to talk about it?'

My initial thought was not really, but it was early in the meeting, and I guessed there was little else to do.

'I went out on Saturday night . . . with this guy I liked. We didn't go out as such, he cooked for me.'

Dr Milton nodded encouragingly. 'And what happened?'

I frowned, shaking my head in exasperation. 'I don't know. Everything was going great. He invited me round to his place, and made this really nice meal.'

I paused, struggling to work out how I was going to tell her about what had happened next.

'That sounds like he went to a lot of trouble for you,' Dr Milton said, filling the silence. 'Like he wanted to make the night special.'

'I know! That's what's so annoying. Because when we were going to—' I paused meaningfully, raising my eyebrows in case she hadn't got it.

'Have intercourse?' she filled in.

I cringed. What was it with medical professionals that they managed to make everything sound so icky? 'Yeah, that.' I looked away, trying to formulate what I was going to say. 'I just . . . well, I couldn't go through with it.'

Dr Milton sat back in her chair and studied me. I could almost see the cogs of her mind whirring.

'That's interesting.'

'Yeah?' I gave a harsh laugh. 'That's one way to describe it, I suppose.' I pulled a hand through my hair. 'I just don't understand it. Why didn't I just have sex with him? It's not like I'm some shy virgin. I've had sex with enough guys before!'

'But this felt different, right?'

'Well, yes . . .'

'So tell me, what's so different about this particular man?'

I frowned, trying to put into words what set Richard apart.

'Well, Rich—' I had to stop myself saying his name – I'd forgotten for a moment that Dr Milton knew him. Although somehow I had a feeling she'd worked it out for herself. 'This man . . . I guess you could say he's a good guy. He's someone I like – someone I could even have a relationship with.'

'Whereas the other men . . .?' she prompted.

I shrugged. 'They were nothing to me. Just a quick roll in the sack. I wasn't looking for anything that lasted beyond one night.'

She was nodding encouragingly again, as though I was just in touching distance of the place she was trying to guide me to.

'So . . . what's the conclusion? I find it easier to sleep with shitty guys than nice ones? I'm not sure what to make of that, apart from that I'm clearly one messed-up individual!'

Dr Milton was usually good at controlling her emotions, but even I could see her disappointment when she heard my reply. There was obviously an answer she wanted from me, but she needed me to arrive at it myself.

'Seriously?' I kicked the designer coffee table in frustration. 'Can't you just do us both a favour and tell me what you want me to say?'

There was silence. Dr Milton didn't reply – and I hadn't expected her to. I just needed to vent my frustration.

'Well, then,' she said finally, once my breathing had subsided. 'Why don't we go back to what we were talking about the last time you were here?'

It seemed like such a waste of time. After what had happened the other night, clearly therapy wasn't helping me at all. But I had nowhere else to go, so I might as well do what she asked.

'You want me to reminisce, then fine.' I folded my arms. 'What do you want to know?'

She quickly glanced over her notes, apparently unfazed by the passive-aggressive note in my voice. 'Now, from everything you've told me, you were still a very sheltered person during that summer we've been talking about.'

'That's right.'

'And yet, by your own admission, sex and alcohol play a large role in your life now.'

'Too true.'

'So I'm just wondering if you can pinpoint when that change occurred? Was it gradual, or was there a trigger point?'

I looked away, and began chewing at my fingernails. 'I'm not sure, really.'

There was a silence, which was Dr Milton's standard response when she wasn't getting the response she wanted from me. 'All right then,' she said eventually. 'If that's the case, perhaps we should discuss the event which in our culture represents the loss of innocence.' I looked up in surprise, wondering if I'd understood her correctly. 'Yes, that's right.' She sat back, so I could see she wasn't budging on this. 'I'd like you to tell me about the first time you had sex.'

I stared at her for a long moment. I'd had no problem talking in detail about my current sex life, but that was different. I opened my mouth to object, but no words came out.

Dr Milton's expression softened. 'I understand this isn't a comfortable subject for you. So why don't we start with when exactly it happened? Was it after you started your art course?'

I knew what she was thinking. I'd told her how sheltered my school was – she assumed that I'd started at university, been around boys for the first time, and it had happened then.

'No.' My voice came out as a croak, and I coughed, clearing my throat. 'No, it wasn't then.' I took a deep breath. 'It was during that summer we've been talking about. At a party. My sister's twenty-first birthday party, to be exact.'

Seven years ago

I sat at a table in the corner of the marquee, pushing a piece of cake around my plate. It was my third slice, and I was only pretending to eat it to give myself something to do. On a raised bandstand at the front, a jazz band was playing, and the dance floor was filled with smiling couples. It seemed like everyone was dancing and having more fun than me.

That evening, when I'd been getting ready, I'd thought I looked good – attractive even. Miraculously, that summer my acne had cleared up, and I'd grown my hair longer. The puppy fat had melted away, and I'd got contact lenses for the first time. These small changes had helped my confidence.

But then somewhere along the way tonight, everything had fallen apart. I felt like I always did – the ugly duckling in a family of beautiful swans. The dress that I thought had looked so good on me now seemed childish. In the shop, I'd fallen in love with the huge princess-style dress. But seeing my sister in a sophisticated, slinky gown, her long, straight hair tied back into a neat chignon, looking effort-lessly chic, I felt like a lumbering idiot, like I'd made too much effort.

I was just wondering whether anyone would miss me if I retreated to my bedroom, when a deep, masculine voice said, 'So, what are you doing all alone over here?' I looked up to see Toby smiling down at me, even more dashing than usual in black tie.

I sat up straighter, pushed the cake away, automatically returning his smile. 'I'm great, thanks. Just taking a break from the fun.'

'Is that right?' The way his eyes twinkled suggested he didn't believe me, but he was kind enough not to press the point. Instead, he held out his hand. 'Would you like to dance?'

I couldn't think of anything I'd rather do than be on the dance floor in Toby's arms, but something made me hesitate. 'It's kind of you to ask, but you don't have to be so nice to me.' I dropped my eyes to the floor. 'I don't want you to ask me out of pity.'

He crouched in front of me, his hand reaching under my chin and tilting it up so our eyes met. 'How can it be pity when it's an honour and a privilege?'

Hearing that my heart lifted. I stood up quickly, in case he changed his mind, and let him lead me onto the dance floor.

As his arms encircled my waist, I rested my head on his firm chest. I closed my eyes, and shut everyone else out. In that moment, it felt like we were the only people there.

After two songs, Toby whispered in my ear. 'Are you bored? Why don't we go out and get some air?'

In fact, I wasn't bored at all. I'd have happily stayed there dancing with him all night. But I didn't want to disappoint him. 'What? Go outside?' I instinctively glanced to the gardens. 'It's going to be pretty cold out there.'

'Hmmm.' He seemed to consider it for a moment. 'Well, we could go somewhere sheltered. What about that old barn?' He said it casually, as though the idea had just occurred to him.

'I suppose,' I said slowly.

'I'll see you there, in say, ten minutes?'

I nodded, not trusting myself to speak.

'Oh,' he winked down at me, 'and let's keep it our little secret, okay?'

As the song ended, we parted. I went back to where I'd been sitting before, and he headed out of the marquee. I chewed at my nails, and obsessively checked my watch for the next ten minutes. Then, once the time was up, I slipped from the tent and into the garden.

There was a chill in the night air, but I didn't care. I felt giddy with excitement as I hurried down to the abandoned barn, slipping on the wet grass in my race to get to Toby. Our secret meeting felt deliciously illicit. And although I had a nagging sense that I shouldn't be doing this, I pushed it to the back of my mind.

I knew it was wrong, but part of me liked to fantasise about Toby being my boyfriend. I felt like we had a connection. He understood me in a way that no one else did. And I liked the fact that he seemed to want to spend time with me over Kate. Deep down I knew he was probably just doing so for her sake, taking pity on her awkward little sister. But for a little while at least I could pretend he wanted to be with me.

The lights from the marquee lit the path down the garden to the barn. I tentatively pushed open the wooden door, and peered into the darkness.

'Hello?' I couldn't see anything at first, and I felt a pit of disappointment begin to form. Had Toby decided not to come? Had I taken too long, and he'd already left?

'Over here,' he called from towards the back.

Relief flooded through me, and I made my way towards his voice. I found him leaning against some bales of hay, smoking. My first thought was that it was a fire hazard, but I wasn't about to tell him that. Especially as he'd never looked cooler. He'd loosened his tie, and as the moon came out from behind a cloud, it highlighted the sharp, aristocratic bone structure of his fox-like face.

'You came,' he said.

I nodded shyly. He held out his cigarette, and after a split second of hesitation I took it from him. I'd never smoked before, but there seemed to be something sexy about sharing a cigarette. I put the end between my lips, my fingers trembling, as I inhaled deeply. The smoke filled my lungs and I started to cough and choke. Toby laughed, and took the cigarette back from me.

'Maybe another time.'

Once I managed to stop coughing, I watched as he continued to smoke. He didn't seem in any hurry, which made me feel nervous. My parents would be furious if they realised we'd disappeared from the party. 'So what are we doing out here?'

He shrugged, a little smile playing at his mouth. 'Just talking. Taking some time away from the crowds. Why?' He frowned a little. 'Don't you like being here with me?'

'Of course I do!' I didn't want him to think otherwise. Then I saw his face relax, and I realised he was only teasing. I suspected he knew that there was nowhere I'd rather be than here with him.

'Here.' He slipped his jacket from his shoulders. 'Why don't we sit?'

He laid his jacket out on the floor, and sat down, patting the space beside him. 'Come on. Don't be shy. I won't bite.'

I hesitated for a moment. I could feel my heart thumping hard in my chest, the adrenaline pumping through me. Part of me knew I should leave, right now, this second. Something wasn't right about me being out here alone with my sister's boyfriend. But then I thought: what's the harm? Nothing's happened. Nothing has to happen. So, swallowing hard, I knelt down awkwardly, so I was facing him.

Toby looked at me through heavily lidded eyes, in a way no boy ever had before.

'God, you look beautiful tonight, Charlotte.'

Heat flooded my face. A frisson of excitement ran through me. They were the words I'd wanted to hear from him for so long, so when he reached out and caressed my cheek, I didn't object. For a second we stared at each other in the dark. I could see the outline of his lips, and the whites of his eyes. I didn't even dare breathe, in case it broke the moment. Then he leaned forward and kissed me.

I'd fantasised about this all summer, and part of me had worried that after the build-up, it would inevitably be a let-down. But it was everything I'd hoped it would be. His lips were soft against mine – light and teasing. My arms tight-ened round his neck, as I felt little fires of desire igniting within me.

He moved closer to me, his kiss deepening. I had so little experience, but somehow that didn't matter. Toby knew what he was doing, so there was none of the clumsiness or hesitation that might have made me stop and think.

One of his hands caressed the back of my neck, as the other slid under my dress. My heartbeat quickened, as I felt him touch me through my knickers. It was the first time anyone had touched me down there – in fact, it was the first time I'd ever been kissed. But instead of pulling away, I found myself pressing back against him, eager for more.

'You like that, do you?' he murmured.

His fingers slipped beneath the elastic of my underwear, and I gasped as he began to touch me again, shocked that anything could feel so good.

And then, quite suddenly, an image of my sister flashed into my mind, and guilt flooded through me.

'Toby, wait!' I managed to pull away a little. 'We can't do this. Not to Kate—'

The sound of her name made him pause for a moment. I'd been expecting him to be as horrified as me, to apologise and maybe reassure me that neither of us was in our right minds. But instead he just shrugged.

'Don't worry,' he said. 'She doesn't need to find out.'

Before I could reply his mouth closed down on mine again, silencing me. He pushed me backwards, onto the ground. And then he was on top of me, kissing me with an urgency that left me breathless.

I closed my eyes, trying to get back to the place I'd been before. But the moment was gone.

'Toby,' I managed to say, as he began to kiss my neck. 'I think we should stop now—'

But he didn't seem to hear me. His hands were on my breasts, squeezing them roughly, as he rubbed his erection against my leg.

When he moved off me for a second, I felt a moment of relief. Then, in the darkness, I heard him unbuckle his belt and unzip his trousers, and he was back on top again, his body pinning me down.

Cold panic seized me. I began to wriggle beneath him, putting my hands against his chest to try to push him off.

'No, Toby. Please. Stop.'

One hand held my wrists, while the other forced up my skirt and ripped off my panties. I struggled beneath him, trying to buck him off, but he was so much bigger and stronger than me. He forced open my legs with his knee, the weight of his body pressing me into the cold, hard ground, crushing me, trapping me there.

'Toby, no . . .'

I felt a sharp pain as he thrust inside me. I bit down on my lip, to stop myself from crying out, as he drove into me again and again.

'Please, stop . . .'

My voice was weaker now. Tears spilled down my face. I could hardly breathe beneath him. I tried to think of something else, to transport myself to another place. But it was impossible.

He was moving faster now, more urgently. Then, finally, I felt him tense. With a deep grunt, he gave one last, savage thrust, before he collapsed on top of me.

We lay there like that for a long moment. I didn't dare move. All I could hear was the sound of him panting in the silence. Finally his breathing seemed to slow, and he rolled off me.

'How was that?' Toby asked.

My dress was up around my waist. I pulled it down and turned onto my side, so I was facing away from him, curling into the foetal position. I felt sore and bruised. I was shaking so hard, my teeth chattering.

Toby laid a hand on my shoulder, and I couldn't help flinching. 'Is something wrong?'

I shook my head, not trusting myself to speak.

He sighed, clearly irritated with my lack of response. 'Well.' I heard him getting up, beginning to pull his clothes on. 'We should get back to the party.' His voice was all businesslike. 'We don't want anyone to start wondering where we've got to.'

Finally I moved. I forced myself to sit up. Toby had his back to me. He was shaking out his jacket, trying to smooth out the creases and the evidence of what had just happened.

'Why did you do that?' I said, my voice little more than a whisper.

'What?' He turned and looked at me, and whatever he saw made him roll his eyes. 'Oh for heaven's sake. Don't start crying. No one ever enjoys their first time.'

Is that what he thought this was? That I just hadn't enjoyed having sex?

'I told you to stop.' My voice wobbled a little as I spoke, but at least I'd said the words.

'Oh, come on now, Charlotte.' He didn't sound unkind – just maybe a little condescending. 'Don't start pretending you didn't want this. You've spent all summer flirting with me.'

I stared up at him. The half-light from the party caught the sharp planes of his cheekbones, reminding me how handsome he was. I felt confused now. Was he right? Was this my fault? I was attracted to him. And when I'd come out here, I'd known it was wrong. Yet I'd come anyway.

Was I so jealous of my sister that I'd seduced her boyfriend? What kind of person was I?

A wave of shame washed over me.

Toby must have been able to seen the uncertainty on my face, because he sighed. 'Look, get yourself cleaned up and come back out to the party. Have a few drinks and you'll forget all about this.' He reached out and chucked me under the chin. 'And it'll be our little secret. Kate won't ever have to know.'

Chapter 25

Once I finished speaking, there was silence in Dr Milton's office. The only sound was the ticking of the carriage clock on the mantelpiece, which seemed unnaturally loud. The tension in the room was palpable. I was suddenly aware of the tears on my cheek. Silently cursing myself for showing weakness, I wiped them roughly away with the back of my hand. There was a box of tissues on the side table next to me, but I refused to take one. Instead I blinked my eyes clear.

Once I'd composed myself, I raised my eyes to meet Dr Milton's. I stared defiantly at her, waiting for what came next.

She didn't speak for a moment, until it was clear I had nothing more to say. 'Is that the first time you've told anyone that story?' Her voice was soft, but still contained its professional detachment, which I was grateful for. I wasn't sure I could have coped with sympathy.

I nodded.

'And do you understand what happened to you that night?'

I tried to speak, but my voice came out like a squeak, so I had to clear my throat. 'I had sex with my sister's boyfriend,' I said finally.

Dr Milton regarded me for a long moment. 'Is that really what you think happened?'

There was that tone she used – the one that people like teachers favoured, when they were trying to get you to reach a conclusion on your own.

'I don't understand what you mean.' I shifted in my chair. My whole body felt tense. I looked up at the clock. The fifty minutes was up, but Dr Milton didn't seem to be interested in finishing on time tonight. I opened and closed my fists, trying to release some of the tension.

'Close your eyes for a moment.' I did as she said. 'Just listen to the story I'm about to tell you, and react with your instincts, without thinking.' She cleared her throat, and then began. 'A girl of eighteen goes to a party and meets a young man. They go outside to talk, and at some point, they kiss. She doesn't mind what's happening at first, but when things start to go further, she tells him to stop, that she doesn't want this to happen. But he goes ahead and has sex with her anyway.' She paused to let the story sink in. 'What would you say had just happened?'

'I'd say that she'd been raped.' I said it instinctively, without thinking, like she'd told me to. Then I realised with a start what the implication of that was for me. My eyes flew open. 'You're saying Toby raped me?'

'I'm not saying anything. I'm asking what you think happened?'

My mind was whirling, trying to process what she was implying. 'But I don't understand.' I frowned, trying to make sense of what was going on. 'If I was raped . . . then why do I behave the way I do?' I looked up at her, and shook my head. 'It doesn't make any sense.'

'What do you mean by that?'

'What do you think I mean? It's what I've been telling you all along. I have sex. A lot of it. With guys I don't know very well. I get drunk. Put myself in risky situations. That isn't what rape victims do. They don't react that way.'

Hearing that, Dr Milton gave an exasperated sigh. That was almost the most shocking moment for me. She usually had such a good poker face, and always behaved like the consummate professional. I think it was the first time I'd seen such an honest reaction from her.

'That's such a common misconception. What you have to remember is that everyone reacts in different ways to trauma. Yes, some rape victims avoid physical contact. But promiscuity is a perfectly normal reaction to rape, too.'

The revelation took a moment to sink in. 'But . . . I don't understand.' I wasn't sure what to make of this. I'd spent so long thinking of myself in a certain way – that I'd led Toby on that night and got what I deserved for flirting with my sister's boyfriend. These past few years, I'd seen my behaviour – the partying and risky sex – as proof that I'd been bad all along. Now I was being asked to see my behaviour as the consequence, not the cause, of what had happened to me that night.

And it made sense. It wasn't long after that night that I'd begun my art course. And that was when I'd started to sleep around. I hadn't really connected my behaviour with what had happened to me that summer. I'd just assumed that it was to do with the freedom of going off to college, of no longer being at an all girls' school. To me, my partying and promiscuity was a way of letting off steam, instead of a reaction to being raped.

I could feel Dr Milton watching me, obviously understanding the thought process I was going through.

'There are different theories about why certain rape victims become promiscuous. Perhaps you were trying to convince yourself that you were fine. Or maybe you were trying to take back control of your sexuality, or prove that the rape didn't matter, because sex wasn't a big deal. It could be any one of those reasons, or a combination, or something utterly different, and you may never figure that out. But I can assure you that having multiple sexual partners is a classic way of devaluing the sex act. Everything you've described – the sleeping around and the way you put yourself in dangerous situations, such as walking down dark alleys – it's your way of regaining control, of not being a victim.

'But what I think is most important for you to understand is that you're certainly not alone in reacting this way. Plenty of women attempt to get over rape by sleeping around, but our society prefers not to acknowledge it.'

I could see her point. It was so much easier to sympathise with a timid wallflower who can't stand to be around men, than a promiscuous party girl – so those were the stories that got printed. That's how I'd felt for so long – that there must be something wrong with me, that it couldn't be rape if I'd reacted the way I did.

But there was something else bothering me about this. It wasn't just about my reaction – it was about why it had happened in the first place.

'But I don't understand. Why did Toby do that? He was already with my sister. They were sleeping together, and she was much more attractive than me. Why would he need to force me to have sex with him?'

Dr Milton sighed again, as though she'd been expecting the question, but also felt slightly frustrated by it. 'What you need to understand is that rape isn't about sex. It's about control. That's what Toby wanted from you. And he was able to get that again by making you feel like what happened was your fault.

'From what you've told me about Toby, he's a very clever narcissist/sociopath who gets off on manipulating people. Half of the excitement for him will have come from getting away with doing this behind your sister's back, and still having everyone look up to him.' She paused, allowing this to sink in, before delivering the final blow. 'In fact, I imagine you'll find that you aren't his only victim.'

I drew a sharp intake of breath. The thought was both horrifying and freeing. For so long I'd blamed myself for what had happened. I'd found it impossible to label what Toby had done as rape. When I thought of rapists, I saw a stranger, a monster in a mask carrying a knife. It certainly wasn't an attractive, well-educated man, who I had a crush on. But now, talking it through with Dr Milton, it began to make sense. I finally understood what had happened to me, and why I'd reacted to it the way I did.

'So,' Dr Milton said after a moment. 'Now that you've finally admitted to yourself what Toby did to you, the question is – what are you going to do about it?'

I didn't remember much about the journey home. There was too much going through my head after today's session.

I now understood why I'd reacted to Richard the way I had the other night. Sex to me had never been something to be enjoyed with someone I cared about. I could only cope with it as a meaningless act, when I was numbed by alcohol. I knew that I needed to explain this all to him, that I owed him that much. I just had to work out what I was going to say first. And I couldn't do that tonight. I was still trying to process all of my feelings about what had happened to me, never mind trying to manage someone else's reaction.

As I walked from the Tube station to my flat, I wondered what to do with the rest of the evening. It was my birthday, which I never much liked to celebrate. Lindsay had suggested meeting me at home, and said that we could go out for a pizza, just the two of us. But I wasn't even sure I could face that. Right now, I just wanted to be alone.

It took all of my energy to drag myself up the five flights of stairs to my flat. As I slotted the key into the lock, a sixth sense told me that something wasn't right. I was on my guard as I pushed open the door.

'Surprise!' Thirty voices shouted out the greeting.

I stood frozen in the doorway, my heart racing at double time. I saw my mother and father's beaming faces, and Lindsay and Adrian, along with Helena and Rex . . . A big banner hung across the ceiling with the words 'Happy Birthday'. It took me a split second to work out what was going on – that someone in their wisdom had decided to throw me a surprise birthday party.

And as if that wasn't bad enough, as my eyes scanned the room, they settled on Toby, his arm thrown casually around my sister, beaming at me as though he hadn't done anything wrong – as though he hadn't lured my 18-year-old self away from my family, forced me down, and raped me. And then, worst of all, made me believe that it was my fault.

My jaw tightened, my hands closed into fists. And I felt white-hot hatred grip me.

Chapter 26

'Happy birthday, darling!' My mother stepped forward, and wrapped her arms around me. I was still frozen to the spot, my eyes riveted on Toby. I was literally shaking with rage and shock, consumed by the realisation that I'd come to tonight about what had happened between us all those years ago. And it was made worse knowing that I couldn't react the way I wanted to, not right now, surrounded by my family, friends and work colleagues.

Fortunately all my guests seemed to have mistaken my cold fury for being stunned into silence by the surprise. My father hugged me next, followed by Lindsay.

'You really didn't guess at all, did you?' she said, beaming. 'I can't believe we pulled it off.'

She looked so pleased with herself that I had to force a smile, and say thank you, and what a wonderful surprise it was . . . pretty much the opposite of everything I was actually feeling.

I spotted Richard to one side – again, someone who I could have done with avoiding.

He came forward to greet me. 'Happy birthday, Charlotte.' He kissed me briefly on one cheek, and I could feel him holding back, as though concerned about my response after what had happened between us the other night. 'This is for you.' He thrust an envelope into my hands. I opened it – it was a two-day trip to Paris on the Eurostar. At dinner, I'd talked about wanting to go back to see the museums, and he'd remembered.

I looked up at him. It was one of the most thoughtful gifts I'd ever been given. He'd put so much effort into it, and I wished I could enjoy it. That was the thing about Richard – even though things were strange between us at the moment, he was never the type to be petty. He was too mature for that.

My heart ached for what might have been between us if everything had been different. And it just made me hate Toby even more, for taking something from me that I could never get back – my enjoyment of physical intimacy.

There was so much I wanted to say to Richard. But before I could find the right words, Kate came over – with Toby in tow.

'Come here, birthday girl!' She hugged me to her. But I hardly noticed she was there – I was too busy staring over her shoulder at Toby.

I couldn't drag my eyes away from him. After that summer night, I'd always disliked him. But somehow what he'd said to me back then had made it feel like it was my fault. I'd felt like I'd led him on – that I'd made him betray my sister. But now I realised the truth – that he had manipulated me, turning an innocent crush and flirtation on my part into something abusive and violent. I'd spent years despising myself, but now I finally felt able to direct that anger where it belonged. My hatred for Toby burned through me. Seeing him schmoozing his way around the room, acting like he was a good person, I wanted to stand on a chair and tell everyone what he'd done to me.

But then, as my sister released me, my heart contracted. As much as I wanted to get revenge on Toby, the problem was it would also mean hurting Kate. And my family, too. How would my parents react when they found out what Toby had done to me? What if the shock caused my father to have another heart attack? How would I live with myself then?

But I also knew I couldn't let him get away with what he'd done. I'd let that happen for far too long already.

'We got this for you, Charlotte.' Toby held out a beautifully wrapped gift. I just stared at the package in his hands. I was shaking so hard that I knew if I took it from him, I'd drop it.

The sea of faces blurred in front of me. My chest tightened, and I found it hard to catch a breath. It felt like everyone was crowding around me, wanting a piece of me. But still, the face I kept seeing was Toby's. It was like some surreal sequence in a film, where everyone seemed to blur into him.

'Sorry,' I said abruptly. 'I'll be right back.'

I hurried towards my bedroom. I rushed in, and slammed the door shut. Then I rested my back against the door, as if to keep everyone out, and sank down to the floor.

I'd been in my room for about ten minute when I heard a soft knock on the door.

'Charlotte?' My sister's voice floated through, and I groaned. 'Can I come in?'

Before I had a chance to tell her no, she'd already opened the door a crack. Seeing I was alone and just curled up on the bed, she took the opportunity to come in.

'What's going on? Is everything all right?'

'I'm fine. Just tired and a bit . . .' I tried to think of a suitable excuse. 'Overwhelmed. But I'll be out in a minute.'

I'd hoped this would make her go away, but instead she came over to perch on the side of the bed. Thankfully my room wasn't its usual disaster area. I presumed Lindsay must have put my clothes away and made my bed, knowing that we had guests coming round. I made a mental note to thank her later.

'What're you doing?' I struggled to sit up. 'Look, I don't really have time to chat. I just wanted a quick break to gather my thoughts. But I've got all my guests here. It'd be rude to hide out.'

'This won't take a moment, I promise. I just want to talk to you about something.'

I folded my arms around my knees. 'About what?'

Kate sighed. She picked absent-mindedly at a thread on my duvet. 'It's to do with Toby.' My heart stopped. What was this? Did she know? 'Look, Charlotte, I know this can't be easy for you. But I really need you to get over this weirdness with Toby.'

'Weirdness?' I echoed.

'Well, I saw you in there. You barely looked at him. And it's not the first time . . . I've been wondering what it's all about and, well, he said you might be jealous.' She blushed a little saying it. 'That you'd kind of had a crush on him.'

'That's what he said?' I laughed bitterly. 'Well, that's hilarious.'

She looked sharply at me. 'What do you mean by that?'

I hesitated. I didn't want to tell her now, not like this. I needed to discuss how to proceed with Dr Milton first. I wasn't sure of the best way to tell your sister that her fiancé had raped you, but it probably wasn't at a birthday party full of your friends and relatives. That is, if I even told her at all.

I shook my head. 'Just leave it for now. Trust me, you don't want to know.'

She frowned. 'Look, I can understand if you're feeling, well, a bit jealous. Everything's working out for me right now – with my job and getting married. And it's natural for you to feel a bit like you're flailing—'

'Oh?' I tried to keep my voice light, but it was hard not to feel irritated by her sense of superiority. It was bad enough feeling like the inferior sibling, without it being made clear that that's exactly how I was perceived. 'Is that how I feel?'

'Yes, and I understand why. I mean Toby told me what happened on my twenty-first birthday.'

I went very still. 'He did?'

'Yes. And there's no need to be embarrassed.'

I saw the sympathetic, understanding look on Kate's face and alarm bells began to ring. 'Kate.' I peered more closely at her. 'What exactly did Toby say happened?'

She sighed. 'Well . . .' She sounded hesitant, so I grabbed her by her arms and turned her to me, so she'd have no choice but to be honest.

'Kate. Tell me what he said.'

'That you confessed to being secretly in love with him, and tried to kiss him, and he rejected you.'

The words were like a slap across the face. It took me a minute to process the lies he'd told, and then I gave a short, harsh laugh. 'I don't believe this. That little shit—'

A pained look crossed Kate's face. 'Charlotte, please. I know you're upset, but—'

'I'm not upset!' I exploded. 'I'm furious. God, you really don't get it, do you?' I shook my head in disbelief. 'I don't fancy Toby! I'm not secretly in love with him! He raped me!'

The words were out before I could stop them. I clamped a hand over my mouth, but it was too late. There was silence. My sister just stared at me, as though she was having a hard time processing what I'd just said.

'I cannot believe you!' The words hissed from her mouth before I had a chance to say anything. 'You nasty little liar.'

She got up then, and headed for the door.

'Kate, wait. Please—' I called, but she wouldn't stop, so I had no choice except to get up and follow her outside.

Most of the guests were in the sitting room, and as we came out of my bedroom, they turned to see us – Kate storming towards the hallway, followed by me begging her to wait. It was obvious we were in the midst of an argument.

I managed to catch up with her by the front door, as she grabbed her coat.

'I'm not lying, Kate. I'm sorry, but I'm not.' I kept my voice low, aware that other people might overhear. 'I'm telling you – Toby raped me.'

She rounded on me. 'And you expect me to believe you?' I was aware that my parents and Richard had joined us in the hallway, to find out what was going on. 'A drunken slut like you?' I recoiled at her hurtful words. 'You've always been jealous of me. This is just another way for you to try and hurt our family.' She looked me up and down, distaste evident on her face. 'You disgust me.'

'That's enough, Kate.' Richard moved between us, so he was facing my sister. 'Whatever's going on, there's no need for you to attack Charlotte that way.'

Kate blinked in surprise at him interfering. Then a look of realisation came over her face. 'Let me guess. She slept with you, too.' She rolled her eyes. 'God, Richard. I thought you of all people would have had a bit more self-respect.' Her gaze moved behind us. I looked back and saw Toby standing there. I felt my body tense at his presence. But Kate ignored my reaction, and walked over to her fiancé and put her arm through his. 'I think it's time we left,' she said to him.

My parents looked between us. It was my father who spoke. 'What's going on, girls?'

Kate answered, which was just as well, because I had no idea what I'd say to him. 'Trust me, Daddy. You don't want to know. But just believe me when I say that Charlotte's gone too far this time.' She gave our parents a brief kiss on the cheek. 'I'll call you tomorrow.'

Everyone watched in disbelief as she and Toby put on their coats and left. Before they could switch their attention to me, I turned and headed into the kitchen, away from the party.

Richard followed me. 'What was that all about?'

I shook my head, unable to speak. I'd known that telling the truth about Toby was never going to be easy, but what I hadn't anticipated was that people might not believe me. But then why would they? Like Kate had said – I was a drunken slut. Wasn't that what always happened in court-room dramas? They brought up the victim's sexual history, and no one believed her story any more. I should never have said anything. I'd kept this to myself for so long now, what was the point of telling the truth? It would just make every-thing worse.

'I need to get out of here.' I said the words almost to myself.

'Fair enough. I'll come with you.'

'No!' That was the last thing I wanted. Once he knew what had happened he'd reject me, just like Kate had done. And I'd rather end this now than hope he might be differ-ent. 'Just for once, can't you leave me alone? As I keep tell-ing you, I'm quite capable of looking after myself. I don't need a babysitter. And I don't need you.'

Before he could say anything, I made for the front door. I could hear him calling for me as I ran down the stairs, but I didn't stop. For the first time in a while, I knew exactly where I was going. Back to The Nick – where I belonged.

Chapter 27

Once I was outside, I started walking in the direction of the bar. I wanted to forget the events of the evening, and getting drunk and doing something stupid seemed the best way to make that happen.

It was freezing outside. I could tell that from the way my breath formed white clouds in the chill night air. But I couldn't feel the cold. I was too numb after what had happened. The events of the night kept running through my head – realising what Toby had done to me, and then revealing it to my sister, only to be branded a liar and a slag. So much for opening up.

I stepped forward, and heard the sound of car brakes being slammed on, along with the long beep of a horn. The noise snapped me back to the present. I looked up, raising my hand against the glare of the headlights, and realised I'd stepped into the road and in front of a black cab. I'd been so caught up in my thoughts that I hadn't been concentrating on where I was going.

The driver, a stocky, bald man in his fifties, leaned out the window, his face contorted with anger. 'You got a death wish or something?' he shouted.

I stared back at him, uncertain how to answer. He shook his head in disgust, and drove off. Other pedestrians were staring openly at me, obviously trying to gauge if I was drunk or not. I bent my head, turning up the collar of my coat, and hurried on.

I made an effort to take it slower and more carefully after that, paying attention to my surroundings. When I saw a bus heading up to Camden, I jumped on it, and ten minutes later it dropped me near the bar.

A blast of warm, beer-soaked air struck me as I pushed open the door to The Nick and stepped inside. It was just before ten, so it was still fairly quiet, but there were enough people dotted around so that the place didn't feel completely empty. Some old-school rock was playing on the speakers – Guns and Roses, and INXS – and there was a low buzz of chatter.

I looked down at myself, feeling out of place. My new preppy look wasn't suited to The Nick. I headed into the ladies' room. As usual, two of the three cubicles were out of order, one of the sinks was overflowing, and there was no toilet paper. I went to work quickly, having no desire to spend any more time in there than I had to. My aim was to do what I could to loosen up my look. The skinny black trousers weren't bad, but the top was all wrong. I pulled off my V-neck grey jumper and stuffed it in my bag. The crisp white shirt wasn't ever going to come close to a tank top, but I rolled up the sleeves and undid an extra button, so you got just a hint of cleavage. Luckily, I'd brought my make-up bag, so I applied some thick eyeliner and another coat of mascara, along with red lipstick. Then I unpicked the elegant French pleat, and turned my head upside down, mussing up my hair. I flipped back up and regarded myself in the mirror. A far trashier version of myself stared back at me. I wasn't completely back to my old self, but it would do.

When I came back out, I headed straight to the bar. There was a new face serving – a tall, statuesque young woman with black hair, too much make-up and an eighties-style punk outfit – and I idly wondered if she was my replacement. She didn't even look at me as I ordered a tequila shot.

As she went to get the measure, I swivelled round on the bar stool to see who else was there. The Nick was the kind of place that attracted a lot of regulars, so there were about half a dozen tables I could easily have gone to join. But then I struck gold. Over by the fire, Gavin and two of his band-mates were crowded round a small table, drinking pints of what looked like snakebite and black. He would be the perfect way to forget tonight and my stupid attempt to try to change my life.

I turned back to the Goth barmaid. She poured the shot, and took my money. I downed it before she'd even come back with my change.

'Two more,' I said.

She didn't register any sign of surprise or interest as she went to get the drinks.

This time, instead of downing the shots, I picked up the glasses, slipped from the stool and headed over to where Gavin was sitting.

'Hey, you.' I tried to make my voice light and playful. 'Long time no see.'

It wasn't exactly the most original line, but somehow I doubted Gavin was a connoisseur of witty banter.

He squinted up at me, clearly having trouble placing who the hell I was. It wasn't exactly surprising, given that he hadn't seen me with this new hairstyle. I hadn't been in here for weeks. The last time he'd seen me was that day I'd screwed up on the PURE campaign. Since then I'd been playing the good girl and staying away.

After a couple of seconds, his expression cleared. 'Charlie? Is that you?'

'The one and only!' I wasn't sure why I was coming out with such cheesy lines, but I think it had something to do with the fact that Gavin actually really annoyed me. It was either these light-hearted clichés or I'd show my exaspera-tion with him.

He squinted up at me. 'You look so . . . different.' Maybe I shouldn't be beating myself up. It wasn't like he was much of a conversationalist either. 'In a good way, though,' he added hastily. 'I like your hair. That's why I didn't recognise you at first—'

'So,' I said, cutting him off. I was already bored of the small-talk. 'Are you planning on asking me to sit down, or should I just go ahead and drink these myself?' I held out the two shots of tequila, and then cast a pointed look at his band mates, making it clear this was a party for two.

His face brightened, as he realised what I was offering. 'Yeah, sure.' He pushed out one of the chairs with his foot. 'Grab a pew. You guys don't mind, do you?'

His friends – poor man's versions of Gavin – gave us a knowing look, and rose and headed off without complaint. Clearly they had a code that made sure none of them would cock-block the others.

I set down the drinks on the rickety table, and pulled up a wooden stool. The pink velvet cover had faded and frayed over time, but I didn't expect anything else from The Nick.

'Well, then.' I leaned an elbow on the beer-soaked table, ignoring the stickiness as I rested my chin on the palm of my hand. I could see Gavin's eyes drop to my cleavage. I allowed my hair to fall across my face in what I hoped was a sexy way. 'What've you been up to since I saw you last?'

Half an hour later, Gavin and I were well on our way to getting drunk. After another round of shots, he'd gone up and got some beers in, and now I was starting on my third bottle of Peroni. It was a bit of a slower pace to obliteration than I'd have liked, but evidently he'd heard about my little regurgitation issue, and had decided it'd be best to keep me away from spirits. It probably wasn't bad thinking. Closing time was at midnight, and I had no doubt by then he'd be inviting me back to his place. After all, we couldn't go to mine, and risk running into stragglers from my birthday party. I had no intention of returning to my flat before tomorrow lunchtime, when I could guarantee that no one would be left.

Gavin sat back in his chair, and played with the ring in his nose in a way that sent shivers through me – and not the good kind. 'I still can't get over seeing you like this. I called you a couple of times, but you never got back to me.'

He looked a little hurt, and I felt a pang of conscience. To his credit, he had wanted more from me than a quick roll in the sack. He'd even talked about taking me to dinner. But that wasn't what I'd wanted from him.

'Yeah, sorry, I meant to call you back,' I lied. 'It was just lucky I decided to come in tonight and ran into you like this.' I walked my fingers up his bare arm. I didn't care that I was throwing myself at him. Right now, this was what I wanted. It had always helped me forget before. Why should tonight be any different? 'So what're your plans for the rest of the evening?'

Before he could answer, I heard the bar door bang open, distracting Gavin's attention. I didn't think much of it until I saw him blink twice, and then grimace as a look of recognition came over him.

Before I had a chance to turn round, a voice said, 'So this is where you're hiding out.'

I looked up to see Richard towering above us, his hands on his hips, his mouth contorted in obvious disapproval. His eyes flicked from me to Gavin, and then stayed there. Gavin shrank under his piercing gaze.

'Tell you what,' Gavin said. 'Why don't I, uh, leave you guys to it?' He reached for his beer and tried to stand at the same time, his knees knocking the small table and spilling his drink in his rush to get away. He wiped at the crotch of his jeans, and then seemed to give up. He bobbed his head at Richard. 'Er . . . nice to see you again, mate.'

Richard didn't respond, he just continued to stare at him. Gavin looked unnerved and rushed away to join his friends. Out of the corner of my eye, I could see Gavin pointing at us, and whispering, as though Richard was some threatening guy.

It was only once he was gone that Richard moved, pulling up one of the seats so he was sitting opposite me.

I sat back and folded my arms. 'Well, thanks for chasing him away,' I said.

'It was my pleasure.' Richard smiled, pretending not to understand my sarcasm.

'So. How did you find me?'

'It wasn't that hard. All your friends are at your flat. There weren't many places for you to go.' He paused. 'In fact, I would've got here sooner, but I thought it'd be best to let you calm down. Plus it took almost that long to get your mother to agree not to start looking for you herself.'

I closed my eyes briefly at the thought of all the fuss. When I opened them again, Richard was still there, looking expectantly at me.

'Well, thanks for dealing with that.' I made my voice deliberately light, as though this was no big deal. 'But as you can see, I'm perfectly fine. So why don't you run along, and let everyone know you did your good deed for the day, and made sure screw-up Charlie was safe. Again.'

His eyes narrowed at that. 'I will go,' he said curtly. 'Trust me, in five minutes' time, I plan to be out that door. Because I have no desire to be in this dive for a second longer than I need to.' He cast his eyes round the room, wrinkling his nose in disgust, before his gaze came to rest on me. 'But when I leave, I want you to come with me.'

Deep down, I'd been expecting him to say that. I reached out, took a sip of my beer, to play for time. 'Now,' I said, replacing the beer bottle on the table. 'Why would I want to go anywhere with you?'

'You know why.' He shook his head in disbelief. 'Are we really going to go through this again? Are you going to pretend that you want to be with that idiot over there?' He inclined his head towards Gavin. 'When we both know that this is just a reaction to whatever went on between you and Kate tonight.'

At that, I glanced away. All around the room, people were joking and laughing, having a good time. It looked so easy for them. Why couldn't it be for me? 'I don't know what you mean.'

Richard snorted a laugh. 'Come on, Charlotte. This is how you always react when something goes wrong. You drink yourself into oblivion and sleep with some guy you couldn't give a damn about. Anything to help you forget whatever the hell is plaguing you. And it's destroying your life. So I'm asking you, this time, not to behave like that. To make the right choice and walk away. With me.'

The invitation hung between us. I dropped my eyes to the table, unable to meet his gaze. It sounded so tempting – more so than he probably realised. I wanted to do what he asked, but it was too hard. It was so much easier just to fall back into old patterns of behaviour.

'I'm not sure I can do that,' I said, in a voice not much louder than a whisper.

Hearing my anguish, his expression softened a little. 'Look, I don't know what happened tonight to make you react the way that you did. But I know you're not a completely unreasonable person, so I'm guessing that whatever it was, it was bad. And I'm not asking you to disregard what happened, or to even tell me about it. I'm just saying – is this really the way you want to deal with it? Because that's down to you. That's your choice.

'The night of the Christmas party, I told you my fears. I admitted the reason that I hadn't let anyone close – because after what happened to my parents and then your brother, it seemed easier to cut myself off than risk losing someone I loved again. But despite that, I opened up to you.' He took a deep breath, and then said, 'And that's because I love you, Charlotte.' I looked up at him, shocked. It was the last thing I'd expected him to say. A rueful smile tugged at the corner of his mouth. 'So help me, I do.'

His words were lovely. They were everything that any woman would want to hear. However, he was speaking them with regret rather than the passion that usually accompanied such a declaration. His eyes were sad, and I could sense a 'but' coming.

'But—' and there it was – 'I can't keep watching you destroy yourself like this. So I'm giving you an ultimatum.

You either come with me now, or I walk away. Because I can't stand by and watch you ruin your life any longer.'

'Seriously?' This felt like more familiar territory. A chance to start a fight. It was easier than letting him know how hurt I felt. 'You're threatening me now?'

'No.' Richard's voice was firm but even. 'At least, that's not what I'm trying to do. I'm asking nicely, even though I don't have to.' He cast a glance around the room, and gave a rueful smile. 'I could punch out these guys and throw you over my shoulder, and force you to leave, if I really wanted. But what would be the point in that? This needs to be your decision. You either want to move on or you don't. I've tried to help these past few months, because I could see you going down a bad path, and I cared about you enough to want to help. But there's only so much I can do. This needs to be your choice. That's the only way it will ever work.

'But equally I need to make a choice for myself, too. You're self-destructive, which makes you the worst person for someone like me to be with. But still I've tried to make this work. Even though I knew it was in my best interests to stay away from you, I couldn't. Because I'm in love with you. But there's only so far that can take us.'

His handsome face was distorted with raw pain. I couldn't hold his gaze. I felt too ashamed that I was the one to cause him such distress.

'I want to be with you,' he went on, 'but you need to want to be with me, too – at least enough to stop acting out like this. Because I can't stand by and watch you destroy yourself. I won't put myself through that.'

He stood then, and held out his hand.

'So, Charlotte, what's it going to be? Are you coming with me, or staying here? Because the choice is yours.'

I looked from his hand to his face and then back again as I considered my answer.

Chapter 28

I continued to stare at the hand that Richard held out to me. It was as though everyone else in the room had faded into the background, and all that remained was us, and the choice he was asking me to make. I wanted so much to reach out and slip my hand into his, to let him lead me out of here. But for some reason I couldn't.

I folded my arms around me. As much as I wanted to go with him, it just seemed too hard. All I could think about was the conversation we needed to have about what had happened to me, and how I'd then have to deal with his reaction. He'd never be able to look at me in the same way again – to him I would always be a victim. And I couldn't stand the thought of that.

I looked up at Richard. My hesitation said it all. He must have seen the decision on my face, and I watched as his expression turned from hope to resignation. His hand closed into a fist and fell to his side.

'All right then.' He sighed wearily. 'If this is what you want.'

I dropped my eyes to the beer-stained carpet, unable to watch as he turned and walked towards the door, away from me and out of my life forever. I felt a wave of emptiness wash over me, a loneliness that was almost palpable. I could feel my heartbeat speeding up, as panic engulfed me.

'You ready to get out of here?' The voice intruded on my thoughts. I looked up to see Gavin standing above me, his hands stuffed into his jeans pockets. He swayed a little, clearly half-cut. I knew exactly what he was offering me: a night of drunken, meaningless sex. Safe in its familiarity.

And then it struck me – what the hell was I doing? Was I really so damaged that I was prepared to settle for a lifetime of empty nights over the chance of something real with someone who cared about me? Because if I let Richard walk away now, wasn't that like allowing Toby to win again? Did I really want him to continue having that power over me?

As Richard had said, this was my choice.

'Wait.' My voice rang out across the bar, over the music and the chatter. As I got to my feet, customers sitting nearby stopped talking and turned to look at me. Richard reached for the handle of the door, appearing not to have heard me. 'Richard, wait.'

He paused. I was already running towards him as he turned back. I saw his eyes light up as he realised that I'd changed my mind. A split second later, I flung myself at him. His arms closed around me, lifting me clean off the floor as he swept me up in his embrace. I buried my face into his broad shoulder, as he kissed the top of my head. And behind us, I heard the pub burst into a round of applause.

Richard drove us back to his apartment. He called my parents before we set off to let them know that he'd found me and I was safe, but after that, we didn't speak. It was as though he realised that whatever we had to say to each other, it wasn't something that could be discussed in the car.

At his place, Richard made coffee, while I perched on the edge of the couch. I knew I should be using this time to come up with a good way to tell him about Toby, but somehow the exact words were eluding me. How did you tell someone something like that? My only experience so far had been with my sister, and look how well that had turned out. What if Richard rejected me, too?

But it was too late to worry about that now, I realised, as Richard carried over two mugs of steaming white coffee, and set them on the low table.

'So,' he said, as he joined me on the sofa. 'Are you ready to tell me what all that was about tonight?'

I took a long sip of coffee, as he left his untouched. Finally I set the mug down on the table. I was aware of Richard studying me, waiting for me to speak. In coming with him tonight, I'd made an implicit decision to be upfront with him. There was no stalling any longer.

'Yes,' I said finally. 'Yes, I am ready to tell you about tonight.' I raised my eyes to meet his. 'I just hope you're ready to hear it.'

It was easier telling the story this time around. Richard listened silently as I spoke. I started at the beginning, and ran through all the events of that summer seven years ago, like I had done with Dr Milton, so he could understand exactly what had happened in the lead-up to the night of Kate's twenty-first birthday.

As I started to talk about meeting Toby in the barn, I could see his face begin to darken, as it slowly dawned on him what had happened to me. As I reached the part where Toby had held me down, he got up from the couch, and started to pace the floor like a caged animal, cracking his knuckles in a primal way that seemed almost alien compared with his usually composed self.

'And you told your sister this tonight?' he asked, once I'd finished. I nodded in confirmation. 'And she didn't believe you?' I nodded again, and he swore loudly.

I raised an eyebrow. 'Wow,' I said, trying to lighten the mood. 'I didn't realise you knew words like that.'

But he didn't appear to hear me. Instead, he pulled out his phone.

I frowned up at him. 'What're you doing?' I tried to keep the nervousness out of my voice.

'I'm going through my contact list.' Richard spoke with quiet deliberation, but I could hear the fury beneath his carefully controlled words. 'I'm going to call that piece of scum and find out where he is. And then I'm going to end him.'

My heart began to pound in my chest. That was the last thing I wanted. As much as I liked the fact that he hadn't questioned my story, had accepted every word I said as true and was primed to avenge me, that wasn't what I wanted right now. Whatever I decided to do about Toby, I knew I needed to give it some thought.

'No, Richard.' I spoke forcefully enough that he stopped what he was doing and looked over at me. I got up from the couch and walked to him. Reaching up, I placed my hands on either side of his face, holding him fast, so that he was forced to look directly at me. 'That's not what I want.'

He frowned down at me, his eyes searching mine, as he seemed to be trying to process what it was I was asking of him. I could feel the tension in his body, his instinctive reaction to what I'd told him. But I kept hold of him, my gaze remaining locked on his as I silently pleaded with him to do as I asked. Gradually his breathing began to ease.

'All right,' he said finally. He slipped his phone back in his pocket, and reached up and covered my hands with his own, gently pulling them away from his face. 'What do you want from me then? Because I'll do anything you ask.'

I smiled softly at that. I'd worried about how he would react to hearing that I'd been raped – that he might pity me, or feel embarrassed, or no longer know how to act around me. But instead he was just offering to be whatever I needed right now.

And I already knew what that was.

'I want us to finish what we started last Saturday night,' I said.

Hearing those words, Richard's body went very still. His brow furrowed as he fully digested what I meant. 'Are you sure that's such a good idea? After everything you've gone through tonight, maybe you should take a few days to think things through. Because, believe me, you've got nothing to prove—'

'I know that. But it's what I want. In fact, it's what I need,' I corrected myself.

I'd realised that tonight. My best revenge on Toby would be to prove to myself that I could move past what he'd done – that I could be with someone that I cared about, and who cared about me.

I looked up at Richard from lowered lashes. 'Right now I need you to help me forget everything. Do you think you can do that?'

Chapter 29

Richard didn't answer. It took me a moment to figure out why. As I met his eyes, I saw the doubt there. He didn't want to deny my request, but he also didn't believe I meant it. He feared it was too soon. While he would never say no, he wasn't going to make the first move either. It was up to me to show him how much I wanted this.

I took a step towards him. He eyed me warily. His lips parted a little, and I almost expected him to voice his objection. But he didn't say anything. Instead he stood there, as still as possible, waiting for me to take the lead.

I placed my hands on his shoulders, wanting to feel the solidness of him in the hope that it might ground me, and then I tilted my chin up and began to kiss him.

My lips were soft and light against his, almost tentative. For all my bravado, even I wasn't sure whether this was a good idea. But as his mouth opened to me, I felt something unexpected – warmth flooded my belly, and a sudden desire for more seized me. My kiss deepened, but even as Richard responded, I noticed how his hands stayed firmly by his sides. He was leaving this to me, making sure I was comfortable with everything, and I felt a surge of affection for this man who cared so much.

I pulled away a little, determined to take things slow, so I wouldn't ruin the moment this time. I felt in complete control as I ran my hands over his strong shoulders and down over his biceps. And still he didn't move so much as a muscle. Emboldened, I began to unbutton his shirt. My hands shook a little as I pulled it open to reveal his ripped chest. I remembered exactly what he looked like from that time I'd walked in on him in his office. He still had that perfectly defined six-pack, like one of the models in an underwear advert. And then I froze, as I spotted something I hadn't been expecting. Across the left side of his chest, over his heart, he had a tattoo – black ink letters that were written in a script I didn't recognise.

I couldn't believe I hadn't noticed the markings before when I'd seen him in his office – but then he'd had a towel thrown around his shoulders, which must have hidden the writing.

I raised my eyes to his. 'What does it mean?'

'*Beauty for Ashes*. It's a Hebrew saying, promising that out of pain and suffering will come happiness. I got it after my parents died.' He gave a wry smile. 'Kit was there when I had it done. It hurt like hell, but you know how competitive we were. I didn't dare let out so much as a whimper, because he'd never have let me hear the end of it.'

Beauty for Ashes. I liked that – the idea that good things could come from bad. I thought of the withered rose that I had on my shoulder. I'd got it after what had happened with Toby, when I'd wanted a permanent reminder of how rotten I was – the kind of person who infected everyone and everything with their poisonous behaviour. Knowing what I did now, I wished I hadn't permanently marked myself with something so negative. Richard's memento of the greatest tragedy in his life was so much more constructive.

I ran my hands across the letters etched on his chest, feeling his heart race under my fingertips, and he drew a sharp intake of breath at my touch.

I raised my eyes. His jaw was clenched, his hands at his side, balled into fists. He was doing everything he could to hold himself back.

'I'm worried you're not ready,' he said quietly.

'I am. I promise.'

'And what if you're not, and you run away again?'

'I can't keep living my life in fear, and neither should you. So forget the past. Stop worrying about the future. And just kiss me already, will you?'

The urgency in my voice was unmistakable. Richard stared at me for a long moment. I think in spite of everything I'd just said, he was still afraid that I might bolt. I half expected him to back away, but then just as I was giving up hope, he cupped my chin in his hands, tipping my face up to him. His gaze held mine for a split second, and then he bent his head and kissed me.

As his lips found mine, my eyes fluttered closed, my mouth opening to him. And before I could think what I was doing, my body was pressing against his, as though it was the most natural thing in the world.

It was all the invitation that Richard needed. With a low growl he finally abandoned his restraint, and he was kissing me wildly, his arms circling my waist, and pulling me to his strong, hard chest with an intensity that left me breathless. His hands were in my hair, his lips on my neck, as though he couldn't get enough of me. I rubbed against him like a cat, enjoying the feel of just how turned on he was already. His grip on me tightened, as he groaned against my mouth. And then he was dragging me backwards, down onto the couch with him, so I was lying stretched across his body.

His hands ran lightly over my shoulder blades and down over my buttocks, sending a delicious shiver through me.

'Tell me what you like,' he whispered, his breath warm against my ear.

I knew what he meant, but I could only shake my head. I'd slept with more men than I could remember, but it had never once been about pleasure. For all my experience, in terms of getting any enjoyment from sex, I might as well be a virgin.

'Seriously? You've never——?' I saw his jaw clench as he worked out the reason why – Toby. And then, with what must have been a supreme effort, he cleared the darkness from his eyes, and managed a playful smile. 'Well, let's see what we can do about that.'

In one practised move, he flipped me onto my back, so that he was kneeling above me. His mouth found mine again, as his hands began to work the buttons on my shirt. As he pulled the thin material apart, he cupped my breasts, his thumbs grazing the nipples in a way that sent little frissons of excitement through me. Part of me wondered if I was being selfish, letting him do all the work, but he seemed totally focused on my pleasure right now, which was fine with me.

My eyes were closed, and I stretched beneath him, giving myself up to his touch. And then his lips were moving down my body, his hands unzipping my trousers and easing them off, along with my underwear. He trailed his mouth across my abdomen. I sucked in a breath, desire pooling at the base of my groin. I shifted restlessly, suddenly impatient to get on with this – not because I wanted it over with like before, but because I needed him to touch me properly, right now, before I exploded.

Instinctively I parted my thighs, and his mouth moved downwards, his fingers fluttering over me as I arched beneath him. I could feel I was on the brink of something, and as tempting as it was to let Richard continue, I wanted us to experience this together, if we could.

'Richard?' It took a supreme effort on my part to choke out the word. He raised his head, and I struggled to sit up. I eyed the bulge in his jeans. 'I think it's your turn.'

'I don't mind . . . I'm happy like this if it's all you want for now.'

It was the sweet, thoughtful response that I'd come to expect from Richard. My answer was to reach for the buckle of his jeans.

I eased down his boxers as he found a condom. And then I was lying against the soft cushions of the couch. He was poised above me, hesitating still, his face a mix of desire and wariness.

I reached up and touched his face. 'It's all right. This is what I want.'

I pulled him towards me; he eased in slowly, moving gently, almost agonisingly so, as though I might break. I knew he was still worried about hurting me, but I was past that now. My thighs clenched at his waist, my hips lifted, urging him to let go.

'It's what I want,' I whispered in his ear. 'Please.'

He gave in. He bowed his head, and abandoned his last vestiges of control.

I felt a white-hot tremor begin to ripple through me. My eyes widened in surprise, and I cried out – a mix of relief and elation. Richard raised his head briefly, and a flicker of contentment crossed his face. Then a second later, his chin dropped, his hands tightened on my shoulders, and with a roar he joined me in the shuddering abyss.

Chapter 30

'Oh, Charlotte.' My mother sighed, and I could hear a lifetime of disappointment in me in the sound. 'Do you honestly expect us to believe that?'

I felt tears gathering in my eyes, and quickly blinked them away. I'd spent some time trying to work out how my parents would react when I told them what Toby had done to me, but even at my most pessimistic, I'd never envisioned this exasperation, as though I was a little child who'd cried wolf one too many times.

I looked around the room. It was odd – I couldn't quite tell where we were. It was an old-fashioned living room, small with a three-piece suite and floral wallpaper, but not somewhere I recognised – certainly not Richard's apartment, or even any of the rooms at Claylands.

'What's she saying now?' Suddenly Kate appeared – which was odd, because I couldn't see a door in the room. She dropped onto the sofa next to my mother. 'She's not telling you that rubbish about Toby, is she?'

My mother and sister were staring at me with undisguised contempt. I turned to my father, who was sitting in an armchair. At least I could rely on him to take my side. But he was looking at me with disappointment, shaking his head. 'You really are a lying little slut.'

His words cut me to the bone. It was so much worse than hearing them from my mother or sister.

And then all three of them were saying it, chanting in unison: 'Lying slut; lying slut.' I covered my ears, trying to block the noise out. 'Lying slut—'

'Charlotte!' Richard's voice jerked me from the nightmare. Panic gripped me. My heart was galloping at twice its normal speed, and the bedclothes were sticking to my body, which was covered in a cold sweat. It had felt so real . . .

I rolled onto my back, and looked up at Richard, who was propped up on one elbow, frowning down at me in concern. He touched my bare shoulder, his hand light and hesitant on my skin. 'Are you all right?'

I realised then that he assumed my panic was to do with him and what had happened between us last night. 'I'm fine. It was just a bad dream.' His frown deepened, and I knew I had to elaborate. I fiddled with the sheets, as I tried to find the words. 'I'd told my parents about . . . well, about Toby.'

'And I'm guessing they didn't react well?'

I attempted a smile. 'You could say that.'

His hand squeezed my shoulder. 'You know it wasn't real, right?'

'I know.' I spoke quietly. 'But it still doesn't make me feel any better about telling them. I don't even know what I'm going to say . . .'

My voice quivered a little. I didn't want to think about what that conversation would be like. I closed my eyes, and all I could see was my sister's face last night when I'd tried to explain everything to her. She hadn't been in touch with me since then, which meant she was still furious. What if my parents had the same reaction? What if they thought I was lying? I dug my nails into my palms, as I tried to fight the rising panic.

'Oh, God.' The words choked out of me.

'Hey, hey.' Richard's voice was soothing, as his hand came up to stroke my cheek. The coolness of his fingers against my own hot skin calmed me, brought me back to reality. My eyes fluttered open, so I was gazing up at his concerned face. 'I know this is going to be hard, but you need to do it. And I think you'll feel better once you've told them. No matter what their reaction.'

He bent his head, allowing his lips to brush mine. I think he'd intended it to be a light peck, just a gesture of reassurance and affection, but as he made to draw away, my hand reached around the back of his neck, drawing him back down to me.

We kissed for a long moment, until he finally pulled away. 'As much as I'm enjoying this, don't you need to deal with your family?'

'You know what?' I stretched luxuriously, from my toes to the tips of my fingers. 'I think it can wait.'

I closed my eyes then, happy to allow him to help me forget, for a little while at least. Usually I couldn't wait to get away from the man I'd spent the night with. But right now, there was nowhere I'd rather be.

Afterwards I made the phone call to my parents. Richard went downstairs, ostensibly to fix breakfast for us, but I suspect mainly to give me some privacy to make the call. I sat curled up on the big armchair by the window, staring at the phone in my hands. I knew I should just dial their number, and get it over and done with, but something was holding me back.

Unfortunately the longer I stared at the phone, the worse it got. My stomach was churning, a sense of dread enveloping me. It was that awful feeling of not wanting to do something that I had no way of getting out of. I thought about putting it off, and going to have some breakfast first. But the idea was only briefly comforting. Even if I did leave it, the prospect of eventually having to make the call would be hanging over me, preventing me from really enjoying anything. It would be best to get it over with.

I took a deep breath and exhaled slowly. I could hear Richard downstairs in the kitchen – the whirr of the juicer, and the banging of cupboard doors – and the sounds of him moving around, and doing something normal like cooking breakfast, comforted me, easing my anxiety. Before I could change my mind, I hit the number for Claylands.

My parents had texted me the previous evening to say that they intended to travel back to the country first thing in the morning. Part of me hoped they'd still be driving back, and that I'd get the answering machine. But instead my mother picked up on the first ring.

'Charlotte?' She must have seen my number on caller ID. 'Is everything all right? What happened last night? You really shouldn't have left your own party like that—'

'I know.' I cut her off, not wanting to get into what she'd see as my rudeness. It would just lead to a fight, and I didn't have the energy for one right now. 'And I want to explain, but not on the phone.'

There was silence at the other end. I imagined my mother had been expecting me to argue back with her, like I usually did – tell her that it was none of her business how I behaved. But instead I'd admitted my mistake, and told her I wanted to discuss it.

'Look, I was thinking of coming to see you guys tomorrow,' I went on, before she could recover. 'If you're free.'

Part of me was willing her to say that they were busy – anything to put off the inevitable confrontation. 'Well, of course,' my mother said, quickly recovering. 'It would be lovely to see you.' She waited a beat and then: 'Is everything all right?'

I softened a little at her concern. 'Everything's fine. I'll explain tomorrow.'

I didn't give her a chance to pry any further. I agreed to be down for midday. She mentioned lunch, but I remained non-committal. I had a feeling no one would have much of an appetite after I told her exactly what had been going on.

I ended the call, and collapsed back into the chair. It was only then that I realised just how tense I'd been. I could still hear Richard in the kitchen, the sound of the kettle boiling and pots and pans clattering, and I knew I should go down to join him. But part of me felt too exhausted to move.

It took all my energy to drag myself up. As I emerged from the bedroom, I caught the salty, comforting smell of melting butter. It lifted my mood a little. I made my way slowly downstairs. When I reached the bottom step, I paused, watching Richard move around the kitchen, enjoying the sight of him being so focused on such a domestic task. He was in the middle of making the pancakes he'd promised, beating eggs and weighing out flour. He hadn't heard me come down, and for a second he didn't notice that I was there. Finally he looked up, and seeing me he smiled.

'There you are.' He stepped away from the mixing bowl, and wiped his hands on some kitchen towel. 'How did that go?'

'As well as could be expected.' I walked over, and slid onto one of the stools. 'I said I'd go down to Claylands tomorrow morning, and that we'd talk then.'

He gave a brisk nod. 'Fair enough. So we'll leave here at nine.'

'You're coming too?' I couldn't keep the surprise out of my voice.

'Of course I am.' He spoke as though it hadn't even been an option not to come. 'There's no way I'd let you do this alone.'

He switched off the hob, and walked over to where I was sitting. 'I know tomorrow isn't going to be easy, but you're doing the right thing.'

'Am I?' I raked my hand through my hair. 'Telling my parents about Toby . . . it's going to rip my family apart. Kate made it clear that she doesn't believe me. So that means my parents are going to be forced to choose sides.'

'And you're worried they won't choose yours?'

I thought about it. 'No,' I said finally. 'I'm just worried that whoever they choose, it will never be the same. It was hard enough for us all losing Kit. Now it feels like I'm breaking up our family again. I feel like . . .' I searched to put into words what I meant. 'I feel like I'm being selfish telling them about what happened. That it'd be easier on everyone if I'd never said anything.'

'It might be easier, but it certainly wouldn't be right.'

I didn't answer straight away. It was hard to put into words exactly what I was feeling. Even after everything that Dr Milton had said, labelling what Toby had done to me as rape, I still felt conflicted. What would Toby say if pressed on the subject? Maybe he'd be genuinely horrified to hear the accusation. I still remembered the crush I'd had on him that summer; how I'd willingly gone with him into the barn that night. Was I simply trying to justify betraying my sister by claiming that Toby had forced me? Had I led him on, and then manipulated events in my head?

'Charlotte.' Richard's voice jolted me out of my thoughts. I looked up and saw the sympathy in his eyes. He'd obviously guessed what was going through my mind. 'You aren't to blame for what happened that night. Toby is. And you need to tell your parents the truth. They'd want to know, so they could support you.'

When he put it like that, it sounded so logical. But still . . . I couldn't shift the nagging feeling that I was doing something wrong. The thought of revealing everything to my parents was going to hang over me today. Because even though I'd spent the past seven years pretending that I didn't give a damn about what they thought, nothing could actually be further from the truth.

Chapter 31

A light snow was falling. Little flakes landed on the windscreen of Richard's car, like confetti, before melting into water. The roofs and trees were covered with a light dusting of white powder. It must have settled overnight, and the pale, cold morning sun was still too weak to melt it.

To my surprise, I'd managed to put the meeting with my parents from my mind and enjoyed the previous day with Richard. Even when I'd woken this morning, I'd somehow been able to block out the prospect of what lay ahead, keeping up a steady stream of chatter as he drove us to Claylands. It was only now, as we neared the house, that I fell into silence. Fortunately, Richard seemed attuned to my mood, and hadn't attempted to make conversation or put the radio on. The only sounds that could be heard were the rhythmic whooshing of the windscreen wipers, and the squelch as the tyres cut through slush on the road.

As we turned off the motorway, and onto the country lane that led to my parents' house, I let out a sigh.

Richard's eyes flicked over to me. 'You okay?'

'For now, fine. But ask me again in an hour. I have a feeling my answer will be very different.'

A brief smile flitted across his face. 'At least you can still joke. That's a good sign.'

We drove for a couple more minutes, but I could sense something was on Richard's mind. 'What is it?'

'What Toby did . . . that's why you never liked coming home, isn't it?'

I nodded. As a child, I'd always loved being at Claylands. A childhood home was meant to be somewhere full of fond memories – a place that you could come back to when you were feeling lost or unsure of yourself as an adult, to remind yourself of where you'd come from. Instead, after that night, it had become somewhere I couldn't stand to be.

Richard reached out and took my hand. 'Hopefully, after this, it'll get better.'

I didn't get a chance to reply, because at that moment we reached the entrance to Claylands.

'Here we go,' I muttered, as we turned into the driveway.

My parents must have been listening out for the car, because by the time we parked, they were standing on the porch, waiting for us. Their faces were grim-set, their eyes wary. Given that I'd walked out of my party on Friday night, they no doubt sensed that whatever I had to tell them was bad.

I walked slowly up to meet them. We embraced awkwardly, our greetings minimal.

Richard stood behind me, like a bodyguard. My mother turned to him. 'We had no idea you'd be coming. We heard the car, but we assumed Charlotte had just got a cab from the station . . .'

There was a question in her voice, and I had no idea how to answer. There was too much already to explain, without getting into that. Richard must have been able to sense my panic, because a second later he took my hand in his. My mother saw the gesture and her eyes widened a little, but she seemed to guess that I didn't want to talk about it yet, because she simply stood back and held the door open.

'Let's go inside to the warm.'

We went through to the main sitting room. With less than a week until Christmas, the preparations for the festive season were underway. There was a six-foot real fir tree which my mother had tastefully decorated with little silver and blue baubles. It was a picture-perfect rendition of an English family Christmas, like you'd find on greeting cards. A fire even crackled in the hearth.

We all settled around the room – Richard and I sat side by side on the couch, with my parents in each of the armchairs. My mother had brought through tea, and poured us all a cup. Thankfully, there was no offer of food, and no attempt at small-talk. My parents no doubt understood that whatever I was going to say was serious. After all, they weren't fools. They knew I wouldn't be here without good reason.

'So,' my mother said, once we were all settled. 'Are you going to tell us what this is all about?'

All eyes were on me. I took a sip of my tea, only aware of how much my hand was shaking as I went to put the cup and saucer onto the coffee table. I looked from my mother to my father. I saw the anxiety on their faces, and hated the fact that I was about to make it worse. But I had no choice. I'd spent too long covering this up.

'I—' I started, but my voice came out as a squeak. I stopped, cleared my throat, and then tried again. 'I have something to tell you.'

'Yes,' my mother prompted.

I took a deep breath and then before I could think about it any more, I said: 'Seven years ago I was raped.' I could have left it there, but I wanted to get it all out before I could change my mind. 'And the person who did it was Toby.'

Chapter 32

'Why didn't you say anything?'

It was my mother who voiced the question I'd been dreading. She was on her feet and pacing the room. It was half an hour since I'd dropped my bombshell, and after my parents' initial confusion, I had managed to give them the details of what had happened to me. Richard had sat quietly by my side throughout the whole thing, supporting me with his presence.

I wasn't sure the gravity of my accusation had quite sunk in with either of my parents yet. They seemed confused, as though they were still piecing the story together in their minds. I wanted to ask them if they believed me, but I didn't dare. I'd got such unconditional support from Richard when I'd first told him. But my family – I felt an uncertainty that I wished I didn't.

'Does Kate know?' my father said suddenly. He'd, of

course, been the quiet one so far, letting my mother take the lead.

It was another question I'd been dreading, because it was inevitably going to lead on to which of us to believe. But it wasn't like I could avoid it.

'I told her the other night. At the party. That's what we were arguing about.'

'Oh, God . . . Kate!'

Something in my mother's voice put me on alert. Her hand was clamped over her mouth, and I could see the anxiety in her eyes. A bad feeling began to form in the pit of my stomach.

'What about Kate?'

'She's due here any minute.' She took a step towards me. 'I didn't know why you were fighting. Like you, she said she'd come down and tell me today. I didn't say you'd be here. I thought if I got you both in one room, you could talk it out. It seemed like a good idea, but . . .'

But that was before she'd realised what we were fighting about.

As if on cue, the doorbell rang. No one spoke or moved.

'Is Toby going to be with her?' It was Richard who spoke first. His body was tense, primed for a fight.

We all looked to my mother. 'No. She's coming alone.'

I noticed Richard relax a little, his fists unclenching. He'd seemed so controlled throughout this whole weekend that I hadn't appreciated just how much my revelation had affected him, too. I had a feeling it was just as well for Toby that he wasn't around today.

The doorbell rang again.

'I better let her in,' my mother said.

I waited in silence with Richard and my father. From the sitting room, we could hear the front door being opened, and the inevitable exchange of greetings. Then there was some more conversation – it was too far away to make out the words, but I could hear my sister's voice becoming increasingly animated. A moment later, I heard the clump of her boots as she strode across the wooden floorboards of the hallway. I couldn't help thinking that it must have been the first time ever she hadn't taken her shoes off to enter the house.

'Seriously?' A second later she burst through the door. For the first time that I could remember, she looked dishevelled and tired. I winced, knowing that I'd done that to her. 'You're telling Mum and Dad your lies now? You really are unbelievable.' My mother was right behind her. Now Kate turned from me to address our parents. 'You know she's making this up, don't you? Toby already told me what happened. She tried to seduce him, and he rejected her, so she concocted this story to cause trouble.'

My heart sank as she spoke. Even to my own ears, the story sounded plausible. Who were they more likely to believe – respectable Toby, with his good job and nice manners, or their wayward daughter?

'You know Charlotte's been off the rails for years.' It was as though Kate was reading my mind. I shrank further in my seat as she spoke. I could see Richard opening his mouth to object to her tirade, but I put a hand out to stop him. My sister clearly needed to get this off her chest. 'She wouldn't miss any opportunity to cause trouble. She's just trying to ruin my wedding because she can't stand everything being about me. She's just a jealous little bitch—'

'Kate.' We all started at the sound of my mother's voice. 'That's quite enough. I appreciate this is very upsetting for you, but you have no right to talk about your sister that way. You know Charlotte. She wouldn't lie. Not about this.'

There was stunned silence. I just looked at my mother. I hadn't expected her to say that – to believe me so readily. I looked over at my father. He was nodding in agreement, too.

Kate made a scoffing sound. 'So if you think Charlotte wouldn't lie, then that means you believe Toby would?'

My mother's chin went up. 'If you're asking me whether I'd believe my daughter over anyone else, then the answer is yes. I'm sorry, Kate, but I'm one hundred per cent sure that Charlotte's telling the truth.'

★   ★   ★

The stunned silence set in again. I continued to stare at my mother, still too shocked to react. Of all the outcomes I'd been expecting today, it certainly wasn't her unmitigated support.

A log shifted in the fireplace, and the unexpected sound broke the silence and made us all jump. It also galvanised Kate into action again.

'Oh, of course you're taking Charlotte's side. She always gets away with everything. I have to be perfect all the time, and live up to your expectations. But she can behave however she likes, and you still forgive her.'

The bitterness in my sister's voice was clear. I'd never realised Kate felt that way – that she believed our parents favoured me over her. I'd always thought it was the other way round. What was the reality? Or did we all just see what we wanted to?

'Well, I'm not going to stay and listen to this rubbish any longer.' Kate began to back towards the door. 'I'm going back to Toby, to the man I love.' Despite her defiant words, I could hear the quiver in her voice and see the tears gathering in her eyes. 'And if you all want to sit round and believe these lies about him, then I suggest none of you come to our wedding—'

'Kate, wait.' I spoke quietly, a deliberate contrast to her increasingly hysterical tone. I think that's why she stopped to listen. It would have been too easy to turn this into a slanging match, and that was the last thing I wanted. Because even after everything that had happened, even though she'd called me a liar and a slut, I felt bad for my sister. She was a victim, too. She was having to accept that Toby, the man she loved, had been fooling her for years. That their whole relationship had been a lie.

I got up then, and walked over to stand in front of my sister. I needed her to see my sincerity when I spoke.

'I am so sorry, Kate,' I began. Her arms were folded defensively, but I didn't let that put me off. 'I know how hard this must be for you to hear. But I wouldn't lie about this. Not after what happened with Kit. I wouldn't do anything to break our family up any more than it already is.' I paused, and placed my hands on her shoulders, hoping that my touch would connect us mentally as well as physically. 'I wouldn't do anything just to hurt you, Kate.'

There was nothing more that I could say. I'd given it my best shot, and now it was just up to her and whether she believed me or not.

Kate looked around at us. Her mouth was still set in a defiant line. For a moment I was sure she was going to storm out. But then a second later her shoulders dropped, and she collapsed like a rag doll, all the fight suddenly leaving her body. I managed to catch hold of her before she fell, and putting my arm around her waist, I helped her over to the nearest chair.

'I just can't believe it,' Kate kept saying. She was staring straight ahead, as though she was talking to herself. Then she looked up at me. 'I'm so sorry for all that stuff I said to you. I didn't mean any of it. I just didn't want to admit that what you said was true.' She closed her eyes and shook her head. 'I mean, what kind of monster is he? And what's wrong with me that I never saw it?'

She started to cry then, softly at first, and then she was weeping into her hands. I wrapped my arms around her, and she buried her face into my shoulder, so I could feel the sobs wrack her body, as she told me again and again how sorry she was.

Chapter 33

Six months later . . .

The courtroom fell silent as the judge took his place at the bench. Word had gone round about half an hour ago that the jury had reached a verdict, and the players in the trial had reconvened with surprising speed. It was almost four o'clock on a Friday afternoon – no one wanted this to drag over the weekend.

I sat in the public gallery, just behind the prosecution. All the people I cared about were with me. Richard sat on one side of me, and my mother on the other. My father and Kate were also there, along with Lindsay. We were all dressed as smartly as possible, hoping to make a good impression.

They'd been here for the whole of the trial – all three days of it. There hadn't been much in the way of evidence

– it was pretty much my word against Toby's. And that's what worried me.

Toby sat across the court, at the defence table, with his army of lawyers. There were a surprising number of onlookers in the courtroom. Word had got out that a high-flying surgeon had been accused of rape. Members of the press had started to attend.

'Now,' the judge began, and the court fell silent. He was a young man – much younger than I'd expected judges to be. But his red robes and wig gave him a commanding air. 'I believe the jury has a verdict.'

The court official went and took the paper from the jury foreman and carried it to the judge. The judge briefly read what was written on the page, and then folded it over and looked up at the courtroom.

I felt my heart-rate speed up, and nervous anticipation set in. This was the culmination of what I had set in motion six months earlier. After that day at my parents' house, I had gone to the police and filed a complaint. It wasn't the easiest of things to do, given that it was over seven years since the 'alleged incident', as the policeman on duty had liked to call it, had taken place, which meant there was no physical evidence. But since voicing what had happened had helped me so much, I'd decided that I needed to make a formal statement – even if it led to nothing.

'Will the defendant please rise?' Toby got to his feet. 'On the count of rape in the first degree, the jury finds the defendant—' I held my breath. 'Not guilty.'

I slowly exhaled. I was disappointed but not shocked by the outcome. Without any physical evidence, it had come down to he said–she said. The CPS solicitor had told me that she suspected the judge and jury were both on my side and believed me, but there just wasn't enough evidence to convict. Her assistant had confided in me that a lot of his boss's colleagues wouldn't have taken the case to trial, knowing that there was a good chance of losing, but that she'd wanted to give me my day in court.

The judge was still speaking, but I had tuned out. Richard dipped his head towards me. 'Are you all right?'

'I am.' And surprisingly, I meant it. When I smiled, it wasn't forced. Even though Toby hadn't been found guilty, I didn't regret coming forward. Partly, it had been cathartic for me to tell the world my story. However cliché it sounded, I'd faced my accuser. Just having the strength to do that had helped me. I no longer felt like Toby had any power over me.

The proceedings ended, and everyone began to file out. The prosecutor, a no-nonsense middle-aged woman named Diane Hall, came up to shake my hand. Her face was grim but determined. 'I'm sorry about the verdict.'

'You'd told me to prepare for it.'

'I know . . . but still.' She flashed a look at Toby, regarding him through narrowed eyes. 'I just wanted to say – this isn't over, Charlotte. I promise you that.'

'I know.'

'I'll be in touch.'

I watched her walk away.

I knew Diane's words weren't idle promises. It seemed my coming forward about Toby was actually much more than a spiritual victory. Inevitably, once the police investigation had begun, rumours had started to circulate about what Toby had been accused of. In the past few weeks, three other women had come forward to lodge a complaint against him. It seemed I wasn't his only victim. From the little I knew, his methods hadn't altered much over the years – he invariably chose emotionally vulnerable girls who had a crush on him, and he would cultivate their feelings for him until the inevitable attack. Like me, they'd been left so confused about whether they'd led him on that they hadn't known whether to label what had happened to them as rape.

Perhaps their cases might have resulted in a 'not guilty' verdict like mine, except it seemed along the way Toby had made a mistake. He'd tried the same trick on a young female patient, during a follow-up visit in his consulting rooms after he'd operated on her. She'd managed to fight him off and had lodged a complaint to the hospital. It had been dismissed at the time, but now the police were looking into it, and while they were, Toby had been suspended from his job. Diane Hall believed that it was only a matter of time before the police found other female patients who'd been targeted by Toby. Dr Milton had said in our last session that she suspected the same.

The Crown Prosecution Service had started to build a case against him. As I glanced over at where Toby sat, I noticed there was a marked absence of hand-shaking or back-slapping between him and his family and legal team. It was unlikely he'd still be a free man this time next year.

Ten minutes later, everyone else had been ushered from the courtroom, leaving me alone with my supporters.

'So I suppose we'd better think about getting you home?' My mother's voice was bright, but I knew she was disappointed with the verdict – probably more so than the rest of us, even. Law was her area – she seemed to be taking the fact that Toby hadn't been found guilty as a personal failing. 'You can bring your car around, right, Richard?'

'Actually,' I said slowly, 'I'm not sure I do want to go home quite yet. I think I'd rather go out and celebrate.'

I knew it wasn't the response anyone had expected from me. I braced myself for odd looks – to have to explain what was going through my head. I knew it wouldn't seem right to everyone, but to me there was a sound logic behind my idea. I didn't want to remember today as a defeat. Coming to court and facing down Toby had been a victory — even if I hadn't got the verdict I wanted. And I needed to treat it that way. I refused to go home with my tail between my legs, regretting standing up and telling my story.

'Celebrate?' It was Kate who spoke. I turned to her, worried that she might be horrified by the idea. After all, aside from me, she'd been the one most greatly affected by what had happened. Toby might not have physically attacked her, but he'd robbed her of her trust and sense of security. Her whole world had been destroyed after finding out what he'd done. She'd been left questioning everything. The idea of turning this into a knees-up might be horribly offensive to her.

But fortunately she didn't look in the least bit put out. Instead she was smiling. 'I think that sounds like a great idea. I could kill for a glass of champers myself.'

'Me too,' my father added.

'Well, all right then.' My mother looked slightly stunned, but recovered quickly. 'So where do you want to go?'

Chapter 34

It was just growing dark when we emerged from the restaurant later that night, the sky a beautiful shade of deep purple. Richard had suggested we go for champagne at Skylon, a bar and grill in the Royal Festival Hall, and we'd ended up staying for dinner. It had been a surprisingly jovial occasion, despite the verdict not going our way. We'd got a table by the window, and watched as the sun set across the Thames.

We saw my parents and sister, along with Lindsay, into a cab, and then it was just Richard and me, standing on the Southbank alone.

'So what do you fancy doing now?'

I thought about it for a moment. There were some obvious answers. It was a nice night for a walk by the river, or we could head back to his place. But I had other plans. 'I've got an idea.'

'Oh?'

'But I want to keep it a surprise. Do you trust me?'

He pretended to think about it for a moment, and then said, 'I suppose I do.'

'Good.' I grabbed his hand. 'I'll tell you where to drive.'

'Oh, God,' he groaned. 'Why do I have a feeling I'm going to regret this?'

I laughed in reply.

We went to his car, and I gave him directions to head into the West End. It was Friday night, and the capital was buzzing. As I directed Richard through the narrow streets of Soho, he had to avoid the drunken office-workers stumbling from the pavement into the road.

'Jesus,' he swore, as he braked to avoid a young lad who fell in front of him. The boy's friends picked him up, and chorused out apologies.

'There it is,' I said suddenly. 'And there's a parking spot too.'

Richard pulled up into the space that I'd indicated.

'So,' he said, once he'd switched the engine off. 'Are you going to finally tell me where we're going? A nightclub? A gig?' He looked round the slightly dingy streets of Soho. 'A sex show?'

I grinned, and pointed at the shop we'd parked outside.

He peered out, blinking twice as he finally realised what I intended.

'Are you serious?'

'Deadly.'

'Fair enough.' He reached for his seatbelt. 'This I can't wait to see.'

An hour later, I finally emerged from the backroom of the tattoo parlour. Richard was waiting patiently for me, leafing through the old magazines that they had lying around. He'd offered to come in with me, but I'd wanted to keep what I'd chosen a surprise.

He stood as I came out. His eyes ran over me, obviously trying to guess what I'd had done.

'So? Are you going to show me?'

I exchanged a smile with the tattoo artist, who retreated into the back, obviously sensing this was a private moment. I turned, drawing my hair to one side, so Richard could see my shoulder.

When I'd first got a tattoo, I'd been in a dark place. The dying rose had expressed the bleakness that I felt. But today I'd decided it was time to show how my life had moved on. My rift with my family had healed; I'd just been accepted again to art school, and would be going back in September; and I had Richard. I wanted to commemorate how far I'd come by marking my body with something more positive.

I'd been thinking about it for a while, and had started making sketches a few weeks earlier. Today I'd brought copies of my idea in. The tattoo artist had understood exactly what I'd wanted. He'd managed to alter the rose on my shoulder, so instead of looking like a flower that was dying, it appeared to be coming back to life. And below the rose, I'd had a phrase written in black ink.

Richard traced a finger under the tender skin.

'*Beauty for Ashes*,' he said.

'Good things can come from bad. It seemed appropriate.' I felt almost shy as I said it. It had only just occurred to me to wonder if he'd mind my copying his tattoo.

But as I turned to face him, I saw that he was smiling.

'You like it?'

'I love it.' He waited a beat. 'And I love you.'

With that, he bent his head and kissed me.

If you enjoyed *Sweet Deception*,
read on to discover

BEAUTIFUL LIAR
by
TARA BOND

Chapter 1

'You here alone?'

The man didn't look at me as he spoke. He was too busy searching through his wallet. He pulled out three notes to pay for his petrol, and slid them under the small hatch. That was the only way we could take payment after eleven at night, because the shop was locked up as a safety precaution.

Our fingers touched briefly as I took his money, and I recoiled at the clammy feel of his skin. I had to resist the urge to wipe my hand on my overall, and instead busied myself at the till, rifling through the drawer to get his change.

I deliberately hadn't answered his question, and I'd hoped he'd let it go. But then I heard his voice, more insistent this time. 'I said – you here alone?' He glanced at the nametag on my striped overall. 'Nina.'

My heartbeat quickened. There was no one else here, but I didn't want him to know that. Especially since he was the first customer I'd seen since midnight. It was the early hours of Monday morning, and anyone with sense was home in bed, resting up for the busy London week ahead.

I took a deep breath, and turned back to face him. 'Manager's out the back.' I forced myself to meet his gaze. 'I'll get him, if you want.'

The security cameras were out again, so if it came to it, the police would be relying on me to tell them what the man looked like. I searched for a distinguishing feature, but came up with nothing. He was white, middle-aged, and had brown hair and brown eyes. He was also average height and weight – the very definition of nondescript. And the way he'd parked his unmarked white van, I couldn't catch the plates.

The man counted his change with painstaking deliberation, before tucking it into his back pocket. He lifted his eyes to mine and I could tell from the amused look that he knew I was bluffing.

'Shouldn't leave you here alone. Not at this time of night. Young girl like you, it's not safe. You tell your manager that.'

He nodded a goodnight, and then walked away without another word.

I stood watching as he crossed the forecourt and got into his van. It was only once he'd driven off that I realised how tense my body was. I breathed out hard, forcing myself to relax.

It was hard to know what to make of the man. Maybe he was genuinely concerned rather than creepy. Most people thought it was wrong to have a 19-year-old female here alone at night, but the late shift paid more than days, and I needed the extra cash.

It was almost 2 a.m., so I forced the man from my mind, and began to go through the process of closing up. I put the meagre takings for the night in the safe out the back, and then shrugged on my jacket, grabbed my bag, and made for the door. I paused for a moment, my nose pressed against the glass as I peered out into the darkness, alert as a gazelle in the Serengeti. I couldn't see anyone lurking in wait, so I flipped the light off. The station plunged into darkness, the forecourt lit only by the fluorescent glow of the sign that loomed out near the road. I pulled open the door and stepped outside.

The smell of petrol hit me along with the cold night air. However long I worked there, I never could get used to the odour. It seemed to get everywhere, seeping into my clothes and skin. After a shift, I'd always spend ages in the shower, scrubbing away, but I still couldn't seem to get rid of it.

I had the huge set of keys for the shop in my hand, the correct ones already picked out for a quick getaway. There were two locks, plus a padlock, and I had the whole process down to thirty seconds. At the end, I gave the padlock chain a quick tug to make sure it was all in place, and then I dropped the keys into my bag and headed off into the night.

As I crossed the darkened forecourt, I stayed on high alert, watching the shadows for movement. It was only once I reached the main road that my heartbeat eased. Most people considered this part of East London to be a no-go area, but I never minded walking home alone at night. Even though Tower Hamlets had notoriously high crime and poverty rates, I'd never had any trouble. I think it's because I managed to give the impression of being pretty tough. Even though I wasn't physically intimidating – only five foot six and naturally slender – in my standard uniform of dark jeans, biker boots and bomber jacket, I didn't look like someone to mess with. Plus with my short dark hair jammed under a beanie hat, I could pass at first glance for a boy.

I set off along East India Dock Road, away from affluent Canary Wharf, and towards less salubrious Plaistow in Newham, where I lived. Usually there were gangs of youths gathered round the kebab shops, but tonight the streets were pretty much deserted. It was late September, there was already frost on the ground, and no one was hanging around outside without good reason.

A couple of girls my age were huddled by the 24-hour convenience store, counting out money for cigarettes. In crotch-skimming dresses, they looked like they were on their way back from clubbing. It was hard not to envy their carefree demeanour. I glanced into the shop as I passed, nodding at the assistant inside. The place was a rip-off, but late at night it was the only way to get the vodka that my mother craved. They'd got to know me far too well over the years.

A sudden blast of sirens broke the silence. Instinctively I looked round, and watched as two fire engines raced by, followed by an ambulance. Five hundred metres ahead, the vehicles turned right, onto my street.

My first thought was: *Oh, Mum. Not again.*

Then I broke into a run.

It took me about ninety seconds to cover the distance. I was breathing hard when I rounded the corner into Hayfield Court, the council estate where we lived. Three soulless tower blocks stretched twenty storeys high around a concrete square. One lone tree stood in the centre, permanently stunted by a lack of sun. I'd just turned thirteen when we moved there – the year my dad died. I'd sobbed my heart out the first time I saw the place. It had seemed such a far cry from the pretty suburban street where we'd lived. But with Dad gone, there'd been no money to pay the mort-gage, and a council flat was our only option.

I instinctively looked up to the fifteenth floor of our tower block. Sure enough, there were firemen on the walkway outside my family's flat. I could guess what had happened. This wasn't the first time Mum had fallen into a drunken stupor halfway through a cigarette.

The paramedics were already loading someone into an ambulance, which meant the lift must have been working for once. As I drew closer, I saw that it was Mum on the stretcher. An oxygen mask covered her mouth and nose, for the smoke inhalation, but otherwise she looked unharmed.

She gazed up at me, her large violet eyes sorrowful, her pale blonde curls framing her delicate face. Even after all those years of pounding the bottle, she was still a beautiful woman, the epitome of feminine. I looked nothing like her, and had taken after my father instead – inheriting his square jaw, chocolate-brown hair and eyes, and olive complexion.

'Where the hell's April?' The paramedic looked over in surprise at my harsh voice, but I didn't care. Any sympathy I'd felt for my mum had vanished a long time ago. She'd brought this on herself – had ruined all our lives with her weakness. Sure, it couldn't have been easy to lose her husband, and be left to raise two young daughters alone. But drowning her sorrows hadn't helped matters. She was hell-bent on self-destruction. My sister was another matter . . .

April was only fourteen years old, and she didn't deserve to be caught up in this.

'Where is she?' I said again.

My mother didn't attempt to speak, but her eyes shifted right to a police car. I followed her gaze, and I felt a rush of relief as I saw April standing there in tartan pyjamas, with a brown blanket thrown around her thin shoulders. She was crying loudly, while a young policewoman tried to comfort her.

April must have felt my eyes on her, because she looked up then. Without any thought to her bare feet, she broke free of the policewoman, and ran across the rough concrete to where I stood, hurling herself into my arms.

'Oh God, Nina. I'm so glad you're back.' She sobbed the words against my chest as I held her tight. 'I knew she was bad tonight. I should've stayed awake, but . . .'

But she was fourteen, and needed her sleep. It wasn't fair to expect her to take care of a drunk 39-year-old woman who should have known better.

I held my sister close, stroking her fair hair. She was the lucky one, who had inherited our mother's looks – although thankfully none of her selfish personality. Outsiders often thought I must resent being the loser in the gene pool lottery, but in truth I was pleased not to have anything in common with our mother.

'Don't you dare start blaming yourself.' It wasn't the first time I'd had to say this. 'None of this is your fault.'

April pulled away, looking up at me with wide, tearful eyes. 'They're going to take me away, aren't they? After this . . .'

She began to cry again.

I could understand her distress. Our social worker had warned us last time that if there was one more incident, April would be placed in a foster home. It was tempting to tell her that she wouldn't be going into care, but I wasn't about to lie to her. Too many broken promises, and you lost your ability to trust. I'd learnt that the hard way. It wasn't fair to take that from April.

I felt a flash of guilt about having gone to work. If only I'd stuck to the day shifts. But we'd needed the extra money, and I'd decided that took priority.

'I'm so sorry, love.' A voice interrupted my self-flagellation. It was our neighbour, Doreen Cooper, a thin, harried mum of five. She'd promised to keep an eye on my mother while I was out. 'I thought she'd gone to bed at midnight. But then the smoke alarm went off . . .'

That was about right. Everyone feeling guilty, apart from the person who should have been – our selfish mother.

I closed my eyes, and wished this whole nightmare would go away.

Chapter 2

'Well, this is quite a mess, isn't it?'

I was sitting in A&E – waiting while the doctors checked April out – when I heard the voice. I looked up to see a short, stout woman in her early fifties, with wild, grey-streaked hair. It was our social worker, Maggie Walker, looking even more dishevelled than usual in an unflattering Paisley dress and long navy cardigan.

'I wondered when you'd turn up.' My voice was hostile. Nothing against Maggie – she'd been fair to us over the years – but her presence here wasn't going to be good for the Baxter family.

Maggie flopped into the chair next to me. 'I thought she was doing better.'

'She was,' I said. 'Sober four months and counting.'

'What set her off this time?'

I rolled my eyes. 'What do you think? She got dumped again.' Since Dad had died, there'd been a revolving door of losers through our lives. Mum moaned about them and fought with them constantly, and then fell to pieces when they left. *You don't understand*, she would tell us. *I need a man. It helps me forget how much I miss your father. I can't stand being alone.*

She often asked me why I didn't have a boyfriend. That was why. Who wanted to be so reliant on another human being that they couldn't cope by themselves?

'So what happens now?' I said. 'To April.'

Maggie sighed, her cheeks puffing out as she shook her head. 'Look, love, I'm not going to lie to you. It's bad this time.'

'Yeah.' I didn't bother to keep the sarcasm out of my voice. 'I kind of guessed that.'

She smiled a little, and then grew serious. 'As of this morning, the court's placed April in foster care. The judge won't make any final decision for a while, but the way things are looking, I think there's a strong chance your mother's parental rights will be removed and your sister will be placed permanently in care until she's eighteen.'

'No.' I was already shaking my head, ignoring the cold, sick feeling in my stomach. 'That can't happen.'

I thought of all the awful statistics about children who'd been in foster care – the high incidence of eating disorders and self-harm. I didn't want that for my sister. In fact, I'd tried to ensure she had as normal an upbringing as possible. I could've gone to university, and left my mum and April to it. But instead I'd chosen to leave school at sixteen and work in a series of minimum-wage jobs, so I could keep our family together.

And now April was going to be taken away from us.

I looked over at Maggie. 'Tell me how to get her back.'

'Very simply, you need to be able to prove that you can give her a safe, stable upbringing.'

'Fair enough,' I said. 'I can do that.'

The social worker pursed her lips. 'Nina, you have to be realistic.' Her voice was gentle – the way it is when someone's delivering news you don't want to hear. 'Right now you don't even have anywhere to live.'

It was true. Weeks of repairs would be needed before the flat was habitable again. Doreen had offered to let me stay on her couch for as long as I needed, but her place was already crowded.

'And your mother needs to get sober,' Maggie went on. 'She needs a more aggressive solution this time. That means rehab—'

'So we'll do that.'

She looked sceptical. 'Come on. You know how long the NHS waiting lists are. The judge will have ruled against you by then. That means twelve weeks at a private facility – which is going to set you back at least ten grand.'

'I'll find a way to get the money. I can stay on a friend's floor—' Even as I said it, I knew how ridiculous it sounded. My work and taking care of my family had never left me time for friends. 'I'll get another job—'

'You've lost your job, too?'

Damn. That last piece of information shouldn't have slipped out.

'I kept being late for shifts.' Dealing with my mother's dramas meant I wasn't the most reliable of workers. When I'd called the manager at the petrol station to tell him that I'd have to miss the morning shift, he'd told me not to bother coming back.

Maggie's grey eyes filled with sympathy. 'Oh sweetheart, be realistic. I know you're tough, but this is too much, even for you.'

'Yeah?' I bristled. 'So you think I should just walk away, is that it? Just forget all about April?'

'No, of course not.' Maggie spoke with exaggerated patience. 'I just think you need to understand what you'd be getting yourself into.'

'Don't worry about me,' I said with far more confidence than I felt. 'I'll do whatever needs to be done.'

Maggie gave me a rueful smile. 'I've no doubt that you will. I'm just not sure you should have to.'

I looked away. I didn't need to be reminded of how hard this would be.

She reached out and squeezed my arm. I turned and saw the concern in her eyes. 'Nina, you can't do this all on your own. Isn't there anyone you can ask for help? A relative or family friend, perhaps?'

'There's no one.' Both sets of grandparents were dead, and my parents were only children, so there were no aunts or uncles around. And my mother had managed to alienate every friend we had over the years with her drinking. 'You of all people should know that.'

Just then, April came out to the waiting room, so there was no more time to talk. She spotted Maggie straight away, and seemed to know immediately what her presence meant. I'd worried that my sister might get upset at the thought of having to go into foster care, but perhaps by then she'd resigned herself to it, because she just gave me a long hug.

'You'll get me out as soon as you can?' she whispered in my ear.

'I will.'

'Promise?'

'I promise.'

Although right then, I had no idea how I was going to keep my word.